Printed in the United States of America.

ISBN 978-0-9978175-5-3

Lady Corinth

Warren T. Dent

Acknowledgments

Heartfelt thanks go to the members of several writers' groups and others for their suggestions and support over the two years that it has taken to put this story together. Peggy McGuire, David Anderson, Amy Irwin, Stan Barnes, John Helmon, and Joan Pasch have all contributed in significant ways. I'm very grateful for their perseverance, patience, and interest in making my tale come alive.

Table of Contents

Lady Corinth

1.   *Refurbishment, voyage preparation*

Portsmouth Dockyard, England. 1816.

The port buzzes with activity. Workers move smartly along the wharves carrying bowed hardwood planks, coils of rigging rope, lanterns, nets, and copper pipes. Shouted orders reverberate across the water as rookie new chums raise and lower sails in training mode. Smoke rises slowly from the chimneys on the administration buildings where officials review orders with captains and detail the allocation of supplies. Two stout militia guards guide a shuffling group of thinly clothed prisoners bound by clanking ankle chains down ancient stone steps to a waiting tender.

"Move along, you mangy lot." The rear guard viciously pokes the last prisoner in line with his baton. The strapping lad, nicknamed 'Dennis the Butcher', turns in defiance and spits at his antagonist, deliberately inviting further harassment. "Do you hit little girls as well, you cretin? Take these chains off and let's see how tough you are."

A blow from the cudgel crunches on Dennis' ribs, just above his kidney. But 'Butcher' is a strong chap, and he shrugs off the hit. Years ferrying sacks of dirty black coal from the colliery to the docks have resulted in wide-set shoulders and bulging biceps. He yells "Stop," and the five prisoners in front immediately do so, for they have been primed ahead of time. The rear guard is unprepared and almost steps on the heels of his goading challenger. Dennis turns swiftly, grabs the man in a fierce choke-hold, and swings him to the ground, banging the bully's head on the moss-covered step. The soldier moans and stays still.

Dennis reaches down and removes the ring of keys from the man's belt. His five comrades in the gang have similarly dispensed with the front guard. They remove his sabre and throw him into the cold water.

"Quickly, mates, pass the key along for the chains and let's get the hell outta here."

There's so much commotion around the wharves that no one nearby notices the incident. Before the guard in the water reaches the boat and his companion sits up warily on the slimy steps, the six youths disappear, racing through the open gates at the port entrance.

Beyond the inner docks a young boy maneuvers his small sailboat out of the way of a large ship which is being carefully warped into one of the repair slips. Horses pull carts laden with barrels of rum and cannon balls. Their clip-clop staccato reverberates along the narrow alleys between warehouses. The air fills with a cacophony as bells ring, whistles sound, hammers clang, and creative maritime curses permeate the workmen's space. The smell of hot pitch applied to damaged hulls wafts back and forth as the wind randomly changes direction.

This busy port is an historic place. Nelson sailed from here and won the Battle of Trafalgar.

It is also an innovative place in ship design, ship building tools, steam engine use, and dry dock construction. Thousands of men passed through this dockyard's crowded facilities over the years. The British Navy, headquartered in the port, is the most prestigious and most feared navy in the world.

Here, damaged ships become sea-worthy again, and new ships are prepared for service. This port maintains a high bar of quality for naval repair and readiness.

* * *

With the Napoleonic Wars now behind, the citizens of the country rejoice.

Most of them, that is.

Many men, seriously injured or dying from fighting on the open seas for the United Kingdom of Great Britain and Ireland returned home through this port. They were honored for serving their country valiantly.

Yet there are hundreds of dead men here who never left British soil. More die every day. They represent the weakest of the convicts incarcerated in the 'hulks' out in the bay. The hulks, old, de-commissioned merchantmen and naval vessels transformed into prisons, are anchored away from shore. They are ugly, deformed remnants of once-beautiful ships.

The Navy's reputation is one of glory. It is bestowed with fame. The extensive port is nationally revered. Out in the bay however, the hulks paint a contrast in disgrace, for they offer only misery and suffering.

"Bring that dead codger over 'ere matey and add 'im to the pile. We'll ferry 'em all to shore t'morrow. 'av you checked 'is pockets fer anythin' valu'ble?"

A fellow guard pinches his nose in disgust. "God these bodies stink. I'll be glad when I'm tak'n off this post. And yes, of course I chek'd 'is pockets. It was easy 'cause 'e don't 'av any. Got a medalyun thingamajig from round 'is neck tho'. You wan it?"

"Nah. See if Walter on shore'll trade more grog for it."

The despised contingent of hulk guards who collect the dead prisoners and transport them to the dock farthest from the main administration buildings is a group of public servants in the bottom echelon of the militia. Most are small-time criminals who've bribed their way to this pathetic form of freedom.

There are all types of citizens who work in this dockyard, from Admirals to grave diggers. At the top end, men of repute and recognized performance execute the highest standards of sea-worthiness to meet naval strategies. At the bottom end, poverty, skullduggery, and desperation weave among the dispossessed who strive to maintain a shadowy form of low-level life. The distinction is appalling.

* * *

The hulks spoil the view and ding the pride of us younger active ships when we look southwards towards the English Channel and the Isle of Wight. Oh yes, mark my words. We ships have personalities, feelings, and needs. It's just that we're usually not vocal about them to the human world. I understand you didn't know that but let me elaborate.

You see, I'm a three masted barque currently moored securely to one of the smaller dockyard wharves where I am undergoing post-voyage maintenance. I was christened *Lady Corinth* at launch eleven years ago. As much as all surface ships are considered 'female', no matter what their name, we are really gender neutral. The materials used in our creation - wood, steel, bronze, copper, wire and rope, are neither 'male' nor 'female', but we don't mind being addressed as 'female'. We view it as a mark of respect.

My repairs proceed well, for the workers have installed better, newer versions of several important components which include the rudder, capstans, anchors, and steering helm-wheel. There are a number of sister vessels tied up nearby who are not as far along in their overhauls as I am. And there's one in the early stages of new construction. This is a very busy and important dockyard, the largest in the nation.

Most of the ships in line with me were all built many years ago. Many of us in dock are closer to retirement than we wish. Between us we've had naval assignments all over the world. We chat and share information and experiences, but it hurts all of us to see those once-beautiful old ships out in the harbour.

The hulks were once magnificent warriors of the sea just like we are. They've been stripped of their dignity and assets, unable now to do anything but float in place and house hundreds of deprived men in terrible conditions. They can't even converse with us, so severe is their mutilation.

They make us wonder about our mortality. Is to become a hulk the destiny that awaits most of us? Frankly, I'd rather be destroyed and sunk in battle than be cast aside as nothing but an impotent wooden floating gaol.

Let me stop being maudlin however and tell you more about myself. A 'barque' is the name reserved for a certain design of ship that has at least three masts. The forward two have square-rigged sails, while the aftermost one is fore-and-aft rigged. That means its sails are set along the line of the keel rather than perpendicular to it. Our 'sail plans' allow us to traverse ocean passages in a manner that nearly matches those of full-rigged ships, but with one major advantage. We get by with smaller operating crews. We're also far more maneuverable in beam or quartering winds, and therefore better able to avoid dreaded lee shores. We take a little longer to get to our destination but we incur far less expense for our naval or merchant owners. As a class of ship, we've become quite popular for that reason.

Barques come in various shapes and sizes. I register somewhere in the middle of the range. My overall length at the waterline is just over one hundred fifty feet, my beam is thirty-five feet, and I draw nearly fifteen feet. Shipyard officials characterize us barques as the workhorses of the fleet, built for long voyages in deep waters, able to carry either cargo or passengers, or both.

I use the word 'passengers' somewhat euphemistically because my next voyage, in addition to transporting a select group of first-class-cabin paying passengers, will include a contingent of male and female convicts. The latter, poor souls, are destined for the penal colony in Sydney, Australia.

They're the citizens who don't rejoice over the end of the Napoleonic wars.

* * *

Three weeks back I was in dry-dock. It was amazing to watch the new steam engines at work as they pumped all the water out. Not that long ago, the workmen used horses to pull wooden spokes around a capstan. Now it takes less than a tenth of the time to get the same amount of work done. Since my previous visit to the dry dock was only three years ago the current maintenance experts didn't expect to find any serious problems on my underwater parts this time. They did clean a nation of barnacles off however, for which I am most thankful. Itchy critters!

So no, I wasn't in dry dock for a check of potential problems below the waterline. I was there to receive the new copper sheathing being added to keels and planks below the waterline these days. Experience has shown it keeps out the nasty Teredo shipworms*[*See Glossary*], helps delay general decay, and mitigates tears and rips caused if one hits a submerged rock. Horrible thought, but nearly all ships have found that the Admiralty charts aren't as up-to-date as the Lords often claim.

In the dry dock next to mine a larger barque was in for repairs to her keel and lower portside hull. She'd been blown by heavy winds onto rocks on the French side of the Channel. They'd torn a large hole. How she was able to limp home amazed me, but attested to the incredible skills of the seamen and carpenters on board. Outstanding seamanship is the foremost pinnacle captains and officers want to climb. To be recognized for creative actions and excellent judgment at sea leads to promotion and better pay. Not all sailors want the renown and increased responsibility of higher positions, but the ambitious few who do provide the leadership that has made the Navy the enviable force it is today.

The coppering process I received in dry dock is not inexpensive. But since mollusks and other small sea creatures can't live on metal, my hull is now protected against heavy fouling. I'll live and serve longer, other things being equal. The copper plates took over two weeks to be put in place, but when they re-filled the dock I floated back into the harbour much cleaner, and more robust than before. I could feel the sheathing soothe my lower timbers. I love practical inventions. I may be repeating myself, but oh my, it really does feel good!

While I enjoyed the cleaning and re-dressing there was one sad incident that detracted from total pleasure. The walls of the dry dock are nearly thirty feet tall. They have to be to accommodate bigger ships than me. Longer, heavier barques often draw twenty-five feet. Inside the dock my decks were a good five feet below the top of the walls, so the access planks sloped downward from the perimeter work area. Short interlocking metal scaffolding surrounded my lower hull where the sheathing was being applied. The empty gap between the solid beams that supported the metal hammerers and the access planks to the deck above was at least fifteen feet. A few specially trained men worked on the hull, three times as many were on the deck repairing the railing and low rigging. That was where the accident occurred.

An apprentice lad, no more than seventeen years old, was replacing worn halyards* with help from two chums. They were hauling the new ropes into position aloft when the youngster's left foot got caught in the rope coils on the edge of the deck. Before anyone realized he was yanked into the air by the rope wrapped tight around his ankle. He screamed as he was pulled upwards. He dangled and swung precariously near the rail, yelling for help. His head hit the rail post just as his foot came free, and he fell onto the access plank. He managed to grab the edge of the plank with his fingertips, but as his mates reached down to grab his arms, he lost hold, and with a terrifying scream plunged downwards.

It was eerie. One second a heart-wrenching scream filled the air. But there was just a soft thud as his body hit the sand covering the rocky bottom. Then nothing. No more screams. Silence. There was no blood to see, just his elongated body with his head twisted at a horrible angle. I watched tears form in a couple of older men's eyes. A life snuffed out so early was not fair to anyone. Tragic.

The surgeon found that the fellow's spine had been broken near the neck. He died instantly. His death, so shocking, stopped work for only a short period however. The Navy had deadlines to meet. Fellow workers, more gracious than I expected for dockhands, took up a collection for the boy's mother to help with expenses. The dry dock

8

supervisor talked to the two chaps who'd been up in the rigging with the boy and who tried to reach him on the access planks.

"You mustn't blame yourselves, lads. It was a freak accident. There'll be no inquiry."

"Yes sir, but it could have been one of us. He was a good chum. We'd drunk a lot of beers together. It was real sad talking to his mother."

"I'm sorry."

* * *

I was glad to be moved finally to my current mooring. Teams of carpenters are now adding strength and detail to the captain's quarters, the dining room and lounge, the brig, the surgeon's rooms, the kitchen, and not least, the first-class cabins.

As I focus on their activities, the shrill blast of the factory whistle screeches throughout the dockyard. It's noon. Lunch time. The men drop their tools and saunter down the gangplanks to the wharf. Half head to the nearest pub for an ale and a sandwich, while the older ones stay behind and form a group which sits on broken upturned oak barrels. They light their pipes and share yarns and lies about their latest good deeds and exaggerated misfortunes, inhaling the camaraderie of fellow workers secure in the King's pay for craftsmen's skills.

It will please me when their work is done. The constant noise of hammer, saw and other work invades my senses. The dust and grime irritate me, especially when the workers' boots grind the debris into the new deck floorboards.

I will admit one thing though. When it's all finished, the above-deck structures will look superb. I've peeked at the naval architect's plans, and he definitely has an eye for style that doesn't skimp on functionality.

Overall, I am impressed. The majority of these carpenters know their trade. A smart official in the dockyard administration must have paid well to get true craftsmen to work on the finer details. No doubt some of the Navy's coins disappeared into that official's own pockets. Corruption occurs at all levels here. To hire experts is much smarter than to employ amateurs who have to be told which nail to use and which plank to measure and cut. How did some of those incompetent chaps avoid apprentice school? The answer is obvious to all us ships - they never went! Rather, they gained a couple of years' experience when they worked for a master carpenter who didn't want to shell out payment for higher quality help.

Mind you, there is one worker in particular I am keeping my eye on. I think he likes his lunch-time beers a bit too much. Several times after the noon break, he has returned unsteadily from one of the pubs across the street behind the main docks. I've made sure to hold the gangplank firm when he comes aboard.

This chap was assigned to complete the corner of a small storage area behind the kitchen where two walls converged. I watched carefully as he nailed the cross boards on the outside of the walls. It was clear he was saving nails, possibly to resell and make money for himself. Nothing I could redress unfortunately. As a result, however, many of the boards are looser than they should be. By the time the insides of the walls were plastered, and the outsides painted over, it was hard to tell. Also, the barrels of salted pork lined high inside the room help obscure the truth. No-one else has said anything, but I know. The sloppy work may lead to problems later.

* * *

In the main administration building Admiral McNulty strokes his meticulously trimmed pepper and salt beard, looks up from paperwork and calls his adjutant in to the office. "How goes progress on *Lady Corinth*? The report from the dry dock on the copper sheathing is excellent, although we lost a tradesman I understand? I hate these accidents."

"Yes sir, couldn't be saved.

"Carpenters are busy on the main deck. Should finish in three days. Work proceeds on schedule, sir."

"Good. She's got a long journey ahead. Let's try out the new lightweight sails on her."

"Aye, aye, sir. Anything else, sir"

"Push those carpenters along. The prison authorities are annoying me with their constant demands for a departure shortly. Also, tell Captain Coubro to stop by, so we can set a date for the sea trial. That's all."

"Yes sir. I'll track the Captain down immediately."

* * *

Let me educate you a bit more about the hulks.

Why, you ask. Two reasons.

One, I fear that I might become one of them some dark day in the future. It's my worst dream. I do not want to suffer the ignominious, debased end predicated by their form. It's a horror that rends my

11

feelings and outlook too frequently. I would prefer to die fighting my country's enemies. Many ships that have never returned are remembered for the valiant contributions and sacrifices they made in war. It's glorious to die in service. It's pathetic so sit impotent in a virtual graveyard.

The second reason the hulks are on my mind is that in ten days' time one hundred seventy-three convicts will come aboard, and some will be transferees from the hulks anchored out in the harbour.

It seems strange to say, but those particular prisoners are probably the lucky ones. I have no clue how the official rules work that govern who gets chosen for 'transportation' to Sydney. Some prisoners will have seven-year sentences, some fourteen, and some life. The latter can never return to Britain, the others may if they so choose once their term of punishment is completed.

From what I've learned from other ships who've been to Australia, most emancipists* will elect to stay, however, because opportunities there are perceived to be far better than those back here. Sad to say, that's an ironic but truthful reflection on the state of our economy and society.

* * *

When old vessels are way past their prime and no longer sea-worthy, the Navy, in cooperation with civil authorities, takes charge. Workmen remove masts, sails, rigging, rudders, cannon, and anything else that makes the ship sailable and defensible. Internally, the holds are reconfigured to create cells for the convicts. Usually there are three levels of flooring, with low-ceilinged iron bar cells, each designed to accommodate six prisoners. The small cages include narrow, short bunks, but often those can't be used, as the prisoners are in heavy

12

ankle chains at night and some can't lift their bodies to the uppermost bunks, as they are weak from malnutrition, illness, and emaciation. Robbery of others' possessions is a common pastime, so fights are frequent. The weak get weaker, the strong stronger.

The hulks' portholes are usually secured shut or boarded over to prevent escape, but this only exacerbates poor ventilation and subsequent disease on board. Prison diets are poor, since they consist mainly of ox-cheek, salted meat, oatmeal, bread, or biscuit. Water is drawn from local rivers, so dysentery is common. Over time, the effect of these arrangements leads to a cargo of human scarecrows. The dead are usually taken ashore every morning and flung into a paupers' pit.

Every day, those prisoners who are still able to walk are ferried to a landing point, where they are put to work, still in chains. They might be assigned to build roads and paths around the harbour, to help out on the docks, or to move ballast from a quarry location to the shoreline. Overseers have an eager desire and practiced reflex to use whips to keep workers from slacking. As a result, many prisoners fall and die from pain or exhaustion.

* * *

To me, it is sickening that humans treat other humans so badly. I'm just thankful that there are no women on the hulks, although even when ensconced in land gaols they do not necessarily fare well.

I wish I could communicate better with those floating prisons, but in the process of rendering them helpless, authorities have essentially made them incapable of speech. No rigging means no rope, no cable, no chains to stretch, rub, and clang to send messages. Dockside, we hear grunts of various timbre, as boards and railings creak but nothing we can understand.

So very sad.

The general assessment is that the hulks are worse than land prisons, gateways to hell.

As I indicated earlier, they spoil my view. In multiple ways.

One thing I promise you. It's easy to rant about the hulks, but woe betide any mean-hearted guard from one of those floating affronts to humanity and decency who sets foot on my decks. I'll work doubly hard to make his life miserable.

What? Not sure you heard right? You wonder how a solid wooden vessel can impact a specific human on board? Ha, just wait and see how slippery I can make deck planks and guard rails... I have other ways as well...

Wait a minute! I'm making an assumption here, so let me check. ...You are coming on this trip to Sydney with me, right? ...Yes...?

Good. I'll show you what I mean somewhere along the way. Be ready!

* * *

The carpenters are long finished for the day, and I'm free of human presence onboard, save for the fire-watch. A few guards walk back and forth on the wharf and between the buildings, making sure no strangers wander into the naval shipyard and sneak aboard a ship or steal materials. Aside from those chaps, things are quiet. Peaceful in fact. I treasure this time because I know once the crew arrives and the prisoners finally come on board it will be noisy twenty-four hours a day. Even if all the prisoners sleep at night, the crew will still be active. The helmsman will pass on orders depending on the wind, and the bells will sound at their programmed intervals.

At this moment however the only external sounds are the slight slap, slap, slap of the waves on my hull and the creak of rope lines as they tighten and loosen on the bollards as I sway with the waves.

All very reassuring.

There are other internal sounds however that I don't like. Scratch, scratch, scratch. Rats! Arrrghhh. What's worse, the authorities forgot to put a cat back on board to hunt them down. There are many things I can do to look after myself. There are others I can't manage. I was totally devoid of the little furry foreigners before I went to dry-dock, but this pair boarded me there.

These rodents are brazen, afraid of no one. They've found a secluded spot on the first level below deck, midway between compartments to port and starboard. The compartments were meant to have a common wall but they don't. One more surprising piece of sloppy construction I'll have to pay attention to if we hit turbulent weather. There's a gap about three inches wide, that tapers to a point ten inches back. Perfect for the rodents. That is, until the pair produces a swarm of wee ones, and they'll need a bigger nest. Where can I get a damned cat? If I don't get one soon I could end up with a major problem. Rats are prolific breeders. I need to keep my structure clean.

Oh, I forgot something about the evening quiet. There are two sea gulls atop my aft mast, their heads tucked under their wings. They clearly feel safe roosting for the night up there. Not all ships are gifted with that privilege.

I interpret their presence as a good omen.

It's heart warming to feel wanted.

2. *Captain, officers, and crew*

The carpenters no longer work here, so the days are now as noiseless as the nights. Two of each pass in relative silence.

It's been dull with no activity so I feel grateful when Admiral McNulty and a tall, hitherto unseen gentleman come aboard. They pause on deck and look around. The Admiral turns to his companion and says, "Captain Coubro, let's tour your vessel. She'll impress you. McNulty has been on board only once before, to check on maintenance progress, but he has an excellent memory and a finer eye for detail than I'd given him credit for. He takes the captain everywhere, starts with the lowest level in the hold, and works his way up to the main deck. He misses nothing; the extra anchors, the new bilge pumps, the heads, improved ventilation ducts, the prisoner cells, locations for food stores, space for the paying passengers' belongings, the rudder, sailors' quarters, the first-class cabins, the captain's and officers' rooms, the brig, the surgeon's bay, the longboats, cannons, capstan, helm wheel, storage lockers, and finally the masts, shrouds and rigging. It is a very thorough tour, and I'm clearly ready for sea. Throughout, Coubro asks penetrating questions about quality, functionality of new equipment, relevant experiences from other vessels, and issues he may need to be aware of. McNulty answers quickly and assuredly, befitting his position and authority.

At the head of the gangplank as he is about to depart, the Admiral pauses, his hand raised under his chin for a moment. "The new sails will be delivered tomorrow. There's thirty of them."

"Thank you, sir. I heard the Navy was testing different material in sails. What replaces the current canvas ones, and why?"

"The ones you'll receive are much lighter, made of cotton and hemp. Should work better, particularly when wet. I'll be anxious to see and hear how they perform."

I'm all ears, for this is encouraging news. The current fabric in sails is finely woven linen made from flax, the same linen which forms the lining of naval officers' jackets. When soaked, flax sails become very heavy. This stresses me, as the weight redistributes along my main axis and affects my ability to change direction quickly.

Lighter sails would also make it easier for the sailors to manage. How those chaps stay aloft and work the sails in high winds and rain, often in the dark is beyond me. I salute their strength, determination and ability to put fear aside, especially when they have to reef or furl the sails in storms.

Formalities observed, the two men salute each other and the Admiral strides along the wharves towards his office.

Thirty minutes later a shout of "Ahoy *Lady Corinth*," comes from the rail. It brings the Captain out of his cabin to meet four men of varied size and dress who've just climbed aboard. The shortest one has a noticeable limp. It's clear from his readiness that Coubro has been expecting them.

"Good afternoon, gentlemen. Welcome aboard. Leave your gear here and let's head to my cabin to introduce ourselves, after which we'll tour this fine lady."

I beam inwardly. Fine lady indeed! I like that appellation. It suits me. And I like Captain Coubro for using it. Yes, sir. Maybe this man will turn out to be first rate. He's approximately six foot four inches, and carries himself with a commanding presence. Square of jaw, with a close-trimmed black beard, a hint of grey in his locks and an athletic figure, his penetrating blue eyes catch one's attention immediately. I learned when he and Admiral McNulty were together that he served in the battle of Trafalgar and since then has captained several navy gunships which sailed between London and New York. The Admiral had praised Coubro, and indicated that he was recognized by the administration as a smart, no-nonsense leader, who was fair with his crew and who looked after the owners' ships.

While Coubro is a Navy appointee, I'm owned by the private shipbroker firm of Camden, Calvert and Richard. The company has an arrangement with the Navy to supply certain officers under Coubro, although the owners are not obliged to preserve the Navy's ranking system and traditional officer responsibilities. Since the firm receives a fixed price per convict transported, the primary focus is to provide a functional crew that will ensure safe delivery of the convicts to Australia.

Once everyone is seated in his quarters Coubro turns to the chap immediately to his left with an inquiring look. The man stands up, extends his right hand and says. "I'm your surgeon superintendent, Cap'n. Name is Arthur Crisp. I have a Doctor of Medicine degree from the University of Edinburgh, now make my home in London. This will be my fourth long trip, the previous ones all to America. I look forward to the challenges that will arise from a mixed contingent of passengers headed to a tough destination. Bring them to me."

"Glad to have you aboard, Mr. Crisp. I must ask, as a physician, wouldn't you find more remunerative work ashore?"

"My father was a captain, sir. Grandfather was a surgeon. This way I please both men."

19

Coubro nods in appreciation of well-understood family influences and obligations.

The surgeon is a handsome chap, an inch shorter than the captain, with a gentle mien, seems a bit reserved and not overly vocal. Close cut curly hair, no beard, long neck. His hands are large, and I imagine they could cradle a newborn baby almost completely, or hold firm a patient's arm or leg that he's about to suture. He exudes self-confidence without being overbearing.

The man next to him speaks without being asked. "Padraig Plunkett, Cap'n. As quartermaster I've plenty of practice dealing with crews like what you'll probably have here. You'll be 'avin' the best team o' men this side of the Blarney, Cap'n. I'll see to it."

Coubro grins from ear to ear. "I know a good Paddy joke I'm sure you'll appreciate, but I'll save it till later."

"I'll look forward to hearing it Cap'n," Plunkett responds. "I like how the name has given rise to hundreds of inane behaviors and actions." He leans back and laughs with an infectious mirth that puts smiles on everyone's face. The thick mat of orange red hair on his head, and the magnificent matching full beard that frames his pock-marked face, bob up and down as he tries to calm himself. It takes a couple of minutes, but eventually he regains his composure. His confidence in laughing so readily in the presence of his new commanding officer, is not lost on the others. It's obvious from their grins and nods that they immediately like and respect the man.

Coubro extends his hand in welcome and says, "We'll get on swell, Plunkett. Glad you're here." It is an important assessment, for the job of quartermaster is to keep the ship running efficiently. Also, more importantly, he represents the crew's interests in hazardous situations.

Should a captain want to sail through a narrow channel between rocky isles as a shortcut, but the crew feels doing so might be dangerous because of high winds known to frequent the passage, the crew could have the quartermaster present their view to the captain. A wise captain would rarely go against a quartermaster's input.

Plunkett has a loud, gruff voice, good for shouting instructions to crew members up in the rigging no doubt. He's of medium build, just short of six feet. The next chap however, wouldn't reach to five feet six inches. Coubro turns his way. "And?"

"Charles Matheson, Cap'n. I'm your Master and Pilot. Pleased to be of service, sir. My home town is norwest of here a bit, sir. Born and raised in Southampton I bin. Lived there all m' twenty-nine years. My father owns a pub, I help out when on leave, am good at the numbers, did fine with the three R's at school, took classes on geography then charts at the naval yard right here. Done sailed to Cape Town once, but now as part owner of Father's pub I spend all my spare time helpin' him out. He's gettin' older, sir, beggin' your pardon. Heard of this trip and volunteered. Would like to see Cape Town again, sir. I can get you there and on to Australia safely."

The Master, sometimes called the Sailing Master, will be our navigator. These pilots, to use an old term, are often the best all-round sailors on board any ship, due to their experience and extended education. They plot the ship's route and make sure she stays on course. Matheson apparently has the right education for his position. Pale-faced, with brass spectacles, his hair neatly brushed, minimal cheek and chin fuzz, he looks more like an accountant than a sailor. His clothes are clean pressed, a silver buckle is prominent on his belt, and his black boots rise to mid-calf. He seems to tilt slightly to one side when he stands.

Coubro scrutinizes him closely, probably wondering if the natty clothes and unblemished hands mean the man doesn't like to work at any outside deck functions. Not that it matters; perhaps a little unusual that he doesn't have the expected demeanor of an experienced man of the open seas.

"OK Matheson, do you have the latest charts from the Admiralty, and have you studied them?" It seems Coubro has decided on a small test of the man's capability and preparedness.

Matheson surprises the men with his answer. "Yes, Cap'n. I picked them up this morning when the Admiral was with ye. There's nothing new in the English Channel nor the seas southwest, sir, but I noticed some changes on the chart for Table Bay at Cape Town. They've identified underwater reefs that weren't on the charts I used last time, sir. That's real good, because the Bay is notorious for violent winter storms when the wind blows on to the lee shore. Being driven on to that reef would be disastrous."

The man oozes self-assurance, unfazed by Coubro's challenge, nor the clearly obvious expectation that he wouldn't have obtained charts before coming on board.

"Glad to have you with us, Matheson." Coubro immediately proffers his hand.

I thought Matheson's handshake was weak compared to those of the others. Made me wonder. Does he consider himself a better man than Coubro because of a superior education? Or is it something else? Do I see something that isn't there?

"Last but not least, Cap'n," the fifth man speaks up. "Duncan Conway, boatswain and Naval agent. When do we sail?"

On this voyage, if it's to be like others my owners have organized, the boatswain, or bo'sun, will oversee the maintenance of the ship and all the resources it carries. Everything from the food, water, rum, wine, brandy, beer, gunpowder, shot, sails, rope, cables, wood, spars, sailcloth, cordage, lines, and tar required to keep the ship and crew fit for action. The bo'sun also organizes the watches, and makes sure the crew is responsive to the bells.

My first impressions of the man...? A taciturn Scot, somewhat controlling, probably very efficient, but with little humor. Heavily muscled with broad shoulders and a thick neck, a full somewhat unkempt beard that reaches past the bottom of his throat. It's easy to imagine him in a clan kilt tossing the caber at the Highland games. Height? Halfway between Matheson and the Captain.

Coubro addresses the four. "I imagine you asked the administration and the company about me, but let me tell you directly about my philosophy of command. First, you all have outstanding reputations, or you wouldn't be here. I look forward to making this voyage with you. I believe strongly in loyalty, obedience, and trust. Obedience in following my orders directly. I trust that you will execute them and manage your responsibilities well. I will give you every freedom to perform, and to do what you need to do to make our voyage as efficient and as comfortable as possible for everyone on board. That means paying passengers, prisoners, marines, and crew alike.

"But hear me well, I will not tolerate repeated mistakes or violations of trust. We are the leaders on this ship. Together, we hold the safety of everyone on board with our directions and actions. Our behavior sets examples for others to observe and follow. Keep that in mind at all times, and we'll have a fine trip."

Wow! Once again, I am impressed. Other captains I've served under let the officers learn their commander's whims and interests enroute. Often the hard way, when the officer did something the captain didn't approve of.

I like Coubro's stated notion of trust. He has made his men feel they are an integral part of his team. While the captain is the supreme authority on board ship, his actions and commands establish a tone, rhythm, and standard of effort and behavior for the rest of the crew. He can be aloof and imperial, he can be a harsh over-bearing disciplinarian, or he can be firm, fair, and consistent, in both judgment and treatment. Coubro must yet prove himself to his officers, but in my view, he's certainly started out well.

After a lengthy tour, and as soon as the newcomers have organized their cabins, Coubro calls them together again in the officers' mess. He makes it clear that it is up to the four to select whatever crew members are needed for the trip. The men are authorized to pick the master gunner, carpenter, cook, and other mates, as well as all the other petty and warrant officers required, along with the able-bodied and ordinary seamen.

He adds a couple of additional qualifications. "Minimise press-gang recruits. I'd prefer that each seaman has been hand-picked by one of you. There should be enough candidates who've returned from the wars to make that possible. I anticipate a crew of no more than sixty."

Press-gangs are small groups of men who capture youths, drunks, criminals, louts and vagabond naïfs from the streets, and drag them into onboard slavery, for which they receive a 'finder's fee' as reward. Coubro wants to avoid a bunch of untrained, coerced individuals who've never been afloat before. He knows there will inevitably be some. In order to avoid the hire of forced labour it will take the officers longer to find experienced men anxious to sail. Another inherent challenge Coubro has set.

"I'd like to personally interview all candidates for cook and carpenter. The carpenter and his mate should have been shipbuilders at some stage, and the cook and his mates should have broad experience. I want someone who has cooked for all the different groups we'll have on board, first-class passengers, officers, convicts, marines and crew. And he'd better be familiar with foods to combat scurvy – we'll want plenty of lime-juice, fresh fruit, kale, and onions available. I'll not have that terrible disease on my ship."

Over the years, I've served under many different captains. They all had foibles and preferences. Most are now shadows in my memory, but a couple stand out. The worst was an older man, who before the ship left port, exhibited the standard capabilities of a captain preparing for departure. Things changed markedly once at sea however.

The crew on the specific voyage I recall were English or Scottish, and to a man formed an intense dislike of the steerage passengers, all of whom were Irish. No, I won't name the ship or the captain or our route. I listened carefully to conversations in the officers' mess lounge. At the end of the first day out of port the captain exclaimed, "I don't care if those Irish scum never see anything except through their portholes. And I hope they are sick as dogs down there. Let them rot."

As I've mentioned, captains have supreme authority over everything under their command once they leave the home shore. Their influence on behavior of everyone on board stems directly from the examples they provide. Ever since that trip I have observed what captains say and do more closely than do any of my sister ships I've talked to.

On the particular trip I remember, after three days of violent storms the seas flattened out, and pleasant, light breezes pushed us through the sunshine. It meant the crew didn't have to work hard.

The captain rationed the passengers' vittles down to the absolute minimum allowed by law, and allocated surplus food to the crew. Over the next two weeks under easy sail the crew members became bored and lethargic. Discipline dropped away. Three of the more daring men smuggled several loose women above deck for sexual congress. When the captain found out, instead of being angry, he actively participated in the debauchery. He'd spend the afternoon in his cabin, either sleeping off his drunkenness or fornicating with one or more of the wayward souls who offered themselves in return for grog.

Incarcerated below deck, with no access to exercise room on deck or to fresh air there, the captive passengers became more and more angry. Ordinary conversations abbreviated into shouts and yells. Differing views on what should be done led to fights. Red-faced men stomped on the floor planks, pulled down timber ceiling boards, and broke them into club-sized weapons. I winced each time they stripped a part of me, yet I sympathized with their cause. My little hurts were of minor consequence compared to what the passengers were experiencing.

The women were outraged that the sluts above deck had no interest in getting better food and medicine delivered to their brethren, especially since many children were ill. The hold reeked from vomit and poor sanitation in the heads. One outraged mother vented, "Who else would like to tie those whores naked under the bowsprit and wash them clean when we reach some heavier seas?" Muttered responses were widespread, a number of a far more violent nature.

The vehemence surprised me. It was an ugly scene.

26

Violence should always be a last resort, but in this case, I had become a prison ship and passengers' verbal pleadings to the food deliverers had fallen on deaf ears up on deck for much too long. I sensed a battle was imminent.

I learned more about the strength of human emotions on that pseudo prison voyage than I'd witnessed before. Ordinary men and women will tolerate a lot, but there comes a breaking point, at which stage emotions can lead to unpredictable actions, sometimes with dire consequences. I now pay more attention to the condition and environment of passengers, criminal or otherwise. It's important that they not become agitated beyond their breaking point.

Not that I can do a lot about human behavior on board. I simply watch, absorb, and prepare for the consequences.

The consequent uprising of the Irish passengers registers vividly in my memory. Strong men beat the sailors who delivered food, then dressed in their clothes, and returned enmasse to the galley, where they overpowered the cooks. The passengers who remained climbed through the deck hatches that had been left open, and in groups threatened to beat the seamen on deck unless they surrendered, at which point those who did were restrained with heavy ropes.

Lunch was about to conclude in the officers' mess when twenty Irishmen broke in. Despite having already drunk too much, the officers retaliated, using their knives and forks to slash and cut. But the passengers jabbed their rough-splintered truncheons into stomachs and faces, and with anger-fueled violence, soon prevailed.

Out on deck, another group of men locked the off-duty sailors in their compartments, and in forty-five minutes it was all quiet. Anyone who protested had a rag stuffed in his mouth and his wrists tied together behind his back.

A small gang of women surprised me with their level of viciousness. They captured the five harlots, cut off their hair, then stripped them and tied them to the masts. Ropes pulled their throats, ankles and midriffs tight against the wood. Their wrists were stretched back and strapped behind the posts, and their mouths were stuffed with pieces torn from their own clothes. As final retribution, hot thick pitch was plastered over their vulvas and painted across their breasts.

Women who were far more reasonable took over the cooking and looked after the wounded, while the men rounded up all the arms onboard, forcibly contained the captain and officers, and through them, the rest of the crew. The captain was encouraged to return to port to explain his actions to the authorities.

I admit I don't pretend to understand the British system of justice. Several trials were held, and although the records were sealed, I learned through untold means what happened. Little recognition of the seriousness of the passengers' plight was recorded. Instead, amazingly, the ringleaders from below deck were jailed for varying periods due to the seizure of private property, the damage they had caused, and the unlawful detention of the sailors. Yet the captain and his officers were given only mild reprimands. They were all permitted to crew again. Conversely, most passengers were denied future transportation on the shipping line, and had to scrounge money to return to Ireland. I was surprised to hear the lack of compassion in the courtroom proceedings. Navy Rule is incredibly powerful.

Even so, that captain better not step on my deck again.

These sorts of incidents leave a bad taste in one's mouth. As the protective outer skin and conveyance on any trip, one of my functions is to safeguard everyone on board. I have to ensure that crew, passengers, convicts, and militia arrive safely at the planned destination, no matter the relationships between the distinct groups. In the end they are all humans and need to be treated as such, even when they are on opposite sides of the law. I acknowledge that different degrees of supervision and behavior are practiced, but extreme differences in treatment are not justified. Despite somewhat contradictory evidence from this particular trip, the majority of men and women are not members of the animal kingdom.

We ships have a role that is defined by service. Our job is to move people and goods from one place to another. As safely as possible. We are not factories that turn out widgets hour after hour. We are not buildings designed to open and shut at pre-determined times for workers' pursuit of business or pleasure. And we are not shops built to offer goods for sale to those who frequent us. Rather, we are time-honored servants, even in war. Carefully designed, and lovingly built; wooden, canvas, rope and chain servants at sea.

We make no major decisions on our own, we respond to decisions made by the masters aboard. We proudly use our sea-faring abilities to execute the orders we are given.

Service.

Ever since I understood what it really means, my motto has been 'I do but serve'.

The actions of a captain affect everyone on board. One of the more public examples is Captain Bligh's cruelty on the *Bounty* in the South Pacific twenty-five years ago which led to the mutiny of most of the crew. Bligh's exaggerated and incongruous sense of discipline and the floggings he imposed for minor infractions of procedure were way out of line. They led to an incredibly drastic response in which he and eighteen sympathizers were set adrift in a longboat. We sailing ships identify strongly with the *Bounty* which eventually made it to Pitcairn Island. She was an unwitting participant in one of naval history's greatest peacetime altercations. Contrary to the court's findings, Bligh goes in our bad books, while Fletcher Christian, the courageous officer who stood up to Bligh, goes in our good books. And the *Bounty*, bless her ancient soul, stands as a sentinel to accommodating service, with the help she provided Christian to find safe harbour at Pitcairn Island. She gave her life when she was scuttled to ensure no one sailed away to the British authorities.

A plethora of incidents over the years that demonstrated outrageous behavior by captains and crew eventually forced the Lords of the Admiralty to create a Code of Conduct for the crews of naval ships, and some of the private shipping lines adopted the code as well. I have no doubt Captain Coubro is well aware of those rules.

In my view, Coubro's early actions portend favorably for a well-managed trip. I particularly like how right up front he delegates authority, and makes it clear that he insists on loyalty from his officers. Smart to support the judgment of his officers in hiring, and to only insist on personal approval of a limited number of hires in important positions. That's what I've seen other good captains do.

I wonder what sort of fellows the officers will round up as crew for our trip to Sydney.

* * *

Everyone says it's imprudent to judge a book by its cover, but I can't help myself. Over the next couple of days, males of varying ages, sizes, and demeanor drift onboard, some singly, some in small groups. Sent by one of Coubro's underlings they are not officially on duty, so they familiarize themselves with my layout, the arrangement of cabins, their quarters, the holds, and the rigging, and help load non-perishable stores.

This emerging band of sailors is a mixed lot, to say the least. Some of the younger ones with rosy complexions don't look old enough to leave their mothers. A number don't even have whiskers on their chins, yet. One pair, with holes in their trousers and jaunty hats, ran up the gangplank and somersaulted several times across the deck. Young men having fun, out to show the world they haven't a care in life. My bet is they'll turn green the minute the first big wave hits my bow and we shudder through a large swell.

An older fellow has one thumb missing. Was he a butcher in an earlier life, or a billiards hustler caught, and relieved of his ability to play? He has a scowl on his face that may be permanent. It hasn't disappeared in two days.

Another chap has a patch over his left eye – reminiscent of pirate tales. There's a scar that runs from under the patch across his cheek. Not the prettiest face to present to the world.

Four chums arrive very drunk. They can't be much over twenty years old. I doubt they've had any sea-going experience as it's comical to watch them navigate the gang-plank. Two crawl on hands and knees, the other two stagger aboard upright. Fortunately, no one falls into the water below. They're coarse in demeanor and language, and their accents brand them as Cockney louts. I'm surprised they aren't sporting black eyes or lumps from altercations. Maybe they are smarter than I suspect, able to keep insults about local ignorant peasants to themselves. At least till well outside the pubs, like now.

31

The chap who brings up the rear sings a raucous shanty. His friend in front turns and implores, "Bag it Tom, we 'eard it enuff t'nite."

"Well, wish I cud play t'cordyun like that chap in the King's Arms done. Nearly as good as some we's seen in London pubs. Not that you would know, Pete. 'Cos you only had eyes for that barmaid with the bleached hair."

A third fellow wraps his arms around Pete's shoulders, and leers at his companion. "Wasn't her hair you was interested in, was it mate?" He turns to the fourth member of the group. "What do you think Archie?"

Archie laughs, a hearty drink-fueled cackling sound. "Cor, lads, did you see the tits on 'er? Mammoth. An' enough room to waggle your head b'tween 'em and go 'brrrrrrrr'. Lov'ly an' pink." His laughter bounces off the walls of the deck cabins.

Tom pipes up. "Ah, yo's all kiddin' yoursel's. She'd never hold still for any city boy. One swat with those thick arms an' we'd be on the floor. Well, maybe not Charles. She might like black boys. Don' see many in these parts."

Charles rises to the occasion. "Yeah, well I wouldn't mind tryin'. Ev'ry gal in there had plenty t'offer. Country broads, right off the farm. Know how to do it f'sure. I lov 'em."

"Ah, put it away Chas," Pete responds. "You've missed y'last chance at braggin'. We're off to see t'world tomorra. In this 'ere ship, *Lady Corinth*. Are ya too drunk to remember your bo'sun friend done recruit us?"

Archie's laugh fills the air again. "Hold up guys, I gotta pee again. Right here into the harbor... Ooh now, that feels better."

I tune out. Heard it all before. Nervous braggards, fortified with grog, trying to convince themselves they can tackle anything by avoiding the subject at hand. Sometimes crude, mean recruits make me bristle. But these drunkards are harmless compared to others. I'll watch how they adjust in the weeks ahead.

All in all, it's a motley group of sailors that has turned up. Some exhale alcohol fumes, some smell of tobacco as strongly as a seasoned humidor, others reek from a lack of bathing. Those need to stand outside in the next rain shower, lest I somehow cause them to tumble overboard.

I imagine most of the youngsters have been recruited for their strength and enthusiastic attitudes, the older ones for their experience and general smarts. I know from past voyages that some of the thinly built older chaps can handle surprisingly heavy loads and outshine tough young fellows in arm wrestling and other strength games. That's because they are all muscle, no fat. I try not to make too many forecasts as to who will and who won't work out, but I've already developed my mental lists of 'yay' and 'nay' men, and have filed them away. Time will tell whether my prognostications are accurate.

The sailors' berths are forward of the foremast near the bow. The quarters are cramped, not only because I taper inwards there, but also because space is needed elsewhere for the prisoners and passengers. Tradition, and experience, suggest that sailors tolerate the sounds of the bow as it slams into waves just ahead of their berths much better than would ordinary citizens, were the passenger quarters established in the bow.

The sailors sleep in simple hammock bunks, end to end, one above the other, with each fellow's head less than fifteen inches from the boots of the chap in front, and the same distance below the chap above.

There are fewer bunks than total seamen, since at any time, some men will be on duty.

The quarters can feel physically intimidating. Especially for those who are new to the life of a seaman, they can generate stress simply because so many strangers are packed so close to one another. With limited ventilation, anyone who smokes quickly makes the tight conditions even worse. A certain degree of tolerance is required of all. Some men are much more flexible and adaptable than others. Bullies tend to rule the quarters at first, but arrangements change over time.

On sight of these sleep arrangements, one of the fresh–faced youngsters, who hoped to earn a living at sea, immediately turned pale. "You won't coop me up in there. I'd be buggered in no time." he yells, proving my point.

He retreats quickly, turns, and races back across the deck and escapes down the gangplank. "Better he's gone now than in two weeks' time," Padraig, the quartermaster, says to the first mate. "Would be a long swim home then."

I agree. Weaklings, or those with a timid character, should not apply to be sailors. It's a tough life. Cramped sleep quarters are the least of their worries. Frequently cold and wet, forced to handle heavy ropes and sails, push the capstan around, climb slippery rigging, launch longboats - all require commitment and energy well beyond the norm of a landlubber. Many newbies only learn from the whip lashings yielded by the supervisory mates.

The best seamen are usually wiry in build, with upper body and leg strength. They have hands that are calloused from handling the ropes in the rigging. I should add they also have a vocabulary that isn't suitable for delicate female ears. Within any crew, a pecking order exists. The top tier consists of those sent highest in the rigging to furl and unfurl the sails while perched precariously fifty feet or more above the tossing deck, regardless of weather. For that work, they need an innate sense of balance, no fear of heights, a blindfolded familiarity with knots, and an innate tenacity to cling tight and survive in high winds and rain. Their mantra is 'one hand for the ship, one for one's self.' Not all sailors can handle the foretop conditions.

Speaking of sails, around noon, great clanking sounds signal the arrival of my sails, carried on a series of old carts drawn along the docks by teams of horses. Duncan, the boatswain, takes twenty men to unload them. He yells to his gang the minute his feet hit the wharf. "Jump to it you lubbers, lift them sails off the carts and lay 'em out on the dock. They're bent on before dark, or you don't eat."

With the new light-weight sails I'll feel ten years younger.

"You," Duncan bawls at the lead horseman, "make damned sure all them 'orses and carts are off them sails when we stretch 'em out on the dock. I don' wan' no 'orse shit on 'em before they're aboard. Any 'orseshit on my sails, his driver eats it! You hear me? Go tell your mates."

The delivery man cowers at Duncan's voice, maneuvers his horse and now-empty cart behind the shed, and rushes back to help his porters empty their carts.

Turning to his crew, Duncan bawls again. "OK, now I want the topsail and the topgallant first. Joe, Willy, find the cart they're on, and get it fast."

He mutters, not quietly, to himself, "Goddamn, I hope these lubbers smarten up. I've got twenty-one sails to bend on and nine more to stow. I'll burn some arse this 'arvo."

Sails are bulky and hard to handle. The ones that hang from yardarms are wider at the bottom than the top. The lowest sail on the main mast is called the main 'course'. It can be thirty feet across at the top and forty feet across at the bottom. Twelve feet high. Nearly four hundred square feet of cloth. Fifty-six sailmaker's yards. A yard of cloth weighs about seven pounds these days, so the fabric in that huge main course weighs over four hundred pounds. To that add the weight of edge seams, bolt-rope, rings, grommets, shackles, reef-points and other trim fittings. Any sailor worth his nightly share of rum can lift eighty pounds or more. Sails this size, wet or dry, take teamwork to move them onboard and up to the yardarm.

Duncan's a true bo'sun. His cusses could make paint peel off the wall. He has terms, bodily references, and family expletives, along with creative phrases of 'encouragement' I've not heard before. A couple of times I see them bring a quick smile to the recipient, who disappears when Duncan repeats his threat closer to the poor man's ear.

Every sail is in place, stretched tight, by the moon's rising, and the crew fed. Impressive. Good work. I really am looking forward to this trip.

We're lucky that there is only the lightest breeze playing. As it is, my timbers creak loudly as the mooring lines pull tight against the bollards.

Twenty-four hours ago, my masts were bare sticks prodding the clouds. Whenever that happens, I feel naked, helpless and exposed. I'm stalled, totally vulnerable to the whims of the tide unless moored to a dock or at anchor.

Right now, with every new sail in place, and momentarily unfurled, I feel grand. The sails gleam in the last rays of the setting sun and send perfect reflections across the bay.

I'm dressed up, ready to party at a ships' society ball.

A puff of wind gently billows the sails, presenting a visage of majestic beauty.

I'm not the only one to notice. Envious vessels in the harbour and docks whisper their approval.

I hope you'll excuse me a little vanity. Only a few times in a ship's life do such moments occur.

Regretfully, my feelings of pride pass too quickly, as my sails are brailed up for the night.

They provide one last shimmer in their bunting out to the bay.

3. *Sea-worthiness*

We've just returned from seven days of sea trials. The best news is that we passed all the tests and are declared fit to sail across the mighty oceans once more. The last page of the Admiralty Lords' report is posted in Captain Coubro's cabin:

'Pursuant to the aforementioned regulations for ships of His Majesty's Navy seconded to civil government requirements, and subject to compliance with the three recommendations in paragraphs 3(c), 4(d), and 6(a) above, and assuming the timely arrival of all allocated militia and convicts, said Barque 'Lady Corinth' is hereby given permission to proceed to Sydney under the sole direction and discretion of her Captain.

May God protect this ship and all those aboard in her quest.
Signed under my Seal
L. L. McNulty
Lord of the Admiralty
On Behalf of His Majesty King George III
God Save the King'

Ah, I sense your thoughts. I am enthusiastic about the report yet you immediately focus on the recommendations. You want to know what went wrong. I understand, so let me tell you.

* * *

The Lords who oversaw the tests surprised Coubro and his officers at one point with an unexpected trial. The crew had had a long day working on myriad turnarounds for tacking* and gybing* procedures, plus defense readiness actions with the cannons. Cannon balls are heavy and hard to handle, and the noise of the cannons firing is deafening. The crew had done well, but they were weary from the demands of repetitive drills. The officers and the master gunner received praise for the crew's performances. A good dinner had everyone in a relaxed mood. The nervousness most of the men felt before the start of the exercises began to eke away.

An hour before midnight, the wind changed direction, and I tugged at the anchor. Thick cloud cover swamped the moon, and a blustery southerly overtook us. Since it had been calm up to that point, only a skeleton crew of sailors was on night-watch. It wasn't enough. The able-bodied seamen who'd worked all day were roused from sleep, and the team was ordered to work the rigging and spars, brailing up the sails. To really test capabilities, half of the men were blindfolded at random. It was a valid, but dangerous, test of teamwork and skills. Good preparation if we ever have to face a blinding wind-driven rainstorm in the presence of heavy seas.

The first two go-rounds on the test were not acceptable, and Padraig was livid. He yelled over the wind at the mates assigned to lead the various teams. "C'mon you scum. Y're supposed to 'ave trained these sea dogs. Useless curs. 'ardly a brain among 'em. 'alf don' know up from down. What the fuck you bin doin'? Get out there and fix this mess, or I'll see you keelhauled."

The mates turned and hurried away without a word.

I won't repeat some of the other phrases Padraig used to berate them. It was obvious from his self-mutterings and crude shouts that repeated failure embarrassed him badly and gave rise to a deep wrath. He who'd promised to have the best team this side of the Blarney. To be shown up twice in front of the Captain and the top men of the Admiralty was totally shameful. His pride was tattered.

On the third attempt the men jumped to their duties, shouting and swearing, and the sails brailed up much faster. Even so, further practice was on the list of the Admiral's recommendations. Of course, in a real situation the men would not be blindfolded. It was a very tough test the brass threw at us. They knew it. We knew it.

The whole experience was sobering and effective. The message clear. The men must always be prepared for the unexpected. I felt relieved that no one had slipped and gotten seriously hurt. Blistered hands, rope burn marks, and twisted ankles were plentiful, all par for the course. Coubro, however, was pissed. His credibility was damaged, his reputation at risk. Over the next day or so, whenever sail management, anchoring, signaling, or longboat launching procedures were less than perfect, he cajoled, admonished, and swore at his officers, Padraig in particular.

"I don't want fucking excuses. Instill a sense of pride in the crew, and generate an attitude where they want to do their best. Promise extra rum for good work, but if a man does not pull his weight, he'll be gone the minute we return to port. Now get to it, you lot. Don't disappoint me further. Make me and the Admiral's team proud of this ship. Move your butts, or you'll be gone."

* * *

The second area where the Admirals noted a deficiency concerned our best bower anchor. Mariners know their anchors are critical, landlubbers seldom give them a thought, and yet the anchor has become the very symbol of the sea. My primary cast-iron anchor is twelve years old. It is attached to one hundred and twenty-five fathoms of chain and rope. That's two hundred and fifty yards. Now listen up. If you are going to travel with us you have to learn many naval terms. A fathom is six feet. Store that in your memory.

Actually, I have three anchors similar in shape, but of varied sizes, to be used in different circumstances such as rivers versus oceans. The anchor currently attached to the capstan is twelve feet long or tall, eight feet wide at the flukes, and weighs fifteen hundred pounds. It's old and rusty in parts and you can see where the barnacles were scraped off. Heavy? You bet.

The Admiral ordered us to drop anchor. No sooner was it deemed to be holding than the Admiral told us to weigh anchor and haul it back up. No rest for the wicked. The capstan at my bow is about three feet high, with a two-and-a-half-foot diameter base and a drum just-under two-foot in diameter. Again, the quartermaster seriously underestimated how many men were required to raise the iron mass off the sea-floor one hundred and fifty feet below. He had to call for reinforcements. That was noted in the Admiral's report. Anchoring was an exercise we hadn't practiced ahead of time, and we paid a small penalty. Padraig did not have a good time.

* * *

Now, come on, careful with your criticism, no ship's perfect. In any list of all possible issues that could have arisen, to mishandle the anchor is a small imperfection. One thing however; it provides a chance for me to talk about something landlubbers everywhere have heard of -- shanties and sea songs.

Seafarers have probably sung comradeship songs ever since two people tried to row a boat together. On a major ship, nothing beats a good shanty to coordinate sailors on heavy tasks, like hoisting yards up a mast, or hauling-up the anchor. The anchor is heavy, and the capstan requires several men on each spoke to haul it up. Even to pull rigging ropes to and from masts over one hundred feet through the air requires several sailors to work together. Shanties create a rhythm that helps the men work in unison, and at the same time distracts them from the heaviness of the task. All hands suffer equally together. The bastard anchor comes up more easily when all put similar mindless effort into the chore.

Shanties have come into vogue more and more over the last twenty years. There are plenty of them now. My favourite is 'Haul Away Joe!'* It includes two great lines: "When I was a little boy my mother always told me...That if I did not kiss the girls, my lips would grow all moldy." The rest of the song tells about a sailor's adventures with women of different nationalities until he finds one that's "just a daisy." I love the sound of the men belting it out as they turn the capstan. I can listen to it anytime.

There are times when we ships almost exhibit human-like qualities. We crave adventure more than does the average man, although we're not in control of navigating towards our destination. We value blue skies, calm waters, and fair winds. We love speed, with our sails driving us on. We accept the crew, working with them to make our journey as smooth as possible, wary of nature's whims. The sea animals are our friends. Porpoises and whales frolic beside us, reassuring us with their presence.

We are man-made, but our home is the sea, and we exist for one purpose, to sail.

We grow old just like humans. When we age, we don't travel as fast as we used to, and our timbers weaken and become thinner, but we still have pride. A ship in full sail regalia, piercing the waves, capturing the wind and running before it, is a thing of beauty. Our lives may be short, but by golly, they can be grand.

And yet, passing by the hulks as we return to port after the trials, I am reminded that our lives may not end in grandeur. Those once-beautiful ladies of sail, broken down, are now forced to serve as ugly, floating prisons until they rot away. I feel sad.

For them and me. Is that my destiny too?

* * *

Enough of these reflections. Everyone is happy to be back in port. It's no small thing to receive Admiralty approval of our sailing skills. It's one of those very positive signs that are great for morale. The crew is encouraged, despite the fact that many were harangued along the way.

But, so saying, I must confess to something that really does irritate and embarrass me. The Admirals found a strike directly against me. It's written in their third recommendation. I have to get a bit technical to explain it so bear with me

We wooden ships are 'blessed' (you understand I use that term euphemistically, right?) with what we call 'devil seams'. The seams occur in two places - where the external hull timbers join the deck planks, and also aft where the hull timbers join at the rudder post. These join points are caulked, or sealed, by jamming oakum fiber into the gaps, then smearing the seam with melted pitch or tar. If one of the seams were to work open in rough weather, a great deal of water could end up in a ship's interior before repairs could be made. It happens, and seamen who make repairs to those open seams often talk about being 'between the devil and the deep blue sea.'

Yes, you've guessed it. In their thorough inspection of my infrastructure the Admiral's team found cracks in the seams near my rudder post. One of their 'recommendations' was that we immediately re-seal those seams.

Frankly, while it was disguised as a recommendation, it was an order.

I don't understand why I couldn't feel those cracks before we left for the tests. I'm supposed to know everything about me, right? Was I blinded by the vanity I described earlier? I'm not sure what I could have done about things had I been aware of them, but that's a rationalization. I guess this Lady who loves to preen in full sail just isn't perfect.

The mention of hot pitch for the seams reminds me of something else you may be interested to know. What's that you ask? No, no, this is not an attempt to distract you. I think you'll appreciate this.

It concerns another phrase that has made its way into your idiomatic English. In every wooden ship the bilge just above the keel is the hottest, dankest, smelliest place in the vessel. It's horrible, and sailors call it 'hell' for good reason. It is regularly re-sealed with hot pitch or tar to prevent leaks. A sailor who is given the task to mop and seal down there to help keep the ship sea-worthy is said 'to pay'. It is the worst job on board and is usually handed out to a crew member who has misbehaved, broken a rule, or has been wayward in the performance of his duties. From the assignment of working in 'hell' comes the saying, 'you'll have hell to pay'.

There you have it, a truth taken from life at sea that applies to life everywhere.

* * *

45

The Admiral and his officers leave us mid-afternoon. Every man on board heaves a sigh of relief, since they have been under close scrutiny for a full six days.

Now they sit in small groups around the masts and railing reliving the plusses and minuses of each trial. I hear laughter at times and see frowns at others.

"That McNulty chap was alright, but his adjutant, whatever his name was, gave me the creeps."

"How so, matey?"

"Always writing notes, and constantly pointing out issues to his boss. He had it in for us before he stepped aboard."

"Whatever. Let it go man, he can't hurt us now."

Gradually, the men relax. They bring out treasured tobacco, stuff it in pipes or roll their cigarettes. One chap plays the accordion. A group at the bow sings a shanty. They've done well and deserve to relax.

I've one last tale to share with you from our days away being tested.

Late afternoon on the fourth day out, from the port side halfway between mid-ship and the stern, came a shout of "Man Overboard" yelled over and over. All seamen fear that cry and it sends chills through the strongest of them. It's a cry of potential death.

We were forging through light rain and oncoming waves, so the man in the water was swept backwards.

Faster than I could imagine, the officer of the watch screamed, "Life-rings away! Man braces!" and the energized crew leaped to it. Two sailors rushed to the rail to keep track of the unfortunate individual in the water. As soon as the crew were at the braces the watch screamed again, "Back Topsails, Clew up Main Course. Man your boat". The rescue boat crew was already aboard the longboat and Boats had it swinging out as he hollered to the Quarter Deck, "Boat ready. Permission to launch." The way was just beginning to come off us as the rescue boat touched water and two men jerked the falls clear.

We all hoped the chap in the water could swim to the life-rings thrown earlier. No guarantee. The rowers paced furiously, each man scared by his own fear of going overboard. Everyone understood the urgency to act quickly in order to have any hope of rescuing the man in the water.

Accidents on board happen. Rarely when the weather is calm. It is when the seas are violent and the deck is plunging and slippery as ours was that men are more apt to lose their footing and fall into the raging waters where there is little hope of survival.

That afternoon the seas were medium, but choppy. Happily, the watchers saw that the chap in the water was a strong swimmer. The water temperature wasn't a threat, and he tried repeatedly to forge his way back to the ship, but the current and the swells held him back. Shouts of encouragement from the stern and the mid-decks rang out as I turned about.

"Come on matey."

"Hang in there."

"Swim, swim."

"We're coming."

"Don't panic."

"You can do it."

Slowly, the distance between the swimmer and the hull lessened as he gradually approached the life-rings. Even so, it was the longboat, managed by six hefty oarsmen, that reached him first and hauled him aboard.

Relief flooded the ship's crew as well as the Admiralty officers. Experienced sailors are a tough breed, but a man overboard is one of their worst fears. The rescued chap was in amazingly good spirits, chiaking* with the longboat team as to why it took them so long to reach him. Onboard he was wrapped in warm blankets, given two shots of rum, and hustled off to the sick bay where the surgeon examined him. The senior Admiral congratulated the longboat crew on their prompt action and nodded to the survivor in acknowledgement of his ordeal.

But let me tell you something. I was smiling inside throughout the whole rescue. Why? Because I knew the event had been staged. Oh, yes! On the first day of tests, Captain Coubro had approached Padraig, the quartermaster. "Keep your ears and eyes open, Plunkett. I want to find a strong swimmer to help with a 'Man Overboard' exercise. Only you and I and whoever is selected are to be involved. The seas are medium and if they stay that way I don't anticipate any real danger if he has the right attitude and is truly fit. If you sense rain will arrive, all the better. Wait for it. Offer him a pound and two days double grog to participate and keep his mouth shut afterwards. Here's a one-pound note. Tear it in half in his presence, and tell him he gets one half after

48

the exercise and the other half in Sydney. That should be enough incentive for him to hold his tongue till then."

Levian Shields from New York had won several swim contests there and was incredibly fit. The reward was large, and after checking the seas he didn't hesitate to accept the role in Coubro's surprise drill. Padraig helped him 'fall' out of sight of others from the slippery deck into the slight chop and raised the alarm. It was so well done that I'd wager that the Admiral's team, and many of the crew, still have no idea of the charade. We gained respect with the Admiral's inspection team for the quick and professional response shown by regular seamen. I'm sure it helped with the mild nature of the recommendations handed down.

Back in port, Coubro comes out of his cabin and calls the crew together on the foredeck. He is all smiles. "Good work, men. Congratulations. I'm proud of you. I've ordered the cook to provide us double portions for dinner as reward, with extra rations of rum for all. You deserve it. We started too goddam slow, but we're through it now."

The resultant cheers would rouse a deaf man.

Coubro takes his time and looks at each man individually in the assemblage. When he speaks again, each seaman thinks he is being personally addressed.

"Well done, and thank you. Tomorrow, we start taking on passengers and convicts, and the last of our supplies. Then it's off to Cape Town. We sail in two days."

4. *Passengers*

Sarah Grainger glowers at the guard standing at the top of the gangplank.

"C'mon you slut," he yells, "Move along."

She turns and looks back at the long line of women prisoners which snakes across the dock to the open horse-drawn wagons in which they've just arrived. The shackles have been removed from her ankles, but the sloping gangway that juts over the four feet of open water to the deck still scares her. She's the first in line, probably put there because she is obviously pregnant. The guard beside her offers a little compassion. "Go on miss, you need to show the others how it's done. Take it nice and steady." With that he gives her a gentle push that starts her upward progress. Step-by-step, holding her belly, she slowly ascends, eyes avoiding the dark waters below. Near the top, the militia man reaches out, grabs her around the back of the neck and viciously pulls her forward.

"Hurry up, we can't wait all day," he yells.

As Sarah stumbles and falls, he slams her hard in the back with his rifle butt. She evinces a sharp yelp of pain.

I cringe. There is no need for this cruel treatment. I'm pleased the surgeon hurries to Sarah's side, pleased to see him exchange sharp words with the bullying guard. The surgeon supports Sarah enroute to the medical office. Sixty-nine more girls and women, and four children are in the line to board. I can plainly see at least two more pregnant women, their condition obvious given their thin malnourished frames.

I feel for all the prisoners. It's impossible to avoid the stench of their unwashed bodies. Many are in rags, some carry small bundles with their possessions tied up tightly. All are dirty, hair unkempt, faces, arms, and legs smeared with grime, sullen and defeated. One by one the big male guards remove the women's shackles, often pawing the women as they do so. The women ignore the intrusions, probably beyond caring, their pride completely destroyed. Probably the mildest form of abuse they've faced in the many months they've spent in prison hell. I wonder what thoughts go through their minds as they board my deck, headed for a long, dangerous journey across two major oceans, to the penal colony in Sydney. Fear, disbelief, disillusionment? Perhaps it doesn't matter anymore for them, their sense of hope for anything positive has abandoned them. I hope I learn the feelings of some of them in the months ahead.

Will it be the same with the male prisoners who are expected to arrive later in the day? A hundred and three more souls -- destination purgatory. One big difference from past circumstances looms for all the prisoners. I am to host groups of the opposite sex, one of the first times the Admiralty Lords have sanctioned such an arrangement on a convict ship. I overheard a couple of officers discussing how females were needed in Sydney because there were too many men. Strange. Authorities want to put convict men and women together there, yet keep them in separate gaols here?

Previously, all the transportation ships carried prisoners of the same sex. Whether it will help or hurt the prisoners in each group to see, maybe even converse with, members of the opposite kind, remains to be seen. Many in both groups have had their families torn asunder due to insensitive court-invoked separation. Will the new situation reinforce sadness for those not seeing their loved ones in the alternate group, or instead will it offer a chance for some to potentially find a new mate? Only time will tell. I suspect the onboard arrangements will dictate strict prisoner management practices along the way.

The river of women and children coming up the ramp slows as a clump forms close to the stern. Sarah emerges with the surgeon who gave her laudanum* for her back pain and allowed her to wash her arms and face. If her hair were to be washed and combed she'd be pretty. She is probably no more than twenty years old, but the caring treatment by the surgeon has produced a tentative smile as she joins the group. It makes my heart glow. There is indeed hope for these poor creatures.

I switch my attention to the bow of the ship where a totally different scene is unfolding. Down on the dock, Sara Goldsmith, the initial first-class passenger to arrive, gracefully steps from a smartly presented carriage and unfurls a delicate cream parasol. It matches the colour of her long dress with its pink lace ribbons back and front. A steward from the Admiralty Office offers his arm and walks with her towards the double-wide gangplank set aft of the bow. She holds her head high, pale face avoiding glances towards the other end of the dock where the prisoners are boarding, probably offended that they are even nearby. Can she smell them? I can.

I guess Sara is about thirty years old. She has an aristocratic bearing, but it is going to be a wearying journey for a lone woman on her way to join her military husband who serves in a senior capacity in the office of the Governor in the colony. I wonder if some of the other adult first class passengers will appear as snobbish as she does. Impossible to tell from the quick peek I got at the manifest.

A cleanly dressed sailor at the top of the gangplank extends a gloved hand as Sara ascends.

"Good morning Mrs. Goldsmith, welcome aboard. Let me show you to your cabin while my men collect your luggage."

"There'd better be a glass of cold champagne waiting, young man. Along with a small savory luncheon. My husband sent a list of my

53

requirements directly to your captain; I assume you received it? Where is the captain by the way? I would have expected him to welcome me on board."

What a contrast. At one end of the pier there are seventy females with hardly any belongings. If one placed their goods and chattels together in one pile it would probably fill only two of Mrs. Goldsmith's ten fine leather suitcases which the porters are wrestling at the other end of the pier.

Sara Goldsmith and Sarah Grainger. S.G. and S.G. Two women, worlds apart in background, life-experiences, fortune, and opportunity. My heart tears a little at the unfairness of the situation.

What sort of world am I helping?

* * *

But, back to more mundane issues. For example, the rats. I watched the rat family closely while engaged in our sea trials, and it was obvious that mother rat was about to offer a litter into the world. The pair had chewed a hole in a sack of corn to establish a major food supply. Nothing I could do about it except hope the cook would find out sooner rather than later.

I believe one of the Admiral's men must have seen one of the rodents at some point because a few hours after the sea trial team had left us, a dock worker came alongside holding two scrawny tabby cats by the back of their necks.

He held them up for all to see. "Courtesy per the Admiral's office."

Duncan, the boatswain, happened to be on the dock returning from the administration offices with the final stores.

"I'll take those mangy critters," he said. "Bring them on deck and we'll get a tasty bite of fish for them. Who sent them?"

"The latest ship in the Battery Basin, *Edinburgh Castle,* sir. She came back to port with cats to spare. The crew there named these two 'Hither' and 'Yon'."

"Well we definitely need them. Pass on our thanks."

And so I have become home for two new residents. They took less than thirty minutes to smell out the presence of the rats. But Hither and Yon couldn't get at them, as the rats were well entrenched. I sense a race. Momma rat to bring her litter into the world versus the two tom hunters looking for a kill.

* * *

The male prisoner contingent was expected to arrive later today, but there's a delay. A messenger has informed the captain that the men will now arrive tomorrow. Perhaps that isn't all bad because more first-class passengers have arrived. The delay will allow the surgeon and the pilot more time to check that the male prisoner compartments below deck are properly prepared, and to arrange any adjustments or fixes required.

Down on the docks, the clip clop, clip clop of a sturdy mare heralds the arrival of an elegant carriage at the foot of the passenger onramp. The driver jumps down and yells for porters. The woman inside pushes the door window curtain to one side. She peers through her prince-nez glasses which are attached to a stem so she won't have to pinch her nose, and looks around. Indignation colors her cheeks. I hear loud commands.

"Matilda, this is disgraceful. Have those men lay a canvas or carpeting over those rough boards. I will not ruin this beautiful dress with dock

55

filth. And make sure the surgeon on board is at hand. I have a dreadful headache from the smell and the horribly bumpy roads we have come by. I need some smelling salts."

"Yes, your Ladyship. I'll do what I can."

Another amusing scene. It's hard to accept the narcissism of some of these 'high-class' women. Based on my limited knowledge of the first-class passenger list this plump twenty-five-year-old who alights with the driver's help must be Lady Hudson-Smythe. She travels unaccompanied, save for her lady-in-waiting, and continues her disparaging remarks as she heads to the gangplank, but I've heard enough. I watch her maid, dressed in well-worn hand-me-downs, rush into the passenger cabin area onboard and yell for the surgeon to come treat her mistress.

That makes a pair of demanding lone first-class women passengers that the surgeon and captain will have to contend with. I hope they have well-honed streaks of tolerance, and are paid enough to remain civil throughout the journey ahead. I don't envy them.

From the next coach to arrive, a young couple alights. The pair appear self-assured, and free of any airs. They are friendly and interested in their surroundings. They ask questions of the dockhands and crew members who assist them with their luggage. Such a contrast to the two prima donnas already on board...

I wonder how everyone will get along.

By nightfall we have all our paying passengers on board. After consultation with the cook, Captain Coubro had him prepare a welcome meal of Dover sole, a dish unlikely to be repeated on the voyage ahead. The guests include one young single male who is a banker, six couples of varying ages, four noisy children between nine and eleven years old, and the two lone ladies, one with maid. No officers are present, being busy with near-final preparations for prisoners and crew. A formal welcome dinner will follow when at sea. The captain, in his egalitarian way, insisted that the maid sit at his dining table with everyone else, much to the chagrin of her employer, who created a nasty fuss as she switched chairs. She pouts throughout the entire meal service.

Oh yes, methinks. Rocky times ahead.

The other adults are all well behaved. They listen attentively as the server outlines the proposed route ahead, and the procedures and rules on board, the most important one being to avoid all contact with the prisoners.

The children are excused to the adjoining lounge where they learn about each other in their own adaptable ways. There's a reserve among the adults, however, as they limit their exposure, and try to assess their status with respect to each other, while providing minimal information. This is standard behavior I've seen many times.

Usually, the first decent storm shakes things up and in short order brings out the good, the bad, and the ugly. I can't wait to see how they all handle one of nature's tempests...

* * *

The next morning, light in the eastern sky has not yet topped the horizon when the sound of bugles, horses neighing, and men shouting, presages the arrival of the male prisoners. As the old horses pull the crude, low-sided, wooden carts off the roadway, the militia's hand-held lanterns cast long eerie shadows across the dock. The prisoners stand shackled in the carts, the heavy metal chains around their ankles clanking with every movement.

It is a scene of utter pathos.

Surrounded by drivers and militia are the helpless individuals raised from their sleep hours earlier. They are shivering in thin clothes, crowded together with no room to sit, clinging to each other for balance, grumbling as they wait to be let out. Threatened by militia whips, they are submissive, heads down, pride beaten out of them, branded as despicable villains of society.

And now they are faced with a long sea voyage, the prospect of weeks in open water, which terrifies all but a few who've had some sailing experience. I feel sorry for them, especially as I suspect some of their 'crimes' have received undeservedly harsh penalties. And, for more than a few, there's a serious question as to whether their health will stand up to the rigors ahead.

But here they are. Broken.

The scum of humanity.

So the newspapers claim.

Mental skeletons of once-loved fathers, brothers, and sons no longer in contact with any family members. Shadows of citizens who've given up hope.

The bedraggled militia guard men add to the air of desperation that now hangs over the dock. Only a few of the guards have full uniforms, the rest have partial outfits. Guarding prisoners is one of the lowest level militia jobs, a duty despised by most soldiers. Many so assigned take out their frustrations by beating their charges, exaggerating infractions, immune to the emotional and physical hurt they inflict. Their self-esteem, both as soldiers and men, has eked away, and as a group they are a sad reflection of the noble intent of enforcing law and order. They too face the long journey ahead, since they will accompany the prisoners to keep them under control. They are doubly unhappy as they also are being sent away from home. Some have juvenile crime records, and are now militia due to their parents' desire to avoid gaol-time for their wayward sons.

As the prisoners top the gangplank and step onto my deck they state their name and where they come from to Charles Matheson, the Master, who records the information in a giant ledger.

"Thomas Guilford, Chatham," "George Berry, Everton," "Henry Harper, Belfast," "Willard Kingston, Middlesex," "Alan Keegan, Essex," and on and on and on. Most prisoners are hoarse of voice and speak softly. The more robust and healthy ones form a minority. Whether necessary or not, guards prod the men along. Some stumble, especially those with chafed and bleeding ankles caused by their heavy chains. A guard beats a chap whose bloody feet stain the deck, and makes him lick the mess. Another guard kicks the man in the stomach. A teenager is grabbed by the hair and pushed back and forth between three guards. The other prisoners file by, seemingly impervious to the treatment.

A small happenstance catches my attention. I am almost nodding off as the names and places keep dragging on... "Stanley Elliott, Kent," "Peter Scarborough, Westminster," Michael Wintergard, Lambeth," "James Robertson..." There is a pause, silence. Pilot waits a few seconds then demands "Where from Robertson? C'm on man, I don't have all day."

Some sort of switch has turned on in Mr. Robertson. Where the other men have been apathetic in their demeanour, he is alert, vital, animated. He shifts his weight from one leg to the other staring the officer up and down.

A savage sneer fills Robertson's face. "Screw you, you bastard. He raises his fist as if to strike a blow. "Put down whatever you want, you suited-up shit." A guard steps forward with baton extended and Robertson thinks better of his intention. He withdraws his arm, then stands back ever so slightly and lets forth a vicious hissing sound. Spittle flies. Several men in the line behind him echo the hissing. It's unnerving in its volume and intensity.

Matheson doesn't bat an eye. "That could cost you scumbag. Just as well I'm Navy and not militia, and in a hurry to boot. If I signaled these guards they'd beat you to a bloody pulp. Now move on. I'll put Portsmouth after your name."

"Up yours, you publican prick. Try and remember me."

Robertson forces his shoulders back, stands tall, gives Charles a venomous look, then turns and spits on the deck. A guard moves to Robertson's side but Matheson waves him off. "He'll keep."

The line shuffles forward, and Charles keeps taking names. The incident doesn't seem to faze him in any way, but I watch Robertson carefully. He is seething. I can see the tension in his face and the quivering of muscles in his arms. He's a big boned chap. and I get a sense that he'd like to wallop Charles. Were he to strike Charles or a guard, after flogging he'd be thrown in the ship's brig without food and water for days on end.

The nearest militiamen have moved to the edge of the deck to ensure prisoners move smartly up the gangplank. Robertsons' words linger with me, however. Two unusual things have registered. Did he call Charles a 'publican' or was that 'republican', as in the Radical Movement? And what did Robertson mean by 'Try and remember me'? Was he referring about the past or was he issuing a warning for the future?

I file the incident away, and vow to learn more about Robertson. I'll keep my eye on him. A couple of the prisoners who had overheard the altercation follow Robertson's example and become testy with the pilot, offering up their own crude responses to his questions. It does them no good.

The slurs, crudities, and epithets roll off Charles' back. I guess he's heard all of the insults before. Only once do I see him look up in response to a profanity and jab the chap hard in the stomach with his slate. It must have been a very personal insult to have evoked such a response. It is clear Charles just wants to finish the list and move on to more important things. Like getting the ship ready to depart.

Exactly one hundred male prisoners come on board, along with eighteen guards. Counting the militia who arrived with the women prisoners, I question how well twenty-three guardsmen can control one hundred seventy convicts, plus four children.

Three male convicts are absent from the original planned muster. I heard the militia commander tell Charles that two on the transportation roster died overnight in their hulk, and that the third, housed in the local gaol, was too sick to stand when they went to fetch him. Makes me wonder how many others might be sick or even near death. The surgeon will have to be fast and thorough when he performs his examinations, lest we depart with men too weak for the long journey ahead.

* * *

Captain Coubro will be paid a bounty for every prisoner he delivers in good health to authorities in Sydney, so he's anxious not to start with sickly specimens.

Supposedly, all transportation convicts are certified by prison authorities as healthy enough to undertake the trip to Botany Bay. Neither the captain nor the surgeon, however, consider the prison officials' declarations meaningful, since those officials generally have no medical education and are simply anxious to get rid of troublemakers and to gain space for future inmates.

Yesterday, the surgeon and his helper performed cursory examinations on all the women prisoners and their children. The checks were designed to detect untreatable conditions, serious communicable diseases, and general weaknesses that might threaten survival of themselves and others during the voyage.

The four children, while malnourished and thin, are otherwise OK. Two of the women, one being Sarah Grainger, are recorded as approximately three and a half months pregnant, another woman five months along, with a fourth due in less than a month.

Five women exhibit symptoms of syphilis or gonorrhea. This is no surprise to Arthur, the surgeon. Women with no alternative means to earn money to buy food turn to selling their bodies. The increased proliferation of prostitution in society has created a plague of sexually transmitted diseases. Venereal diseases are a pestilence. They're not exclusively contained to the prostitutes and the males who purchase their services, but are also spreading to the wives and children of the latter.

Regretfully, the surgeon also identifies three women with consumption. Some surgeons believe consumption is easily spread from those afflicted to others, while younger surgeons are much more hesitant about cause. The Navy, however, takes the view that due to the confined spaces in which transportation convicts travel, the possible contagion risk is too high, and therefore, anyone with it is not permitted to remain on board. The Navy also applies this to private contractors' ships.

While the male prisoners are in the process of boarding, the captain meets with authorities to return the eight women with consumption and venereal diseases. One is a mother with young child. My soul is tormented. Returning to a land gaol is essentially a death sentence for the mother, and a vagrant's life for her child once her mother dies. Diseases can linger for months, even years, but damp prison cells with unsanitary conditions will hasten the effects. The removal of all the sick women means sixty-two remain, along with three children.

As with the female prisoners, the male convicts receive simplistic health checks. It takes all day, and Arthur's report to the captain in the early evening is guarded.

"Captain, I am truly saddened by the state of the male prisoners. In general, they are emaciated, robbed of spirit, physically weak, poorly clothed, and scarred with whip lesions. A few have retained some strength, but they are the minority. Most are devoid of ambition, deprived of hope, and feel disgraced by society. They have been caged in land prisons or floating hulks for nearly two years. Thankfully none have sexual diseases, since they haven't been with women during their incarceration time. But seven men either have consumption or will die from other causes within days. It's disgraceful what's been done to them. It shocks me."

Coubro puts his sherry glass on the desktop and smiles sympathetically. "Our politicians and bureaucrats don't know how to deal with all the crime in the cities these days, Arthur. It's getting worse, not better. There aren't rehabilitation programs for these men and women once they are incarcerated. They only get out of gaol when their time is up. And then, more than likely, commit the same crimes again. I regret I don't have useful suggestions."

The surgeon clinks his glass against Coubro's. "Me either, sir. All I can do is make this trip as comfortable as possible for the prisoners who leave with us tomorrow. I need another hour to complete my prisoner reports, but I would like the cooks to prepare some meat-filled broth immediately for the men and women alike so I can start on a better diet for them. It's terrible that so many passengers are ill, but we don't want deaths on board, and given how long this journey will take I feel we must leave the ones I've mentioned behind."

"Doctor, I respect your findings. Talk to the cook while I head to the commander's office in the administration building. It's late, but they should still be there. I'll need the names of those seven men."

Crisp nods. "Thanks for your support. The eight women and lone child have already left, and the seven men will probably have to stay overnight – I'll quarantine them in the brig. That will leave us with ninety-three males, for a total of one hundred and fifty-eight prisoners. I'll do a quick look over the militia contingent in the morning. One chap holds his arm by his side all the time, and one shuffles, rather than walks normally. I need to find out why, but I should be done with them in ninety minutes. I suspect they'll all be healthy enough to travel. Should be buttoned up well in time for a noon departure. Would that work?"

"Not a minute later doc! The ebb tide turns shortly thereafter. Now, I must be off, but have your assistant catch up with me along the wharves in case there are questions about diseases I can't answer."

Sometimes I listen to these verbal exchanges in depth, other times my attention is required elsewhere. Listening to these two men, however, is a pleasure. They care. It makes me want to care too. We ships look for inspiration and leadership. The ships in Nelson's armada, which returned to port here eleven years ago when I was still more shell than ship, were proud to have served the man and the country. I talked to a number of them, many in sad shape, torn apart with cannon and fire damage. But they'd all follow Nelson and the HMS *Victory* again without reservation.

Coubro and Crisp are leaders. How many doctors would consider getting convicts healthy? I admire both of them.

* * *

There's much to tell about how the convicts are housed. They'll be on board for four months, so there is plenty of time to describe their accommodations. Right now I have to check that the cook's fire is burning safely, and watch the militia for any mistreatment of their charges.

Tomorrow we sail.

It will be great to be under way.

5. *Under way*

Three bells have just sounded in the afternoon watch. We're well down through the Solent, west of the Isle of Wight. The marine mist has lifted, and the greyness of the morning is on the wane. Random rays of pale sunshine struggle through gaps between low hanging clouds, adding fleeting sparkles to curling wave-tops.

I feel grand, happy to be under way. This is what I was born to do. Sail!

My hull slices smoothly through the waves, minimal wake trails behind me. Foam sprays in graceful arcs to port and starboard. The wind in my sails pushes me on, the twenty fathom depth hardly aware of my shadow. It's a sweet ride.

Many hands are aloft, and at sheets and braces. They're helping me fine tune a southwesterly course along the Channel in order to skirt Guernsey and île d'Ouessant and enter the Celtic Sea. The maneuver completes and the helmsman locks on the new course. Steady as we go!

In a dark corner of the female prisoner compartment a youngster about ten years old sits and lowers her head in prayer, her hands clasped beneath her chin.

"D...dear God, p...please help this ship take us safely across the seas. A...and d...do not let these guards hurt m...mummy like the men in gaol did. She...she is a good person. She... she loves you always. I promise we will be good."

There's a long pause and I wonder if there's more to come, for her head stays bowed.

Yes. Her lips purse. "Thank you L...Lord for getting us on this ship. It...it is already better than the gaol. P...please make it stay that way. Your humble servant Diana, Amen."

I will watch this little girl closely, in the hope that I can at least provide safe shelter and reasonable comfort for her. It will be up to God however to decide how mild or strong His storms will be along our route.

* * *

Coubro strides to the front of the assembled prisoners and militia. Convicts crowd the foredeck between the bow and the main mast, shoulder to shoulder. Militia guardsmen patrol the perimeter of the vast gathering. A few of the first-class passengers watch through the lounge windows.

I have an uneasy feeling. The militia were very heavy handed as they brought the prisoners up through the hatchways. Several convicts stumbled as they transited the narrow openings, each one received blows from the cudgels the guardsmen carried. Cries of pain emanated from all four exits onto the deck. About ten prisoners, still whimpering from the blows they'd borne, are supported by comrades. Three of them are women. The convicts are unnerved, wondering why they are gathered together.

The captain steps up on a bench to be better seen. Charles, his pilot, hands him the brass speaking trumpet.

"Prisoners, I am Captain Coubro, in command of this ship, the *Lady Corinth*. We will be together in close quarters for several months. There are a number of rules you must follow to make life on board more tolerable for everyone."

He eyes the crowd and takes in their murmurs.

"LISTEN CLOSELY," explodes like cannon fire from his lungs.

Heads lift and look directly at the captain. Perhaps the harshness of his voice makes the convicts sense they are about to be harangued and threatened as is usually the case when called together in large numbers.

Coubro continues. "My job is to get you all safely to Botany Bay. The worst thing any of you can do is get in the way of that goal."

He pauses for effect, then shouts "KEEP OUT OF THE WAY OF MY CREW!" The volume and intensity cause eyes to rivet on the man and his trumpet.

His next statement catches crew, militia, and prisoners by surprise.

"Hear me well now. I make no judgment of your crimes. I repeat. I MAKE NO JUDGMENT OF YOUR CRIMES."

A nervous tittering, unsure they've heard right, rolls through the prisoners. Clearly, this is highly unusual.

Several of the guardsmen apparently think the statement is comical and snort at the notion. Coubro silences each one with a direct, withering look. His eyes blaze as he focuses on the commander of the guard unit, who is shaking his head side to side, smirking as he does so.

Coubro turns back to the main body of the crowd. "The militia's responsibility is to ensure you behave, per government decree. However, I will closely oversee the militia's role on this ship."

By now, the crowd, as one, is hushed. All listen closely as the Captain raises the speaking funnel again. "The other man responsible for your well-being is Dr. Crisp, our Surgeon. His job is to ensure you arrive in Sydney in good health. Listen up! One good thing to that end..." He pauses again. "Better chow than you've experienced in any gaol."

A lengthy, soft murmur extends into a cheer from most of the group. Some, however, are guarded, mute in response, as they wonder if they are being served yet more false promises.

With well-recognized hand motions the commander gestures to his troops that he thinks the captain is crazy. Coubro notices but proceeds.

"The doctor will help with health issues. You will be treated equally in so far as that is possible. Food for women and men will be the same except for women who are pregnant or nursing."

I see relief on the faces of those women who are clearly pregnant. Recognition of special needs. Unbelievable!

Coubro continues. "You will get regular exercise. Punishment, if warranted, will be the same for man and woman if the crime is the same. I have no love of the cat of nine tails and would prefer it to remain unused."

At this point there is audible snickering among the guards, clearly as an indication of disagreement on withholding the whip for punishment. The guards' behavior makes me feel uncomfortable. On a previous trip I heard similar statements of responsibilities and commitments presented to convicts, but Coubro has added some extra touches. The militia, who should remain silent, are showing open disrespect that borders on hostility.

Apparently Coubro recognizes this and says, "Guards, listen well. Be sparing in your administrations. Heed my words."

He lets his words sink in and invites the surgeon up beside him. Prisoners shuffle feet as they stretch in place, and I also notice some of the sailors shifting positions. They usually hang around and observe the prisoners from a distance out of curiosity, the females especially. A few sailors seem to move with purpose. Unusual!

There's an expectant silence as Coubro speaks up again. "Dr. Crisp will now present the rules. Listen closely." Coubro hands the speaking trumpet to the surgeon.

"Rule number one. Cruelty to your fellow man will not be tolerated. You will use surnames to address each other, and there will be no derogatory name calling. You will be divided into 'messes' of about six persons each with an elected leader. The leader will see that mess members receive equal treatment. A leader can be relieved of duty if a majority of mess members complain.

"Rule number two. You will attend divine services on Sundays. A number of Bibles will be supplied for your use. As well, we will seek out teachers among you and establish classrooms for those who can't read or write. This is a perfect opportunity to be educated."

Murmurs of appreciation rise in the crowd, and a few tentative smiles appear. A male voice cries out loudly, "I'm a teacher." A guard wields his baton, wedges into the milieu and whacks the man on the arm. The prisoner turns with a look of disdain on his face, unafraid. He moves forward, stands nose to nose with the guard, and berates him. "Shitface weakling, like a little boy with no hair on his balls. Back off." Nearby prisoners hiss, emboldened by their compatriot's defiance.

71

Two large sailors separate the pair before serious conflict occurs. A soft buzz precedes a new calm across the deck.

It's a brave man who has challenged the guard. I look closely and identify him. Robertson. This is the man who made a scene as he boarded. He'd better watch himself. He may be strong, fit, and confident, but the guards are powerful. Robertson moves to the front of the group and repeats himself, louder this time. "I'M A TEACHER."

Crisp acknowledges him with a nod, and continues his spiel. "Rule number three. Cleanliness. You live together in tight quarters. The militia will check on ventilation each morning. Do not close the scuttles, 'portholes' if you know not that term, unless ordered to. You must bring your bedding topside once a week and brush and air it. Wash your clothes weekly and sweep out your quarters at least weekly.

It's a lot for the prisoners to absorb. They've heard nothing like this before. Crisp isn't finished.

"Mess leaders will organize a rotation of cleaners for the heads. Our two cats, some traps, molasses, and other arrangements should help keep cockroaches, rodents, and lice at bay, but do not leave food behind after meals. The cleaner the better."

I see heads nod up and down and neighbors murmur to one another. They are becoming fatigued from standing, but remain attentive. A couple of women are supported by comrades. Crisp raises the trumpet again.

"We plan to stop at Cape Town to replenish provisions of food and water, and make necessary repairs. We should arrive there in just under two months."

72

Soft cries of "yeah", "good-o", echo across the deck. The surgeon smiles at the response.

"On to rule number four." Crisp's face hardens. "You are prisoners of His Majesty's government. Any attempt to escape or to cripple the ship's progress for such intention will be dealt with harshly. I might add that escape overboard in the middle of the Atlantic or Indian Oceans requires a very long swim home."

Muttered acknowledgements, heads nod, and even muted titters run through the crowd.

"One last point. The captain, commander of the guards, and I, must note any untoward behavior on the records we provide the authorities in New South Wales upon arrival. It behooves each and every one of you to do your best to comply with the rules and avoid any negative marks made against your name when you arrive. We cannot undo the reasons you are aboard, but it would be unwise to add to them."

Now the prisoners are showing restlessness. They've been standing long enough, and mention of the unknown land and arrangements ahead is bothersome because of the uncertainty and ignorance they all feel. Unfortunately, the surgeon doesn't help with his next set of words.

"We cannot control Mother Nature, who will undoubtedly test us along the way. Trust the crew when conditions become harsh. FOLLOW THEIR COMMANDS."

Coubro takes back the bullhorn. "Commander of the guards, step forward."

No one moves, but the prisoners' heads turn as one to where the commander leans against the starboard railing.

"Commander Mullens, come forward."

Warily, the huge man in a tight red coat over a bloated belly, saber dangling at his side, pushes through the crowd and climbs up beside the captain, who turns to address him.

"Do you understand, sir, how I expect your men to treat the prisoners?"

The commander's face turns the color of his waistcoat, and he yells so everyone can hear him without use of the speaking trumpet.

"You scum-faced dogs of criminals are the pits of humanity and a disgrace to our society. My men will treat you according to the commands and understandings we have been issued, and will punish anyone who violates the rules to the maximum letter of the law. It's our duty to do so."

The prisoners are stunned. One minute, Coubro and Crisp appear as compassionate leaders who offer a touch of humanity to prisoner life aboard. The next instant, it disappears and is reversed through the uncouth and threatening statement of the commander.

Shoulders slump. Smiles crumble. Hopes fade. Oppressive silence follows.

Coubro is irate. He drops the speaking trumpet and turns to the commander. "You miserable cur! You're just one-step above dog shit. Let me reiterate. You and your men will treat all prisoners fairly. Understood?"

The commander sneers and a couple of his guardsmen snigger. Coubro issues a command that is heard clearly across the deck. "Quartermaster, seize this man's weapons, gag him, take him to the bow, lash him to the capstan, and hold him till I join you."

At the captain's command, the commander reaches for his saber, only to find the captain and first mate pinning his arms to his side.

A deafening cheer, even louder than before, arises from the prisoners, accompanied by a number of rough grunts of approval. The noise partially obliterates the commander's instructions to his compatriots: "SOLDIERS. DRAW YOUR WEAPONS AND TAKE CHARGE!"

The shouted command is to no avail. Coubro has clearly anticipated trouble, for two able-bodied seamen who stand close by each soldier disarm them of rifles and sabers. Suddenly, twenty-two soldiers stand totally embarrassed as their leader is dragged away to the bow.

Coubro uses the trumpet again. "As for you remaining soldiers, which of you is next in command?" One chap struggles to shake himself from the sailors who hold him and steps forward. Coubro observes he's the man Crisp had remarked, for his left arm hangs limp by his side. "That would be me, sir, Corporal Tomkins."

"Good. Is there anyone else in your regiment who feels the same way Commander Mullen does?" No one moves.

"OK Tomkins, you may escort the prisoners to their quarters below deck."

The prisoners willingly head for the hatches, thankful for the captain's intervention. I have no doubt Coubro's actions will be discussed at length during the afternoon.

I feel relieved. Clearly Coubro had a sixth sense about the worthiness of the commander ahead of time to have had the sailors ready to respond.

As if to corroborate my thoughts, Crisp steps forward and whispers, "Very courageous, Captain. And a brilliant tactical move. Now the prisoners are with you, and the crew's respect as well. Though I wager you'll hear from the military high command when they learn of your actions. Of course, by then, more pressing matters will occupy their attention, I'm sure."

Coubro apparently has one more activity in mind. He approaches the bound commander, ignores the venom in the man's scowl and the muffled curses behind the gag, and asks him, "Can you swim? If so, nod your head up and down." Fear registers in the man's eyes since he interprets the captain's question as a threat to throw him overboard. He thrusts his head and neck to and fro sideways in an obvious and desperate expression of inability.

It's Coubro's turn to smile sardonically. "OK Mullens. I have no intention of pushing you overboard and leaving you to swim, as that would make me as much a bully as you. I merely wanted you to experience the sort of fear at the edge of the hell you promised the prisoners. Which you are about to realize in a different way.

"Sailors, remove his uniform and undergarments, and tie him securely under the bowsprit. It looks to me like the waves are building. Let's see how well he likes being face to face with some of them. Have the surgeon check him at eight bells and bring him to my cabin."

76

* * *

Like the captain, I sense that the waves are increasing in size, as the swells roll slowly beneath us. There is a storm in our path. Perhaps it may catch us overnight, or maybe it will simply peter out. In any event the commander's head and torso will be washed repeatedly, he will taste lots of salt water, and be truly scared. Ultimately, he will fume over both his punishment and the humiliation in front of his men, but I'm sure he won't treat prisoners harshly for fear of worse punishment at the captain's behest.

The militia certainly have a role to play onboard. The crew is responsible for the ship. The militia is responsible for managing the convicts.

Coubro has made it clear he is managing both crew and militia. By establishing his position after leaving the docks, rather than before, the commander has no ability to report the issue to his seniors, unless he demands a longboat to get back to port, which request Coubro would undoubtedly deny.

One good reason for employing the militia onboard is that they have training and experience in the firing of cannon. You might wonder why we even have cannon on board? Pirates still operate in the southern Atlantic Ocean, especially out of South America. The risk seems to lessen each year, but just in case rogue marauders approach us, we travel prepared. I hate the thought of having foreign cannon fire at me and splinter my hull and deck. I'd prefer to flee than fight, frankly, but it all depends on who has the faster ship. Not something I care to dwell on.

* * *

As direct proof of his words, the captain orders lamb stew for the prisoners' evening meal. Fresh bread, large steaming pots of meat, and tin bowls and spoons are distributed by sailors and militia throughout the prisoner quarters. Dire warnings are delivered to mess leaders to share the food evenly among their charges.

I watch carefully. A couple of the stronger men ask for bigger portions. They are denied, but create no fuss. In several messes, weakened men cannot hold their bowls steady. Others spoon-feed them. That is a good thing to see. The women are just as considerate. Probably the best meal any convict has had since their confinement. There are even a few wary smiles as plates and spoons are collected afterwards.

But an even bigger surprise awaits everyone. Coubro sends down a double ration of beer for anyone who wants it below decks. You may be surprised to learn, that like the men, a majority of the women take the drink. In land gaols, thirst is satiated with either beer or unfiltered river water. Inmates learn quickly that beer causes far fewer intestinal problems than does the polluted water.

* * *

Most of the men and women of good breeding who can afford first-class passage on a ship of my caliber have no idea what life is like in a gaol.

In their city mansions or on their rural estates there might be a keg of beer available for poorly paid workers, but at dinner, the beverage of choice for the owners and patrons will usually be a fine wine, imported from France or Italy, with brandy or sherry from Spain.

The offering at the captain's table onboard will be closely scrutinized and either decried or praised in letters home. Indeed, the respect accorded to the captain may in part depend on the quality of wine he serves. Astonishing, isn't it, considering the passengers have placed their lives in his hands?

I'm an interested voyeur when Mr. Mullens is brought back to the captain's cabin after his stint kissing the waves beneath the bowsprit. The surgeon has checked the commander over and declared him little the worse for wear. The commander's hair is unkempt and salt-water drops run down his cheeks. But the sailors at least have allowed him to put his clothes back on.

His dignity has suffered most. Coubro hastens to add another ration to the man's chagrin. "Mullens, you have been warned. On this ship I am in charge. Of the crew, of the passengers, of the prisoners, and even you. Your views with respect to treatment of the prisoners are despicable and totally contrary to mine. I do not trust you.

"From now on, your home will be the brig, away from your men and al prisoners. You will receive limited rations Ordinarily, a commander would join the captain's table for dinner each evening. That privilege is denied you. Furthermore, Mr. Tomkins will replace you in the formal interviews we are required to perform with each prisoner.

"Your saber will remain locked in my possession. You, and any of your men who want to follow you, will be put ashore in Cape Town, whence you can find your own way back to England. I will choose a new set of soldiers there to help manage the prisoners.

"Dismissed! Be gone from my sight."

6. *New companions*

In the captain's dining room, the four children, all boys, are served at a separate table away from the adults. The boys are boisterous, intent on trying to outdo one another verbally with respect to their backgrounds, lineage, estate sizes, schools attended, and privileges. I am surprised at how important it seems for them to establish their social pecking order at such young ages.

Greater entertainment, however, is provided by the adults. Coubro, in full captain's uniform, takes his place at the head of the table. As soon as everyone is seated, he rises, raises his glass of dry Fino sherry, and offers a genuine smile. "Ladies and gentlemen, it's a pleasure to have you all on board. I bid you a warm welcome in the name of *Lady Corinth*. We have a long journey ahead, and my fellow officers and I will try to make it as enjoyable as possible. This elegant ship is one of the finest seconded to His Majesty's service and I'm proud to be her captain for this journey.

"I'm ably assisted by four officers who are recognized as top men in the positions they hold. Let me introduce them to you."

He praises each officer, describes their backgrounds and defines their functions. Each man stands and bows as Coubro introduces him. By the time Coubro is finished, pea soup with pickles and bread has been served. The sets of glasses that held the pre-dinner sherry are replaced by crystal goblets filled with the first course Montrachet wine. The captain hasn't partaken of any of the food offerings at his place.

"And there's one other member of the crew I'd like you to meet. He has one of the most important jobs on board." He stands, and nods to the surgeon, who slips out of the room.

A minute later the dining room door opens and the surgeon re-enters followed by a large man wearing a white apron and chef's hat. The passengers applaud as Coubro announces, "This is Mr. Stephen Gateshead, responsible not only for your meals, but also those for everyone else on board. Keeping over two hundred people well fed is not an easy task, and while he has three helpers, one of whom you've met, he's the man in charge of the galley. It takes a wide range of skills to provide a first-class meal for you all and to feed the prisoners at the same time. Mr. Gateshead's experience is varied. He's worked in the Admiralty's offices, as well as having been the chef at several major hotels and restaurants over the last twenty years."

Gateshead's face flushes scarlet but he smiles, lifts his hat up and down, turns, and quietly exits to more gentle applause. The passengers murmur among themselves, and Coubro takes a few bites from his still full plate.

Sara Goldsmith waves a gloved hand, "Captain, begging your pardon, some of us observed your restraint of that dreadful man who heads the marine militia. I hope he will not have anything to do with us during our trip."

"I assure you, Mrs. Goldsmith, that his province is entirely with the prisoners. He would ordinarily dine with us, but given his views about the prisoners I doubt any of us here would relish his company. Therefore, he will not be in attendance, and has been isolated to the brig until we reach Cape Town.

"With respect to the unfortunate individuals in the deck below, they will appear on deck from time to time – for the purpose of exercise and also to air their mattresses. You may see them from a distance through the lounge windows but you should have no occasion to interact with them, although it is possible one or two may manage to slip by our supervision.

"If that happens, I urge you to seek the assistance of a nearby officer or the purser immediately. The convict may simply be curious, but we cannot risk the notion that he, or she, may have unpleasant intentions in mind. I aspire to keep the prisoners as busy as possible, make them look after themselves and improve their station, but there is usually at least one rotten apple in any bunch."

A tight smile flits across Mrs. Goldsmith's face. Relief? Maybe, but she suddenly asks another question. "And that big convict man who stepped forward and claimed he was a teacher. Is that true, or was he just trying to get attention?"

Dr. Crisp straightens and turns to Sara. "It's quite possible he is indeed a teacher. We haven't interviewed him yet. But many of the convicts, male and female, were employed in semi-professional positions as governesses, cooks, ladies-in-waiting, coachmen, butlers and teachers, before incarceration. Those who held such positions of authority often stole from employers or made other mistakes as they sought money in order to buy food for their families. Not all the men were labourers or all the women maids and seamstresses."

Sara lowers her head. "I'm sad to hear that. Most sad. I hope that teacher man helps others learn their **three** R's as you promised, Captain."

Matilda, the maid, lifts her face and mumbles, catches her breath, then bravely speaks up, "Her Ladyship wonders whether she might be permitted to interview some of the prisoners to learn their stories for a book she intends to write."

There's an immediate rebuke. "Shush Matilda. That subject is for me to raise with the captain. This is a sensitive topic beyond your ken, and needs considered exchange. I will pursue it with the captain later."

Coubro turns and faces her Ladyship, admiring her more than ample cleavage. "Lady Hudson-Smythe, I'd be happy to discuss your interests in the days ahead. Please see me in my cabin at four bells any afternoon."

Matilda blushes with embarrassment. The distinction between her and her fashionably dressed mistress is heightened. As the main course of pheasant is served, madam presents a haughty visage to the other diners, signaling her prowess in the grant of a private invitation to visit with the captain. Savouring her modest victory, she remains silent for the main course and lets others chat peacefully.

Timothy Blaine, the banker, just twenty years old, has a question for the captain. "Mr. Coubro, when I studied the globe in our London offices, it seemed to me that the shortest route to Cape Town would be southward down the west coast of Africa. But I overheard Mr. Matheson tell the helmsman to steer so'-so'-west, towards Brazil. I'm sure there must be a good reason. Could you help me understand, please?"

"An excellent question, Mr. Blaine. Mr. Matheson is our pilot, I'll let him explain."

The little man stands. "I appreciate your interest in our route, sir. Please bear with me as I introduce some nautical terms. 'Pilotage' is the art of sailing along a coastline using known landmarks. And while it is true that the shortest route to Cape Town would be southward down the west coast of Africa as you surmise, it is often the case that the shortest route is not the fastest route. Sail ships like ours need wind and favorable currents in order to make progress toward their destination. Both the currents need to run, and the winds need to blow, in the right direction.

"At the moment, we have the winds obliquely behind us." The pilot points rearward with his arms outstretched, then pulls them forward close to his chest. "We know that around the equator, well off the Brazilian coast, the winds switch direction and blow out of the northwest." His arms move again in a different arc. It's those winds we seek. They will drive us all the way to Cape Town. And the art of sailing long distances out of sight of land, which is our plan, is called 'navigation'."

"So, it's strong winds you'll be looking for way out there?" Mr. Blaine says. "I see. Then what about this 'tacking' I've heard so much of, Mr. Matheson? I must have heard the word a dozen times since stepping aboard."

"Tacking is one of our means to keep the ship travelling generally in the right direction. Suppose the wind comes directly from the south, which, unfortunately, is almost opposite to the direction we want to go. We can't sail directly into the wind, but if we turn twenty, thirty, or forty-five degrees to the east, the wind will blow across the sails at an angle from the right. In so doing the wind creates 'lift', it fills the sails with air and moves us forward. If we continued in the new direction for too long, we'd veer way off course to the east, so we turn the bow back through the wind, redirect the sails and head off in the other direction, up to ninety degrees different. That is what we call 'tacking'. We make a zig-zag pattern across the water instead of a straight line. Sometimes you will hear the term 'points', a point is 11 ½ degrees."

"Thank you, sir. Makes sense."

I must digress for a moment. Mother rat just delivered six youngsters in her little cubby hole. The cats smell their arrival and are crazed with curiosity and frustration. I have a feeling it won't be long before one of the rat parents gets caught as they forage further afield to feed their pups.

But back to dinner. Mr. Blaine seems satisfied with the explanations he's received. Obviously a thoughtful, intelligent fellow. I noticed how Matilda hung on his every word. He is a dashing sort of chap. Probably attractive to the young lady, but somewhat above her station, I daresay.

The plates for the main meal and the accompanying red wine glasses, empty of Bordeaux, have been cleared away and now the servers offer apple tart, coffee, and port. The captain is asked a number of questions about Cape Town, and he gives Mr. Conway, the bos'n, the floor, since he's traveled to the city twice before.

I'm surprised at how well Lady Hudson-Smythe is holding her tongue. I expected her to show off more, as some upper-class women are prone to do. Perhaps she's saving her talents in that regard for her private interaction with the captain. She looks at him every now and then, rather than pay attention to the others when they speak.

Whoops! An altercation erupts between two male prisoners below. I hear everything, you understand. This is indeed a busy evening.

Ah, it's not something to get worked up about, just a man in one of the messes complaining about his portion of food. Tom Collins has been a troublemaker since arrival. He always tests the boundaries of the rules, and complains over tiny issues. He picks up his tin dish that holds mashed potatoes and throws it at Paul Knightbridge, the mess leader. Paul catches the dish, although some of the meal slides to the floor.

Collins yells, "Not enough to feed a baby. You've cut me short again. Why do I deserve less than the others?"

Paul responds calmly. "Look at my portion Tom. Same as what you got. I'll give it to you. That make you feel better?"

Tom takes two steps forward and cocks his right arm back, as if about to throw a punch. "I don't want <u>your</u> food, I just want more." Two other men jump up, pull Tom's arm down, and hold him tight. Tom slowly calms down and hesitatingly takes Paul's plate, retreating as far away as possible, deliberately making loud noises as his spoon scrapes across the tin bottom. I imagine it won't be the last time he becomes irrational about food.

When strangers are enclosed in tight conditions there's always adjustments to be worked out, so this is nothing unusual. It will happen again.

Such a difference from the decorum and abundance gracing the captain's table.

Back in the dining room, I notice the surgeon whisper to the captain, who nods in apparent agreement with whatever is said. The surgeon clinks a spoon several times against his wine glass, quelling the murmurs of the guests. "I'd like to introduce a custom that navy men in the company of women partake in at this stage of dinner. Would the gentlemen please gather your wine glasses, and move to your right, to occupy the space left by the gentleman two spots ahead? This makes it easier for everyone to get to know each other. If you haven't done this before, it may feel a bit strange, but please indulge us."

Lady Hudson-Smythe can't resist, "Am I to gather that this will be the routine at every meal, Dr. Crisp? It seems most unsettling."

Before the surgeon can reply, one of the young fathers, about to sit beside her Ladyship, responds. "Madam, I welcome this opportunity. I'm a publisher, and am most interested to hear about your proposed story. James Winthrop, at your service." He dips a slight bow.

I watch James' wife, Nancy, beam with pride as her husband's potential importance and value register in her Ladyship's face.

The surgeon doesn't get a chance to answer the question about how often the walk-around will take place. One of the other married men, about to sit next to Sara Goldsmith, adds his two pence' worth.

"I'm sure my wife Carolyn will welcome the chance to be rid of me," he laughs, "and talk to someone more interesting. And since I now get to catch the surgeon's ear, I have some government policy questions about prisoners' rights that I can ask him more readily. This rotation is a wonderful idea."

Carolyn smiles, with a laugh in her voice, "John Pennington, in your haste to get away you left your coffee and port behind." She reaches across the table and hands him both. "What would you do without me?"

"Stay sober," he replies with a wink.

The merriment at a construct new and simple catches on. Most of the women are as enthused as the men. At the far end of the table, sits a young woman with a flawless complexion that sets off her startling blue eyes, rosy cheeks, and cherry lips. Her face, framed by golden locks which flow down past her shoulders, commands attention with its beauty.

Clarinda Finsbury speaks softly. "Captain, can you tell me what's in store for the women prisoners in particular? Through our church back home I worked with a number of parish women who were in gaol for various reasons. Based on that experience, I have some empathy for those incarcerated in the deck below. What helps most is to have something to do. You mentioned the need to keep the prisoners busy.

Is there spare cloth on board that the women could use to repair garments or make new clothes?"

The captain thinks for a moment before he responds. "Madam, I'm delighted to meet you and your husband, Tristan, and may I commend you on your charitable work in the prisons. I'm sure Lady Smythe could learn much about prisoners by talking to you."

A strident voice cuts across the table. "Lady *Hudson* – Smythe, Captain."

"Humble apologies, my dear," Coubro responds. "I shan't forget again. Have you any experience akin to Mrs. Finsbury's interactions with prisoners?"

Her Ladyship looks disgusted as she pushes back a little from the table. "I certainly do not. I wouldn't go anywhere near a common gaol with all those criminals housed in filthy conditions."

Coubro gently prods further. "But you apparently are prepared to go below deck here Madam, and interview some of our prisoners?"

Lady Hudson-Smythe responds harshly. "Good heavens no. I expect any prisoner I'm to interview to be brought to me in chains, with a guard present. I wouldn't trust one close otherwise. And I hope they would be washed as well."

"That's most unfortunate, Madam," Coubro parries. "Because the only prisoners who would be in chains on the *Lady Corinth* would be those in the brig. It seems we really don't need that discussion about your wish to interview the prisoners after all, does it?"

Lady Hudson-Smythe's face falls. A look of incredulity flits across her countenance. Her mouth gapes wide, then closes noiselessly.

Clarinda Finsbury raises her hand. "Maybe I could write a book about the prisoners. I have so much I could talk about and ask them."

Lady Hudson-Smythe can't resist. With a pained tone she asks, "Do you have the credentials to be a writer, Mrs. Finsbury? I've been taught by the best tutors in the country. It's important to have experience."

Clarinda hesitates. I think she's contemplating how best to counter the condescension just directed at her. Silence settles as everyone waits. A couple of women glance down, most likely to hide their embarrassment. Finally, Clarinda smiles and says, "My father, sir Ivor Kenny, is the Downing Professor of Law at Cambridge University, Madam, and I have benefited markedly from his tutelage. Over time I've assisted him in writing several of his longer briefs. No doubt you know of the impact his writings have had on the Laws of England."

Her Ladyship looks away and after an awkward pause focuses on her maid. "Matilda dear, I do believe we are finished here. Let us retire. We'll say goodnight, everyone."

All the men rise, and the two women slowly file out. A loud *"hurrumph"* follows her Ladyship's form.

I doubt that many meals will be as intriguing as this one. We'll see. In any event, I will leave you for a while now as I feel the wind shifting direction and the air pressure rising. I'm sure Padraig, the quartermaster, is alert to the change.

The storm I had expected never materializes, probably blown away by the strong new wind coming from behind off the port quarter. The terror that a major storm would unleash on unsuspecting passengers and convicts will clearly be delayed. Everyone is spared this first night at sea, although most don't realize it.

Just to further reassure you, this is a positive change that's on the way. It suggests we will have fair weather and smooth sailing for the next five days or so.

That's good for all on board.

7. *Onboard activity*

The first 20 days at sea pass with fewer issues than I had anticipated. The weather has been delightful, the seas calm. While that has helped everyone's general demeanor, it's a problem in some respects because prisoners and passengers alike feel they have already become accustomed to sea travel. Which means the shock will be greater when we hit rough water or a storm.

Out of my control of course.

Based on my past experience, this captain and his officers have performed commendably with all on board – crew, militia, passengers, and prisoners. The crew still undergoes exercises to improve their sail handling and watchkeeping skills. I sense the first signs of pride in the new recruits as they become more skilled and confident in their tasks. Some of the older salty dogs have even smiled when a newcomer does a good job. They say nothing however.

When off duty, the old hands play cards, dominoes, or checkers, and enjoy teaching others how to play. Amazing! One pastime that for some reason seems to be reserved for a select group of eight veteran sailors, is chess.

Samuel Hammond is a seasoned sailor with wrinkled skin, tanned from years of at-sea exposure to sun and wind. His movements are deliberate, as if he doesn't have many to spare, but bright blue-grey eyes are beacons that light up his face with an almost permanent smile. I enjoy watching him as he sits against the foremast and retrieves his highly polished wooden St. George pieces one by one from a well-worn cloth pouch, tied with a faded gold ribbon, and which never strays far from his side. A simple black and white wooden board, perhaps 10 inches square, completes his set.

Pipe clenched between stained teeth, Sam sets the pieces on the board and mumbles to his opponent, "Ok, matey, choose whichever color you prefer, and then remove any three of my pawns and one of my bishops. Put them back in the bag."

His tone is friendly, neither condescending nor showing off. Rather, he's mentioned that he wants to make each game fairer based on others' skills. After a win, he explains to his opponent where he could have made better moves. No doubt that is why he is popular. In the rare event where he loses, he's sincere in his congratulations, as he loves to see players progress in their abilities. His patience and thoughtfulness are already well respected by new crew members who watch and talk among themselves.

"Crogan!" The yell comes from the Second Mate. "What the hell do yer think yer doin'?"

"Watching t' chess game, sir," comes the hesitant reply.

"Yer on lookout duty, Crogan." The mate lashes his small multi-tailed whip across Crogan's back.

"Move yer bloody arse up topmast before I thrash you prop'ly."

The youngster moves quickly, climbs the rigging as if his pants were on fire.

Ship life to date has been easy for the new recruits, and some have become too relaxed and lazy. More canings for the ship's boys under 18 years old and more short lashes for older sailors are needed, for any crew performs best under tight discipline. The mates and bos'n will feel Coubro's wrath if order is not kept up.

The first-class passengers have settled into comfortable routines. It turns out that Mrs. Pennington, and her son, Graeme, play the piano well.   Twice they've performed duets at dinner time to rousing approval. As soon as someone hums a tune, the boy has the ability to play an excellent rendition directly afterward. Another boy, Paul Winthrop, plays the fiddle.   The pair of lads managed one short impromptu 'concert', much to the enjoyment of the adults.

And, as if that weren't enough, we learned first-hand that Mrs. Goldsmith has a fine voice when she sang Robbie Burns' "Highland Mary" with Graeme at the piano. She handed a copy of the lyrics to the captain as a memento of the occasion.

Music is pleasing to everyone apparently. Even Lady Hudson-Smythe was able to smile and participate in the applause that evening.

At the upper end of the spectrum of social classes, her Ladyship works hard to raise her stock with Captain Coubro. She's switched her proposition from wanting to write about prisoners to a desire to write about sailors. Seems that she now feels she can write a book that will attract young men to the sailing profession. I wonder how she'll react after her first visit to the seamen's quarters with all those hammocks so close together, where she will smell smoke and human sweat and other signatures of tight company.

She's certainly tenacious. I give her credit in that respect. She's made it clear to her first-class companions that she's convinced she has a charter to do good in this world. Her intentions are laudable, but I'm not sure how realistic they are.

The other passengers have finally elicited her purpose in taking this trip. She tells them, "I want to be one of the first unmarried free-settler society women to travel to Sydney and set an example for others to pursue their dreams there. As I understand it, unlike earlier governors, Governor Macquarie wants to convert the town into a thriving city, well beyond its current status as a penal colony."

I surmise from overheard conversations and gestures that some of the other passengers are still scratching their heads as they try to figure out what she means by that. The woman doesn't seem the innovative type to go out and establish a new business. And the colony has only been in place for just over 25 years, so it's not as if there's a large upper-class society in place that will embrace her presence and goals.

John Pennington, the lawyer, is subtle. "That's very noble, your Ladyship, but surely you will disappoint a number of squires back home who might treasure your attention and vie for your permanent acquaintance."

"Perhaps, Mr. Pennington, perhaps. I appreciate the sentiment, but I am a woman of the world and must pursue my dreams."

After this exchange, I pay close attention to a discussion between three of the other women that takes place over coffee in Carolyn Pennington's suite. Carolyn follows her husband's lead. "Given her Ladyship's demeanor I wonder if she may have frightened away potential suitors. As I remember, no-one came to the wharf to see her off, unlike our friends."

Heads nod, minds busy assessing this notion. Finally, Clarinda Finsbury puts down her cup, and speaks. "I think we all feel there's more to her story than what she has shared so far. Forgive my directness, but given tales my father spun over the years, I am wondering if she might have been banished from home for some reason. Could this trip be a penance for some ill-advised indiscretion?"

Heads nod again, and there are murmurs of agreement. Nancy Winthrop says what's probably on all their minds. "Surely Matilda knows."

As if they were still back in London, that poor girl is at her Ladyship's beck and call sixteen hours a day. I've seen her sneak out at night when her mistress is asleep, and sit by the main mast to enjoy the cool air. One evening, she and Timothy, the banker, spent a couple of hours together. Matilda seemed glad of his company. The difference in class doesn't seem to bother him. In fact he wrapped his coat around her shoulders at one stage when she complained about the cold. Her clothes are very thin, almost see-through in places. I have a premonition they'll find more time for each other in the future.

I think everyone has sufficient sensitivity not to challenge her Ladyship directly with regard to her intentions. They'll wait patiently for some future revelation that will shed credit or doubt over her obscure journey goals.

But, enough about the good folks in their first-class cabins. Let me bring you up to date on other aspects of our voyage.

Just after noon each day Captain Coubro pins a chart on the wall in the Common Room that shows our approximate location, along with a statement of how far we've travelled, and our average speed over the past twenty-four hours.

With respect to total distance covered, I would say we're right on schedule. We've made good speed with no significant mishaps of any kind. New crew members certainly hope that that will continue to be the case. Based on past experience, however, it's a pipe-dream to expect everything to stay rosy. In fact, it won't be long before the

97

ambient temperature rises to almost unbearable levels and we enter a wind-less area near the equator. Many will be unpleasantly surprised.

Today the convicts are on deck in groups of 20, using carpet beaters to air their mattresses. Their hour topside allows them to enjoy the sunshine that never penetrates below. From each group, Dr. Crisp examines three or four in a more detailed health and life assessment than the cursory one given when they first arrived on board. The groups alternate between men and women.

The next group of men is climbing up the rear companionway ladder as the women descend through the forward hatch. **The doctor's assistant selects four men at random, one of whom is James Robertson, the chap who claimed openly that he is a teacher.** I've watched this man closely since our departure. He definitely behaves differently than the other prisoners.

As the male prisoners share their stories with one another, most act as if there's little chance for anything of redeeming value to occur in their lives again. They project an air of resignation, and are genuinely dispirited. Tales include being torn from homes, families, and their country, left with few or no attendant personal possessions, experiencing sickness and mistreatment. Most complain strongly about the unfair and cruel justice system. Many are physically weak from the deprivations of land gaols. All are aware they are headed to an unknown destination with no idea what's ahead of them, although they anticipate it cannot be good. They are locked in a crowded ship among strangers, many of whom are small-scale petty criminals, while others may be rapists, or even murderers.

Robertson, however, stands out. He's a mess leader and empathizes well with the others in his group. He makes sure the food is shared equitably, and encourages the others to exercise. A couple of them try to emulate his routines, but the other three aren't up to it yet. One reads daily from one of the thirty Bibles Coubro arranged to have brought on board before departure.

Robertson met with all the male mess leaders and indicated his willingness to teach anyone who wishes to learn how to read and write. Clearly, he has smarts and a genuine disposition to share his knowledge, coupled with an urge to keep busy. He's not one to pine away like the others. At the moment he only has two students, who are a bit on the slow side. He's been given pencil and paper and a hard, smooth board to act as backing for the paper when he writes. He also has a small chalkboard, but uses it infrequently.

Here's what has raised my curiosity. He uses the paper in class very sparingly, but when there's enough light in non-class times and the others in the mess are asleep or out of the area, he makes copious notes on what has become a private hoard of single paper sheets. What is he writing about? I wonder, but I can't see any detail – he's very secretive and careful to keep the contents hidden from prying eyes, even mine!

At any moment in time I'm aware of what is happening in every corner and space of my structure. My attention fluctuates however, especially when there's a lot going on. Which, frankly, is most of the time. There is a myriad of important components vital to forward progress and direction that need constant attention – the helm, the rudder, the sails, masts, rigging, and so on. Only when I'm assured those aspects are working well can I turn my attention to the elements of human behavior and interchange. Which is why I have only seen glimpses of Robertson's work.

I know he numbers the pages, and that the lines and sentences are set out meticulously with lots of room between. Once in a while he crosses out a whole sentence, and on one page he has drawn some kind of image. He's been slow and thorough about constructing the drawing bit by bit. I've seen curves and shading but not the whole piece. Is he writing a book about this voyage, or something else? He has set me a fine challenge. I'm intrigued.

At the moment he's in the doctor's exam room, putting his clothes back on. I listen in to their conversation.

"Tell me, Robertson, where are you from and what is your crime?

"Southampton was home, sir. Teacher at King Edward's. I shot a fellow. Life sentence."

"How long ago? Killing's a serious offence, Robertson."

"Oh, I didn't kill him. No, sir, definitely not. He's still very much alive. Incident was only nine months back."

"If you've been in gaol, how do you know this?"

"Because the man is here on this very ship, sir."

"You mean he's a fellow convict? Come, come, we're not that gullible, Robertson."

"No, sir. I didn't mean that. He's one of the crew."

"What? We don't check the backgrounds of all the crew, but I don't remember any discussion among the officers of a man who's been shot. What's his name?"

"I'd rather keep that to myself for the moment, sir."

"Why? I hope you don't have plans to accost him again."

"Not at all, sir, although he committed a crime which he's gotten away with."

Crisp smiles. "I hear good things about your willingness to teach the three R's to others, Robertson, but we hear these kinds of stories from convicts all the time. Don't push it."

"I understand, sir. But at some point I hope you might give me time to explain. Meanwhile, same as for the prisoners, I will teach any sailor who'd like to learn to read and write. They may feel uncomfortable to fraternize with a convict, but the offer is sincere. And I assure you the man I shot can read and write already. He's not a target pupil."

"You're a strange man, Robertson. I'm fascinated by your story, and I appreciate your offer to teach crew members. I will definitely discuss it with Captain Coubro. Meanwhile, you seem to be in good health, which is encouraging. Perhaps the fact that you served only a short time in gaol is a factor. You are dismissed."

Robertson gets up to leave, but pauses at the doorway, turns and address the doctor. "Sir, I notice the wooden flute hanging on yon wall. I lost my flute in gaol. Stolen. Too bad. Songs like 'Derry Down', 'Rakes of Mallow', 'The Sun Beams', 'Speed the Plough' – I could play 'em all, sir. That looks like a well-used instrument."

Crisp points to the wall. "Go ahead, try it." Robertson fits his fingers easily to the holes, sends a steady breath across the mouthpiece, and fetches forth a rich tone. He blows a few more notes which indicate a skillful familiarity with the instrument. Crisp nods in approval. "You have the touch, fellow," he says.

Robertson produces a few simple chords, then a couple more complex ones, smiles, and hands the instrument back. "Well preserved doctor, it has a mellow sound. Thanks for letting me play it." He wipes his sleeve across his mouth and departs without waiting for a response.

Crisp is right. Robertson is definitely an unusual chap. Teacher, musician, and with a secret story. I wonder which sailor was his victim. I'll have to listen more closely to the bunkhouse conversations in case some chap boasts of surviving a shooting. I love intrigue.

Robertson hides his document, and won't reveal who he shot. No one else seems as secretive as he is. On second thought, I take that back. Before I elaborate, let me describe the prisoners' accommodations.

In the first deck below, two side by side passageways run roughly along the centerline of the ship from a point fifteen feet aft of the bow to a spot ten feet forward of the stern. At either end of each passageway, stairs climb topside. Each passageway provides access to sixteen 'rooms', each about eight feet wide and fourteen feet deep, bordered by the curved inside of the hull. There is a porthole about six feet up on the hull, and each room holds six mattresses. There are no solid walls between areas for privacy, just a wooden strut across the deck that indicates a boundary.

In each defined space, attached to the hull, are two bunks with skinny mattresses, one above the other. Each bunk is about six feet long, the lower one eighteen inches off the floor, the second bunk eighteen inches higher. The porthole is within a stretched reach for the chap in the top hull bunk. The other four mattresses occupy floor space, easily pulled out of the way when not in use. Prisoners sometimes rotate sleep positions.

From the passageway, access to each 'mini room' is through a four-foot wide 'doorway' between vertical struts. The other four feet in the passageway 'wall' is comprised of struts spaced maybe eight inches apart. The timbers provide obvious interior frames that define each 'room'. Guards need to see multiple people and rooms in one glance to identify quickly where any problems may have occurred. Privacy means nothing here.

On each side of the ship, nine rooms are reserved for men, and seven for women, each of the two sets of rooms referred to as a 'compartment'. Between those two compartments, solid bulkheads and a hatch in the passageway separate the men from the women. The heads are beyond the stairs at both ends of the passageways, as are militia quarters, and there are two locked connecting doors between the two passageways – one forward, one aft.

I might add that there's a second deck below the prisoner deck that holds small quantities of cargo, food, medicines, and other supplies for the voyage, along with household goods of the paying passengers. Much narrower than the prisoner deck of course due to the shape of my hull. And believe me, you would be surprised at what some of these pompous first-class travellers have insisted they take to the new land.

Then there's the bilge and a half deck below the cargo deck. Below water level, it's an unpleasant area full of rope, pitch, pulleys, brooms, shovels, extra sails, spare spars, boards, cannon balls, tools, two extra anchors and all sorts of other items needed for maintenance and repair. There's a large hatch forward which allows access between the second deck and bilge area so that heavy or large items can be retrieved via tackle and winch. To haul anything upwards is not a job for the faint hearted, which is why many sailors perform strength exercises in their spare time. They do chin ups from the spars, and balance cannon balls while they stand on one leg. Competitive arm wrestling is where they reveal their prowess.

Earlier, I mentioned there are folks who are almost as secretive as James Robertson. In particular, there is this thin, wiry chap named Peter Cooksey. He has paired up with a convict woman named Betsy Willows, who has managed to preserve a larger girth than most. The couple has found an inventive way to 'get together', let's say. I'm unsure how they met but they've formed quite a bond.

Whenever a guard opens the door that separates the men's and women's quarters, there are folks on both sides of the door who try to see each other and communicate. It often requires two guards to control the prisoners. Once in a while a man manages to sneak through, and when the door is re-locked, the guards have to ferret him out. He's supposed to be punished severely but I think the captain's message has been well heard. At most, the guards may hold the errant chap down and pummel him with their fists, but they never report him, which would result in prison isolation.

I think I know why the men who slip in with the convict women are not reported. Three of the guards try to be friends with certain women themselves. They understand, and so are more prone to forgive when a male prisoner tries to do the same. I'm not saying the guards have the best of intentions, but that's my assessment.

Two guards, however, are not sympathetic to any prisoner's situation. They haven't absorbed the captain's message about fair treatment. Both despise the women. Do you remember the guard who belted pregnant Sarah Grainger in the back as she boarded? He's one of them. Miserable rogue named Millstone. I've seen him push women out of his way, stamp on their toes, and toss their personal belongings around. I don't like him and don't trust him.

But back to Peter and Betsy. These two are interested in sex, plain and simple. As I understand it, sex is a natural aspect and activity of human life. Most of the prisoners have been denied it for a couple of years. Oh yes, I have no doubt some of the prostitutes on board were active in gaol, as probably were some of the other women who sought favors. I'm not making any judgement, just observing what appears to be normal human interactions. It's what they needed to do to survive.

Peter must have been very athletic before he was incarcerated. Also, very creative. Still is. The door that divides the passageway between the men's and women's sections is tall – maybe seven feet high, but it doesn't go all the way to the top of the passageway. Peter has found a way to scale the struts at the side and squeeze through the narrow opening above the door. It's a gap of at most twelve inches, but his skinny frame makes it through. He climbs over in the middle of the night when most convicts are asleep. He tiptoes into Betsy's 'room', where she's usually awake waiting, and together they head to the end of the corridor. Beneath the stairs they've found a tiny space for togetherness. It's a bit of a struggle to fit, given her size, but they work it out. When they're together, I worry that Millstone will discover them.

As you see, there's no end to the variety of entertainment on the *Lady Corinth*.

8. *Not quite routine*

As the week progressed, the previously calm seas slowly changed. At first, small waves appeared; they hardly raised any interest among those on board. By the end of the week as the breeze picked up we were sailing through two and three foot waves, much to my enjoyment. We produced more wake, with noticeable curls spreading away from the bow. Every now and then I'd get a nice splash along both sides of the hull which washed me down. The sails filled out, and I developed a regular lilting pitch up and down. Most folks became accustomed to it in short order.

Two of the passenger boys had established a routine where they twice half walked, half ran, the perimeter of the ship at a fast exercise pace each morning before breakfast. One morning, after just one rotation they rushed back to the lounge with excited yells: "Porpoises, porpoises. Come see!" In various stages of alertness the passengers headed for the port railing where they stopped and admired the frolicking airborne leaps, and the way the animals matched their speed to that of the ship. Most of the group returned to their cabins, got fully dressed, grabbed a cup of tea from the breakfast table and returned to watch the graceful mammals. They stayed alongside for nearly two hours which also gave the prisoners a chance to see them through their portholes. What many had only seen pictures of in books were now real, a pleasant surprise of reality.

I'd spied the pod behind us a full day ago. I'd chatted only briefly with a couple of members in the pod, for while I understand a number of marine animal languages, my 'dolphinese' is scratchy at best. This was a group headed south of the equator to breeding grounds. They liked to 'play' with ships, seeing how well they could match their speed and how close they could come to the hulls and avoid scrapes. Sea life was pretty boring otherwise so ships were welcome distractions. Porpoises and dolphins are different species but it's hard for everyday humans to tell them apart. Wasn't something I could communicate to anyone on board of course.

Whoops! Of course! I see from the puzzled look on faces that you had no idea I could talk to marine life. Ships are easy fellow communicators, but there's a common primitive language between sea birds, mammals, fish and other sea creatures that I understand. Sort of akin to your 'pidgin English'.

When the sleek creatures turned up a second day, some enterprising sailors broke out their fishing equipment. For three days, fishing for dolphins became the pastime 'du jour' for off-duty sailors. I regretted that many of the friendly creatures suffered. I tried to warn them to be aware of fish that didn't move in a normal fashion, but some got caught anyway.

Several porpoises yielded fresh, but tough, meat which was not universally enjoyed. The much smaller bonito fish were tastier and easier to catch. The fish caught by sailors were shared with the crew first, and only if there was enough left over did the prisoners get any.

Whenever the prisoners were allowed to exercise on deck, they became enthusiastic supporters of the crewmen fishing, urging them to bring in multiple catches so they might have fresh meat, too.

A day after the dolphins disappeared a remarkable phenomenon occurred; a number of flying fish leapt out of the water and smashed against the hull. Sailors quickly used nets to fetch the stunned animals from the water and placed them in buckets. A few fish jumped higher and the sailors yelled with mirth as they skidded across the deck. A few hit the seamen directly. Others simply landed wriggling on the planks. More pails were gathered and the fish loaded into them. The dense 'shower' went on for fifteen minutes, at the end of which there were twelve pails of fresh food taken to the cooks. Many of the crew had seen the phenomenon before but none of the passengers or prisoners had.

Once again the crew, militia, passengers, and prisoners dined well.

In the passenger lounge that evening, the boys finally completed their sixth 110 piece puzzle. The small 30 piece dissected maps of Britain and Europe had lasted no more than a week but the larger images of formal landscapes like St. James Park, sporting events such as horse-racing and boxing, large foreign buildings, and well-known people had provided greater challenges and entertainment. Looking for something new to do, one youth asked his mother if she had packed their checkers game in the luggage. She replied negatively, and voiced to the other adults how she felt embarrassed that in the nearly four weeks they'd been on their trip no-one had even mentioned such games.

The adults had occupied themselves reading books or playing cards once they had identified mutual interests. Now, suddenly, those with children tried to recall whether any board games were packed in their suitcases in the hold.

Sure enough, two sets of parents had packed some games in anticipation of their use once the families were settled in Australia. It hadn't occurred to them that the games might come in handy while on the open seas for a lengthy period.

Sailors were dispatched to retrieve well-described suitcases. One family's goods were buried so deeply that none of their belongings were readily accessible. They promised to shop for items in Cape Town. But the other couple eagerly opened the box and suitcase brought to their cabin and recovered boards for peg solitaire, checkers, the game of the Goose, and tric-trac, also known as backgammon. Their son ran to his friends' cabins and shared the news.

At breakfast the next morning Clarinda Finsbury comes up with a suggestion. "Now that the boys have new games to play with, I imagine we can hide all the puzzles that have kept them happily occupied to date."

Several heads nod and a couple mutter "Makes sense", "Yes indeed."

But Clarinda is not finished. "I'm sure you remember that I once worked with incarcerated women and indicated how they need to keep busy. I know the puzzles belong to several of us, but I wonder how you would feel about letting the prisoners have them instead of stowing them away in some cabinet out of sight?"

Forks are downed, fingers of toast halt mid-flight between plate and mouth, spoons are returned to the serving dishes of marmalade and raspberry jam, and silence descends. So obvious, why on earth hadn't any of the others thought of that?

Voices rise in unison, but Nancy Winthrop stands, her face flushed. "That's a wonderful suggestion, Mrs. Finsbury. I feel so selfish not thinking of others as you have. Thank you for your generous idea. The prisoners are most welcome to the puzzles Tristan and I brought along."

Others follow suit with promises and declarations, and a relieved, benevolent air settles across the room.

* * *

We're hundreds of miles off the coast of Africa, many days southwest of the Azores, and have picked up the Northeast Trades south and west of the Cape Verde Islands. Soon we'll head almost due south towards the equator, where we hope to avoid a long stay in the no-wind zone before we reach the Southeast Trade winds and can sail closer to the coast of Brazil. There is nothing to see but foam-tipped waves, blue green water and skies decorated with thick cumulus clouds. The repetitive sameness has become boring for most folks.

In the last hour, however, wave and breeze action has picked up. The sailors have noticed the sails filling out more, which brings about a slight increase in speed, although it's the prisoners in their claustrophobic compartments who have noticed more marked up and down bow movements as the wave heights have increased.

I'm conscious that time and distance between waves has lengthened and that the bow sometimes pierces the top edge of a wave after which a deeper trough follows. We're amongst six to eight footers at the moment. They're steady but not very comfortable. Several convicts feel a bit nauseous.

Suddenly all my senses go on alert. Three miles ahead there's a serious swell in water volume. A rogue wave is forming, gathering its prodigious power from the depths, and there's no way we can avoid meeting it. I have no means to warn the crew, but as the distance closes and the wave looms larger the lookout finally yells "rogue wave!" The seemingly vertical wall of water rises steadily before his transfixed eyes. The deck falls silent at first, then bursts into frenzied activity as line-handlers pull their belaying pins, top-men race aloft to furl their sails, and the Captain and Sailing Master on the quarter-deck shout orders to reduce sail as quickly as possible.

Traveling at ten knots, we cover ½ a mile in four minutes. Men swarm the rigging, in an attempt to furl sails in time to slow our speed, and reduce wind resistance. Others sprint to cover the boats and to clamp chests and lockers closed on deck. At least no prisoners are out exercising. Urgent shouts urge sailors everywhere to furl whatever they can and then hold tight. I hear the brawny Boatswain shout, "Pray, men. Pray for your salvation, and the safety of our ship."

During this turmoil the Surgeon quickly leaves his cabin with convict teacher Robertson and two students in tow, escorting Robertson back to the hatch to return below deck.

I slam unchecked into the huge wave, shuddering with the impact. My bow tosses up nearly three times its normal height above water. I stall on top of the wave and hang suspended for a second, all lines and a few open sails trembling at the collision. Then I plunge sickeningly down into a trough at least twice as deep as normal and bury my bow deep into the sea. The jarring force as I bottom out throws everyone topside onto the deck in bewilderment and dismay. One man falls headfirst down a hatch mistakenly unlatched, others slide towards the ship's rail as my bow careens upward again with the deck at a crazy angle. Two unlucky men are thrown from the rigging into the sea, never to be seen again. There's no way to save them.

The Surgeon is one of the first to straighten back up. He rushes to the companionway in response to the yells of the man who has fallen through, then turns happily away when the chap rubs his shoulders and stands shakily. Two marine guards in the passageway have trouble getting up as their muskets have become entangled with their legs. One enterprising convict tries to grab one of the guns. He is hit over the head by a third guard's baton and falls near the base of the stairs, moaning heavily.

Robertson and his students bounce and slide towards the main-mast along with a guardsman who'd been behind the surgeon. As Robertson clambers to his feet he looks up and is stunned to see a sailor twelve feet above him swinging crazily from a thick line. The line he had been handling now coils in a double tight loop around his throat and the chap's own weight keeps pulling it tighter.

Without hesitation, Robertson grabs a boathook from its cleats on the rail and starts climbing into the rigging. As soon as he is high enough he reaches out with the hook and catches the line above the sailor's head. Using all his strength and adrenaline, and timing the ship's natural roll to advantage, he hauls the poor chap to the side, grabs him tight, lifts him and attempts to loosen the noose about his neck.

The man's face is a brilliant red. His breath comes in huge gasps as he and Robertson both work to remove the coils. Once off, they reveal ugly burn marks. Robertson's seamen students have scrambled upwards and now help him steady the young sailor and release him from his near-death escape. Close up, Robertson realizes the chap is just a lad, probably no older than eighteen. He looks closely at the rope marks on the boy's neck and says "You'll be Ok son. You are lucky your windpipe isn't crushed. You'll have some heavy bruises for many months yet but in time they'll disappear."

The four men carefully descend to the deck where the surgeon immediately takes over and inspects the young lad. He checks the victim's breathing and applies a salve on the burn marks, coming up with a similar assessment to Robertson's. "You are lucky this prisoner acted so quickly," he tells his patient. "A minute later and I don't think you'd be alive right now."

The two sailors who'd assisted clap Robertson heartily on his back and shake his hand. "Thanks matey. You sure done a good job."

The embattled lad, breathing more easily, sits on a large tool box, reaches up and extends his hand as well. He rasps a weak "Thank you" and struggles to smile.

The surgeon peers with respect and appreciation into Robertson's face. "You are full of surprises my man. I think it's high time you told me your story."

9.   *A visitor*

Sail Ho!" The lookout shouts down from the crow's nest. Repeats his call, points aft. "Sail Ho – abaft the beam."

"Distance?" the First Mate retorts.

"Five to six leagues, in the haze, sir."

"Colors?"

"Can't tell. A ship, still hull-down."

The Mate looks aloft at the sails, shouts "steady as she goes", and swiftly climbs the ratlines to the masthead. He returns 10 minutes later and sends a messenger to Coubro's cabin.

"Officer of the Deck's duty, sir, and he reports a ship overtaking on the port quarter, sir. Too far off yet to see her colors."

"Call All Hands as soon as she is hull-up. Fetch Corporal Tomkins to meet me on deck. Secure all prisoners and passengers in their compartments. Carry on!"

The ship comes alive. Topmast men climb high onto the uppermost spars to check their rigging and lashings. Others sidle across the deck and remove cannon covers, close open rigging chests, and help the gunners roll back the cannon.

On the quarter deck Coubro asks Tomkins, "What could your men hit with so little practice?"

"Precious little, sir."

"Very well. Load all with double-shot grape and chain. We may not be able to repel, but by God we can damn sure defend this ship. Carry on."

"Aye, sir."

"I want to hear cannon fire in ten minutes. Understood?"

Coubro seeks his most trusted officer, the surgeon.

"Arthur, pirates aren't known to operate in these waters, and generally they're in smaller ships. Even if this over-taker is flying British colors, they could be a ruse. If we're attacked, you are bound to have to treat both men and women. Make ready for female casualties in the orlop, as we've discussed."

"Aye, sir." The surgeon wheels and disappears to his quarters.

The prisoners below hear the thumps of more boots than usual on the main deck, and the rumble of heavy equipment being moved around. The extensive activity leads them to unusual murmurings and conjecture as to what is going on, until a guard locks down the hatches, and tells them an unknown sail has been sighted on the horizon, and no one knows if it is friend or foe.

That news, coupled with the extra hustle and bustle above makes many of the prisoners nervous. Twitching faces, shaking leg muscles, worried looks and whispered conversations change the atmosphere. Fears of capture or slaughter by foreigners spreads quickly. Women cry, men yell. The air fills with a cacophony of wails, swearing, and arguments over what might happen.

Fifteen minutes after Coubro's command the boom of the forward portside cannon reverberates around the superstructure.

The thunderous blast assaults the prisoners' eardrums in their confined space and turns apprehension into panic. Men try to force open the hatch to the main deck, to no avail. They beat on it with fists and try to lever with staves they discovered stuffed behind the heads. Paul Knightbridge, one of the mess leaders, climbs ahead of the throng at the top of the companionway. In a loud voice he yells, "Men. Calm down, it's too soon to know. Maybe the militia are just getting ready. There's nothing we can do here. Let's wait a bit. We'll know soon enough."

Peter Cooksey, the skinny lover, climbs through his high access gap above the door and gives the women Knightbridge's message. For a moment, across the compartments, there's a pause in the anticipated terror as anxious ears strain for news.

Up above, a shout from the lookout "Merchantman sir, full canvas, French colors."

Coubro mutters, "At least he's not a pirate or a frigate."

The other cannon fire in quick succession, and Coubro orders Tomkins to fire them all again. He joins his quartermaster by the main mast. "Padraig, hostilities with France are supposed to be over. Could this be a rogue captain who has vowed never to surrender?"

"Thought crossed my mind, Cap'n. But, as a betting man, I think unlikely."

"What's your bet?"

"She rides low in the water, sir. Hard to tell, but from a glimpse of her hull, I see few cannon ports. Same as us – perhaps only four. She's not a fighting ship. Cargo clipper I suggest, ably skippered and crewed. Maybe all ex-French Navy. Possibly bound for South America. Isn't France about to recognize Brazil's independence? Maybe this is a test of new relationships."

Coubro looks to his own gun crews, scans the set of his sails, turns and says, "Good thinking, Paddy. Let's hope you're right."

He is right.

I could have told Captain Coubro that **three** hours ago, if I'd had a way to tell him. We ships frequently broadcast our positions and courses through the waters we travel in. The freighter is named 'Le Soleil du Matin' and she's been recently refurbished in Lorient, France. No other vessel is within 55 miles of me at the moment. She'll be alongside in three more hours.

An hour later, it becomes clear to the crew that the visitor is definitely no man-o-war, but a heavily laden freighter making surprisingly good speed with her four masts fully rigged. The gunners are probably more relieved than the sailors. From the conversations within each gun crew, it was clear none of them relished a fight. As I mentioned before, many of the guards are ex-criminals themselves, signed up to avoid further gaol time, not to fight any enemies of the King.

For the convicts, four cannon firings from both sides of the ship and the long silence afterwards have calmed immediate fears. Conversations are back to normal levels, and while there's still an undercurrent of concern, face muscles relax and worry creases smooth. The general rationale shared among folks is that were a battle imminent there would be much more activity and preparation.

118

Relief is palpable when the ship slows and a guard unlocks the hatches and tells all that the visitor is friendly.

Half a mile astern, *The Morning Sun* furls her sails, dips her ensign and salutes our colors. We, heave-to so that she can lie aback and send a boat across the intervening stretch of water to us.

Coubro greets his visitor with grace and tact. "Bonjour monsieur. Bienvenue abord *Lady Corinth*. Je m'appelle Coubro, à votre service."

"Captain Perouse, sir. I'm 'appy to speak English."

"Then, please come to my cabin."

"Thank you, mon Capitaine."

The two men meet for an hour. Their discussion covers the peace which now holds between their countries, weather expectations, present position calculations, personal histories and backgrounds, and their mutual concern over the conditions ahead as they enter the tropics. *The Morning Sun's* primary cargo is a wide selection of French wines and cheeses. A major portion of her load was landed in Plymouth where she picked up British textiles, along with a range of metalware and hardware, all destined for Brazil. In return Perouse hopes to bring back raw commodities and materials, especially wheat, sugar, butter, flax, and rice.

Captain Perouse gifts Coubro two bottles of white wine. Coubro responds with a flask of 12 year old Scotch. He conducts his guest through the paid passenger accommodations and introduces the French Captain to an assembly of them in the common room. The men

119

and women graciously nod to the visitor across the room, but Mrs. Finsbury steps forward, and addresses the two captains.

"Excuse me gentlemen, but may I ask Captain Perouse a question?"

"Mais oui, madame, s'il vous plait. Comment puis-je vous aider?"

"Captain, I'm sure Mr. Coubro has informed you of our unusual cargo. We carry sixty women convicts who wear rags. I wonder if you might have any spare material of any form in your cargo that we could purchase to clothe them properly. This may seem a strange request. We have some spare canvas but that's not suitable for the women. Even if it were, we still have thousands of miles to travel and storms to survive. Replacement clothes may be essential for them. These women may be prisoners, but they are still human beings. I propose to treat them accordingly. Perhaps we could trade some fresh fish for a few bolts of English cloth if you have any."

Captain Perouse's smile is kind and understanding. "That's a noble thought madame. I vill be delighted to help. We do in fact carry a variety of textiles from Yorkshire, as well as a variety of metalware. I'm sure we vill find an error in ze count of ze 'undreds of product bales as they were placed on board. Vood you prefer cotton or wool? You say nearly 60 female convicts? So perhaps two large bolts of each cloth? Beige, blue, or green? If Captain Coubro vill impart a few more bottles of scotch in return we vill call it an even trade. Oui?"

Coubro nods affirmatively. "D'accord, monsieur."

Clarinda's eyes light up as she registers unexpected surprise. "Oh, sir, you are most kind. Blue please. Heartfelt thanks from all of us. Vous etes absolument un vrai gentilehomme...."

Carolyn Pennington waves her hand in the air, and attracts Captain Perouse's attention.

"sir, you mentioned metalware. Is that just table and serving cutlery and pots and pans, or by any chance does it include scissors? The ladies will need to cut the cloth into various shapes and sizes, and I doubt they have such implements with them."

"Madame, I will check when I return to my ship. If we have some I will happily include them with the bolts of cloth. Adieu et bon voyage, Mesdames et Messieurs."

The captains turn and depart as the passengers enthusiastically applaud. Congratulations pour over Clarinda for her initiative in approaching the foreign captain.

Half an hour later, enough material to clothe a majority of the convict women arrives inside two large burlap sacks. Coubro asks Clarinda how she would like to present the goods to the prisoners.

"I'd like to consult with Corporal Tomkins and Doctor Crisp, sir, as I suspect between them, they may have knowledge of a competent seamstress with a genuine interest in others' plights."

Tomkins does not know the occupations of the women, but the surgeon provides names of two possible candidates based on discussions during their health examinations.

Betsy Grantham and Molly Sandstone are escorted to one of the storage boxes, where they meet Clarinda. The surgeon accompanies her in order to reassure the two prisoners that nothing negative is in store, and to calm their anxiety. Clarinda asks the women for details about their seamstress experiences, and then tells them of the availability of two bolts of cotton material. She knows as the ship approaches the equator that it will get much warmer, and cotton will serve better in the heat.

Betsy is overwhelmed. "Cor, miss, tha's unbeliev'ble. T' young girls are emb'rassed wif their breasts on show and no und'wear. We could fix 'em up proper in no time. And..."

Molly interrupts. "Plus, many of t' adult clothes are torn and filthy. Thems would love new clean dresses. Oh my, we'd all be so 'appy."

Betsy again. "Did you say two whole bolts ma'am? Ain't seen that much cloth 'cept in tailors' shops. What color?"

"It's a dark blue, perhaps not the most feminine color," Clarinda replies.

"Oh ma'am. It don' matter at all. What t'ink you Molly?"

"Ev'ryone 'appy anythin' new. Hate to ask, but needle an' thread? Thimbles and scissors?"

Clarinda nods. "My lady friends and I will provide half of our sewing kits. You will have to be judicious in how you use our gifts I'm afraid. I need to talk to Dr. Crisp about the scissors."

Betsy squints, and wrinkles her face. "What 'chudishus' mean ma'am?"

"It means be careful, sparing. We have a very limited supply of black and blue thread. Other colors are more plentiful."

Molly has a thought. "Any brown thread ma'am? If we prop'ly wash discards p'aps we could make slippers for some ain't got no foot cov'rin's."

Betsy's face colors, she hangs her head and mumbles. "Mr. Surgeon, can you leave for a moment?" Crisp walks away to the railing. "Ma'am. Hate to say, but some need monthly strips. 'portn't as clothes, you know."

Clarinda nods. "I understand. You all decide. Now, you wait here, and I'll go get everything." She motions to Dr. Crisp to return and tells him it's time to give the women the bolts and supplies.

"sir, the good French Captain also sent two pairs of steel scissors to us. I don't know what the rules are for the prisoners, but scissors could be used as weapons. Do you want to allow them? I don't know how the ladies could produce clothes without them I must admit."

"Very astute, Mrs. Finsbury. I will talk to the Captain and the Corporal and get their opinions. I'm inclined to let the ladies have them, as long as they understand that any abuse and the scissors will be confiscated. Perhaps they could elect someone to be responsible for them whenever sewing sessions are complete, and return them to an officer. I'll let Betsy and Molly know when I take them back to their compartment."

To her new first-class female friends who have watched through the lounge windows, Clarinda summarizes her exchange with the two prisoners and then heads back with a bolt under each arm and a small box of sewing supplies in one hand.

Tears form in Betsy's eyes. "You dunno what t's means dear lady. We t'ank you from the bottom of our 'arts."

123

Molly is overcome and sniffles as she picks up a bolt and caresses it on both sides "Lov'ly" she purrs. "We'll look like new people in this. Thank you ag'in. Yo're ver' kind."

She and Betsy wave to the women watching from indoors as Crisp escorts the pair back to their compartment.

At dinner that evening Clarinda provides a summary of the day's good deed, appropriately filtered for the menfolk. The discussion is buoyant, although Matilda, her Ladyship's maid, is somewhat withdrawn as she listens intently.

During a lull in the conversation, she speaks up, "You have done something wonderful for those poor women and girls. I know they have committed some crime, but that doesn't mean they shouldn't have reasonable clothes. I wonder what they are all saying now. I imagine many of them won't believe what they will look like when they see themselves in a mirror in a new dress. I know I wouldn't. That material you provided was of excellent quality. When I grew up, I learned all about various cloths, as my mother was the top seamstress in our village."

She pauses, then muses wistfully. "My, what I could do with a few yards of that cotton."

Carolyn Pennington inquires, "Exactly what would you do, Matilda?"

"I'd make me a going-out dress with full gathered skirt, Mrs. Pennington. The top would be tapered to my waist, so it would be as cute as what you have on, but with ruffles at the shoulders and flares that drooped at my wrists."

"That sounds lovely, dear girl. I know we'd all love to see it. What do you think Lady Hudson-Smythe?"

Lady Hudson-Smythe looks up. "The guests admire your service to me, Matilda, and they all wanted to reward you. So here's one of my small purses with enough coins inside from the ladies to buy some lovely cloth when we reach Cape Town. I do hope you like your little surprise."

Matilda's hand reaches up and covers her mouth in disbelief. Her eyes open wide. "For me?"

The evening ends happily. There's little variety in the things the passengers can do to relieve boredom, so anything outside of regular routines and activities can offer rewards. Today has provided an unusual opportunity to experience something vastly different from the everyday norm. It's been good for everyone.

The female prisoners are ecstatic.

I watch faces glow, I watch tears run, I hear joyous cries of disbelief and thanks.

And in a dark corner I hear little Diana pray. "D... dear God, I am to have a new frock, and m...mummy a new chemise. We will look so pretty. So I don't know why mummy is crying. Please bless the kind ladies upstairs. Amen."

10. *Empty seas*

We are becalmed in clear blue waters one degree of latitude north of the equator. Every inch of sail is up and ready to catch the slightest stir of a breeze. During the past week, the temperature rose steadily, and our progress became slower every day. It is very hot. Ninety-three degrees Fahrenheit. The surface of the deck is too hot to walk across in bare feet. The shroud wires that hold the masts in place almost burn the hand when touched. Everyone is miserable. Me too. The sun beats mercilessly on all my woodwork – hull, masts, spars, deck, railings, passenger cabins – and dries out the deck planking. Another day or so and some timbers will start cracking, possibly tearing and even splintering. I shudder at the thought.

As if that is not enough, salt from the seawater dries in crystals on my hull, the deck, and the lower sails. It's like a second prickly skin, or an irksome rash of tiny blisters. I need to plough through some big waves to wash everything down. Or get drenched in a rainstorm. And soon. Before I become very irritable.

Prior to the rapid rise in temperature a few sailors tried their hand at fishing with surprising success. Several small bluefin tuna, and a baby hammerhead shark found the larger hooks. But the supply has now disappeared and the fishing rods have been stowed away.

It's exercise time for the male prisoners. Perhaps fifty of them have ventured topside, but none are doing any exercises. They've come instead to escape the stifling environment below, where the thermometer reads one hundred and five degrees, and the odors are malignant.

As they have done for the past four days, the men sit shirtless in the shade of the sails, hardly talking, fanning themselves with the shirts they've taken off. Sweat drips off their bodies. For some, the welts and cuts across their backs from past whippings stand out in vivid horror. They itch, but it takes too much energy to scratch them.

Sailors and prisoners rarely mix, except as necessary for organizational purposes – food deliveries, opening and closing of hatches, minor repair work to the compartments. The militia have more engagement with the convicts than do the sailors. In the past few days of almost no wind however there have been some new interactions. The heat affects everyone. No one likes it. When on deck, the prisoners watch the sails, as do the sailors, each person hoping to be the first to detect the faintest movement in the limp canvas that might signal a change. Watchstanders chat to each other about the size and shape of the sails, which ones will be most likely to detect a breeze first, and whether the lookout man high aloft will feel something before those on deck do. It takes energy to talk. The deck is mainly quiet.

There is one notable exception to this inactivity. James Robertson sits in the shade near the bowsprit where he reads Jane Austen's "Pride and Prejudice" aloud to two young sailors who listen attentively. The book is one of several in the doctor's small library, which he has made available to the teacher. Robertson has a unique relationship with the surgeon, for the doctor has also offered his cabin as a classroom when otherwise not in use. Before the current heatwave arrived, three convicts and the two sailors gathered there daily for reading and writing lessons.

The men resting within earshot of Robertson's voice pretend a lack of interest, but inadvertently reveal they are listening with snickers at some of the customs and actions of Austen's characters.

Elsewhere on deck conversations are desultory and limited.

But that's about to change.

In early evening the temperature drops to the low-eighties, and the sailors organize some self-entertainment. Swimming races!

Coubro breaks the traditional rules and invites all the prisoners on deck at the same time. He even invites the first class passengers to come watch and reserves an area for them forward towards the bow on the port side. Four soldiers are strategically placed to intercept any prisoner who might be a little too curious about the high and mighty societal patrons.

There are two types of swimming contest, one sprint-like, the other endurance-oriented. Coubro explains the sprints to the prisoners who gather between the two after-most masts. From where Coubro stands, the passengers can also hear him.

"Two men will stand on each platform on either side of the rudder. At my signal they will dive in the water and swim forward along the hull, two to starboard, two to port. They will cross at the bow and swim back along the opposite side of the hull. The first man to touch the rudder on return wins the race.

"The prize is an extra ration of rum for the next two days. We have fifteen participants, so there will be four events to give us four winners. Those four will then race to see who's champion. The champion wins more grog and an oilskin that was one of several donated to the ship owners by the Admirals before we left port."

Whoever thought to hold this little competition should be congratulated. The crowd seems galvanized by the idea of something novel. As Coubro concludes his speech, the crowd cheers, and myriad discussions break out as a sense of excitement builds.

I haven't seen these sorts of races before, so am intrigued to watch and learn. We need a distraction from the heat, and this is a brilliant one.

I've seen other races- there's one in which two sailors start from opposite sides of the deck and see how fast they can climb the rigging to the lookout's cage, retrieve an item, and return to the deck. There's a bit of danger associated with that one, but some of the men are like monkeys the way they scramble up the nets. Swimming is far more appropriate in this heat though.

The fifteen contestants parade across the deck. They wear only their long pants. Chests and arms are bare, caps gone from their heads. They challenge each other with good-natured taunts, "Joe, who you kiddin'? You're too old. I c'd swim backstroke an' beat you."

"Oh yeah, the on'y t'ing keepin' you afloat mate will be y'r britches. You'll sink with tha' huge stomick."

"Stand back fellas, look at this chest and these arm muscles. P'wr evryw'r. Wanna' give up before we start?"

The onlookers get in the spirit, cheer loudly as each man in a foursome takes up his position, flexes his arms, and waves to the crowd. The swimmers hold on to the rail with one arm, leaning backward, the other arm pointed down to the water twelve feet below. Coubro steps close by, and with a loud yell calls, "Ready?" Four hearty affirmations come back. Coubro raises his arm, drops it, yells "Go", and the four men leap off their platforms. Two are skilled divers, two jump and make huge splashes. The crowd above laughs and cheers.

Men and women rush to the rails on both sides, sailors and convicts intermingling, nudging each other aside to peer over the rails and urge their favorite swimmer on. The decks, cooled by buckets of saltwater, reverberate with their joyful shouts and cheers. I relish the sounds of laughter, of good-hearted camaraderie, of enthusiasm and fun. There hasn't been much of that to date. But clearly the prisoners are as human as the sailors. Convicts and seamen alike are enjoying themselves. For a short period there is no distinction between the haves and the have-nots. The crowd moves forward, peering over the outer railings, in order to keep pace with the men in the water.

At the bow there is not enough room for everyone, but in the spirit of sharing, those who have an advantageous position shout to those behind them.

An older sailor with a patch over one eye and a strident voice calls, "Ben from the port side is first around, a length ahead of Louis."

His red-haired friend leans out along the bowsprit and adds, "Both touch the anchor chain and are off again."

Others chime in. "Charlie from starboard has just come into view."

"Come on Charlie!"

"Pete is way behind Charlie. Ben and Louis are out of sight."

The crowd splits and retreats to the opposite sides of the ship as their favorites head back to the stern. Their cheers escalate as Louis gains on Ben and as Charlie puts on a final sprint. A few verbal bets are traded between companion sailors.

Sailors around the rudder post keep up the commentary.

"It's Charlie versus Louis."

"Go Charlie!"

"Faster Louis, go man!"

"Louis wins by an arm's length!"

The victor climbs the rope ladder ahead of the other three swimmers, and loud congratulatory shouts ring out. The cheers are accompanied by back-slaps and hand-shakes among contestants and onlookers alike.

The second heat starts off like the first, all four men thrashing through the water, devoid of style, but full of energy and determination. The crowd loves the atmosphere. As the men converge under the bow halfway through the course however, one gets jostled and hits the bowsprit guy-wire head-on. The wire consists of strong twisted strands, stretched taut. It is immovable and very hard. Much harder than the swimmer's head. He stops, gasps, reaches for the top of his head and comes back with a bloody hand. Not a serious injury, but certainly headache-inducing. He's sufficiently shaken that he swims slowly to a rope ladder and climbs aboard. Dr. Crisp checks him over, makes him sit in the shade, and arranges for a beer. The swimmer gets a short bout of sympathy from the crowd, but once declared fit, he's forgotten. Back to the race.

And so it goes on. Four heats and then a final race. I'm impressed that the enthusiasm continues across all five events. Some prisoners are becoming hoarse by the end. Eventually Coubro crowns the ultimate winner – a short athletic seaman named Rupert. He gets well-deserved applause from the crowd as well as his grog and oilskins.

Coubro senses the positive spirit of the crowd and responds with an offer of free beer for all. He receives a roaring ovation with his announcement.

* * *

The merriment is wonderful to see and hear – who would have guessed that prisoners could actually enjoy themselves to this extent? And as much as I'd like to stay and watch, a small crisis is unfolding below deck that demands my attention. Screams and moans rent the air in the

132

female prisoner quarters, unheard above deck over the spectator din. Arthur, the surgeon, once summoned, quickly gulps the last of his beer and rushes to the side of a young woman, Susannah Moore, who is in labor. Her cries sound desperate, for she's very frail, not a robust individual at all. She suffers terribly with the incredible heat. Arthur, along with Susannah's friends have rallied around her day after day, making sure she drinks plenty of fluids, fanning her to keep her cool, applying cold compresses to her brow, supporting her when she has to get up and walk to the head, and watching over her as she sleeps. Her moans are constant now, interjected every few minutes with piercing screams. Her thin frame is distended in front, elsewhere her bones are obvious beneath her thin, pale skin.

* * *

The temperature continues to fall as evening progresses, although the sun is still well above the western horizon. Back on deck, new friendships are being forged among the prisoners as they sit and relish their beer. Men who have only viewed each other at a distance across the messes below now sit side by side, sharing backgrounds and experiences. Females tend to gather in bunches rather than couples, perhaps a little unsure of their safety with so many males around them. But they chatter volubly and with apparent purpose. Those disinterested in new relationships, or with a preference for their own company, sit alone on the capstan or the rigging boxes with their feet dangling over the side.

As one might expect with a loosely supervised mingling of the sexes, a few mixed-sex groups have formed. From the snippets of conversations I overhear, their topics focus on family members left behind. There's a common anguish, not always angry, but certainly reflective. I sense relief in both males and females to be able to share similar feelings. Perhaps there is indeed some value for prisoners of both sexes to be on board – as long as they are allowed to socialize.

Maybe I'm merely optimistic and hopeful, but a few men seem calmer after these group exchanges. I also anticipate some pairing may be the result of these gatherings.

Of course, as in free society, there are always those who will test the limits of allowed behavior. Two men who've consumed more than their fair share of beer approach the first-class passenger group making derogatory remarks about the snobbery of people in the upper classes of society and how they feel they are better than others. Several female passengers look embarrassed and irritated, and with a request to the militia, the two troublemakers are shepherded away.

A teenage boy and girl join hands and disappear down a back hatchway. I'm usually well aware of any couplings on board, but this one is new to me. They seem to be happily attracted to each other and share caresses in a dark corner. I have sensors all across my frame, so I see and feel many things that occur simultaneously as a natural happenstance. The boy runs his hands up under the girl's chemise and she doesn't object. They share lengthy kisses with each other, and his hands move elsewhere.

Coubro once again addresses the crowd. He announces a new and different swim race. It's over a long distance, and requires endurance rather than speed. The contestants will be rowed in the longboat approximately three quarters of a mile away and will race back to me. Coubro calls for volunteers.

This race is a more grueling event than were the sprints around my hull. The distance will be more than ten times that required to circle me. And there may be ocean current to contend with farther away from my keel, although probably much deeper than will have any surface impact.

Three men immediately step up on the platform beside the captain. Two I recognize but am surprised at the third who seems substantially older than the others. There are cries of "Forget it old man," and "Come on Thompson, who are you kidding?" But the old fellow smiles and waves. With a parting of the crowd a fourth contestant approaches the platform. He gets a loud cheer when recognized. Do you remember the chap who jumped overboard during the sea trials? It's him – Levian Shields – definitely a worthy competitor who will probably be the favorite.

Padraig, the quartermaster, ties long, wide colored sashes loosely around the four men's belts. One is red, one blue, one green, the last one white. They are to help the watchers identify the men once in the water since it will be hard to tell who is who at a distance.

A tall prisoner elbows his way to the front of the crowd and calls to the Captain, "Mr. Coubro?"

The captain turns from the contestants and responds, "Yes, Mr.?"

"My name is Grant Wembly sir. Can I compete in this race?"

"I'm sorry Mr. Wembly, but no, this is only for crew."

Those prisoners within hearing immediately start booing and hissing. The message spreads and there are shouts of "Unfair," "Let him compete," "Why can't he race?"

Coubro is surprised, as are the four sailors waiting to proceed. One of them speaks up. "Alright by me cap'n. Sh'dn't hurt nuffin'. May do some good."

The other three murmur agreement, so Coubro steps down from his platform and seeks out the surgeon. The pair talk in soft voices for several moments, then Coubro returns and addresses Wembly directly.

135

"What makes you think you can compete, Mr. Wembly? We're not in the practice of rescuing prisoners on the verge of drowning."

"I did a lot of swimming when I was twenty or so, sir, and am still in reasonable shape despite a year in gaol. I've swum across the Solent from Hurst Castle to Colwell Bay three times sir, once in winter."

"How far is that, Mr. Wembly?"

"About a mile and a quarter, cap'n."

Grant Wembly is a courageous convict to speak up so. He is shirtless, but sports a dark cap. Curls peek out from under the cap on both sides of his head, and sweat glistens across the light hairs on his chest. His demeanor is friendly, and a smile makes the scar on his right cheek scrunch up and almost disappear. Coubro can't hide his admiration of the man.

"Very well, Mr. Wembly. We'll make an exception. You may compete."

He turns to the acting head of the militia. "I'll take responsibility for allowing this digression and bending of the rules, corporal."

Tomkins snorts derisively. "Your ship, Captain."

Coubro turns away. "Quartermaster, give Wembly two sashes, one blue, one red tied together. OK, gentlemen, time to board the longboat. We'll fire a cannon to signal the start of the race. Good luck to each of you."

Grant hands his cap to a friend and follows the sailors down the rope netting on my port hull into the longboat. Cries of "Go blue," "Go red," and so on, cheer the swimmers as the longboat pulls away.

The sea is like a mirror, flat and featureless. My port side is to the east so it's easy to see the progress of the longboat as it moves away perpendicular to our setting. Six oarsmen make light work of the task, and in twenty minutes we see the boat turn sideways as the rowers ship their oars.

There are nearly one hundred people standing along my port rail. I list slightly, but not at an angle that worries anyone. The five contestants slip over the side of the longboat and hold the gunwale with one hand. From the stern a rower stands and holds up a large white cloth – the signal that the swimmers are ready.

Coubro nods to Padraig, and a cannon fires, a cloud of smoke rises into the rigging. The watchers are silent since all they can see at this distance is heads bobbing and streams of white foam behind legs and feet working overtime. The sailor in the lookout atop the main mast suddenly yells. "It's Levian in green in the early lead. The others are bunched close behind, bluey next." Blue is the color of the sash on the older sailor. The crowd murmurs surprise.

A few minutes later the lookout yells again. "One hundred yards gone. Blue and white are pulling away. Prisoner falling back." A few of the sailors make serious bets with each other, usually about the amount of grog to change hands. Levian's name is bandied about frequently.

At the halfway mark a pattern emerges as positions start to firm up. Best guesses of the lookout man have Levian five yards ahead of the blue and white sash wearers, with the red sash wearer and the prisoner ten yards behind them. The crowd's focus is on whether anyone can catch Levian.

A few observers with good eyesight have climbed twenty feet up in the rigging from where they can actually see the color of the sashes for themselves. Several sailors now provide commentary. Positions in the water are changing as the rear swimmers increase their pace. Excitement in the callers' voices indicates the last two hundred yards will involve a sprint to the finish.

Once again, the red-haired spectator calls the race, "Levian is slipping back."

His friend with the eye-patch is not to be outdone, "Blue man just hit the front. This old codger is terrific."

As before, others take up the commentary cause, "Prisoner is now third behind whitey."

"Looks like Levian is out of it."

"Prisoner gaining on whitey."

"Looks like a two-man race — whitey and prisoner. Come on people. Cheer them on. They can hear you now."

At less than one hundred yards out the crowd goes wild, yelling their throats dry, waving their arms, exhorting both leaders to go faster. Two sailors climb down the rope net to greet the contestants. Forty yards out and it's dead even. The shouts get louder, reaching screaming pitch. White versus the convict Wembly. The prisoners chant, "Wembly, Wembly, Wembly" over and over. The sailors respond with loud cries of "Whitey, whitey".

A seaman at the bottom of the net yells "Whitey wins!" and the sailors at the rail clap each other on the back. There's good humor in their praise for Grant Wembly, who climbs wearily over the rail and sags in the arms of his convict friends. Old man 'Bluey', who came third, walks over and shakes Wembly's hand. "Great race mate. You have powerful strokes. Who knows what would have happened if you'd been free and more fit. My name's Roger. We'll chat again. Well done!"

On this rare evening, all is right with the world, at least above deck. Sailors have relieved their boredom, the prisoners have had more fresh air and entertainment than since they became criminals, and the passengers have watched two classes of humanity mingle as though equals, more easily than they would ever have guessed possible.

As quiet slowly falls across the deck, several persons hear the female cries from below. Brows furrow, and concern etches faces, especially the women's, as they recognize the reason and source of the yelling. I disregard the peaceful atmosphere on deck and re-focus on the room where Susannah lays panting, sweating, and screaming as she pushes to bring new life into the world.

She grabs the arm of the nearest woman and squeezes hard, while Arthur takes the mother-to-be's pulse. Susannah's waters broke 24 hours ago, dilation is now well complete and her body arches as she strains to deliver. She's nigh on exhausted, yet the little mother to be is urged to push once more, and she screams each time she does. Such is the way with some births. The process continues for another twenty minutes until at last Arthur eases the baby's head into view, and Susannah cries with relief. Her daughter is so tiny she's cradled in Arthur's hands. He carefully inspects the infant, who lets out a weak yell. The attendant friends smile in recognition of a new life among them.

Mother and baby are both feeble, and it's not clear whether Susannah will be able to offer her child any milk. Arthur is concerned that her breasts are not swollen with any meaningful offering. When he finally leaves her side, he immediately heads to the kitchen to check on the supplies of cows' and goats' milk. But there is none. What was drinkable was used up well over a week before.

The outlook for the baby is not promising.

* * *

The prisoners' lanterns burn longer than usual this night, as men and women alike re-live the mingling with the sailors, the fun of the swim races, and the captain's permission for one of their own to compete. Grant Wembly is the underdeck hero and tells his version of the race over and over.

Just past three bells in the morning I hear a soft creak of timbers, and feel my stern shift ever so slightly. A breeze has struck. Sailors, attuned to movement, wake. They remain quiet, breathe deeply, share questioning looks and careful smiles, not meaning to offend, or change the potential for wind. Duncan Conway, boatswain, is at the helm, having offered to take the quartermaster's turn as a gesture of comradeship. He's half asleep, but the soft voices and new movements stir him to action. He immediately sends a junior helmsman to inform the captain.

I hardly raise a wave at my bow under this zephyr of a breeze. Initial excitement among the crew fades as everyone realizes it is not going to blow harder. I'm sure if the prisoners were on deck there'd be a giant celebration, no matter how slow our speed. But no-one goes down below to wake them. Maybe some have guessed from the footsteps overhead or from the slight movement of the hull. On the other hand, perhaps they'll just think the extra beer they consumed is giving them strange dreams. Whatever, come morning, they'll no doubt celebrate.

Over the next two days the breeze lifts to five, then **seven** knots, gently moving us forward and providing some mild relief from the heat. We finally reach the equator, that invisible line around the earth that separates the northern and southern hemispheres. Zero degrees of latitude, a truly unique location. And one that has been recognized for centuries as a spot for celebration.

King Neptune resides in the depths here and every sailor who crosses the equator for the first time must pay homage to him and his court for the privilege of entering the kingdom of the southern seas. The price of entry is not cheap. And those who have crossed the Line before are ready and eager to extract it from the uninitiated.

11. *Commitment*

Twenty-one sailors who are part of the crew have never crossed into the Southern Hemisphere. They are held in the prisoner passageways, where they await their introduction to the Neptune Rex and his royal court. A cannon has been moved to center deck upon which quartermaster Plunkett, as Rex, sits clothed in a long flowing black robe. He is adorned with a grey horse-hair wig which stretches down his back and which has a cardboard crown, painted gold, on top. A pitchfork represents his trident.

Another cannon sits eight feet in front of him, and to this the first inductee seaman is led blindfolded and seated across the barrel facing Plunkett, held firmly in place by two of King Neptune's 'attendants' who have roped the inductee's ankles together. The boatswain, Conway, who stands off-center between king and subject, has at his feet a pail of foamy seawater polluted with chicken guts, old fish heads and left-over cooking grease. Behind the novice, a giant sail has been rigged in the form of a mammoth bath which holds gallons and gallons of seawater filled, bucket by bucket, by those who've been through the ceremony before.

The passengers form a gallery behind Plunkett. Plunkett booms at the first man nervously poised on the cannon barrel.

"Welcome to King Neptune's court Able Seaman. State your name."

"Christopher Winters, sir."

"Whence do you hail, Mr. Winters?"

"Newcastle on Tyne, sir."

"Good, now listen carefully you pollywog*. In order to become a shellback*, you must state your allegiance to the laws of my Kingdom. Understood?"

"Yes sir."

"Repeat after me. 'I promise to uphold the laws of King Neptune, his Queen, Amphitrite, and his helper, Davey Jones, so help me God.'"

As the man utters the first words "I promise to..." the boatswain swabs his face with a brush dipped in the foul mixture at his feet. The seaman gags, and spits.

Neptune continues. "I didn't hear you, pollywog. Speak up. "

Winters tries again and receives the same treatment. The process is repeated until he realizes he has to swallow, which he finally does and immediately vomits the contents all over his clothes. He curses mightily and struggles to get up but is held in place, as he is now allowed to complete his oath. The passengers and veteran sailors shout 'welcome' on cue, and clap noisily.

Neptune speaks again. "Well done, seaman. But your appearance is scruffy. You must look good for Queen Amphitrite."

At this point two burly sailors pinion the man's head and a third shaves part of his whiskers with a broken iron band previously used to hold the staves of a barrel in place. Blood drips down the inductee's chin from an errant swipe. He thrashes wildly, whereupon the men remove his blindfold and push him backwards into the giant bathtub behind him. They hold him down for a few seconds while he struggles and chokes, then let him emerge rinsing off his face and what's left of his mangled beard.

The sailors who are gathered around laugh, clap him on the back, and welcome him as a soul-mate who has survived a hazing that earns respect from his peers.

I've seen similar 'celebrations' on other voyages. This one is no worse than others but it still gives me pause. Is it really necessary? I suspect it's mainly for entertainment and retribution for those who've already been through a similar rite of passage. I can't see any tangible benefits, unless it's less beard to maintain. Unlikely, given the way the 'attendants' hack at the whiskers. The whole process is a bit too barbaric for me, and I cringe when the men are forced to swallow and then regurgitate the foul 'soup-of-the-deep'. The sooner the ceremony is finished the better, although it will take at least ninety minutes, I know.

Like me, some of the passengers are unsure of the treatment, and Sara Goldsmith retreats indoors with two of the other ladies. Surprisingly, Lady Hudson-Smythe stays in place, watching.

Aha, I notice that smile on your face. You've remembered she wants to write a book about the sailor's life. Good for you.

I can't help but eavesdrop on the retreating ladies' conversation. Sara, clearly a well-bred woman, is aghast. "My husband mentioned there'd be a ceremony for sailors crossing the equator for the first time. He called it 'a memorable occasion'. Ridiculous! Unbelievable! He must have been drunk at the time. That poor sailor, victimized with that scrungy, filthy drink poured down his throat. How utterly vile. The whole affair was disgusting."

Carolyn Pennington coughs and splutters. "When that man started throwing up it made me want to do the same. Why are men so cruel to one another?"

Nancy Winthrop responds. "I think they euphemistically call those episodes 'becoming one of us.' I'm sure glad women don't have any equivalent. I'm like you Carolyn, thoroughly disgusted. I want to complain to Captain Coubro, but I doubt he'd do anything, especially as her 'high and mighty' Hudson-Smythe is still sitting there. She must feel differently than we do."

A smile crosses Carolyn's face. "Witch. At the moment I think she'd do anything to get our dear captain in bed. Have you seen the coquettish looks she throws his way anytime she addresses him at dinner?"

Sara's face flushes, "Really? I hadn't noticed."

Nancy adds her two bits. "Come on Sara, are you blind? The woman's knickers are half-off already. She swings her breasts close by his face every chance. So obvious. You just watch, one day she'll parade around with a giant smile on her face like the cat that ate the canary." Nancy smiles at the thought.

I turn my attention back to the front deck. A second novice sailor is brought up from the lower deck and the award ceremony performance repeated. This goes on until all inductees have been welcomed and initiated into the kingdom, at which time, barrels of rum and beer are brought out, and everyone drinks to the health of the new members. Enough grog, and the taste of the boatswain's brush is forgotten.

The cats, Hither and Yon, have become mascots for the crew. They are brought forth and given savory bits of chicken and fish. The new shellbacks are encouraged to pet and hold them, adding to the approval process.

I reflect further on the induction ceremony. It is one of those sea-going traditions which has both a fun and a serious side to it. The limited amount of fun occurs for the men who are already shellbacks, initiating

146

others. The serious aspect is to see if the newcomers are worthy shipmates, and that they understand that they are at the whim of the gods of the oceans, whose actions are not always understood, but deserve respect no matter what. It's a comradeship experience whose value becomes clearer over time as participants suffer the intangibles and unpredictability of nature at sea.

A number of militia guards witness the ceremony. However, as the proceedings die down with the last individual, one of the on-duty soldiers takes the opportunity to vent his wrath against a female prisoner. Of course I know what is happening, but have no way to intervene. The guard, Millstone, is the one who has a thing against women.

For whatever reason, he's had it in especially for Sarah Grainger ever since she came on board. Maybe he hates pregnant women because of some event that happened earlier in his life. Maybe he doesn't even know the reason. I watch him on patrol in the women's quarters where he confronts Sarah in the passageway and blocks her way.

"Well, if it isn't little Sarah, the whore in a new dress. Where do you think you're going, missy?"

"To the toilet. Let me pass."

Millstone doesn't move, and instead, pokes Sarah in the stomach with his night-stick, forcing her to back up a step. "You're just a slut who fucked one too many times. I know your type. Just a man-serving bitch." He pulls his baton back and smirks as he drives it up hard between Sarah's legs. She gasps as pain emanates from the tender spot and shoots throughout her body. She folds forward, clutching beneath her belly, almost stumbling into the guard.

Panting, she yells between breaths, "You filthy pig! What a coward you are to hit a defenseless woman. Pig, pig, pig!"

She raises her voice so others will hear. "Move aside you bully. Let me pass or I'll report you to your leader. You'll be placed in irons. You've gone way too far this time, pig."

Two women rush up behind Sarah, one quietly urges her to retreat. "Sarah, he's too big to fight. Don't get hurt more."

Millstone stretches his face forward and spits on Sarah. "Whore, fucking whore!" He doesn't budge position, still blocks her progress. Then, with a swift motion he punches her hard on her swollen left breast. She screams in agony and falls to the passageway floor. Two more women arrive and comfort her, yelling for more help as they do so.

Millstone glares down at Sarah, draws his leg back to kick her, but relents, turns on his heels, and marches off down the corridor, his chest puffed out in disdain for the women behind him. Friends cradle Sarah, helpless to relieve her pain. One of the more daring women follows Millstone up the companionway ladder at the end of the passageway to the deck and calls for the surgeon. A sailor at the ceremony hears her, rushes to the hatch, gets the message that the doctor is needed urgently and finds the surgeon who is watching the induction proceedings. The doctor doesn't hesitate. He picks up his black bag from his position by the pollywogs' cannon, and heads to the companionway.

As it does for those who witness it, Millstone's behavior makes me sick. The female prisoners have been abused enough in their lives. While managing them requires order and discipline, personal vendettas have no place, especially given Captain Coubro's announcements at the start of the voyage. I wish I had some way to hurt Millstone as much as he has hurt Sara. I'm filled with rage, but powerless.

The doctor arrives, concerned and sympathetic. His ministrations calm Sarah and her angry supporters, but he is aghast at the sight of the bruise already coloring on Sarah's breast. The doctor hurries up on deck and pulls Coubro and the militia corporal aside. Coubro is furious, while the corporal is a little defensive, although he doesn't object when Coubro suggests the man be given fifty lashes and placed in the onboard brig until we reach Cape Town.

Nor does Coubro delay the punishment. He forces the corporal to bring the other active men in his force to where the Neptune ceremony has just completed. He dismisses the passengers and calls for a volunteer from the militia to be the flogger as he hands the cat-o-nine-tails to the corporal. None want to flog a fellow soldier, so Coubro approaches the bos'un, one of the bigger sailors in his crew, who willingly agrees. The sailors generally don't care for the militia, as they represent a controlling government force that is not liked anywhere. The flogger hates what he has been told about the assault below deck.

Millstone is dragged before the group, man-handled by four huge seamen as he kicks and screams. He is strapped over the cannon barrel recently used by Plunkett as his King Neptune throne. The shirt is torn off his back, and his britches are pulled down to his knees. Coubro walks around in front of the man, pulls his head up by his hair, and stares him in the face.

"You are not fit to be a guard on my ship, Millstone. You are no better than a mongrel dog, a cur of no value. I despise you. You are lucky I don't have you keelhauled, or simply thrown overboard. Instead you will suffer fifty lashes, and bread and water in the brig until we reach Cape Town, where you will be handed over to the authorities. No one beats a pregnant woman and gets away with it. You will rue this day for the rest of your life."

Coubro walks back to the militia corporal, takes the cat-o-nine-tails from his grip and is about to hand it to the bos'un when he stops and says, "No, it should be one of your men, corporal. Your Commander wouldn't have hesitated to use the 'cat' on the prisoners. Get him out here and have him flog his own man."

The beast that is Mullens has no hesitation in punishing his soldier. It's an opportunity to vent his rage for his incarceration. The cat is made up of nine knotted thongs of oiled cotton cord about two and a half feet long, designed to lacerate the skin and cause intense pain. Millstone screams as the commander lashes with fury. At the end Mullens is breathing hard, and Millstone's back and buttocks are a maze of bleeding cuts and welts. The man's fellow guards cart him away to the brig.

It's an ugly end to the day, but serves its purpose. From the look on the faces of the other guards, a clear message has been given and received. Crisp returns to the women's quarters to check on Sarah and to announce that Millstone will bother her and other women no more.

* * *

In the days that follow, prisoner harassment ceases, but a new problem emerges with the heat that affects nearly everyone.

Cockroaches!

Before we left Portsmouth I knew there were nests in the deepest part of the hold. But while the vermin multiplied over time, they stayed in the bilge area. Unfortunately, the hot days we've experienced around the equator have driven them upwards for some unknown reason, and they are now invading the prisoners' quarters, and elsewhere. They scurry silently along the skirting boards, their ugly bodies viewed with disgust and horror.

These are large, bold, insects that seek food wherever they can find it. They usually come aboard in the various barrels and crates of supplies and are difficult to detect at the time of loading. I can't remember a single voyage where they haven't been present. We seem to have two different genera on this trip – identified by their distinct mating habits. No, I'm not going to elaborate, other than to say in one species the females are the aggressors; in the other, the males. There are only two ways to get rid of them, and both require a concerted effort. The obvious one is to crush them underfoot, but that doesn't work when everyone is sleeping.

At night the convicts ensure their rooms are free of crumbs, and construct small pools of flour and molasses in pathways where the vile creatures are observed as they sneak under the woodwork. The cooks have been generous in granting supplies, as they want to keep the devils below deck and not have them enter the galley. It's easy to scoop up dead and dying roaches from the traps each morning, and eject them overboard. The prisoners have been at it for three days now, and I'm pleased to say that sightings have fallen off dramatically.

Some inmates initially thought the cats would hunt the cockroaches, but Hither and Yon seem to have had more fun killing rats and mice. Since the sailors keep feeding the two furry felines tidbits of human food, they seem content to kill the rodents but not eat them. Many a below-deck resident has awakened to find a carcass deposited as a 'gift' near their bed in the morning.

There's one ironic twist to Millstone's punishment that very few persons know about, but who would rejoice if they did. The brig into which the blaggard was thrown has two cells, defined and separated by a thick wooden partition. The cells are dingy and cramped, with only a small high port that lets in minimal light when the heavy oak door is bolted shut. Mullens has occupied one stall, but now has a new cellmate next door, who, on arrival, immediately attracts the attention of the other brig residents, hundreds of cockroaches!

The place is overrun with the ugly creatures. They immediately swarm on Millstone's back, eating blood clots and tearing at moist strips of skin. He stomps on the multitude with his boots, but hardly makes a dent in the infestation.

Days later he still yells as the filthy vermin climb all over him, but his cries are ignored.

He who handed out terror so readily, now faces his own.

12. *Southern Atlantic*

We're proceeding on a south-easterly course now at a gentle eight knots. A pleasant change from the miserable time spent stationary around the equator. The first breeze that finally found us there was a gentle zephyr that barely stretched the canvas of our sails. It propelled us slowly southward, but our lack of speed frustrated everyone on board. Not until we were two degrees south of the great hemisphere dividing line did we finally pick up the Southeast trades we're running before now.

We've established a course aimed directly for Cape Town. Each day, the wind on our beam grows steadily stronger. The charts Coubro affixes to the saloon wall with thumb pins show us traveling more miles every day.

At dinner in the middle of the sixth week at sea, the discussion is all about the ship's speed.

Mr. Finsbury addresses the captain. "sir, I'm amazed at today's chart. It indicates we covered 240 miles in the last 24 hours. That means an average speed of 10 miles per hour. Just how fast can *Lady Corinth* go?"

I hold my figurative breath, waiting for the answer. Locked in my memory are the maximum speeds I've achieved on every trip I've made over the last twelve years. Coubro doesn't know what I can actually do, although he could probably make a shrewd guess based on his experience in other barques and his assessment of the wind and currents we'll be facing on the remainder of our voyage.

I wait anxiously to hear his reply, but he doesn't respond immediately, and I have to curb my frustration. He points his chin towards the pilot. "I think Mr. Matheson needs to tell us more about speed and measurement."

Charles speaks up. "We put those charts up, Mr. Finsbury, with the distances listed in miles. That makes it easier for passengers like yourself, who are accustomed to see mileposts along the country roads and who know it is 20 miles from Portsmouth to Southampton, say.

"But, because they match the distance between parallels of latitude, in the maritime world we actually make all our measurements in 'nautical miles' which are 15% longer than land miles. Over time, the term nautical miles* has become abbreviated to 'nauts', which is much easier to say. And to measure speed, rather than say 'nauts per hour', we lazy sailor-types used the word 'knots'. A knot* is 15% faster than one mile per hour."

Matheson pauses, and Finsbury speaks up. "Sounds very confusing Mr. Pilot. Why have two different measurements for distance and speed? Who benefits?"

Pilot responds. "Good questions, Mr. Finsbury. Are you all ready to learn some maritime lore?"

Several heads nod around the table, but Sara Goldsmith grimaces and asks, "Will this involve an understanding of mathematics and science Mr. Pilot? I'm not well versed in those subjects."

"I'm afraid so, Mrs. Goldsmith. But I will make it as simple as possible for you."

"Thank you, sir, but even with your good intentions, I suspect I'd have a headache very quickly. So, begging your pardon, I'll excuse myself and let the others enjoy your lesson."

Sara pushes back her chair, and demurely leaves the table. Following her example, the other women rise one after the other and murmur similar concerns. Lady Hudson-Smythe adds advice, "Come on,

Matilda. This would be straightforward for me, but extremely difficult for you. I do not want you to be stressed. Let's return to my cabin."

Matheson smiles at the gentlemen who remain. "I'm sorry to lose the ladies, but I do understand. For those of us who sail regularly, it's all very obvious of course, but sometimes the uninitiated find it hard to grasp. Since we all enjoy the faster speed these days, I'll show you how that's calculated."

John Pennington has been concentrating hard. He has stayed silent, except when bidding his wife goodnight. He stands, walks to the chart on the wall and fiddles with the pencil strung along its side. He writes out a string of numbers then turns around triumphantly.

"The chart indicates that we've averaged ten miles per hour for the past twenty-four hours. So, in terms of knots, it's ten divided by 1.15, which is about 8.7 knots. Is that correct, captain?"

"Sounds about right to me, Mr. Pennington," Coubro replies. "But let me challenge you gents, officers excepted. What do you think is our speed right this minute? Any idea?"

It's James Winthrop's turn to add to the conversation. "I guess at least nine knots, since we've been gradually picking up speed the further southeast we travel. But how can we find out?"

Padraig rises. "Come on gents and I'll show you how the chip log works."

He leads the four men to the stern of the boat and motions to two sailors to come along. "Swenson, Holmes, bring the chip log."

At the stern Padraig points out a large wooden reel that holds a very long coil of light line, called the log line. It's nothing like other coils the passengers have seen at various places on deck. It is much bigger and there's something odd about the rope itself. At the open end of the coil, the rope is spliced into three single thread lines. These are attached to the points of a quarter-inch-thick triangular piece of wood whose sides are roughly 5" or 6" long. The bottom of the wooden piece is slightly longer and weighted lightly with lead. The apparatus looks like a very small kite, a frame made of wood, but with no cloth.

Swenson tosses the wood into the water. It floats tip-upright, with about two thirds of its height under the surface. The chip log acts as a drogue which remains roughly in place vertically while the breeze in my sails moves us forward and away from it. Steadily, the gap between the chip log and my stern increases, and the line pays off its reel.

Padraig turns to Holmes. "Tell them about the knots in the line matey."

"As you can see gents, there are small knots at large intervals in the rope line. They've been carefully placed so the distance between each of them is identical. Now, as Swenson watches the board, and the rope passes through my hands, I count the number of knots going past my fingertips. If you look carefully at Swenson's right hand, you'll see he holds a glass sands timer. It's the same hourglass you use at breakfast time to make sure your eggs are boiled to perfection. The sands slip down from the top end to the bottom in exactly 30 seconds even. Let us show you."

He turns to Swenson. "You ready Andy?" he asks.

"Aye, matey, on my mark. Go." He holds up the timer and inverts it. The sands start to run down through the narrow neck in the middle.

Holmes starts counting as each knot passes his fingertips. "One, two, three, four, five, six, seven, eight, nine, ten..."

...Andy shouts out, "Trip!" All the sands are in the bottom half of the timer.

Swenson jerks the line strongly to release two of the strings held by a pin to the chip log and starts to haul the kite board back across the surface of the sea. Holmes explains, "The knots in the rope are exactly 50' 8" inches apart, which is why the reel is so large. It turns out that the distance between each knot is calculated to represent one knot of speed. Nice huh? A knot for a 'knot'. I counted out ten, headed for eleven. That means our speed is just over a wonderful clip of ten knots. That's pretty fast gents, believe me. Look at those full sails. Any questions?"

John Pennington steps forward. "Impressive Mr. Holmes. And so simple, although clearly the distance between knots is critical. Thanks for showing us. I wonder who invented that small device. Mr. Plunkett, can we go back to the chart and play with the numbers again? I'm thoroughly intrigued with this procedure."

Back inside the lounge, Pennington steps to the chart.

"Let's make this simple. Suppose the ship moves only one length of rope, fifty and two thirds feet between knots, in the 30 seconds. At that rate, in one minute, twice as long, one hundred and one and a third feet would run out. So in an hour, 60 times that length would play out. Let's see if I can do this multiplication correctly. Check my numbers men. 60 times 101.33 is 6,080 feet.... Now, if I divide that number by 5,280, the number of feet in a land mile, I get 1.15. Unbelievable. Just what Mr. Matheson told us – that a nautical mile is 15% longer than a land mile. So, we've verified that every rope knot does indeed represent one knot of speed. Some mathematician must have worked backwards initially to determine the need for just over fifty feet between knots."

Coubro has remained behind patiently awaiting the return of the men from the stern. He enjoyed a glass of port in their absence but immediately responds to their eager jabbering when they re-seat themselves. "You must remember that all of the measurements we make are approximations. But they are sufficiently accurate to measure our speed. A man named William Bourne invented the 30 second timer in 1574, though alternate hourglass times are currently proposed for consideration.

"Directly related to our speed of course is the distance we cover. To calculate distances however requires use of the sextant. You've probably seen Mr. Matheson and me sighting the sun at noon and stars in the evening to determine where we are. I'm afraid using the sextant and converting its angles to a plot is a lesson we'll avoid for now. It's not simple at all."

James Winthrop rises. "We're all very appreciative of your willingness to have your officers educate us Captain. A special thanks to you and Mr. Matheson and Mr. Plunkett." He raises his glass. "To your good health, gents."

The words "hear, hear" echo around the room as the other men join in the toast.

* * *

Away from the dining room turned classroom, a far more meaningful event below deck holds my attention. Women passengers are gathered about, wearing black scarves, holding handkerchiefs. Some are sniffling. There is much sadness in the room where Susannah Moore's baby daughter, Alison, has just died. Despite copious beer consumption, Susannah's milk never came in, and with the heat as a constant torment, the wee child struggled daily since birth, failed to gain any weight, and finally simply stopped breathing.

Tears stream down Susannah's face as she gently holds Alison. She looks down at the baby's placid countenance, wondrous at its serenity and innocence. Rocking back and forth, she cradles the infant tenderly against her breasts. Close, warm, deeply loved. The air is still, save for the soft murmurs of the gathered women and the to and fro swish of Susannah's chemise.

Her friends, who have been seated on the floor by her side for the past three hours, weep softly, distraught at the baby's passing, and their inability to do anything that might have prevented it. Their grief is palpable in their facial expressions, as understanding of the finality of the little girl's death renders them momentarily incapable of further soothing and supportive words. They hold on to each other and envelop the mother and child in a circle, unified in sorrow.

Janet Whittington mourns Susannah's loss a little more empathically than do the others, as she also is a victim of a jailer's repeated demands for sexual favors in response to his providing handouts of extra food. She turns to Susannah, points to Alison, and asks, "May I hold her?"

Susannah looks up in surprise, hesitates, then passes the doll-like infant across the intervening space and mutters "Thank you." She wipes her eyes and watches as Janet cradles Alison and kisses her on both cheeks. This open, human expression of empathy is not lost on the other women present, and in turn they too kiss Alison on the forehead or cheek as she is passed among them.

Janet takes Alison back in her arms and lovingly rakes her long bony fingers through the baby's thin blonde hair. "She's beautiful Susannah, just like you. Here, I'm sure you want to hold her again."

Susannah finds her voice, and amid sobs says, "You're all so kind to me, thank you. Thank you. I've lost my baby though. I've lost my little girl. Nothing can make her alive again."

She tries to blink her tears away, but fails, overcome by despair. The sobs turn into an eerie wail that echoes up and down the passageway in its intensity, stopping others in their tracks. It's a keening few have ever heard, unmistakable in its rendering of grief. More women troop to Susannah's doorway in response, and as a gesture of comfort. Two of the friends who sit with Susannah are particularly affected as they too are pregnant, although their due dates are at least several months away. Their nerves are rattled by the high-pitched ululation and they move to hug Susannah and utter sympathetic words designed to silence her cries. "God will look after you Susannah, and one day there'll be another baby. She'll have a good father who will love you both very much. Save your tears for now."

Susannah sees things differently however. "No," she shouts. "God is punishing me because I sinned in gaol. I created a new baby in that horrible place and now he's punishing me by taking her away. Why couldn't He have taken me instead? My baby knows nothing of my sins. She is innocent. She has the face of an angel. God should have let her live and taken me instead for my past wrongs. I want to die."

Exhaustion is setting in and Susannah's cries soon become a whimper. Only the supportive arms of her friends stop her from falling backwards. Her eyelids close, and those around her cease all noise, hoping she can rest, if only for a brief period. The women lift her onto her bed, and lay Alison beside her, wrapping the pair with the same blanket to keep them close to each other.

It's a grateful pause time. The five friends hug each other and two of them retreat from the room as they feel they can do no more. They spread their sadness to others along the corridor as they return to their own rooms. One climbs the stairway and talks to a guard who walks to the fo'c's'le with the message. A seaman there indicates he'll let the captain know and heads to Coubro's cabin.

Sarah Grainger, well recovered from her beating, and now emerging as a leader in representing the female prisoners' needs, remains behind to watch over Susannah and Alison. In light of Susannah's plight she vows to herself to keep up her exercises and to eat as well as possible in order to do the best for her unborn child.

She and her boyfriend, the baby's father, were caught stealing food, but were sent to different gaols. Despite the pleas of both families to have the pair transported together, the petitions were ignored. Sarah clings to the hope that Rodney may follow her to Botany Bay at a later date. I suspect she feels a twinge of guilt, as she recognizes, that unlike Susannah, she has two additional people to live for, Rodney, and the baby they created together.

As much as we ships are made of inanimate materials - wood, rope, canvas, pitch and metal - we're not impervious to feelings. Ask any sailor about the spirit of his ship.... We are attuned to our own needs, and react to problems in ways similar to those you humans use. But I've never been exposed to the depth of pain and breadth of social reaction that the death of Susannah's baby has caused. I have seen sailors die from accidents, and I've seen soldiers die from battle injuries, and we have even had scurvy and other diseases aboard. But the loss of a baby, taken before it has had a chance to experience life, affects everyone far more deeply. Its departure is so premature, so contrary, so unexpected, and against nature, that it makes all those who have been close to feel as if a great cruelty, beyond their ken, has been perpetrated, with no earthly justification. Susannah's feeling that a punishment has been served her is understandable.

I've been a patient observer of Susannah's crisis for days, weeks actually, but the poignancy of the last few hours makes me realize there is so much I don't understand. In an attempt to comprehend human feelings, I try to rationalize what it would mean were a vitally important part of me to be taken away. Suppose my rudder were deliberately destroyed without explanation. I'd be totally at the mercy of the elements. How would I survive? Maybe my friends of the deep would nudge me along for a while, but not forever. Just as Susannah's friends can be supportive for a period, her loss is permanent, not temporary. Like mine would be. If I were somehow to make it to port in time, a new rudder could be built and fitted to my stern. That would be akin to the notion of Susannah finding a man and creating a new baby with him. But the original loss would never go completely away.

I wish I could help Susannah overcome her emptiness.

* * *

Susannah knows that her baby must be given up to the sea, but is understandably reluctant to let her go. The surgeon visits her twice a day, trying gently, but so far in vain, to get her to agree to a funeral service for her daughter. Susannah clings to the baby, and refuses to hand her over to Dr. Crisp. It is difficult for Susannah's friends to console her, as they understand the strength of a first-time mother's love, while recognizing that nothing can bring the baby back. Susannah continues her laments that God is taking the baby away from her as punishment, but instead of shouting, she mutters continuously with her head down close to the baby in her arms. Her rants that God should have taken her instead, and let her daughter grow into a strong woman, are rendered as whimpers. Susannah doesn't eat and sleeps randomly for only minutes at a time.

For two full days she refuses to permit Alison to be buried. But when the faintest odor of putrefaction pervades the room and passageway and other prisoners complain, the surgeon intervenes and forcibly removes the baby from Susannah's grasp. Though exhausted, Susannah weeps and, stolidly, her friends rally to look after her. They spoon feed her, wash her face, brush her hair, wrap her in warm blankets, and watch over her as she sleeps fitfully.

On the fourth day after Alison's death, Susannah is sufficiently composed to participate in her baby's burial service. The women provide her with a fresh, quickly sewn new dress for the occasion. After lunch, the quartermaster rounds up the crew members of the active watch and has the marines invite sympathetic prisoners to attend the burial ceremony. Robertson, the teacher, climbs the companionway and once on deck seeks out the surgeon. After a short conversation between the two men, the doctor goes to his cabin and returns with his flute, which he hands to Robertson. Once everyone is gathered on the foredeck, the quartermaster orders the crew members present to remove their caps. The surgeon whispers to Captain Coubro who then initiates the service.

"Brethren, we are present here this afternoon to say goodbye to one of God's tiniest children. Susannah, would you please bring your daughter forward?"

Susannah steps forward unsteadily, tears streaming down her cheeks, her daughter held before her in outstretched arms. She falters momentarily, and Sarah Grainger quickly falls in alongside, adding support.

Coubro takes the baby and cradles her in the crook of his left arm, so she faces the people gathered in front of him. He places his other arm soothingly around Susannah's shoulders.

From memory he recites,

"The Book of Lamentations, 3: 31-33.

For no one is cast off by the Lord forever. Though he brings grief, he will show compassion, so great is his unfailing love. For he does not willingly bring affliction or grief to anyone."

163

He uses both arms to hand the baby to the surgeon. Dr. Crisp wraps her securely in a large shroud of canvas, which holds a cannonball. The child so bundled is placed on a plank balanced across the port railing.

Coubro holds Susannah again and speaks with firm voice.

"In sure and certain hope of the resurrection to eternal life through our Lord Jesus Christ, we commend to Almighty God our sister, Alison Moore. We commit her body to the deep, to be turned into corruption, looking for the resurrection of the body when the sea shall give up her dead and the life of the world to come, through our Lord Jesus Christ."

He signals to Robertson, who steps forward, nods to Susannah, then turns to the audience, raises the flute to his lips, and gently plays the haunting Macpherson's lament*. Several sets of lips in the audience mouth the words and a number of heads drop in reverence.

Robertson reaches outwards and touches the small bundle with the flute and retreats to the throng of watchers.

Coubro raises his face to the heavens, then back down to look lovingly at the small form laying on the board. She is miniscule, the vastness of the sea to the horizon providing the final curtain on her life. Coubro stretches his left arm towards her, and addresses her directly, his voice somber in its pathos.

"Numbers 6: 24-26. Dear Alison Moore. The Lord bless you and keep you, the Lord make His face to shine upon you, and be gracious unto you, the Lord lift up His countenance upon you and give you peace.

Amen."

The assembled onlookers reiterate "Amen" and the surgeon tips the plank so that baby Alison slips swiftly and quietly into the sea.

Susannah wails uncontrollably, and Coubro wraps his arms around her, offering soft words of consolation. Sarah and other friends come forward as a group, thank the captain for the service, and gently escort Susannah away.

The congregation splits into two groups – sailors and prisoners. Many eyes are moist, even among the hardened sailors.

For the prisoners there is a new harsh reality affecting them – the lack of any marker or monument at the location of the burial. Susannah can never sit by her daughter's gravesite, or bring flowers in remembrance. All she has is the memory of the service. She will remember that forever, but it will take years for her to stand tall and love herself once again.

Most of the sailors present are God-fearing men, sensitive to the death of any person with whom they may be acquainted, in whatever minor capacity. Some may have seen a companion die from injuries in an onboard accident, or from battle or disease. Sea burials of such victims can be distressing, for they can heighten superstitions and emotional bonds of sailors related to a need to both honor and protect themselves from the spirits of their dead companions.

I've seen a number of sea burials over the years, none easy to witness. This one has been harder than all others. My empathy for the desperation of a mother losing her baby has heightened dramatically.

As a ship, I have only one advantage over humans in this domain, in that I know exactly where a burial takes place. For I'm constantly aware of the bottom of the ocean we sail above. And because there are animals of the sea always about, they help me pinpoint where a body comes to rest.

For now, my only solace is that I can do something humans cannot.

13.   *A rude awakening*

It's the start of the seventh week afloat, and fat raindrops splatter the deck. Driven out of the clammy, tropical air behind us by the strengthening breeze, they feel warm on the sailors' skin. The sea, placid until now, begins to show whitecaps. A group of seamen looks heavenward, heads nod, voices grumble, and the men quickly head to their midday meal. It's noon, and the sun shines weakly overhead. Miles astern however, lightning flashes between dark clouds. Faint thunder reaches the ears of all on deck seconds later.

Coubro nods to the duty officer, then strides forward to the main mast. He calls to the militia corporal and points to the port side of the ship where the last of the female convicts seek shelter under the overhang from the guardroom. "Get those women below now." The corporal hurries in their direction, his crimson jacket loses its bright luster as the rain spots increase in volume and density.

Padraig is already in motion. He exhorts his team, which scales the rigging on the foremast. "This wind will come up fast lads, watch your grip." Padraig is covered with one of the newly designed waterproof jackets called oilskins. They are primitive and unsophisticated, made from worn-out sail canvas and painted with a mix of linseed oil and wax. They have a yellowish tinge. Their color contrasts with the red-brown patina of the wet mast.

The men who climb the rigging are bare-chested. Their caps drip and their trousers are soaked. Coats would be cumbersome aloft. Padraig turns to a second group of men held at the ready, awaiting the Captain's order. I think they're both trying to assess how strong the storm will become. The order comes and Padraig relays, "Hands aloft to reef maintops'ls – go!"

He hastily organizes and dispatches four more teams. The earlier training has clearly paid off as the men move smoothly and without hesitation to their stations. Padraig's face reflects a twinge of pride as he observes the fluid movements of the men in the rigging. But he dismisses it immediately. The sails still have to be fully reefed successfully. Getting to the yardarms from which they hang is one thing. Furling the canvas is another. He races to the railing to help a sailor tighten the halyard that holds one of the top spars. The seaman lying along the yardarm up above acknowledges the help with a balled fist.

Duncan, the boatswain, sprints from the on-deck storehouse towards Coubro. "Prisoner portholes all secure you are, sir. Hatches next."

Coubro pulls the man to his side, faces away from the rain, turns and speaks directly into Duncan's ear. "Have the cooks serve out storm rations to each mess – enough to last two days. I don't like the look of what's coming."

There's a marked sense of urgency in his voice. "Make sure each room has at least one or two pails. Throw extras down. Secure four large barrels of water in the common areas as well."

Duncan's "Aye, aye, sir" gets whisked away by a strong gust of wind. Behind it, the rain lashes the ship, no longer warm to the touch. It's not as if the storm gently sweeps along the length of the ship from stern to bow. Two minutes after the first few droplets arrive, the whole ship is engulfed in a pelting deluge. It's as if God is sending a dire warning to those still standing, shooting icy drops at them from a million slingshots.

Heavy clouds have moved directly overhead. They darken the scene in all directions except forward. Between clouds ahead, the sky is momentarily pale, anemic, helpless to avoid the encroaching maelstrom.

A sailor on the far side of the ship shouts at the top of his voice for Plunkett. His voice is unheard. The wind starts to howl. It whistles through the rigging, the masts moan as they sway, and the lower sails slack and fill with loud pops. It's becoming more dangerous anywhere in the rigging as the intensity of the wind increases.

Charles, the pilot, emerges from the navigation station and turns to the helm. He assigns another man from the at-watch team to relieve the young helmsman, and takes command. "Well done," he screams at the man. "Go find the Captain and see if he wants to heave-to, or run before this wind a bit longer."

The chap is white-faced and scared. He hurries forward, clutching at any secure object along the way for safety. With good reason, for I am starting to roll and pitch markedly now. The wind has increased and changed direction over the past hour, which is what gave us the first indication of an imminent weather change. Now, as the storm heightens, it drives the waves more fiercely. Foam flicks my stern as the waves crash into the transom. Dark green water slaps angrily at the rudder. The skies darken further. I pitch mercilessly up and down ten to twenty feet at a time as the waves grow larger.

All the sails are down except the reefed lower courses on the three masts. The fore and aft triangular jibs and stay sails are tightly furled. Seamen, down from the rigging, wring their clothing in their quarters, as they know full well they may be out in the tumult again soon.

Coubro has decided to run before the wind and keep it on the starboard quarter. As a bonus it is taking us in the right direction, and the bow has not yet breached a wave. He sends the apprentice helmsman back to Charles with his message. Lamps have been turned on in the passenger lounge, their beams surprisingly bright in the darkness that now encompasses the deck. Sailors hang more lamps and check to ensure storage chests are fully locked and barrels of food and water are doubly secured. The cannons have been run up to the bulkheads and keepers attached. Cannon balls have been struck below to the magazine.

Coubro, Padraig, and Duncan struggle back to the wheelhouse, clearly conscious of the slippery, slanted, pitching deck and the corkscrew path I am forced to follow in the turbulent seas. At one stage they move hand over hand, carefully guiding each other past obstacles. Water streaks down their oilskins and their hoods are blown back, having failed to stay tightened around their heads. Their hair is matted and slicked down, as the rain is more like a sheet waterfall than individual drops.

The wind shrieks. In one mighty pitch the bow crashes into a trough, throwing green water aside as it plunges. Down, sickeningly down, black depths hiding the bottom of the drop. It smashes into the base with a crash, then lifts up again, flinging the curl of the wave into the rain above. Up farther, pauses, then slides down again to repeat the performance. Every old hand knows worse is to come.

Below deck, the prisoner compartments are in turmoil. No one has experienced anything like what is happening. My frame pivots up and down, and throws men and women off balance against the passageway struts or onto the deck. They cling desperately to anything solid that is nailed or bolted down. Personal items, drinking vessels, pots, and pans fly across and between rooms. Several people already have minor cuts and developing bruises from slamming into walls or berths or from airborne projectiles. One young boy has a four inch gash across his forehead that oozes blood. His mother uses a patch of towel to pressure the wound.

The doors that separate the male and female compartments have been flung open and swing wildly on their hinges, crashing back into the framework and adding to the noise. Screams of fear from the women sound along the passageways. In the men's section swearing replaces screams. People smash into one another as they lose their grip on the stanchions. Some lie on their beds, where they seek confinement and safety, nursing shattered stomachs.

The pregnant women fear the fierce jostling will hurt their unborn babies, and group together to support each other. The three children are quickly mustered and stuffed under the lowest bunks while adults sit on top to contain them. One child slides out anyway as the floor rears up through twenty plus degrees. He crashes into a stanchion on the other side of the room. His cries are heard only by those close by as the hull shudders, water hisses its warning as it streams by the portholes, the timbers groan, and the wind shrieks loudly through the rigging above deck.

Tiny Diana, under a cot, clings desperately to her mother's ankles planted firmly in front. She cries, "Mummy, I'm going to be ssss..ick," and vomit streams across the floorboards to the center of the room. Mother reaches down and adds a reassuring hand to her daughter's face, a cloth wiping her mouth. "It's Ok dear. Just hold on tight. I'll be right here until the storm passes."

Two tiny lanterns throw meagre light from the bulkheads. Their beams hardly penetrate the overwhelming darkness. Other lamps lit earlier are now cast aside, their glass cylinders broken from being flung about. Shards of glass cut hands and legs.

A woman screams in horror as she removes a furry blob from her face, a dead rat tossed from its hiding place. In the men's compartment, a bucket of vomit tips over, men stand and collide, their feet covered in the mess. Fear and shock are palpable. Dismay and helplessness punctuate stunted conversations.

In thirty minutes the world below deck has plunged into terrifying chaos. No rhythm regulates the jostling pitches and rolls. Unable to see waves coming, there is no way for the prisoners to anticipate when the next one will arrive nor how violent it will be. Everyone would like to be prepared, but it's not possible, and surprises abound as the sea toys powerfully with my frame.

You ask what I can do to mitigate some of the horror for these wretched convicts. Very little. We are at sea, is the answer. The captain has done what should be done. I'm not worried about running before the wind and its waves – that's much better than running into waves. I concentrate on dampening the side to side roll. That depends a lot on how evenly the waves are formed, and how much they come from the same direction each time. As the helmsman moves the rudder in anticipation of each wave's direction, I add a little reinforcement or restraint if I think it will mitigate the amount of roll. So far, I must admit, Charles is doing an excellent job.

You certainly wouldn't think that, however, if you were within earshot of Lady Hudson-Smythe's ravings. "Help me, I'm dying. Someone help me. Doctor Crisp, where are you? I'm sick. My life is passing in front of me. Help!"

After a few deep breaths, a new approach. Ultra-loud desperate shouting. "Matilda, girl, where are you? Go find the surgeon at once. I'm dying." She groans and moans as if in terrible pain.

Poor Matilda, in her closet cabin next door, is more seasick than her Ladyship. Vomit stains spread across the top of her maid's tunic, and several viscous chunks of regurgitated food are caught in the end of one pigtail. Vivid brown bile dribbles from one side of her puckered mouth. She reaches for a glass of water, but before she can get it to her lips, another violent heave from her innards sends little opaque food projectiles into the basin and across the tiny counter, where they smear the bottom of the mirror.

Matilda's stomach makes unpleasant sounds, her lips and mouth are sore, her skin is a pasty color, and her hair has developed new sets of tangles. She's barefoot for no reason she can remember, and her knees keep knocking together. Sitting on the deck wedged against her bed, she is in no shape to help her mistress and wonders if she'll die with her. Feeling another attack coming on, she stands and leans over the basin hanging on tight to the edge of the sink as the cabin lurches yet again. Her eyes focus on the mess decorating the mirror and she dry-heaves, her stomach tightening, her delicate frame shaking from her shoulders to her toes. She slumps back to the floor, lowers her head and weeps copiously, adding dark wet circles to her tunic.

None of the paying passengers are in any position to help anyone but themselves. Mal-de-mer has claimed twenty victims without discrimination. The four boys try hard not to cry. Their macho veneers are stripped away and replaced with whimpering requests and concerns. "I'm scared Mother." "Hold me Father." "Will we sink and drown?" "How long will the storm last?" "Can't the captain do something?" "I hate being sick." "My stomach hurts." "This is awful. If we pray, will it help?"

The parents have little to offer in response other than "The captain will get us through. He's been in storms like this before. Have faith." The adults swab cold washcloths across the young boys' pale faces and urge them to sip water, as they themselves have done.

Not that the wise suggestions always work. With the vile smelling vomit bucket and the sink being used alternately by different family members in their closed quarters, heaving by one member makes others follow, so contagious is the affliction.

Many can faintly hear her Ladyship's pleadings from further down the corridor. They too want to know where the surgeon is.

He's actually below deck administering to more than 150 poor souls with the same problem. Some are worse off than those upstairs, some less so. It depends how long ago they last ate and how much they ingested. The pails thrown down for the purpose of vomit collection are filling up in any event. The place reeks of foul odours. There is no escape from the ugly stench. The screams, the moans, the shouts, reverberate around the compartments, adding to the unnerving conditions. It is dark, wild waves hammer on the portholes, the timber stanchions and ceiling boards groan ominously, water drips from the deck above, and the howl of the wind outside is terrifying. Bright flashes of lightning illuminate the quarters for brief seconds, and thunder peals across the sky. It's only the presence of the doctor that provides reassurance that perhaps they all may survive God's wrath.

The false bravado some of the drunken seaman recruits displayed when they first boarded back in Portsmouth, has totally disappeared. The initial attempts to ignore the churning in their stomachs have succumbed to recognition that avoidance is futile. Risking all, they head for the rail and lurch to vomit over the side. A couple miscalculate and the wind throws it all back into their faces. It's a horrible experience.

The militia, to a man, turn pale green in the face and contribute to the single red and white bucket. Their superiors back on land would not be impressed.

Dr. Crisp rises tentatively through one of the hatches, moving carefully and holding tight to ensure it doesn't blow wide open. He makes a dash with his bag to the passenger cabins, but gets soaked anyway. Inside, Lady Hudson-Smythe's pathetic calls assault his ears.

"I'm dying! Matilda, Dr. Crisp, help!"

Arthur knocks on her cabin door and pushes it open without waiting for a summons. Her Ladyship, sick as she is, is affronted. She hastily reaches for a robe and holds it in front of her. It covers far less than were it on properly.

"Do you always enter a lady's chambers without knocking, Doctor? As you can see I am in a state of undress. Please return in two minutes."

Crisp has seen it all before of course, although her Ladyship has more bountiful offerings than most. He notices the half-full pail of discharge on the floor and several towels around it with evidence of queasy misfirings.

"Madam, if I leave, I will spend time with all the other passengers before I return. Do you want to wait that long?"

"What can you give me to help? You must have something. My stomach feels twisted, my throat is like parchment, and my shoulders and chest ache from bending over and heaving. I need you to take that pail out of my sight."

Crisp wets a facecloth and passes it across her Ladyship's noble countenance. She says nothing. He rescues a glass from the cabinet, and half-fills it with water.

"Sip, madam. Sip. Nothing more. If it stays down, in ten minutes two sips again." He reaches in his bag. "And here's some ginger you can chew on. It will help your stomach. Just a tiny bite, then wait. Sit on the deck, with your head down, and hold tight to the bed post."

He turns to leave. She yells. "What about that obscene pail? It must be emptied, and these towels washed."

Crisp pauses at her door. "I agree madam. I'll be back in an hour to see how you are managing."

It's not hard to read his mind from the looks of disdain and disgust on his face. No thanks offered by the woman, just demands. Let her live with herself for a bit.

I doubt he'll be back in an hour, if at all.

He heads to the next cabin and knocks on the door, opens it without pause. He checks on the family within, reassures them of his support if needed, and moves on to the next cabin. Most of the occupants are scared and have contributed with gusto to the collection buckets, but are now quiet in their acceptance of the conditions. They have used towels to cover the pails, and while pasty-faced, aching, and uncomfortable, they work at reassuring each other that the storm will pass and all will be normal again in time. Crisp offers no guesses on how long they might have to wait.

No one but experienced sailors have been spared, but Carolyn Pennington and son Graeme, the piano players, seem to have suffered badly. For whatever reason, their constitutions are not as robust as the others and both are writhing on the floor of their cabin in considerable distress. The surgeon feels they'd be better off in their bunks and helps them back there, and gives them some ginger to chew. His caring attitude makes his patients appreciative, and they thank him repeatedly.

Now, at last, the pitch up and down seems more rhythmic, even though it's at least a fifteen-foot movement each time. The regularity will help everyone's equilibrium adapt. Bodies will stabilize a little, but even so, the consistency of pitches won't assuage the terror and feelings of helplessness that the prisoners especially feel in their claustrophobic space.

Up on deck, the wind still howls. Three heavy crates holding hawsers, clamps, and heavy chains have moved, and are sliding on the sloshing deck, crashing into each other with each roll, and lifting on the pitches. A seaman rushes from the jumble back towards Coubro and his team, swearing in pain. His left arm hangs limp, the hand at its end crushed and bleeding. "Surgeon", he shouts, his face pale and streaked with dirt and rain. Coubro dispatches a helmsman to find Arthur, then sends the man to the surgeon's cabin with the messenger of the watch.

Crisp arrives there in short order having been close-by in the passenger cabins. He gently holds the man's arm, but even so the seaman winces in pain.

The storm rages on. All we can do is run before it, hoping it will eventually leave us alone to clean up from our miseries.

* * *

It is two full days before we begin to find a lull. The passengers, prisoners, and militia were affected most, unaware ahead of time how lengthy and devastating storms at sea can be. Those sailors who experienced their first major tempest have gained a new respect for Neptune, Poseidon, and the perils of their occupation. A christening every sailor must experience. The smarter ones now move more purposefully, as if a sense of pride and knowledge has been newly instilled.

The rain eventually stops completely. The wind steadies to a regular beat, and the sun peeks meekly through the few clouds that remain. Now relaxed, the waves reduce in pattern to a regular chop, and the rigging begins to dry out. In the steady breeze the sails puff out and begin to draw easily, reassuring all that smooth sailing is once again the norm. We use our steering wheel to move away from the storm.

I've been in storms like this one before, and in others far worse. It's the head-on ones I dislike most. Winds from behind push us along in the general direction we want to travel, but winds from the sides and ahead always push us off course, sometimes into more dangerous regions. We have less control when God throws challenges at us head-on.

In the storm just passed, I didn't sense any real danger. Uncomfortable for all aboard, certainly. But minimal chance of sinking or being capsized. Even so, I always prefer smoother seas. Who wouldn't?

Coubro and the surgeon have encouraged all the prisoners to come on deck, males and females simultaneously. It is a time to regroup, to bring laundry and bedspreads up from below, get colour back to their cheeks, to have them feel alive again, and to experience warmth from the sun, however weak.

It's a ruse to distract them all by getting both men and women to remember old social habits and occasions. The women revel in the opportunity. The men are more wary.

The storm has frightened every civilian. No man, woman, or child has emerged untouched from its onslaught and the effect it has had on their minds and bodies. Even now, many stomachs still complain. Those concerned are urged to eat slowly. But all now have something in common – a deliverance from recognized fear. Few can articulate it, which doesn't matter. The bond exists anyway.

A few small mixed-sex groups form, as they did once before during the swim races. Conversations are stilted and awkward at first. The majority of men and women have not been together with the opposite sex in years. In some new groups individuals look from face to face until some brave soul asks another his or her name and where they are from.

The militia are watchful, but stay their distance per Coubro's orders. Paying passengers watch the gatherings from the dining room windows. The boys want to be outside to play. For the moment, they are restrained. Soft smiles wash across the ladies' faces as they observe the blooming efforts at new prisoner to prisoner communication. Sara Goldsmith stands by Lady Hudson-Smythe's elbow and whispers, "It's nice to see isn't it?" She's rewarded with a one -word response. "Perhaps."

The party outdoors eventually clears, and Coubro joins the passengers in the lounge.

"It's good to see you all up and about. That was an extremely nasty storm. But it had one unexpected benefit. The wind was so strong that even with nearly all the sails down the waves drove us forward at a faster pace than we made before the gale. We should make Cape Town a couple of days earlier than expected. I know that will please you all."

Hands clap. Light cheers greet the welcome information.

Lady Hudson-Smythe speaks up. "Are we likely to encounter more storms, Captain? Are they more prevalent in the Southern Hemisphere than the Northern Hemisphere? We had no problems north of the equator."

"Storms can occur anywhere, Madam. We were most fortunate to avoid them in the North Atlantic. I wouldn't be surprised if we encounter more tempests here in the Southern Atlantic, and we'll be very fortunate if we don't strike one crossing the Indian Ocean. As you've seen however, *Lady Corinth* is a strong ship. She'll get us through."

Ooh, how I love a little praise.

Clarinda Finsbury speaks up, "*Lady Corinth* may be tough and eminently sea-worthy Captain, but I think she had some leadership and skill at the helm as well. We thank you and all the crew for getting us safely through that gale. Are all the crewmen safe? I don't know how they work in those terrible conditions."

Murmurs of "yes, thank you," "well done sir", "great job", sound out around the table.

Dr. Crisp speaks up, "Speaking of the crew, we had one incident...."

Coubro interrupts. "The crew did a superb job. All the men got a good soaking, and there are a few cut hands, and many bruises, but they'll recover."

He turns and faces the surgeon directly. "There's one chap who had a small accident, and we're watching him carefully. He'll be OK. Right now the men are scouring the ship to see if there are any problems below deck."

In her naivete Matilda misses the deliberate deflection of the Surgeon's spiel by the Captain and asks "What was the incident you mentioned Dr. Crisp. Is that the accident the Captain referred to?"

"Yes", Crisp replies. "But we don't have to go into details."

Matilda is persistent. "Was someone hurt? What happened?"

Coubro sighs, and raises his arms in a gesture of resigned response. "The deck is a very slippery place in a storm. While we came through well, we did pay a small price. One of the sailors had his arm and hand crushed as he tried to stop a heavy storage crate which came loose and slid across the deck towards the railing. The surgeon has had to amputate the arm below the elbow."

Matilda's face turns white, and she sobs heavily, large tears splotching her chemise. Sympathetic moans echo around the room. Clarinda Finsbury covers her eyes with curled-up fists, Timothy Blaine puts his forehead down on the table. Everyone is shocked.

Carolyn Pennington stands and says "How terrible. I will pray for him."

With the wind taken out of their metaphorical sails, the small group breaks up. Some stray into the fresh air, others retreat to the sanctity of their rooms.

Lady Hudson-Smythe speaks quietly to Matilda. "Come my dear, let's read from my bible."

* * *

I need to attract the good Captain's attention. We have a problem that may become serious. Actually, I wish I could attract any officer's attention, most particularly Conway's, as the problem is in his domain.

In the deck below the prisoner compartments, alongside the passengers' household goods and other miscellaneous cargo, there are multiple barrels, crates, and sacks of food. Initially, they were packed together in orderly fashion, but the storm moved the supplies around a bit despite the thick ropes and strong wooden chocks designed to hold them in place. After the storm, sailors immediately checked the cargo hold and have been in the area double-checking several times since. They re-established orderly arrangements of the supplies, with a special eye to ensuring the worthiness of the kegs of rum and beer.

But even though their lamps provided good light for the many different sets of eyes involved in the re-allocation of space, especially for kitchen goods, none have seen what I can feel. At some point in the storm when a larger than normal wave hit, one of the supply barrels in the upper tier was squeezed upwards and sideways, and slammed outward into the hull. It hit at a point where the hull slopes inward just above the tops of the barrels in that tier. The heavy barrel that moved caused a deep gash and splintering in one of the internal hull planks. The cut is sufficiently large that one can see the outer hull plank clearly. The gash is up high near the ceiling of the hold and not easily discernible in the dark storage environment, even when lamps are held high.

It bothers me enormously, because any more damage there could easily open a hole to the sea. The location is not far above the water line, so large seas could easily enter, possibly even enlarging the hole, and flooding the lower deck. If undiscovered, and sufficient water pours in, the bilge pumps may be unable to handle the volume of water cascading further down inside and we could end up in a very dangerous situation.

Perhaps you think I'm exaggerating. Believe me, I'm not. If we were talking about a hole in the prisoners' section of the hull, I would worry far less. Partly because it would get discovered easily, but also because it would be far above the sea-water level.

At least for the moment the hole I'm talking about is totally internal, but a barrel with its metal edging thrust hard against it, could easily make it larger, and a second thrust could then damage the outside hull.

You think it couldn't happen again, perhaps? Sorry, that kind of thinking is risky. Weak spots in any structure seem to be targets for further stress. I've seen ships with amazing hull holes being repaired in port. Their stories are similar. An initial freak event created a problem, which grew worse with a follow-up incident. Somehow, I must avoid that happening to me.

If found soon, the gash could easily be repaired with pitch, and a new piece of plank could be added by the carpenter across the vulnerable spot.

It's the 'if' that bothers me. I struggle with how to alert someone to the problem. So far I have no solution. It's very disconcerting not to be able to communicate my concern. I focus on the issue frequently, and that's not good for maintaining a smooth sailing experience.

As if my concern over the gash in the interior hull lining isn't enough, I sense another mishap pending. Remember the carpenter who did a shoddy job on the aft corner of the galley? Too few nails were used in the construction, those saved disappearing into the man's pocket, probably for resale onshore somewhere, or home use perhaps. We'll never know.

I have been aware of light creaks and ripping sounds for two days now from that corner. The hot days we suffered near the equator dried out and expanded several wood sections so that many of the nails no longer hold things together. Then the storm, with its furious winds, managed to push a number of planks farther apart. Once again, I'm frustrated because I can't tell the cook and his assistants about the problem. I think within a week that whole corner will collapse and cause part of the ceiling to come down with it. I just hope none of the barrels of flour and salted meats fall over and split open. I don't have fingers of course, but if I did, they'd be crossed.

It probably wouldn't hurt for you to cross your fingers, too. By now you should have a good understanding of what being at sea in the middle of a vast ocean means. After all, you've witnessed a death onboard, the rough initiation of novices into Neptune's Kingdom, sailors' self-entertainment, and you've survived relentless heat, and an incredibly frightening storm. What else is there? A staged mutiny by crew, a prisoner uprising, a fire, pirates, or a collision with an iceberg....?

Let's hope none of those incidents visit us in the southern reaches ahead. Given the breadth of your exposure already, I'll let you make your own observations from here on out, although if something really awkward or unusual crops up, I'll be back in touch.

Based on past experience, I doubt my silence will last long.

14. *Unusual happenings*

Another two days and it's as if we'd never been in in a storm. We're sailing like we did before God turned his vengeance on us. Steady breeze, calm waters. Everyone is much relieved.

Well, maybe not everyone.

We had an unexpected incident this morning. Nicholas Albright, one of the first-time sailors, failed to turn up on his assigned post at five bells in the morning watch. He'd been in high spirits during the previous day, telling everyone over and over how thankful he was to have survived the storm. His constant chatter annoyed his mates, who, while also thankful to have come through, had put the experience behind them and were now back at their regular duties. "Stow it Nick," "Cut the gab mate," "On with your work swabbie," "Get over it chum," were among the well-intended pieces of advice Nicholas received.

All of which he ignored.

It was as if he had experienced a life-changing catharsis. His incessant rants grew louder and became more obnoxious to all who worked near him. At one point he sat down, banged his head repeatedly against the foremast and fell sideways, laying prone, yet he continued to mutter. Two men lifted the poor fellow and carried him to the surgeon's cabin. A sedative soon had him in a cot fast asleep, although Crisp wondered out loud to his assistant whether the chap might have suffered a brain attack or so-called apoplexy. Night fell and shipboard routine continued.

Until early this morning.

The doctor had had Nicholas returned to his bunk in the crew quarters after dinner last night, and he'd been observed there at three hours

185

after midnight. As word that he was now missing spread amongst the crew in the dawn's early light, most feared he might have been lost overboard – perhaps had woken sometime in the night and wandered in a stupor to the railing and fallen over. It could have happened one hour ago or eight hours ago with no hope of ever finding the man alive were they to turn around and try to retrace their route.

A quick search failed to find any trace of the man, and fears grew. Coubro was notified and immediately ordered a repeat search. Sailors accompanied militia and together invaded the prisoners' compartments, waking and annoying many with shouts of "Nicholas, show yourself." All officers and mates were awakened, and the surgeon began gently knocking on the doors of the first-class passengers' cabins to check that no surprise visitor was within.

Groups of unhappy, fearful men went into the holds with extra lanterns, but all came back empty-handed. Sail boxes were unlocked, searched and double checked. No sign of the man. Those off-duty gathered on deck, shocked and mournful. They assumed the worst and were downcast at the realization they had lost a shipmate. Six bells sounded and while those in one watch headed back to their quarters, those of the next watch trooped to the mess room for breakfast. A young chap in front suddenly blurted "Has anyone checked the boats?" With the canvas covers tight and seemingly undisturbed, no one had thought to check inside the boats. The group dispersed quickly and two minutes later a joyful cry echoed across the deck, "Found him!"

Joy turned to anger however as details of the find were shared. Nicholas was fast asleep under a canvas sail in a longboat, with two empty bottles of wine by his head, hair a mess, mouth askew, shirt covered in red stains, and he'd clearly wet himself. Disgust travelled through the group as several men pulled him from the boat and laid him unceremoniously on the deck. He blinked as he struggled to comprehend what was happening.

For nearly all the observers, what should have been relief that the chap hadn't fallen overboard, was masked by feelings of annoyance, even rage in some instances. One sailor vented his anger by kicking Nicholas in the ribs, but was quickly restrained. Coubro was fetched and ordered the man to be tied to one of the masts until he sobered up, at which point he'd be given 20 lashes for stealing and drunkenness.

The surgeon shared with the captain his concern that perhaps some form of mental illness may have precipitated the apparent celebration Nicholas had initiated. Even so, Crisp realized the thrashing should proceed as an example to all the others. Coubro made sure that all off-duty crewmen witnessed the flogging with the cat-o-nine-tails. It left a bad taste in everyone's mouth.

* * *

Crew meals this evening are sullen, silent affairs. Even Coubro excuses himself from dinner with the paying passengers. The ugly prospect of 'man overboard' has touched the crew markedly. To find the 'lost' seaman drunk and hiding was not only embarrassing, but detrimental to others' relationships with him. I suspect it will be a couple of weeks before anyone trusts Nicholas again, if indeed he is in a healthy mental state.

The whole negative episode was distressful, but unfortunately more angst is in store. It's now nearly seven bells, 3:40am and the watch will be changing in less than 20 minutes. I recognize a rogue wave ahead, not massive, but significant. The helmsman has no inkling of it, given the dark cloudy night. One of the assistant cooks just started a fire in the sheet-iron galley stove. The stove is one of the most complicated machines on board. It includes a hot water tank, three ovens with cast iron doors, four heating surfaces for pans and kettles surrounded by an iron pipe railing, and an iron and copper smoke pipe equipped with a damper.

The galley can be a dangerous place. Fire is an ever-present concern. To prevent heat descending to the wooden deck, beneath the fire hearth is a layer of sand with stone slabs. Most cooking is done in the ovens but the pork and beef is boiled in large round pots which sit in huge round holes on the top of the stove. The cook and his assistants all sport marks from burns, some more serious than others. Cooking for over 200 people is no trivial feat, and the cooks work long hours.

The clock ticks past 3:45, my bow rises up on the rogue wave, then falls with a sickening crunch into the following trough. The sound of tearing wood, breaking glass and shrieking metal roars through the galley. The assistant cook is bowled over as the walls at the far corner of the storeroom pull apart, the room's ceiling collapses, and a rush of air accompanies barrels of vegetables and meat rolling from the pantry into the galley proper. The noise, coupled with the turbulence of the wave, is enough to wake officers and regular seamen alike. In less than a minute, 10 men race to the galley to see what has happened. One helps the assistant cook to his feet. He wrenches free and stumbles across peas and potatoes scattered across the hearth to immediately check that the fire he just lit is well contained behind closed doors. A lantern has crashed to the floor, and broken glass litters the entryway to the storeroom with its now dangling ceiling.

The head cook arrives, checks that his assistant hasn't been hurt, and pushes aside overturned barrels and boxes and forces his way as far as he can into the storeroom. Two faces peer at him from outside the room through the now well exposed open corner point. He tells them, "Call the carpenter, we need to shore up this overhead before more of it falls." The men retreat and in just a few minutes the bleary-eyed carpenter is standing outside the corner. He takes one look inside, and tells the cook, "I'll be right back. Need my assistant and some planks for temporary support. Best if you stay away from that ceiling my friend."

There's no reward in having my negative predictions come true, although this mishap occurred a little earlier than I expected. It was the rogue wave that really caused the problem. Hitting the bottom of its trough jarred my frame mercilessly. I'm just glad it didn't happen an hour later when all the oven fires would have been raging and water boiling on top. Someone in the galley could easily have been scalded or cut by an airborne carving knife.

It will take the best part of the coming day for the carpenter and his helpers to fix the storeroom walls and ceiling. While food supplies are strewn across the storeroom and galley floors it seems all are still usable.

All small favors are gratefully received.

* * *

Another day and all is shipshape again. The winds are steady and sure, driving us directly towards Cape Town, a week or so away. Captain Coubro starts interviewing all the prisoners, one by one, adding details to the register he must hand to the authorities when we arrive in Sydney. The militia commander is usually present at all interviews, as his signature is required alongside the captain's entries. Coubro, however, is using Corporal Tomkins, the militia second-in-charge, given Commander Mullen's hateful disposition towards the prisoners, and his current incarceration.

The interviews are short unless unusual circumstances arise, since nearly 160 must be conducted. The Surgeon is also present, often speaking on behalf of nervous prisoners who are in awe of the Captain and who stutter or become tongue-tied in his presence. For some convicts the doctor offers a medical assessment for the record, especially for the pregnant women. Limited physical descriptions are included and any distinguishing marks or deformities noted.

Most interviews proceed routinely, but, based on the surgeon's persistent requests, Coubro reluctantly agrees to set aside extra time when it's time for the prisoner James Robertson to be interviewed.

When summoned, Robertson enters the cabin and is seated. Coubro and Tomkins go through their standard list of questions about name, age, domicile, profession, crime, parents' names, date of conviction, and sentence, then check the surgeon's notes about physical condition and behavior. Robertson has an air of calm self-confidence, not seen in most other prisoners. His beard is neatly trimmed and his hair combed. His clothes are old, but are clean and tidy.

Based on the surgeon's prior input, Coubro compliments Robertson on his leadership of the mess to which he's assigned, his willingness to teach others how to read and write, and most especially his effort to save the crewmember caught in the rigging. The surgeon has indicated five students, including two sailors, have responded well to the weeks of daily reading and writing lessons. Coubro notes that Robertson has brought along a sheaf of papers covered with neat handwriting.

"What's that?" he asks.

"These are my notes I wanted to speak to you about, sir. I use this technique to help me remember important points in my lessons as a school teacher."

Tomkins speaks up. "OK Robertson, you get a little extra time based on the surgeon's unusual request. What is it you want us to know?"

"sirs, you are aware that many of us prisoners believe, rightly or wrongly, that we've been convicted unjustly. I'm no different. The only reason I want to tell you my story is that I believe one of your crew, Captain, is responsible for my being here, because he lied when making statements to the judge. He's a thief, and as such, I'm not sure he

190

deserves his status as a man in good standing under chartered assignment to the Royal Navy."

Coubro's facial expression is a mixture of respect and dismay. It appears he is impressed and irritated at the same time. This fellow is articulate and rational – at least so far. At the same time, Coubro is clearly offended that a good navy man's actions are being impugned, even though he's been warned about Robertson's story that he has shared in friendship with the surgeon. Robertson's notes are in small but legible hand-writing. He's clearly well educated.

"That's a heavy accusation Robertson. You'll need strong evidence to back it up. Which crewman are we talking about?"

"I'd like to hold his name in reserve, sir, until you and maybe others have heard my story."

"Be careful how you test my patience, Robertson, but continue. I'm listening."

Robertson tells an interesting tale. Coubro and Tomkins rarely interrupt, and in each case only for clarification. They make no judgement. Robertson is sure of himself. He speaks with conviction, minimizes emotion, and only checks his notes when he needs to reinforce the factual aspects of his story.

When finished, he reorganizes his notes, and stands up, waiting for a response and dismissal.

Coubro is pensive, digesting the information presented. Convicts, as with prisoners everywhere, are prone to exaggerate their cause. The fault is never theirs, always someone else's. He's heard their tall tales before and wonders whether he's wasting his time continuing the discussion.

Robertson, however, has remained calm, controlled, respectful, and realistic. His recounting seems highly plausible. Which suggests there are some grains of truth in it. Coubro decides he may as well proceed and asks Corporal Tomkins for his opinion on what he has heard. As expected, the Corporal is skeptical, having heard oodles of convict stories. He points out weaknesses in the prisoner's tale and bits that don't ring true.

I've been an avid eavesdropper to this intriguing exchange and the account Robertson has presented. Now I understand why he is always making secretive notes on pieces of paper originally intended for use in classes. I give him a lot of credit, for he has been listening patiently to the latest exchange between Captain and Corporal, and controlling his emotions. However, he can't hold his silence any longer, although still appears calm.

"You are right gentlemen. There's much I cannot prove now. I told my story to my solicitor and to the judge. I hoped other witnesses might remember the incident. But all feigned total memory loss. Remembered nothing about the evening and the event in question. I was on my own.

"What I've told you is the truth, but like I said at the outset, many convict stories are false or exaggerated and judges and solicitors alike are prone to discount them. Just as you have corporal."

The corporal smirks.

Something stirs in my memory about Robertson. Maybe as far back as when he first came on board. Or came forward declaring he was a teacher. For the moment however, I'm failing to recall whatever it was that may have caught my attention earlier. It'll come back eventually.

I refocus on the foursome in the captain' s cabin. Coubro rests his chin in his hand for a few seconds, withdraws it, and writes a series of sentences on a blank piece of paper on his desktop. He turns back to the prisoner.

"What is it you want, Robertson? I can't undo your trial or conviction."

"I understand, sir. That's not what I want."

"Then tell me, man. Speak up or be gone. What *do* you want?"

"I want a trial of the crewman, sir. I accuse him of theft and perjury. He's as much a criminal as many below deck who've been convicted of stealing. That's what I want."

"Come on Robertson, we don't conduct legal land-based criminal trials on board ship. You must know that. I'm a captain, not a civil judge. You are starting to sound ridiculous."

"Sorry, sir, you misunderstand my request. I want the man tried in Sydney where we will once again be present under British rule. I also think the man should be held in prison until we get there."

"Good heavens Robertson. What possible evidence could you have that would lead me to support your case with the authorities in Sydney and lock a man up until then?"

"I have two pieces of evidence, sir, that I think will make you and others believe me. And I have a suggestion about how to go forward."

Coubro stands, red in the face, eye to eye with Robertson, who stands perfectly still and does not back away. "Are you daring to tell me what to do on my ship, Robertson? You'd better be very careful in what you say next."

"sir, I mean no disrespect. I understand that one of the gentlemen first class passengers is a highly respected lawyer."

The corporal stands alongside Coubro and interrupts. "Where on earth did you hear that Robertson? You have no business with the paying passengers."

Robertson responds calmly, infuriating the corporal even more. "I understand, sir. That doesn't alter the facts."

Coubro takes a step forward. "So what, Robertson? Who is this person you so badly want to have tried? I need his name."

"I would like to repeat my accusations, sir, in front of the crewman, but with the gentleman lawyer present as an objective observer. That's all. I believe it would be in all our interests to have someone neutral present. I will provide his name if you agree to these conditions."

Coubro pauses. Opens his mouth to speak. Thinks better of it. Closes his mouth, pauses again, then says, "Okay, Robertson, you have my attention, but this is highly unusual. My authority is such that I am not inclined to grant such requests to prisoners. Still, you have conducted yourself in a solid fashion. I will take it under consideration."

Coubro has calmed down, and in fact I believe appreciates that the prisoner's demeanor has remained respectful and reasonable throughout the encounter, and that his demands are far from ridiculous. His behavior is in fact commendable, given the circumstances.

But he is a prisoner, nothing more.

Coubro gestures to the doorway, indicating it is time for Robertson to return below deck. "I will let you know my decision in due course. Keep your notes, prisoner. They serve you well. You are dismissed."

The corporal shuffles, prepared to take his leave. "It's a long way to Sydney, sir. Plenty of time to decide how to proceed once there."

As the door closes behind the departing guard, Coubro's eyesight latches onto the large world map on the adjacent wall. He smiles to the surgeon. "Yes, indeed, a very long way, but I have an idea."

15. *Tough times*

Coubro informs his paying guests that another heavy storm is approaching. They are surprised since it's only been a week since the last tempest. In this part of the southern Atlantic Ocean successive storms are not uncommon. Sharp-eyed lookouts have identified a threatening cloud mass to the southwest. Coubro states that he has no idea whether there'll be even more storms after the one on its way. Given the storm's travel direction he indicates it has the potential to drive them closer to the African coast in either an easterly, or, heaven-forbid, a northerly direction, depending how strong the winds are. Closer to the coast the trade winds would be well diminished, adding time to their journey. He suggests that the passengers make sure their cabins are secure, and that they are well prepared to sit things out over many hours. Even though they've already suffered sea-sickness and think they may now be immune, more discomfort may follow. To minimize that possibility, they should all eat lightly over the next several hours.

The militia corporal and his men are sent below to deliver a similar message to the prisoners. Sailors diligently fasten items on deck and rig storm-preventers to the main mast, after top-masts have been struck onto the deck. As a further precaution, boatswain Conway sends two teams to check that food supplies and cargo are also well secured in the holds. A frontal storm that drives huge waves towards the bow has the ability to create greater instability than a storm from astern. Waves can randomly change direction and size, and the wind direction is almost totally opposite to the desired course. A succession of waves that suddenly come nearly broadside have the ability to turn the ship side-on to the turbulent seas. Lying vulnerable in the trough between high crests can be a death knell, often the last position held before a ship is capsized or broken apart as huge waves smash the entire length of its hull and deck from above.

While I don't look forward to weathering what looks like a much shorter, but extremely violent storm, I'm pleased that the galley storeroom walls and overhead have been repaired. Even the new coats of paint have dried, and there are almost no signs on the outside that anything has changed.

Regretfully, however, no one has yet discovered the gash high up in my inner hull in the storage area for supplies. The nascent storm is definitely bad news. Based on his experience Coubro is undoubtedly well aware of what's ahead and he's painted realistic expectations for the passengers and prisoners with his choice of words and phrases.

With the gale bearing from the southwest, our current course exposes my forward starboard hull, right where the injury is to the inner woodwork. There's a high chance that the problem will worsen given the direction of the storm. Heavy waves that pound directly at the weakened point of impact could break it open and let saltwater in. The picture that presents is not pretty. I have lots of varied sea experiences so don't scare easily, but how I wish I could tell the captain.

The storm clouds far ahead are deep black and well defined. They have abrupt, straight edges, almost like the sides of a box. I hear the sailors estimate the base width at two miles. Usually the patterns of rain in a storm are far more extensive, up to ten miles or more across, creating a grey wall that often obliterates the whole horizon from view. This storm is different, and the one thing none of us can readily discern is how far back the black clouds extend. Within those clouds we anticipate the winds will gust ferociously. The clouds are tall so the winds can be funnel driven, bringing intense rain downward, along with towering waves.

* * *

Earlier, soon after first sight of the dark clouds, Coubro had the sailing master change our direction to an almost easterly course in the hope that we might reduce suffering by being at the edge of the system heading down on us, rather than at the core. But, now, four hours later, the fore-winds of the storm are already slowing us down, and most of us realize the course change was too little, too late. We won't avoid the full impact of the oncoming fury.

There's a dilemma as the sails start to slap wildly. Do we keep them up to try to gain extra distance eastward, knowing full well it will be far more difficult and dangerous to furl them as the wind force strengthens? Or do we furl them immediately, cutting our risks and being better prepared for the onslaught heralded by the approaching blackness?

The strong winds are a warning that we haven't interpreted well enough. In thirty minutes they gust randomly, accompanied by massive rainfall. Coubro resets the course to quarter into the gale, exposing our starboard flank to greater danger, as Plunkett sends his teams aloft to fully furl the sails. With a following storm some of the sails can be kept up, using the wind to drive us forward. With a head-on storm, wind in the sails would be disastrous. I see a tension in Coubro not witnessed before. He has spent considerable time by the helm observing the strength of both the wind and waters coming at him. I know he's concerned.

My senses are suddenly alerted to a freak wave building half a mile ahead. The landlubbers on board will wonder if we provide some special attraction for monster waves when it hits. This one is coming in fast, and I fear the crew is not ready. Unfortunately, its direction is nearly twenty degrees to starboard of our new path, meaning it will knock me down when it hits. There's no way for me to let the crew know although I attempt to move the rudder, spinning the wheel momentarily out of the helmsman's grasp, but not enough. He looks up and sees what I see. It's too late.

The wave crashes into me with an immense jarring motion. It slams into the starboard hull forward of the main mast, and sends a massive fountain of foam over the entire deck. Two sailors standing by the main mast are knocked off their feet and slide towards the port railing. They manage to clutch onto it and lie prone as a huge second wave washes over them. They yell to each other, checking for injuries, but both are OK, and they quickly get up and rush to the foc's'le.

The sails are all furled, but many crewmen are still working their way down the rigging as the first wave hits. The ferocious rain temporarily blinds the men. Most stop their descent and hang on with arms, legs and hands to shrouds and stays, waiting to assess when they can best move again between wave hits.

The second wave follows the first faster than one man aloft anticipates. He stretches for a lower hand hold, but the mast sways him out of reach and his momentum carries him off balance. He tries desperately to straighten and regain a hold on the tight line around the sail he's just secured, but his hand slips on the wet canvas. With loss of all support, he plunges down to the deck with a horrible scream that is torn away in the howling wind. He lands on his back across a coil of rope, but his head swivels incongruously, and there's no other movement in his body. Crewmen rush from their quarters and kneel to examine him. A slick of blood oozes from the side of the fallen man's mouth and his eyes are glazed. A rescuer places his fingers on the still man's neck, and shakes his head when he feels no pulse. The deck continues to buck and heave beneath them.

Three men pick the dead man up and carry him hurriedly to the surgeon's quarters. One of the bearers is crying, most likely a close companion of the deceased. In my experience, it takes a lot to make an

Able Seaman cry. Death is not uncommon from onboard accidents, and while most men are inured to it, a few show their feelings more easily than others.

I feel sad at the young man's death, however, and it takes me a few moments to refocus and reset my vigil. I'm reminded of the Admirals' warnings at our sea-worthiness trials. One must always be alert and grip securely when in the rigging, even more so during storms. The crew has paid a price for less than perfect execution in its tasks. I empathize with them.

I suddenly remember the starboard side inner hull gash, forgotten in light of the Able Seaman's fall. Did those first two waves weaken my planking or is it still intact? More waves have arrived – large ones, each throwing tons of water at me with horrendous force. I check and find my fears are well founded. The impact of the waves has created a hole no bigger than a two-shilling piece in the outer skin, as if a small knot in the wood has been blown away, and a limited amount of water has flowed in. Far too small to be dangerous, but the full-on pelting against the hull has also weakened the inner planks, so the internal gash is now bigger and more substantial. This is a growing problem. If the outside hole gets bigger, more water will pour through. Forget the supplies. Some will get wet no doubt. More urgently, if the flow of water coming in increases in volume we could have a flood in the bilge. Despite our turn quartering into the wind, waves are pounding against my side. I have to arrange a rescue effort before we are in serious trouble.

They say necessity is the mother of invention. I've stewed on the problem for several days now, hoping for inspiration, and have come up with a risky plan.

The prisoner deck has long passageways running fore and aft in the center of the ship. There are no such passageways on the cargo deck below. But toward the stern and bow there are wide sets of stairs leading down from the passageways. The railings on both sides of the stairways are formed with vertical wooden spokes. In order to stop prisoners getting into the cargo section there's a very large locked hatch in the floor of their deck that acts like a trapdoor above the stairs down to the cargo, blocking access to the lower hold. The underneath support rim around the hatch rests in part on the tallest support posts of the staircase railings.

There's no time to waste. I wait for a slightly larger than usual wave forming ahead of us. As it hits, I naturally list to port, but I help exaggerate the degree an extra five percentage points, and then bounce back in the other direction as hard as I dare. I hear a satisfying grating noise amongst the barrels. I know everyone on board is thinking we were just smashed by a huge wave. Not really – I deliberately added the effects of increased listing in both directions. The passengers, prisoners, and crew alike are surprised, hoping that what they just experienced was a one-off incident. It wasn't. I need them to understand. I need them to awaken to my warning.

I feel bad, but they're about to be frightened further. As the next wave roars in, I do it again, exaggerating the natural list the wave causes, and bouncing back hard to a full upright position. More grating noises. I keep this up over the next fifteen minutes. Roll and recover. Roll and recover. Harder and harder. The violent rocking bothers everyone, but I dare not stop. The barrels in the cargo hold are starting to shift a little which is what I want. Meanwhile, the hole in the hull has opened to the size of a small dinner plate and water pours in with each wave hit. I keep the violent maneuvers up for another fifteen minutes as the deck under the barrels becomes awash with cold seawater which then floods down to the bilge. That's part of the risk I anticipated. Finally, I hear the ropes snap around the group of barrels holding the salted pork. I'm nearly there!

Now I pause, mainly to give all the humans a break, but not for long. It's time for my final effort.

I'm patient as I wait for another larger than normal wave. It's scary waiting, as water still pours through the widening gash with each intermediate wave. But it's now or never. The oncoming wave I select builds evenly, and as it hits I roll even farther than before with the list, and then apply every ounce and speed of momentum I can muster to rock back way past vertical.

Several of the loose barrels fly across the cargo hold. They slam into the railing of the stairs. Just as I had hoped. The railing is smashed with the combined force of the heavy barrels. It collapses on one side. As a consequence, a corner of the trapdoor drops into free space.

Two prisoners who brave my massive rolls, peer through the gap into the hold. It is dark, but they hear water sloshing back and forth. The unexpected sound terrifies them. Water outside the ship is one thing, water inside the cargo deck signals potential disaster.

"We must have a hole in the hull," the man shouts. "We're doomed."

"We're going to drown alive," shouts the woman. Another woman screams and races back to her room.

More prisoners race to the aperture revealed in the deck they stand on. They look at each other hopelessly, fear etched across a half-dozen faces. One, held by his friends, stamps his foot hard on the dislodged corner. The hatch splinters around the edges and causes nearly half to fall and dangle in space.

"We're trapped," a young male yells. "Rats in a sinking ship." He turns and nearly bumps into an older man who carries one of the few lanterns still alight. Now, the small crowd can observe broken barrels and pieces of stair railing afloat in the water below them. At the fringe of the lamplight, a pile of barrels sways and the top ones splash into the water. One onlooker is startled and screams in surprise.

"The devil must be in there. Let me out of here."

Chaos ensues. No-one knows what to do.

The man with the lamp is a sailor of old. He remembers that two of the militia guards didn't make it up to the main deck before the main hatches were bolted down when the storm broke, and sends others back to get them. They find the guards sitting in the port corridor outside the male prisoner compartment. Initial stilted conversations between prisoners and the guards have graduated over the past hour or so to friendly exchanges on a personal level, including sharing stories of growing up. There's more similarity than either side would have expected.

Prisoners demand the guards take charge and find a solution. The pair confer, but neither has any extensive maritime experience that suggests an appropriate course of action. What is clear is that the quartermaster, Mr. Plunkett, and his engineer and carpenter need to know immediately. Everyone gathered around the trapdoor hole agrees. The question is how to raise the alarm with the vicious storm raging above, and the pitches and rolls which still continue. Fear and panic are evident in the faces and voices of those who can see the water level rising below.

The issue has spread quickly throughout the prisoner compartments. The guards unlock the intervening passageway doors in the desperate hope that a convict will come forward with a suggestion. I wait anxiously, expecting that someone will volunteer to go topside, despite the risks. I don't feel I can do anything more. Perhaps I can help determine the best time for someone to scramble across the deck, as I work hard to eliminate, or at least smooth, some of the rocking and rolling.

Looking down through the hatch opening one of the guards gets an idea. He asks someone to get him one of the long-handled brooms used to sweep the rooms. He lies on the floor and drops his torso through the gap with two strong men holding his legs securely. With the broom upside down he maneuvers the handle under one of the ropes that pulled apart as the barrels broke free with the violent swaying movements. Once he has a sufficient length hanging down he slowly lifts the broom handle until another man can reach down and grab the rope and haul it up.

Between them, they've done an excellent job, especially as the rope must be ninety feet long, having encircled a group of barrels possibly three of four times. Two male prisoners come forward offering to climb through the top hatch to the main deck and slither across it to alert an officer. They feel confident that they can tie the rope securely around their waists and be hauled back to safety if things don't work out. One of the men is Peter Cooksey, the very skinny and nimble chap who climbs the scaffolding around the passage doors to get to his lover's room. The other is Grant Wembly who swam against the crew in the races near the equator. He argues that he has unusual upper body strength that should help him pull himself across the deck using small handholds along the way.

The men are cheered for their willingness to fight the elements. Several women pray openly for their success and safe return. The ropes are tied securely, Grant in front, and are anchored to a stanchion by the open trapdoor. Three men force the top hatch open by striking it repeatedly using pieces of wood retrieved from the carnage below. They hold the hatch against the wind while others boost Peter and Grant through the opening.

Now it's my turn. The men will move forward when they are ready. As soon as I sense both are stable and have an action plan, I brace myself for the next wave, turning into it head-on and avoiding any tilt or listing at all. Grabbing each other tightly the pair scurries to the shelter of a large sail storage chest. They sit and catch their breaths. I like the fact that they calmly take their time, despite the urgency of their quest. The wind sweeps around the big container, ruffling their wet clothes and hair. They chat and reassure each other, talking with hand signals about their next movement. I understand their intentions and applaud their decision. Strapped together they rise to a crouch position and get ready to head to the main sailors' quarters.

Just as the pair is about to creep forward, serendipity strikes, as a seaman opens the door to the foc's'le and peers out. He sees the pair, realizes their intention, and immediately calls into the interior of the crew's quarters for help. Once again, I turn the ship straight into the next wave as strong sailors form a human chain four men long, and grab Wembly and Cooksey as they stumble across the deck into the fierce wind.

I rest, tired from my exertions, but happy that the pair have reached safety. The prisoners have been watching, and send up a cheer. No one above deck hears it. The topside hatch is closed, and relief is felt all round, knowing help will be coming in due order.

Fifteen minutes later a small army of crewmen descends the ladder to the prisoner deck and proceeds below to the cargo hold, a multitude of lamps held aloft. They search first for the source of water in the hold. It's found quickly. Canvas is plugged into the outside hole temporarily, while the carpenter determines how best to proceed. The main pump and two bilge pumps are set to work, with the men planning to switch off every 15 minutes. I leave them to it. They are a competent crew, acting surely and with determination. There is no panic among them. I'm happy that disaster has been averted. It won't be too long before we are in Cape Town, and more permanent repairs can be made. The two prisoners who took their lives in their hands on the open deck are treated as heroes, and the crew gives grudging respect to their bravery and determination.

Me, I'm pleased to see my little scheme worked.

* * *

The storm continues but the crisis in the hold has been thwarted. Back when the first massive waves mashed into my hull the passengers and prisoners were all taken by surprise at the storm's severity, even though they'd been warned. Many in beds and bunks were unceremoniously tossed to the floor. Now, six hours later, my frame still lurches and shudders with each massive wave. Ferocious squalls momentarily obscure the helmsman's view but cleanse me from bow to stern. Torqueing pressures on my hull, both below and above the waterline, and on the swaying masts, create ominous creaks from the sturdy beams, rigging, and planking that holds me together. It's disconcerting, but I'm sure the men who designed me and the shipwrights who built me did an excellent job. I'm confident we will come through unscathed. Especially now that the one major problem of the hole by the waterline has been taken care of.

The first-class passengers were smart enough to make new arrangements in anticipation of the storm's arrival. The four boys were placed together in the Pennington's cabin where they played checkers and other board games on the deck. When the roll of the deck caused puzzle and game pieces to slide off the base board, the boys argued about the pieces' original positions as they tried to put them back correctly. So far there's been little angst, mainly laughter. I hope it stays that way.

John and Carolyn Pennington, he the government bureaucrat sent to improve process to colony affairs, relocated to the Winthrop cabin.

James, the publisher, keeps score for the four adults seated on the floor playing 'five hundred', a card game I do not understand. They all seem to enjoy it as I've heard several peals of laughter from behind their door. And the two prima donnas – Lady Hudson-Smythe and Sara Goldsmith must have found something in common, as they are in her Ladyship's suite reading. Both appear to enjoy the Robbie Burns' poems. The suite is big enough to boast two comfortable lounge chairs. They are fastened to the deck so do not move when I lurch to one side or pitch up and down through waves and troughs. The occupants shift a little but seem reasonably comfortable. Her Ladyship has groaned a few times at the turbulence, but she hasn't complained that she's dying like last time, and that she needs a doctor. We should all be thankful for such small mercies.

Well before the storm had been sighted, Lady Hudson-Smythe had given her lady-in-waiting the day off. Matilda, happy to be out of uniform, spent the morning on deck, far away from any freedom-ending becks or calls from her mistress. She'd put on her only light cotton dress and cloth topped shoes, meaning to take advantage of the sunshine that never penetrates indoors. She walked around the deck several times, enjoying the exercise, then sat at the port rail, dangling her feet over the side, fascinated by the patterns of the water swirling away from the bow.

I enjoyed watching her smile as the breeze played with her golden locks. She spread her skirt across her knees, placed her hands in her lap, and tilted her face to the warmth of the sun. It was if she was tasting the air, drinking in its refreshment like a little girl licking an ice-cream. It was only the fourth free day she'd been granted on the trip so far, and it seemed as though she was determined to use it to relax, and act as a passenger in her own right, rather than as an appendage to 'Her Highness', the personal label she applied to her Ladyship.

As the winds heralding the storm kicked up a boisterous chop, she became sullen and pouted childishly. One could almost read her mind. How dare my limited pleasure-time be interrupted so? She pulled her arms around her chest, wrapping herself like an immobile statue, challenging the elements to upset her further.

The storm, inevitably destined to spoil the latter part of her free day, takes no notice. Defiant, she stays outside on deck until a caring sailor warns her that if she remains there longer she may end up in the drink. Her face crinkles at the message, her hair matting with the first rain drops. Annoyed, but grudgingly appreciative of the advice, she makes her way cautiously back to the passenger cabins.

At the entrance she jerks open the heavy oak hatch. A strong gust of wind catches it and wrenches it from her grasp. She swears, although I'm the only one who hears. Unbalanced, she falls backward. Her left foot catches under the door, and her head hits the deck. I hear the thud and feel for her.

Timothy Blaine, the banker, has just exited his cabin heading for the toilets, and feels the surge of wind rush into the passageway. He turns, and seeing Matilda fall, rushes to her side.

She lifts her head dizzily and reaches behind to feel for a bump. Timothy leans over her face and checks her disposition. Her cheeks redden as she quickly reaches down to clutch her billowing dress that reveals tattered drawers not fully covering her private parts. A gentleman to the core, Timothy ignores her struggle. "Here, let me help you up Matilda. We'll go to my cabin and check your foot and head. Does it hurt anywhere else?"

"Thank you, Mr. Blaine, the wind surprised me. It grabbed the door and made it fly open. I'll be fine I'm sure."

Together they limp to Timothy's cabin where he seats her in the soft lounge chair. He quickly examines her head and finds only a small bump. With a smile in his voice he says, "I think you'll live, but let me see if I can persuade the cook to make us some tea and find a powder for you. Your ankle has a small scrape, but we'll attend to it when I return."

He's back five minutes later with tea and headache powder. Matilda has regained her composure, along with better color in her cheeks.

"This is very thoughtful of you, Mr. Blaine. I appreciate your consideration. I looked at my foot and used one of your towels to wash it. I hope you don't mind. It's just a scratch really and has already stopped bleeding."

"Good, but please let me double check."

He gently lifts her foot until her leg is straight out, and looks at the cut. It is insignificant.

To his surprise Matilda is blushing. She flashes a coquettish smile and blurts, "You didn't see too much when I fell down did you, Mr. Blaine?"

Timothy considers his answer carefully. He'd seen plenty but chooses gallantry over honesty. "Nothing beyond the pained look on your face. Now, my dear, rest up while I pour you a cuppa. Sugar?"

"One teaspoon please. I'm glad I don't have milk in my tea as we've run out. Her Ladyship complains all the time about its absence. I tell her we'll get more in a week when we dock in Cape Town."

"I admire you Matilda. You must have been born with a reservoir of patience, the way you serve her Ladyship. I simply could not do what you do for her."

"I know on the surface she appears blustery and pompous and demanding. I put up with it because she pays me well, and a part of me feels sorry for her."

"You surprise me when you say she pays you well. That isn't my experience with the remuneration of servants and maids like yourself. To many of us, she uses you shamelessly."

"Well, the wage she provides is indeed tiny, but every now and then she will give me a bracelet or small clutch purse she no longer favors. I turn those into cash at the local pawn dealer and am building a nice little savings pile. One day I will be able to leave and look for a secretarial position, or apply to be a teacher somewhere."

"You also said you feel sorry for her. Why is that?"

"I've probably said too much already, Mr. Blaine. I don't want you to think poorly of me."

"Oh, come now, Matilda, if you help us understand your mistress we may appreciate her more. The others are very confused about her real goals for taking this dangerous journey. I can only guess at her age, but why would a woman of high breeding, apparently in her early twenties, be on a ship like this, all alone? She can't be much older than you."

"It's a bit of a story so listen carefully, sir. I've been her Ladyship's maid for three years, so I have knowledge of all her likes and dislikes, and the feelings she has for select relatives and immediate family members who live in the mansion. I also know her relationships with certain friends, as well as a myriad of other little secrets.

"You probably aren't aware that the Hudson-Smythe estate is in the parish of Wallingford in Berkshire, bordered to the east by the Thames. The village's history goes back to the ninth century, and in fact I'm named after the Empress Matilda, who lived in the village in 1141 and

211

whose father was Henry I. I don't know exactly how the current estate came to belong to the Hudson or Smythe families. All I know is that they own acres and acres of forest and meadows, and that the actual village and tenant farmers are all under their dominion.

"Those parts of the estate not selected to grow grains and vegetables or used to breed sheep and cattle are beautiful. Foxes, deer, rabbits, pheasants and grouse make hunting a frequent sport for the mansion residents and their visitors. The house itself is very old, but half of it has been renovated and has all modern conveniences. That's where the family lives. The other half is not used, other than a place where sometimes we maids and servants sneak for a smoke or an ale away from family demands and needs."

Timothy interjects. "Sounds like a lot of tradition and history govern the estate. I'd love to see it sometime, but please go back and talk about her Ladyship."

"Oh, yes. I get carried away because I love the Hudson-Smythe family. I was raised in the village and the Earl and Countess took me into the main house soon after I turned eighteen. I was an only child to my loving mother and father. Father tended crops and mother was a seamstress, as I've indicated before."

"I imagine after some initial training you were assigned as Lady Hudson-Smythe's lady-in-waiting. Is that correct?"

"Yes, the current lady-in-waiting announced she had to return to her home up north where her father had recently died and her mother was ailing. She taught me her Ladyship's idiosyncrasies and personal needs for two months, then left. I was lucky to have so much time with her."

"I think all ladies-in-waiting must have special characteristics to abide by the trust shown them in their serving capacity. I guess that something not so good must have happened that causes your mistress to be unchaperoned on this ship."

"It's a very awkward circumstance, Mr. Blaine. You see, there was a giant ball at the mansion last year celebrating the bountiful harvest. All the villagers and tenant farmers were invited, for the Earl and Countess were very good to their people. It was a truly wonderful evening with bands inside and outside, dancing under a marquee on the front lawn, enough food and drink to feed an army, gas lamps lighting up the rooms and lawns. It was very romantic and exciting. The party was still going when I climbed into bed around three am.

"A few hours later that morning the only ones up were a few of us servants. The mansion was very quiet. I went down to the service area in the basement sometime after nine am and helped prepare the light luncheon that was being organized for any household members and guests that might appear. The bells that usually summoned us were silent.

"Eventually, my friend Daisy was summoned to the Countess' bedroom, and one by one after that guests rang or sauntered into the main dining room for lunch. At one pm when I still hadn't heard from her Ladyship, I went quietly up to her room to see if she was stirring or whether she needed anything.

"I was shocked to find she wasn't there, but across her bed lay her night dress and undergarments. Excuse my indelicacy but I think you've seen what I mean. Her beautiful evening dress was hanging in her wardrobe, but a thin cotton robe was missing.

"I fled back downstairs and asked my best friend Evelyn, who served her Ladyship's older sister, what I should do. She suggested that I wait in the hallway that led to her Ladyship's bedroom and help her dress the minute she turned up."

Matilda's voice lowers, and her speech slows. Timothy looks closely in alarm. Was the bump on her head more serious than it seemed? "Go on," he says, and leans forward to encourage her.

"No. I should stop. The memory is unpleasant, and I talk too much. 'Her Highness' will kill me. Another time, Mr. Blaine. Can we talk of something else please?"

* * *

The storm still rocks my frame unevenly. One minute there is a short list to port, and then starboard, as the next large wave assaults us with unmitigated force. Matilda and Timothy are conscious of the upheavals but scarcely seem to notice. Timothy lies flat on his bed, Matilda remains seated in the lounge chair.

The silence between the pair is heavy. I imagine Timothy reflects on the story but is anxious to know more, while Matilda worries that she has already said far too much.

The episode is clearly on her mind for out of the blue she adds a footnote. "Her Ladyship has her eye on the Captain as someone who might save her. I hope the man is prepared to be seduced. My mistress is not above it."

The look on Timothy's face is one of amazement, but after a while he relaxes, as he realizes that from Lady Hudson-Smythe's perspective it makes sense. He says nothing.

He rises and makes his way to the inbuilt desk and retrieves a board and a box of checkers. "Do you play?"

"Oh yes, down in the basement of the estate we often spent our spare time putting puzzles together or playing board games."

Timothy speaks without reflecting sufficiently. "I guess you are pretty good at draughts then?"

Matilda blushes, looks directly at Timothy, summons up courage. "Not bad."

Her companion smiles. "Well, I hate to be beaten, so be nice to me. You go first."

* * *

Elsewhere, I can sense a need to offset new problems the gale is causing. The backup chains to the rudder have slipped off the metal strap bolted to the rudder-horn. We need to fix this in a hurry or lose our reserve for steering control. It's happened before, and extra sailors are being assigned to help. I need to be aware and to add what force I can to keep us stationary as the chains are refitted.

Reluctantly, I turn my focus to sea-safety, and leave the young pair chatting amiably in Mr. Blaine's cabin. One day I suspect they might indulge in more than just chatting.

16. *Respite*

With the first call of "Land Ho" 20 miles off the coast of South Africa, excitement spreads through all quarters of the ship – including the prisoners' compartments. While they will not be allowed ashore, they realize they will be relieved of the tedium of the side to side rolling and the up and down motion of the ship for several days, and that food and water supplies will be refreshed. They also expect to be given more time on deck to absorb some sunshine and get more exercise.

Coubro must have had a briefing about the politics, economics, and history of South Africa before we left Portsmouth, for he gathers the senior crew after dinner one evening and passes on what he knows. I listen in, anxious to know what to expect when we finally arrive.

Cape Town congregates around Table Mountain Bay, where reflections of the flat-topped mountain are ever present. It's actually an historic time. For while the British secured the town from the Dutch in 1806, it wasn't until 1814, just two years ago, that the colony was ceded outright by the Netherlands to the British crown. By then the colony extended to the mountains in front of the vast central plateau, and some 60 thousand residents lived there, a mixture of white settlers, free Khoikhoi*, and slaves. While formal transfer was initiated in 1814, remnants of political and economic change are still taking place in current times. If one talks to the citizens, one may find many of them confused about what the new political climate means on a day-to-day basis.

In 1815, the important Cape Town naval base was moved to Simon's Town, a spot 45 miles south from the commercial part of Cape Town, beyond Table Mountain. For those on a ship, it involves sailing around a peninsula, the actual sea-route closer to 70 miles. Much to the chagrin of many on board, Captain Coubro has decided to anchor off Simon's Town before heading into Cape Town proper.

We sail 50 miles south along the coastline, turn east around the peninsula's Cape Point, and proceed 15 miles north to an anchorage in False Bay. We drop anchor in 20 fathoms, five hundred yards offshore, directly in front of the Royal British Navy's one-year-old building which combines mast-house, boathouse and sail loft.

The Commander of the Cape Station, Admiral Sanders, bids Coubro and his officers a grand welcome, delighted to have a friendly ship in view directly opposite the station's front door. It takes well over half a day for Coubro and his officers to recount sufficient details of our voyage to make the station officials feel they are well informed. A gala dinner is quickly arranged, for Coubro has told the Commander he proposes to sail back to Table Bay tomorrow in order to effect repairs and replenish supplies, notions well understood and appreciated by the local Naval officials.

The laughter and merriment from the dinner scene floats fulsomely into the bay. Our senior crew is thrilled to be back on *terra firma*, eating fresh food and drinking the popular world-renowned wine from the nearby Constantia area.

After dinner, Coubro and Admiral Sanders take a walk along the foreshore. I catch only a few snippets of their conversation. Part of it is about the Militia Commander that Coubro punished, and what to do about him. Another discussion relates to the repairs and maintenance Coubro wants for me. He has a list of items that the Boatswain and First Lieutenant have decreed need attention, all of which I agree with. Most lively, however, is a discussion about the prisoner James Robertson and his request. It is clear from the intensity of the Admiral's questions that he is perplexed as to how to proceed. Coubro apparently offers a suggestion, because just before the pair return to the Navy building there is a lot of head nodding and a warm, lengthy handshake between the two men.

Early the next morning we weigh anchor and head out through a mild southwesterly. We are bid farewell by a five gun salute send-off. I think the local Naval command rarely gets a chance to play with the big guns, and our departure is unanimously deemed an acceptable cause. The crewmen of the *Lady Corinth* line the starboard rail and raise their caps in response. Unnecessary, but they are glad to be near civilization again. Sort of stirring – a symbolic rendering of British tradition thousands of miles from home. Touching.

Before daybreak, I'd heard two riders leave on horseback. I suspect they headed north to announce our pending arrival in Cape Town, and to alert officials and merchants about Captain Coubro's needs.

We have many miles of sea path ahead. At the eight knots we've averaged for the past two weeks, it will take us about eight hours to make the trip. Coubro, in his caution and good seamanship, has enticed a Pilot from the Navy station to conn us into Cape Town. We do not want to chance a grounding at this mid-point of our voyage. Our trip will be far longer than it will take the two horsemen to ride less than 50 miles north. Ah, the benefits of land access.

I'm looking forward to anchoring in Table Bay and receiving due attention. The major issue for me is my rudder. Its chains came off once, and the rudder has worked a bit loose from the harshness of the two consecutive storms we endured. I felt it more than the helmsman did at the time but have made the crew aware by moving it back and forth a little while stationary. We are only half way through our journey, and without thorough tightening we could be in serious trouble if we encounter more severe storms.

Fortunately, the shipping company has an agent in Cape Town who has relations with repair shops and suppliers that will both keep costs down and speed up the process of meeting Coubro's requests. The agent has clearly been active all day, for he greets us in a small boat along with a couple of chandlers anxious to get to work.

I do know of one planned event though that is highly unusual. Since Cape Town is now a bona fide colony of the British Empire Coubro plans to have convict Robertson's case against the crewman heard by the city's judicial authorities, rather than wait until we get to Sydney. He shared the idea with the Surgeon who gave his support, as anxious as Coubro to have the issue resolved.

Coubro informed Robertson of the decision after breakfast this morning. Robertson is appreciative that he will have his day in court much earlier than expected, but is justifiably reserved and somewhat hesitant, given the newness of the practice of British Law in the territory.

It's mid-afternoon when we drop anchor in Cape Town Harbor. There's a lone jetty, and goods and people must be transferred between ship and shore by boats. Table Bay is notorious for violent winter storms, with damaging winds that blow directly onto the shoreline. Admiral Sanders tells us it's the end of the storm season, else we would have stayed in False Bay.

Maybe we were just unlucky to experience two southern Atlantic storms so close together. Perhaps they were the last two in the area. I'm sure Coubro hopes so, as the major marine resources reside here at Cape Town, not in False Bay.

As for me? I'm tired. We've covered thousands of miles of open waters, struggled through oppressive equatorial heat and scant winds, and weathered two terrible storms. Not to mention serious enroute repairs to the galley and hold. On the emotional human side, we suffered the amputation of a seaman's arm, and experienced the death of a prisoner's baby girl, plus those of two young seamen.

I need a good fresh-water wash down and scrubbing to remove the dried salt and attendant tiny critters on my hull, deck and the masts. Several shrouds have worn and need to be replaced, along with the running rigging, especially for the main course and main topsail. Many sails need to be mended, and I heard Coubro talk with the Admiral about possible replacements for the two jibs that blew away in the storm. The copper sheathing on the underwater hull and keel needs to be checked, and a number of spars have exposed cracks and worn fittings. They should be replaced and the crow's nest on the main mast needs to be revamped. The winds up high have loosened its holdings, and the topmen are uncomfortable with its present state. Some fresh line and small stuff is all that's required. Also, I'd feel better if some local shipwrights examine the repairs made at sea, at least to the forward starboard hull.

As for my interior, the stairs to the cargo area need to be fully repaired, of course, as well as the hatch on the prisoners' deck. Numerous prisoner rooms need bracing timbers replaced, and several portholes have sprung leaks. The heads and the doctor's rooms need to be fumigated, and broken lanterns replaced.

Most of the workers from the resident chandlers will be native, speaking a local tribal dialect, although a few will speak Afrikaans and will be able to converse on occasion with any sailors or convicts present, if Coubro so allows. I know a number of sailors will welcome the outsiders but many will feel strange, exposed for the first time to an unfamiliar foreign culture.

As soon as we anchor in Table Bay all the portholes and hatches are opened to the sea breezes and bedding is struck topside to air out. That helps remove the smell of sulfur brimstone used in fumigating, but later, those same breezes permeate the lower decks with the aromas from bunches of fresh bananas and other fruits that traders have brought alongside in their small boats. The fragrances assail the prisoners' receptive senses, and bring hopes for new items in their diet. Along with fresh milk for the pregnant women, it's enough to bring smiles to the faces of many.

Conway, our Boatswain, had shared his list of stores and supplies for the ship, and the Purser relayed our required food and drink replenishments through the Naval command when we were in False Bay. No doubt our agent here in Cape Town has already placed orders with city merchants to meet the demands. I know they will be eager to complete our orders. As well, Conway wants a few more sail palms, needles and thread, belaying pins and a fresh Ensign and company flag to replace the tattered remnants left by the storm. In anticipation of the journey ahead he already has two work parties in the hold opening chests and breaking out more cold weather jackets and coats for the crew.

After conferring with Coubro this afternoon, Conway also receives approval to order more agricultural tools and implements as personal trading stock to add to the ship's cargo. There is room in the hold for them, and both men anticipate that once we arrive in Sydney they'll be able to sell double the amount of such goods the Portsmouth officials and company business agents had allocated them to carry. The pair also plan to buy more laborers' tools – axes, saws, wheelbarrows, crowbars, chisels, shovels, and rakes, etc for the same reason. Nothing improper about seeing an opportunity and taking advantage of it. "As long as it doesn't interfere with official duties," Coubro affirms.

The stay here is definitely warranted, and is consistent with my owners' orders and their contract with the British Navy. It is a time for everyone to relax a bit, catch their breath, and then get on with the myriad tasks involved in preparing for the next part of our trip. Undoubtedly, there will be challenges ahead.

* * *

The first day at rest, Quartermaster Plunket recommends, and Captain Coubro agrees, to grant leave to half the crew to spend in town. A number head for the brothels, many to the wharf-side pubs, others to the marketplaces to see the different wares offered, and to survey the various types of people present there.

Passage for the first-class passengers includes a land-based stay at the four-year old Dutch Manor Hotel, a short distance inland from the waterfront. Small, with comfortable rooms, it offers a delightful, stable, fragrant, and dry change from the onboard cabins. All 20 passengers are taken there with suitcases filled with clothes to cover a three-day stay. Many include clothes to be laundered. The sailors who manage the transfer of the passengers to the hotel share tales of stumbles and awkwardness as the privileged few struggle to find their land-legs once again. Those who elect to walk alongside the horse-drawn carts which carry their belongings find their sea-legs disappear faster than those who ride on the carts. The walkers quickly welcome the fixed, immobile surfaces beneath their feet.

It doesn't take long for nearly all the passengers to become enthusiastic voyeurs of everything that is different in this colonial outpost. From the wide streets to the Victorian architecture, much of it recently constructed, to the civilized shops and apartment buildings. Reminders of England, but with none of the pollution, dirty alleyways, and braziers of coal on major street corners. In fact, bright sunshine forces many to shield their eyes, as the overall color of buildings is white rather than red-brown or dull grey, and reflects the sun more readily.

In the hotel dining room, familiar dishes from back home are served, embellished with local ingredients and adaptations. They provide a welcome change from the ship's diet, and there is talk of desire for a lengthier stay.

There are innumerable requests brought back aboard ship for different clothes, and personal artifacts left behind. Some experienced crew members find themselves engaged as friends and helpers to travelers who have never previously left England.

Coubro, Corporal Tomkins, and a contingent of sailors escort several soldiers to the city's military reserve. The group includes Mullens, the Militia Commander, Millstone, the guard who was whipped, and two other men, loyal to Mullens. At the militia headquarters Coubro explains to the Officer-in-Charge his detention of commander Mullens, and the thrashing and imprisonment of private Millstone. He presents the signed papers he has drawn up that detail his reasons for the various guards' dismissal. He asks whether four replacement men are available and willing to travel to Sydney. He then departs, leaving Tomkins behind to finalize any new arrangements and arrange for the new men to come aboard.

On deck, the remaining guards are diligently patrolling, guns at ready positions. Prisoners have been allowed to leave their quarters and enjoy the fresh air in groups of about 20 at a time. The guards watch for anyone who looks like they might be thinking about diving overboard and swimming to freedom. It has happened on other convict ships. But no one has ever escaped completely. While the guards on board are watchful, the local constabulary is also vigilant. A few policemen actually wish someone would try for a break and provide some unusual excitement in their job. Chaps who are strong swimmers would have the best chance, but even Grant Wembly, who competed in the long-distance swim race near the equator, shows no desire for freedom.

Around 10am next morning, a small tender brings an unusual group of officials alongside. The Mate of the watch assigns several sailors to help the strangers climb the rope ladder that hangs down my portside hull.

It is clear that most of the visitors have not had to board a ship for some time.

Coubro is present to greet these august town officials. The group includes the city's senior Magistrate, as well as the highest ranking constable who reports to the Magistrate, the Naval Commander-in-Chief from False Bay, the militia garrison Commander, and two clerks of the court. One of these assistants carries an official staff with the Union Jack furled around it. The other assistant is clearly a scribe as he holds an oversized ledger, a sheaf of papers, and two pens and inkwells. The Magistrate wears a court wig, which makes him look younger than is probably the case. There is also a very large nondescript fellow who accompanies the constable. A bodyguard perhaps?

This array of arrivals indicates that Robertson is about to have his day in court. Soon, the crew's dining room is overcrowded, for Coubro has ordered all his officers and their direct subordinates to attend the meeting. Members of the latter contingent, comprised of the cook, master gunner, carpenter, and other mates, look bewildered, perplexed by their Captain's command. There are not enough chairs, so Coubro makes his men stand, as does he.

Once all are assembled, he stills the idling sideline conversations, and introduces a sense of gravity.

Having talked with each visitor on deck as they came on board, Coubro quickly introduces the visitors by name, title, and function. He asks that the prisoner Robertson be brought in and offers him the seat which has been reserved at the far end of the table.

There is a palpable tension in the air as the strangers eye each other with a sense of anxiety and uncertainty. Sailors fear the claustrophobia of what is now obviously a defacto courtroom. Townspeople feel uncomfortable in the presence of a group of swarthy, unkempt crew members who clearly would prefer to be elsewhere.

Coubro establishes the purpose of the meeting.

"Gentlemen, thank you for coming to this unusual gathering. I appreciate that the city officials among us are all very busy, and that they have acceded to my unique request on very short notice. I am obliged to those who have had to make marked changes in schedules and commitments.

"For those of you unfamiliar with our legal system, Mr. Simpson here is the chief Magistrate of Cape Town. He acts as a justice of the peace, with authority to issue orders pertaining to providing aid and/or punishment to citizens, as may be warranted. We will be engaging here in a court of inquiry under his oversight.

"Are there any questions before we commence the legal hearing?"

The room remains quiet. All eyes are on Coubro, but not a mouth twitches.

"No? Then I now call this meeting to order in the presence of His Honor, Mr. Simpson. I will summarize the reason for the meeting as succinctly and fairly as possible.

"Prisoner James Robertson is being transported to Sydney for holding a loaded pistol to a man's head and threatening to harm that person. The incident took place nearly two years ago in Southampton, and Robertson's sentence is 14 years. He claims that at his trial a witness committed perjury and was actually involved in a theft of goods Robertson aspired to. In itself, while not remarkable, Robertson also claims, and indicates he has proof, that this man is a member of the *Lady Corinth's* crew."

Murmurs erupt around the room. Coubro looks reproachfully at some of the men and forcefully says "Gentlemen, hold your tongues until these proceedings are complete." He turns to the Magistrate. "I apologize your Honour."

Mr. Simpson nods in acknowledgment and waves his hand to indicate Coubro should proceed.

"Inasmuch as we are a chartered vessel, we are under contract to the British Navy, thereby bound to serve her needs and act as a responsible vessel in her fleet. Officers, while privately hired, must conform to, and be governed by, Naval laws and conditions. No felon may serve as an officer."

He pauses. Silence falls heavily across the room.

"This proceeding is to hear prisoner Robertson's charge and for the court to decide what action, if any, should be taken in response to such charge. "

He turns to the Magistrate.

"Your Honor, would you like to add anything?"

"Thank you for that summary Mr. Coubro. I may have questions for clarification as we proceed, but otherwise I am prepared to hear the prisoner's story. Since this ship is in British protected waters, the major laws of the mother country apply directly here. As Captain Coubro has stated, this meeting is called to assess the prisoner's case for a potential trial of his so-claimed antagonist, and to deal with any appropriate actions as a result."

Coubro steps forward. "Mr. Robertson, please repeat the story you told Mr. Tomkins and me two weeks ago."

17. *Vindication*

All eyes turn to look at Robertson, who slowly rises from his seat. Polished deck planks creak and his chair scrapes, jarring in the hushed atmosphere. A number of the crew, irritated by the proceedings on behalf of a prisoner, cast hateful looks at him. The Magistrate and his accomplices wait patiently.

"Your Honour, it's like this. Me and my friend, Ben Carson, were out celebrating one evening at the Barrel & Anchor pub down by the wharves in Southampton. We'd been in a couple of other pubs, but liked this one better."

Mr. Simpson interrupts, "When was this exactly, and what were you celebrating?"

"Beg pardon, sir, this was 18 months ago. Ben's wife had run off the week before with a man who'd promised her a better life in London. The toff apparently had plenty of money, so all she took with her was her clothes and purses and jewelry etc., leaving everythin' else behind."

Robertson pauses, but the Magistrate signals with his hands for Robertson to continue.

"My friend, we'll he's a simple chap, doesn't need much. So he gathers everything up in the house and pawns the beds, tables, chairs, sideboard, household implements, chamber pot, serving dishes, sheets, pillows towels, and so on. He moves in to the seaman's almshouse. Much cheaper to stay there.

"Anyway, he and I were out celebrating his freedom. Ben carried a large sack with all the other small objects from the house. These included silver candlesticks and cutlery, pewter mugs, and personal items like hairbrushes, ashtrays, ornaments, picture frames, etc. He planned to pawn those the next day. As well, in a pouch on the inside of his belt he had a bunch of money hidden – near 10 pounds worth – a veritable fortune for Ben. And to protect himself against robbers he'd just bought a small pistol. He gave it to me to hide in my big jacket."

The Magistrate asks, "Where did your friend get the pistol?"

"In exchange at the pawn store, sir."

"You may continue."

"So Ben and I are having a great time. Ben has found a new freedom with his missus gone. I'm watching him closely because he's drinking more than usual. The barman keeps plying him with full glasses and eventually calls over one of the bar girls, who sidles up to Ben real cozy like. Well, the two of them get friendly and it isn't long before she leads him upstairs.

"I turn to watch the chap playing the piano. He's good, the place is crowded, and there's lots of singing. It's a happy group that night. We sing a bunch of songs together.

"At some point, I head outside for a pee, and as I come back in I see the barman sneaking out of the door of the room upstairs where Ben's being entertained. That was okay except for one thing. The barman is carrying my friend's sack of silver. Thieving bastard!

"I yell at him to stop, and head across the floor to get to the staircase. But he tears down full force and knocks me over. Hits me in the ribs with the sack, hurts something awful. Then he heads for the back door. Ben is now out of the room on the balcony, holding up his pants, hollering that his stuff has been stolen. Including his money belt. He's mad as hell."

The Magistrate nods his head up and down. He's undoubtedly heard many variants of this sort of tale. His clerk speaks up, "You mean the barkeep snuck in the room, took the belt from Ben's britches while he's busy plugging the girl, grabs the sack of candlesticks and all, and is making off with the takings? Surely the theft is obvious to all? You said there was a big crowd, right?"

Robertson looks down at his notes, pauses, runs his finger down a page, turns it over, scans the next page and says. "Yes, sir, that's how it was. Just checking to see if I've left anything out. Oh yes, here it is. Bargirl's name was 'Tillie'. At least that's what she called herself. Big eyes, frizzy hair. Tall, big tit... bosom. Drank like a man, sir."

The clerk speaks up again. "Okay, so the barman barrels into you and knocks you down. No one tries to grab him?"

"I guess no one wanted to get involved, sir. Except me. Barman no doubt had friends in the crowd I imagine. I get up and chase the bastard thief. I push through the crowd and out the back door. I'm yellin' to him to stop. But he doesn't. He's maybe no more than 10 yards in front of me. I start to catch up to him since he's got the heavy sack to carry and it slows him somewhat. I pull out Ben's pistol from the inside pocket of my coat, point it at him, yell that I'll shoot, but he keeps running. So I fire, and lo and behold the bullet catches him in his calf, and he goes down. I run up and stand over him pointing the gun at his head. He glares at me, and tries to stop the bleeding from his leg. He's cursing like crazy because of the hurt."

"So what happened next?" The Magistrate sits straighter in his chair. Robertson consults his notes once more.

"Ben comes running up, red in the face, cussing like crazy. He kicks the robber hard in the ribs several times, punches him in the head, and tries to retrieve the belt the little bastard had put on. But, of all things,

231

and here's the rub, sir, around the corner come two constables. They must've been on their regular beat, because I'm sure no one in the pub had time to go fetch them. They blow their whistles, and I know I'm a gonner.

"Now, my friend, Ben, has had a little run-in with the law previously, so he's in no mood to hang around. He grabs for the sack on the ground, but the robber is half lying on it, so Ben gives up and takes off. It's sort of comic actually as he's hauling up his britches, but the cops are on me in a flash, because I'm the one with the pistol at the barman's head.

"A crowd gathers. My friend, Ben, who I was trying to help, has deserted me, the coppers take the pistol, and next thing my hands are cuffed in those new handcuffs they call 'flexible' links, and one of the coppers is marching me to the local gaol. Last thing I see is the barman having his wound attended to by someone with a dish of water and a towel come outta the pub. The other copper is writing in his notebook as he gets the barman's story."

Robertson pauses and catches his breath.

The Magistrate holds up his hand to stop Robertson from saying more. "Okay Mr. Robertson, I follow your story. The police had every right to immediately take you into custody, given the gun in your hand."

"Yes, sir. I understand."

"But your point is that the barman stole your friend's possessions, and you were trying to recover them. Is that the essence of your position?"

"Yes, Your Honor, plus the fact that in court, the thief lied about the sack of goods, and claimed I stole them from my friend."

"And you further claim the barman thief is serving as a member of this ship's crew. Is he present at this moment?"

There's an ominous pause in the proceedings. The silence weighs heavily throughout the room. Everyone is focused on Robertson, edgily awaiting his revelation. He fixes his gaze on the Captain, then the Magistrate, slowly rises, and points behind him.

"Yes, sir," he responds. "He's the Pilot, Mr. Charles Matheson."

There are gasps all around the room. Old memories assail my brain. Matheson actually walks with a limp and claimed on arrival that he sometimes helped his father who owns a pub. Could it really be him? He's a senior officer whom Coubro depends on heavily.

Matheson shouts, "This is ridiculous. I've never seen this man before. What's your purpose here, Robertson? You are making a mockery of yourself and wasting the time of these important visitors. You're insulting one of the highest officials in the land, impudent fool."

Robertson responds calmly. "You may not recognize me Mr. Matheson, for at the time of this incident I sported no beard, and my hair was cut very short."

The city officials and other crew members whisper among themselves, clearly surprised.

The Magistrate bangs the gavel on the table, and the noise slowly subsides. "Continue Mr. Robertson," he prompts.

Robertson turns towards the Pilot. "Mr. Matheson, do you have a scar on your left calf?"

Matheson is red in the face, and starts for the door. "This is preposterous. Captain, I'll not be subject to his attempt at humiliation."

Mr. Simpson bangs the gavel again several times. "Mr. Matheson, this is a defacto court of law. No one will be dismissed until I say so. if you

233

have no injury, this meeting is over. It's a simple request. Please haul up the left leg of your britches."

Matheson cowers, and his crewmates look at him expectedly. A Second Mate cries, "Come on Charles, get this over and done with." But the Pilot is defiant and doesn't move.

The Magistrate speaks again. "Must we do this by force?"

Matheson mumbles, "I have a serious mark on my calf, put there by a deranged sailor on one of my voyages. He attacked me with a knife and carved a chunk out of my leg before others pulled him off me. The wound took months to heal properly, and I've never been able to walk perfectly since."

Coubro steps in. "So, Mr. Matheson, you say the mark on your leg was caused by a knife, not a bullet? Mr. Robertson, perhaps you are accusing the wrong man."

Robertson will truck no argument. "I know otherwise, Captain. I don't believe Mr. Matheson for a second. I suspect if one pressed hard on his leg one would feel the bullet still lodged under the skin."

"We're not going to do that, Robertson. We'll take the word of an officer," Coubro responds. "If that's all you have to offer, this meeting will adjourn."

"I have more, sir. I believe the belt Mr. Matheson wears belongs to my friend, Ben Carson."

Matheson's outburst comes immediately. "Another ridiculous assertion! One of the barmen in my father's pub found this belt in the toilet closet when closing up one night. Some poor drunk probably never knew he'd lost it. The finder gave it to me. Could be anyone's belt."

The Magistrate leans forward. "So you do work in a pub when not sailing, Mr. Matheson? By chance is it the Barrel & Anchor in Southampton owned by your father?"

Matheson is quiet, says nothing. The Magistrate asks again, "What was the name of the pub where you claim the belt was found Pilot?"

"I don't remember, sir."

"Do you work in many different pubs, Mr. Pilot?"

There's no response. The Magistrate turns to Captain Coubro. "I think from your Pilot's silence, Captain, that his father owns the Barrel & Anchor, and he works there. It wouldn't be hard to verify once back in England."

Everyone is now staring at Matheson's belt. It's a leather belt, not that unusual, except for the buckle clasp, which is almost circular and larger than most, about three inches in diameter.

Robertson remains standing, patiently waiting. He speaks again. "If in fact that is anybody's belt then I wouldn't know anything about it, correct?"

He hasn't addressed anyone specific with his question, but Mr. Simpson sits forward. "That is correct Mr. Robertson. What exactly are you trying to say?"

"I know something unique about Ben Carson's belt, Your Honor. I'll describe what I know and you can see if the one Mr. Matheson wears matches the description. From the little I can see of the buckle, I believe it is my friend's belt, stolen from him at the Barrel & Anchor as I've described."

Mr. Simpson is intrigued. "Mr. Matheson, indulge us and bring your belt forward to this end of the table. And please note, sir, we won't take 'No' for an answer this time."

Matheson explodes again. "You think I will let some wayward prisoner who's been apprehended for threatening a man's life play games with my belt? This whole issue about a belt is a distraction, it's the pistol held at his victim's head that is relevant to his crime and penalty."

The Magistrate disagrees. He's not to be trifled with. He sends the senior constable and his burly henchman to the other end of the room where they quickly restrain the much smaller Pilot, relieve him of his belt, return, and lay it on the table in front of the Magistrate, the local naval Commander, and Coubro.

The Magistrate nods to Robertson. Robertson shuffles the pages of his notes, rifles through them until he finds what he's looking for. Silence envelops the room. Matheson's face is red, his cheeks puffed. He stares daggers at the Magistrate, snorts, and stamps his feet. Onlookers do not know what to expect.

Robertson looks up. "Your Honor, I will describe my friend's belt based on my memory and my notes. First of all, it had a double clasp, the interior silver clasp being about 1.5" diameter. On it is a carved image of a knight in armor. I have drawn as best I can my recollection of roughly what it looks like on this piece of paper." Robertson holds it in the air and the constable retrieves it.

Everyone wants to see what Robertson has drawn.

I'm flabbergasted. This whole episode is unbelievable! Two days ago I was just another ship sailing across the world's seas. Today, I am an official floating courthouse, fascinated with all that is happening. I have a quick flashback and remember that when I had become curious about

Robertson, I saw part of an image one day, drawn on a piece of paper the Surgeon had given him. No wonder he was so secretive about the thing.

Robertson continues, "On the back of the outside clasp are the initials B.C. They are intricately engraved."

At the head of the table Mr. Simpson speaks up. "Everything you describe so far appears as you say on this belt. You have an excellent memory. Your drawing is a close approximation."

Matheson shouts from the other end of the room. "Means nothing. Hundreds of men have the initials B. C. Why even on board there is a prisoner Barry Chambers, and our gunner beside me here is Brendan Carlisle. The fact that the prisoner guesses the initials is of little importance. I have no doubt the prisoner has seen the front clasp open at some point when he's noticed me on the foredeck. I don't always close that clasp, since there's a second one."

Robertson turns and looks at the man. ""I suppose that's possible, but I'd hardly have seen the back of the second clasp would I, Mr. Matheson? As you know, I haven't had the freedom to sneak into your quarters."

For the first time in over 30 minutes, there is suppressed laughter around the table. It eases some of the tension.

Robertson continues, "I'll describe what's behind the inner clasp."

It occurs to me that there is a subtle change that has taken place. Maybe others sense it, too. Robertson no longer proceeds with a memorized description of his friend's belt. He's confident that what he has offered up so far is damning enough evidence of the belt's ownership, but he's about to make it incontrovertible.

"On the back of the inner clasp are the initials C. C. They stand for Catherine Carson, Ben's wife, who gave him the belt as a wedding gift. In this case, Mr. Magistrate, you'll notice the scratching across those initials, as my friend Ben vented his anger when his wife left him."

The Magistrate raises his eyebrows as he stares at Matheson, who says nothing.

Robertson starts to speak again, but the Magistrate raises his hand in a stop position. He speaks directly to Matheson. "Anything to say, Mr. Matheson?"

"I've wondered about those initials ever since I got the belt, Your Honor. They prove nothing."

"Anything more to add, Mr. Robertson?"

"Yes, sir. As I said, this is a special belt, given lovingly by Ben's wife to him. He was initially both angry and sad when she left him. Even though he vandalized her initials, the belt served as a lasting memory of Catherine that he refused to part with and pawn. It was to be his lone reminder of better times.

"There's another unique feature of the belt, Your Honor. Hold the front clasp out at 90 degrees and give it a hard twist clockwise so that it lays parallel to the table."

The group is surprised to see the buckle turn so, Matheson included. His mouth sags.

"Now, pull up the clasp gently. You should see a narrow slit about two inches long stretch open in the top of the leather."

"I see it. What is it – a second money slot?"

"Yes, Your Honour. I wouldn't be surprised if you pry it open and find a one-pound note. Ben carried a pound there for emergencies, unless of course Mr. Matheson stole that too, like all the money in the main pouch."

The Magistrate is handed a small knife and prises the slit open, looks inside and carefully retrieves a single -pound note. He holds it up for all to see. Matheson gapes, then hangs his head. It is clear he had no idea of the secret cache.

The Magistrate sits up tall in his seat. "Mr. Matheson, there is obviously no question that this belt belongs to Mr. Robertson's friend, Ben Carson. Mr. Robertson claims his friend was wearing it in the pub where you worked and outside of which Mr. Robertson was arrested. You have possession of the belt, which rightly belongs to Mr. Carson. It was stolen from Carson by you, or your so-called bar help, whom I suspect is imaginary. I find no alternate explanation of why you were wearing it.

"It is disturbing to learn that a man of your trusted position has been involved in a robbery, which, had it been committed by any ordinary citizen, would have resulted in incarceration. I find you guilty of robbery. If you falsely testified at Mr. Robertson's trial, then you committed perjury, as well. From what we have learned here, I suspect this is indeed the case. Mr. Robertson chased you and shot you in a perfectly understandable effort to retrieve his friend's belongings, which you stole. His actions were somewhat justified, and he should not have received the level of sentence he did."

Feet shuffle again and whispers break out, but His Honour silences them with a tiny 'shush' and a disapproving, haughty look. He pauses, confers quietly with his clerk, then stands, turns and faces Matheson directly.

"Mr. Matheson, you are sentenced to three years in prison for the robbery, and will no longer be permitted to serve in His Majesty's Navy. A government physician will examine you to determine if a bullet is lodged in your calf. Evidence of such bullet will only exacerbate your leanings to mendacity and will lengthen your sentence."

He pauses again, to let his words sink in. Despite the previous admonition, numerous conversations fire up all around the room. The other crewmen are visibly upset. Several group around Matheson, pat him sympathetically on the back, or shake his hand. Mr. Simpson turns to Captain Coubro and Admiral Sanders, clears his throat, bangs the gavel twice, silencing the room once again.

"Mr. Coubro, although Mr. Matheson is your Pilot, and could be helpful on your continued journey, he will serve his prison time here. I regret your loss, since I doubt whether a replacement Pilot is available. In light of same, Mr. Matheson will be allowed to stay aboard until tomorrow so you may confer with him on any aspects relevant to the remainder of your voyage.

"With respect to the prisoner, we recommend that this belt be given to him on arrival in Sydney, but until then he should remain with the other prisoners. My colleagues and I shall write our position in detail and provide a sealed copy for your safekeeping tomorrow. It should be presented to the authorities in Sydney since that is Mr. Robertson's official transportation destination. Court officials there will be responsible for a final judgment, but we will suggest that Mr. Robertson's conviction for shooting Mr. Matheson be reduced to two years, which period he will have served by the time you arrive in Botany Bay. Is my position clear?"

Coubro responds "Yes, Your Honor. Thank you for hearing this matter. I am much obliged."

The words convey a readily understandable sense of relief. But Coubro's eyes are downcast, and he slumps. Several of the crew head for the exit and push past him brusquely, avoiding eye contact and muttering between themselves. Their demeanor is sour, and once outside there are raised voices expressing displeasure at what has transpired. Exclamations abound. 'It's not right', 'How can a prisoner get an officer convicted?', 'What was Captain thinking?', 'Legal sham', and 'Doesn't seem fair'.

Mr. Simpson, the Magistrate, gathers his entourage but stops in front of Coubro before venturing outside. "Captain, I regret that our ruling leaves you in an awkward state of affairs. And I don't refer simply to the loss of your Pilot. Most regretfully, it is a prisoner who has brought about the unseemly result of the conviction of an officer. That will not sit well with a number of your crew who have a positive relationship with your Pilot. Those men will question the reasonableness, and certainly the justification, of trying a member of your crew halfway through your voyage."

Coubro nods in agreement. "This is certainly a unique situation, Your Honour, with an unprecedented outcome. I suspect we'll have a challenging time ahead."

"We wish you well Captain. I don't envy you your position. Adieu."

Coubro, Admiral Sanders, and the Surgeon see the visitors disembark, then retire to Coubro's cabin. The trio downs successive tumblers of whisky in silence, each lost in his own thoughts. Coubro swallows a glassful, and finally speaks, "Admiral, I am embarrassed, and I apologize. I had no idea an officer of mine was a criminal, same as the very prisoners we carry. I am responsible for my choice of officers, and I should have checked the Pilot's background more thoroughly. Makes me wonder if there are other surprises hidden among my men. My sense of judgment is shaken. I am shamed by this outcome."

Sanders hesitates before responding. "May this be a lesson we all learn from Captain. Pilot is a dishonest man. It is most regrettable that you didn't discover this before you left Portsmouth. But justice has now been served, and we must move on. Our immediate focus is to find an alternate Pilot, if at all possible."

18. *Moving On*

The atmosphere onboard in the aftermath of the unusual legal hearing is both strange and strained. Below deck the reaction to Robertson's victory is mixed. He is congratulated by most of his fellow inmates for a triumph against the civil justice system, which they all detest. He re-tells the story of the belt over and over. Yet there are some who are jealous and wonder how he received the special treatment of a second hearing. They wonder if in part he has been rewarded for passing on observations of certain ill-doings in the men's quarters. I hear guarded murmurings in dark corners.

I'm fully aware of course that there are several men who prefer other males over members of the opposite sex. Those individuals are disliked and disrespected, but left alone by the others. The homosexual men's fears of exposure are totally unfounded, as it is clear Robertson has absolutely no interest in such men. He ignores their withdrawal from group engagement and their disinterest in the details of his changed situation. He proudly holds up the image of the belt buckle he showed the Magistrate, but makes sure his notes stay steadfastly within his grasp since he doesn't know whether he'll need them again.

In Coubro's cabin it's clear from Admiral Sanders' facial twitches that he is visibly disturbed by the revelation that a common crook was serving as an officer under Coubro's command. As a realist however, he promises to check whether any of his colleagues or acquaintances in town can suggest a replacement Pilot. He leaves in haste.

Coubro downs another drink. He dismisses the Surgeon, and shakes his head in bewilderment. His fingers drum incessantly against his desk's roll-top cover. His head sags. It seems his heart is heavy with grief, his soul wrenched with embarrassment. He summons Matheson to his cabin, refusing to extend a handshake as the man comes through the doorway.

"Matheson. Why?"

The Pilot faces his Captain squarely, responds readily. "Frankly, sir, I don't remember the circumstances all that well. I do remember being shot. It hurt like hell."

"So you even lied about that. No knife wound?"

"No, sir. I had no idea the two men had a hidden revolver. Had I known, I suspect I would never have tried to steal their goods."

"But why did you go after the sack in any event?"

"I've been trying to think back to the night in question. I have a vague recollection that the prisoner's friend, Carson, called me a name, or made fun of my size, or threw some other insult at me that really irritated. The details elude me."

"So you approached Tillie to take Carson upstairs and while he was busy with her, you stole whatever you could? Clearly this wasn't a new arrangement with Tillie. That's one of the other things that bothers me. You'd done this before. You're nothing but a regular thief. I'm beyond disappointed, rather, disgusted.

"You have made a mockery of the esteem in which ships' officers are generally held. And you have embarrassed me mightily in front of the local Admiral. You've tainted my name with your behavior. I feel like placing you in shackles as an example to the others. How can a respected officer stoop so low? You are no better than the prisoners below."

Coubro shakes his head again. "I just don't understand."

"Yes, sir. I am sorry you had to learn this. I swear to you that that was the last time. Being shot scared me into changing my ways. My father

244

disowned me as a result, and refused to have me serve in his pub any more. My sister will now inherit the pub when he's gone."

"I'm sorry too Matheson. You are a damned good Pilot. I guess once you get back to England your only option will be as a Pilot on a private merchantman. You'll be shunned by the Navy, but at least you will survive."

"It won't take long to pack my things tomorrow, Captain. I will leave all the charts in my cabin, but obviously keep my sextant. I wonder how it will survive a gaol term.

"As for the next part of your voyage to Sydney, I feel I owe you a few words of advice. First, steer well south as you round the Cape, for the wind and storms there will fight you. Second, in the Indian Ocean I would head for St. Paul Island to avoid being pushed south into the iceberg fields that flow out of Antarctica. And last, I'd be doubly careful as you manage Bass Strait between the mainland and the island called Van Diemen's Land. The south-westerlies in that region blow hard if it's stormy and there are a number of small islands you need to avoid."

"I thank you for those thoughts, but wish I didn't have to remember them. Like I say, Matheson, you are a damned fine Pilot and the Navy is losing an excellent sailor. It's too bad you will never serve again.

"I'm encouraged to hear you've seen the error in your ways. But for now you must pay the price of poor choices in the past. I will not be present when you leave tomorrow.

"You have disgraced this ship and my command. Dismissed."

Matheson leaves without a backward glance. As the door closes behind him the perplexity of the situation registers even more fully with Coubro. He wrings his hands, his shoulders slump. He mutters something unintelligible. He sits momentarily, then stands and pummels his fists against the soffit above his sleeping alcove. I feel his anger.

He beats on the fine oak crosspiece and talks to me. "Well, my Lady, I'm cursed. One of my finest officers has betrayed me and embarrassed me in so doing. I've been thoroughly duped, and my reputation may suffer. We have dangerous waters to traverse still, and I am without Pilot.

"If I'd never agreed to hear Robertson's story, I'd still have a first class Pilot to help guide us. Yet his actions in the past are inexcusable."

Coubro pauses, lifts his head and addresses an unseen moral entity, for which I am a surrogate. "Probably not much different from other publicans. But he got caught. Makes me wonder how many other prisoners, both here and in gaols back home, have been falsely accused. Far too many in all likelihood. I wish I could help change that."

He searches his drink cabinet, retrieves another bottle of Scotch and pours himself a large measure. He swallows it in one continuous gulp.

"Damn the world to hell," he curses, and thumps the glass down on his desk.

* * *

I've watched the Captain and his crew for two months now. Never in that time have I seen him act in such a manner as he has over the results of the onboard inquisition. He has revealed that he is a proud man, confident in his leadership. He values highly the spirit of loyalty and togetherness he has instilled in his crew. However, in soft words spoken to himself, he worries now whether his men will grant him a continuation of their past respect.

A veritable procession of able-bodied seamen passes down the passageway by the officers' cabins to visit Matheson and wish him well. Most are stunned with the news they are digesting, knowing only the experience of being onboard with the man. Some question why the Captain even held the hearing for a convict, and blame Coubro for Pilot's demise.

Matheson must realize full well however that he is a victim of incredible coincidence. That Robertson should be on the same ship, recognize him, and then have the wherewithal to convince the Captain to hold a hearing, is a set of events of such low joint probability that it is incredible. Matheson must wonder who on earth, or on the seven seas, would have guessed that such circumstances could ever have come together as they had? He shakes his head as he bemoans his fate to his friends. He eats alone in his cabin in the evening, one of the cook's attendants hastily delivers food and avoids eye contact. Matheson starts to feel lonely as the frenzy of visitors tails off. He has a restless night.

Coubro is disconsolate. Distraught over the court's findings, distraught at losing an excellent Pilot, after supper he is rowed to the jetty and wanders the shoreline. From my anchored position I see him walk past the warehouses, chandlers, pubs, and brothels. He stops at the doorway of one of the brothels and chats with the girls, but resists temptation and saunters on. Eventually he is lost from my sight as he disappears over a small hillock on the far dunes.

* * *

The main part of town shuts down early, but harborside establishments stay open well into the early morning. Along the promenade on top of the stone levy, gas lamp flames sputter in the light breeze, casting more shadows than light. The Captain returns from his sojourn and is quickly rowed back. Both he and the oarsman are cold, their jackets fastened tightly, canvas across their knees, as the temperature has fallen, and a light mist adds to the pair's discomfort.

The Captain pours himself another glass, downs it quickly, and heads to bed.

The next morning on the dock there is much noise. Small carts pulled by horses arrive with fresh foods, most coming directly from nearby farms. The Purser is up early, checking the quality of the supplies and supervising the loading of the tenders. I hear a bleating sound across the water and on searching, spot a cart with a pen that holds four goats. Is their milk destined for first-class passengers' tea, or for pregnant convict mothers and their babies-to-be? The next cart in line contains many large barrels, probably full of fresh, or reasonably fresh, water.

Loading goes on all morning. Men from a couple of the chandleries spread across my frame. They make minor repairs, replace frayed lines, check the rigging, stitch and patch minor rips in the sails, and generally give me a good sprucing-up. A dedicated team works on the gash and the temporary repairs to the hole in my hull. They even have pre-bent planks of the right width and thickness, although their length has to be trimmed to fit. I didn't know ahead of our visit just how busy a port Cape Town is and how extensive the maritime industry is here. It's very fortunate.

About 2:30 pm a clerk from the Magistrate's office arrives, accompanied by two very stout constables. The clerk hands two envelopes to Coubro, one sealed, the other not. The sealed envelope contains the Magistrate's summary of the Robertson proceedings and, as a result of the findings, his position on actions taken, along with recommendations for future consideration. In the unsealed envelope is a copy of what has been sealed, along with a personal note to Coubro.

Matheson is sent for, and as he walks across the deck towards the two constables, shouts of "Good luck", "Chin up", "It ain't fair", and "God be with you" fill the air. A number of men have even come back early from leave to say farewell. They discount his crime since it happened well before they knew him. They respect his seamanship and are nonplussed at his departure. Some think Coubro should have challenged the Magistrate's ruling, and looked for some leeway to keep using Matheson's skills all the way to Sydney.

Matheson is grateful for the support. He acknowledges the reception by raising his cap and waving it in the air. A weak smile lights up his face. Coubro is nowhere to be seen.

At the hotel, according to messages from the runners to the bosun, the first-class passengers are busy writing letters home. A cargo ship, the *Sea Hunter*, which arrived from Sydney several days before we did, is taking on goods for its onward trip to London. It will carry many sacks of mail that contain a variety of personal, business, and official government matters. Several of the better-educated crew members have also written notes to family back home.

I'd love to have been able to see what was written in some of the passengers' letters. How much did they vilify me? How much was I to blame for the rocky paths through the storms? Why didn't I go faster to make up for the stalled days north of the equator? How much am I to blame for the structure of the rooms they are forced to exist in on board, and the leaks and creaks of passage?

I'll probably never know. I do hear stories about the passengers in the hotel of course. Runners speed between the hotel and the passengers' rooms back here onboard, the men and women and children requesting items left behind. At Coubro's insistence, the runners also provide a sense of security for the passengers, discreetly following them, watching for pickpockets and others who might try to take advantage of the tourists. Apparently, Lady Hudson-Smythe and Clarinda Finsbury, the woman whose father is a Professor of Law, have deepened their friendship. They have been seen walking the town arm-in-arm on several occasions, clearly all the earlier tension between the pair now totally removed.

Among their purchases, her Ladyship has bought a beautiful hat adorned with colorful feathers of local native birds, and Mrs. Finsbury has proudly negotiated a good price for an elaborate wooden carving of lions fighting. As a result of this new togetherness, Matilda, her Ladyship's maid, has been given extra time off. She feels closely protected when Timothy Blaine accompanies her on the streets. During a stroll through the local marketplace she admires a fur purse made of tiger skin. Apparently, on a whim, Timothy buys it for her. She protests. "I don't deserve this Mr. Blaine. It's very generous of you, and I love it." Impetuously she pecks him on the cheek. "Let's take it back to the ship for safekeeping."

I hear this from discussions between the runners later. It helps me understand Matilda's remarks to Mr. Blaine when they surprisingly come aboard. Matilda runs to her cabin and on return to the railing where Mr. Blaine waits she blurts, "Thank you again so much, sir. But I'm embarrassed, for there's no way I can buy something for you to reciprocate. I'm in your debt."

"Tell you what, Matilda. Finish your tale about why her Ladyship is on board, and I'll consider any possible debt fully paid."

A frown crosses Matilda's face, and her eyes close as she hesitates. Finally, after a lengthy pause, she reluctantly asks, "Well, where exactly did I leave off, Mr. Blaine? Had I gone upstairs to my Lady's bedroom the morning after the ball?"

"Yes. You'd discovered her missing and her clothes strewn about."

"Oh yes, I felt awful, because I had a very good idea of what was going on."

"I waited outside her room nearly 30 minutes. Finally, she appeared at the end of the hall, looking very disheveled, tiptoeing quickly from the male guest quarters. As soon as she saw me, she put her fingers across her lips for silence, although I wanted to tell her to retreat. Coming up the staircase was the Count himself, apparently looking for one of the guests he had invited. I desperately waved my hands, signaling her Ladyship to go back, but it was too late."

As Matilda paused, a furtive look in her eyes, Timothy eased her embarrassment.

"Let me guess. Her Ladyship had spent the night with the very guest her father was looking for. What was an amazing coincidence turned into a scandalous event."

"That's right, but it got far worse. The Count was regarded as very gracious and generous, highly supportive and forgiving to the people in his village. But he was a strict disciplinarian with respect to his family's behavior. He felt they should revere old-fashioned values, and practice standards that were exemplary to others. He and her Ladyship rarely spoke after the incident, as he was clearly embarrassed and disgusted by her conduct.

"Unfortunately, a month later, her Ladyship went up to London and stayed overnight again with the Count's friend. I accompanied her, of course. Somehow the Count found out about the arrangement, and it was too much for him. His anger was impossible to moderate – threw ornaments and papers around, swore as I'd never heard before. Despite pleas by the Countess, and her Ladyship herself, the Count banished her Ladyship from the estate and sent her away. That's why she's on this ship to Australia. An exile, tainted with shame, bearing

251

internal scars you and I will never fully understand. She was given a generous income and endowment, but at the moment has no idea what she will do once we arrive in Sydney.

"I should add that the Count felt betrayed by his so-called friend, and, through various means, fairly quickly forced the man's business interests into bankruptcy. The Count has powerful and influential acquaintances in government, the royal court, and industry circles that he called on. In the end her Ladyship's lover was publicly shamed and lost all standing in his former societal circles. I didn't know the Count could be so vindictive. While I love the Countess I'm glad I no longer have to live in their house.

"Now you know why I feel sorry for her Ladyship, but please, you mustn't reveal the past to anyone else. I will be in serious trouble if she ever determines I've told you all this."

Timothy puts his free hand on Matilda's shoulder. "I see how difficult it has been for you to share this story with me, Matilda., I promise it will stay with me alone."

While Matilda is a sweet, devoted young woman, she reveals naivete at times. It's just as well she doesn't see Timothy's crossed fingers behind his back.

* * *

It's now early morning, and Cape Town is coming alive. The cargo ship *Sea Hunter* should leave within the next day or so for London, so the activity around her will intensify today. She still needs a few minor repairs and more cargo waits to be loaded. As my new friend, we have shared tales about our trips here. *Sea Hunter* ran into a massive storm as it rounded the Cape of Good Hope. She was battered continually by huge waves. The gale force winds ripped her sails apart, and blew away her main mast top, down to the cross-trees. I should add that *Sea Hunter* is 10 years older than me and has seen a lot more service in all the oceans. Originally a passenger ship, she now sails much slower and carries cargo only.

The broken mast had sprung, and was fished with inferior hemp during an earlier tempest in the southern Indian Ocean. So it was no surprise when it broke completely, although the break hurt badly. *Sea Hunter* suffered from heavy bruises until three days ago when they removed the top. I can imagine how painful it must have been for her. She lost the uppermost yardarm at the same time. The Captain and Bos'n decided not to replace the whole mast, just repair what was possible. They did so yesterday afternoon as Pilot was led away to gaol. I doubt he noticed.

As *Sea Hunter's* silhouette takes form in the soft light of dawn I stifle an internal groan as I observe her damaged outline. I hope she gets a full mast replacement quickly once tied up in the London docks. Her looks are a little embarrassing right now.

Mid-morning, Admiral Sanders boards the *Sea Hunter* and spends an hour with her Captain, following up on information that the ship arrived with an extra Pilot in its crew. Sanders is clearly wondering about the second Pilot's qualifications and availability. Unfortunately, he learns what I've already been told, that the extra Pilot is a young chap and only an apprentice. He's been with the ship for several voyages acting as backup Pilot, getting on-the-job long-distance training in order to meet the requirements for a certified Pilot's commission. The plan is for him to assume the role of Pilot-in-charge on the trip to London. If successful in navigating homeward, he will be recommended for full Pilot status.

According to my new ship friend, the Admiral hoped that the *Sea Hunter's* primary Pilot might be interested in changing plans to help

Coubro out on the leg to Sydney, allowing the apprentice Pilot to manage the route back to London.

The freighter's parent company, however, requires a registered Pilot to be on board for every voyage. Two pilots are not necessary but an apprentice cannot guide the ship in foreign waters. The cargo is too valuable to risk any navigational mishaps.

The Admiral boards me to share this disappointing news with Coubro. The pair sit at a corner of the Captain's dining table and have lunch. The cook, Stephen Gateshead, carries dishes in and out and hears snatches of the men's conversation. He serves a light blancmange as the final offering and speaks hesitatingly. "Beg your pardon, sirs, but I wonder if I may speak about a possible solution."

Coubro looks up. "This hardly concerns you, Gateshead."

"Yes, sir. I apologize for the interruption. I realize I do not know all the circumstances of the issue. But.."

Coubro interrupts. "Get on with it, say your piece."

"This will sound strange, sirs, but what if Mr. Matheson were permitted to go back to London on the *Sea Hunter*, and serve his time in London rather than here. He's fully qualified as a senior Pilot and the freighter is not a naval ship, so he wouldn't violate the terms of his sentence as I understand things. He could supervise the apprentice on the return trip, and free up *Sea Hunter's* regular Pilot if that gentleman is willing to navigate us to Sydney."

The Admiral and Captain look at each other, their faces simultaneously registering embarrassment at their oversight. Coubro slaps his forehead. Recognition engenders wry smiles and the pair hurriedly push their chairs back and stand tall. Coubro speaks first. "Gateshead, that's ingenious. I can't believe we never considered the idea. Incredible!"

Sanders breaks in. He's already donning his bicorn. "Captain, you go visit the *Sea Hunter* and see what the Captain and the senior Pilot think, while I go rouse the Magistrate. As a fellow citizen, I might have a little more sway than you in convincing him to adjust Matheson's current arrangement. Let's rendezvous again at eight bells."

The pair exit, Gateshead clears the leftovers. He hums and smiles to himself. I suspect he's thinking similar thoughts to mine: 'Sometimes our leaders over-complicate things.'

* * *

Two days later we're once again under full sail. It feels wonderful to have the wind filling the canvas on high and driving us sou-sou-east then southeast to round the Cape.

Perhaps the only people unhappy to be under way again are the prisoners. The limited dose of stability and the sight of civilization that they experienced for five days lifted their spirits. But the bouts of laughter are now fewer and farther between. From overheard conversations, they are aware that the next stop is Sydney, and many have retreated into self-pity. They are only half way through their voyage, but suddenly, the second half is viewed with feelings of trepidation.

By all but Robertson of course, for whom arrival in Sydney means freedom. He's careful to contain his enthusiasm.

He thanks the Surgeon profusely for his help in convincing Coubro to hold the onboard court hearing. He muses in front of the doctor about whether he should return to England to re-engage as a teacher there, or alternately, whether Sydney might have enough attraction to encourage him to seek a position as teacher at one of the church-run schools there. He wonders how well convicts who've served their sentences are accepted in the colony. Just how real will his freedom be?

He has many long days to worry.

Contrarily to the prisoner's angst, the crew snaps to their tasks, seemingly happy to be at sea again, refreshed by the stopover and the repairs to my frame and fittings. There are still thousands of miles to go but this is the life the men have chosen. They're living it again. We have several new militia, although we have one man less than when we left Portsmouth. Even though these men are not sailors they too prefer movement and potential adventure ahead. Their demeanor is unaffected by Matheson's exit. The crew are more positive since the old Commander, Mullens, and his cronies, are gone.

At dinner on our first night after leaving port the first class passengers meet the new Pilot, Mr. Jacob Nagle. In his introduction, Coubro describes the last-minute negotiations that led to a swap of Pilot positions with the *Sea Hunter*. He praises Mr. Nagle's willingness to join us on the long eastern leg of our journey. It was late in the negotiations that Mr. Nagle revealed he had been the Pilot on a freighter to Sydney not a year before, such a valuable experience to bring to *Lady Corinth*. He'd also piloted a number of British navy ships from England to the Americas before his trips to Africa and Australia, so he has an extensive sea-going background.

Unlike Mr. Matheson, Jacob Nagle is a tall man, with a lined face, as craggy as the rocky shoreline we are passing, above his mouth he constantly fingers and preens a smooth handlebar moustache. He is less reserved than Matheson, and has a friendly, outgoing disposition, making the passengers take to him quickly.

256

"Happy to make your acquaintance," he says to the passengers, after the first course is complete. "If I can answer any of your questions about the ocean we have to cross to get to Sydney or about the town itself, I'd be happy to do so. You will find there are some primitive aspects to the colony, but it's amazing how far the place has come in 30 years."

Mr. Pennington responds first. "Perhaps tomorrow night you can elaborate a little for us Mr. Nagle. But for now, if it's not too impertinent, I'd be interested to learn why you accepted the Pilot position on *Lady Corinth*. I ask because I presume you were on your way back to Britain on the *Sea Hunter* with good reason. I'm not sure I could make such a major change on the whim of the moment. I applaud your flexibility."

"Perhaps it does seem a little strange," Jacob answers. "I was headed back to London to sell my house there, and make financial arrangements in order to move to Australia. I've become infatuated with the country, its wide-open spaces, blue sky, adventurous people and the opportunity to run my own business.

"When this opportunity on *Lady Corinth* arose, I immediately wrote and asked my brother back home to see to my affairs, since working here allows me to get back to Sydney at least eight or nine months earlier than I would have been able to otherwise. I also wrote several other letters, in a hurry, to bank managers, sales agents and certain authorities, I must admit."

Mr. Finsbury sits forward, clearly intrigued. "What sort of business are you considering in Sydney, Mr. Nagle?"

"I'd like to be involved in the shipping of freight somehow. With years of experience on cargo ships, I could run some form of cargo trade business. One option would be to set up a brokerage and warehouse to manage imports and exports. A couple of firms already exist, but I believe trade will increase between Australia and England as well as certain countries in Asia, such as China, and Batavia. Though Sydney is still a penal colony, I believe it will attract more and more free settlers like yourselves, as people back home learn of the opportunities in the new land. Newcomers will need all sorts of supplies, and most must be imported for some years yet."

Mr. Pennington joins in again. "A number of us present in this room would certainly agree with you, sir. Sounds commendable. I can see demand for all sorts of domestic and commercial building materials, and goods to make those buildings and homes attractive. But what does the country offer that will fill the holds of cargo ships when they return to England?"

"Good question, sir. There is some risk, for sure, in that respect. But last year over 60,000 sealskins were sent to London. Seal fur and elephant-seal oil is in demand in both China and England. As well, very productive farms are already established outside Sydney. If we can solve the preservation problem, food exports represent major potential. Grain is one commodity I think will increase in volume. The same with wool. I understand a new strain of Spanish Merino sheep produces super fine wool which is attracting attention in the mills in northern England."

"What other options have you thought about, sir?" Mrs. Pennington asks.

"Well, the one at the top of my list is to own a medium sized cargo vessel with optional accommodations for passengers. You may already know that in Australia there's another town besides Sydney that is starting to receive convicts. A place called Hobart, in Van Diemen's Land.

"At one time, there was a settlement at Port Phillip, way south of Sydney on the northern shore of Bass Strait, but it was abandoned 12 years ago. Similarly, there was once a penal colony on Norfolk Island, 1,000 miles northeast of Sydney. There's talk that these settlements may one day come back. In any event, there'll be more coastal towns that spring up in the years ahead as explorers find new places with appropriate resources supportive of population growth. Both people and goods will need to be transported by sea between towns. As these places grow, along with towns on navigable rivers, trade between them is inevitable, and shipping will be the only viable conveyance for years to come.

"I don't have the funds to buy a ship outright, but possibly I could be master of one that is owned by the same company that owns *Sea Hunter*. Or perhaps there is a local consortium of businessmen in Sydney who would want to invest in a ship along with me."

Timothy Blaine has been sitting quietly, but now leans forward with obvious interest. "Your thoughts parallel those of the principals of my bank back in London, Mr. Nagle. I represent their desires to invest in commercial enterprises in Sydney. Perhaps we can talk further about your goals and needs. I'd be happy to be of assistance."

Mr. Nagle's comments make me wonder about my role in the future. Once I deliver the convicts and passengers to Sydney what will I do? Return to England with a load of grain, or something else? I don't even know what options might exist. I conclude that I will listen to Mr. Nagle as often as possible in case he offers other useful information.

Moving away from business interests, he warns the passengers that rounding the Cape will be far from a smooth ride. They should be prepared to hunker down in their cabins for at least half a day while we transition from the Atlantic to the Indian Ocean. He avoids mention of the wild storm *Sea Hunter* just experienced, probably in order not to scare the passengers unduly.

He warns that it will get very cold as we travel east and strike the currents from Antarctica, so that everyone should dig out warm, woolen clothes in anticipation. He wonders out loud who will so inform the prisoners. His interest in their well-being is widely noted by the listeners and Dr. Crisp immediately asks Jacob to accompany him so they can jointly deliver the information below deck.

One gossipy side-note from dinner is the amicable relationship between Lady Hudson-Smythe and Mrs. Finsbury.

The latter tells everyone that she has agreed to help her Ladyship write her book about sailors. Moreover, the pair conducted their first interviews with two seamen the previous day. One man was well-seasoned, the other on his first voyage. With genuine intrigue, the group encourages her Ladyship to read aloud the first few paragraphs she's written with Clarinda's input and advice. Her Ladyship has Matilda retrieve the diary from her mistress' cabin.

> 'Sailors do not live in the present, but in anticipation of the journey's end, and the satisfaction of a job well done. The most important topics of their conversations are the strength and direction of the wind, and how soon they will reach their destination. The greatest pleasure of a voyage is its end, for the cry of Land Ho! is always heard with joy. Even so, many have such a fond disposition for their profession that they would go to sea the next day again.
>
> Although it is not the sea itself that attracts them, other than providing the connection to other countries. The sight of a foreign land or town for the first 24 hours is enchanting. But no such sight is cheaply purchased

given the long imprisonment at sea. And even when all lands have been seen, there is none like home!

Those who go to sea face many deprivations and are rewarded mainly by long-lasting relationships and camaraderie with fellow seamen. All suffer the noise of constant creaks of the masts and bulkheads, plus the crack of sails whipped by the winds high above. Better if their noses are plugged, for the odors on older ships from cramped quarters, tobacco smoke, and stale provisions are far from agreeable. One must like the taste of fish or be doomed, and have the ability to climb rigging like a monkey with no fear of heights.

A sailor's best companions are warm sunshine, the breeze in his hair and a mug full of rum. He is a creature rewarded more by solitude than is his peer on land, and is a fierce protector of his way of life, so be careful in initiating any criticism of same. He is wiry, tough, and stronger than you may realize, for he easily carries barrels of food on his shoulder, and pushes on the capstan as hard as any man can.

Except in very rare situations he is also intensely loyal. Do not disparage the officers he serves if you value your pretty face. And do not snitch on behavior you may not condone. Able seamen constitute a brotherhood of proud men. One must earn their respect to be invited to join them. Tread carefully.'

Gentle applause greets the end of the reading, although I notice Mr. Blaine does not join in. Her Ladyship beams with delight and explains that the next section will deal with loyalty and more detail on the rewards and values that keep men sailing. She's clearly pleased with her audience's reaction.

I watched Mrs. Finsbury's face closely throughout the reading. Despite her best intentions, there were several instances where her lips tightened almost imperceptibly, and her nostrils flared a miniscule. These tiny qualms made me wonder if she actually had had much influence on the story, for it seemed to be written in a somewhat rambling fashion that I wouldn't have expected from a Professor's daughter.

Maybe she and Mr. Blaine have some reservations in common. Or perhaps, given what he knows about her Ladyship's past, he's concerned about the two ladies' relationship?

* * *

As time passes I notice Coubro's officers grant their new Pilot a grudging respect. He has an easy-going style, laughing off any slightly contentious remarks made to him, never criticizing, and is very positive about the charts Matheson left behind.

Captain Coubro has confided in the Surgeon that he is apprehensive about the new Pilot due to the *Sea Hunter's* loss of topmast and sails during the storm they encountered at the Cape. Similarly, I'm hesitant about the man. Will his orders to hands at the helm be as sure as Mr. Matheson's? Will his voice of command be equally decisive whenever he sets a new course or trims the sails? Will he deal as effectively with the Bos'n as with the Captain? *Sea Hunter* assured me before she departed that I would have no worries. Even so I wait anxiously to see how Pilot will handle the first challenges to be thrown at us.

Coubro stands beside Mr. Nagle at the helm the whole 10 hours of wild pitching and rolling as we push through the Cape's heavy seas. The ride makes it difficult for all on board to sleep. Coubro permits himself no rest, except for short visits to his cabin for a nip of rum to warm his insides. He carries a small flask back for the Pilot each time.

Two months sailing on the turbulent Atlantic Ocean has conditioned everyone on board to feel more confident in high shrieking winds and stormy seas. They are almost inured to the consequent perturbations of my apparent instability. Prisoners and passengers alike cringe, but are stoic in their tolerance of the things they cannot change.

I am their safe harbor, of course, so I work hard to minimize the impact of heavy waves on my bow and hull. This region of the southern seas is strange. There's little pattern to the wind and waves. With no islands in the way for thousands of miles to temper their onslaught, the Roaring Forties drive cold currents north from Antarctica. Just as I think I've deciphered the sea's behavior, the elements throw a new wind direction or wave height at me. The helmsman and I constantly double-guess what the sea gods have in store for us. All we can do is react to the thrust of each wave, take it on fore or aft quarter, and square away into the trenches between waves so we neither broach nor run bow-down too deep into the trough.

I give the new Pilot, Mr. Nagle, credit, for his orders on steering and sail handling are firm and timely. I like the way he responds quickly to changing conditions. Sometimes a driving sleet attacks us as the heavy clouds drop lower and fling their wind and stinging spray our way. It's a wild ride, and there's a collective sigh of relief when waves start to smooth out, and random gusts of wind abate, leaving a strong, steady breeze in their wake. The moon shines through cracks in the overcast, and once in a while enough bright stars appear through the gloom for the Captain to fix our position accurately enough to maintain the proper course.

As dawn breaks and calmer seas greet us, Nagle calls the crew to unfurl reefed sails, turns a few degrees north of east and targets St. Paul and Amsterdam islands more than 3,000 miles ahead.

The crew quickly acknowledge a sharp drop in the outside temperature, and most add a layer of clothing accompanied by disparaging language about the "damned Roaring Forties." I expect the passengers and prisoners will soon wake and respond similarly making use of the extra blankets Coubro has ordered distributed.

We face a long, unappealing path ahead, fraught with danger from strong, biting cold winds and massive random itinerant icebergs set adrift in freezing waters. Tough conditions we've not faced before will test us all.

19.   *Cold*

The distance between the Cape of Good Hope and Sydney is about six thousand miles across the bleak reaches of the southern Indian Ocean. For some unknown reason, almost exactly half way along our route, God has planted two tiny islands which we are now approaching. Despite initial wary expectations, we've been pleasantly surprised and fortunate to have had the initial cold, gusty westerlies replaced by strong, favorable winds which have driven us forward at a healthy clip under wonderfully clear skies. I hear Nagle warn the sailors not to get complacent, that conditions can get much worse. Pessimist!

Coubro has shared his limited knowledge about the islands with his officers, and I've been listening.

The history of these islands is shrouded in uncertainty as few explorers have written about visits there. The Dutch were probably the first to discover and name Amsterdam Island in the seventeenth century, while the French gave St. Paul Island, 50 miles to the south, its name a century later. This more southerly island boasts a peak which rises 1,618 feet, and supposedly can be seen from 60 miles away on a clear day.

Sailors off-duty scan the horizon hoping to be the first to sight the small mountain.

These islands are incredibly remote and their existence in the middle of nowhere is a surprise, welcomed by captains. Their latitude and longitude have been duly certified over time. This provides a check on the accuracy of navigational instruments and calculations used on ships sailing between the Cape of Good Hope and China, or the Cape and Australia.

St. Paul is actually the top of an inactive volcano, rocky, with steep cliffs on the east side. The most recent information Coubro had access to is from 1796, 20 years ago, and indicates the thin stretch of rock that used to close off the crater collapsed maybe 30 years before that. The sea was then admitted through a three-hundred-and-thirty-foot-wide channel only a few meters deep. Coubro is a curious man, and wants to anchor outside the inlet then go ashore and experience the active thermal springs around the crater's edge.

The lookout sights the peaks of St. Paul Island about 20 miles out and we carefully sail three miles eastward along the southern coast then turn northwest along the east coast, and anchor in 15 fathoms directly opposite the opening to the caldera*. Sailors, passengers, and prisoners alike spend time viewing the unusual coastal formation.

At dinner Coubro has a surprise announcement for his passengers.

"Tomorrow I will take two longboats to the entrance of the lagoon and hunt for rock lobsters. I will have room for two men, if any of you would like to join us. You will get wet, but I can provide oilskins that will protect you a little. We shall wait until low tide which should be just past the lunch hour, as best we have determined. Anyone willing to risk a dunking? This is a unique place, nothing like it known elsewhere."

Timothy Blaine almost yells his interest. "I'll go. I don't mind if I get wet. This will be terrific."

"Count me in," says Tristan Finsbury. "I've never seen live lobsters. But I've heard that rock lobsters are smaller than regular lobsters."

His wife, Clarinda, looks at him with concern. "Are you sure sweetheart? I never thought of you as the fisherman type."

"No, but just think. I'll be able to tell people I helped catch lobsters in the middle of the Indian Ocean. How many people in the world will be able to say that?"

The new Pilot, Jacob Nagle, speaks up. "Not only catch them, but maybe cook them as well. You see, right by the rocks marking the entrance, there are volcanic vents. If the tide is low enough, you'll be able to hold the lobsters in a net over the bubbles and at least turn them red. The cooks will finish preparing them back on board. The lobsters are small, but delicious. We might all get a small portion depending how many are caught."

Heads turn at Nagle's revelation. This man has been here before! Why didn't he say so? I wonder whether he's added to Coubro's initial source of information. No matter, the passengers are intrigued.

Next day at about 1:30pm, the longboats leave my side and make their way swiftly to the caldera. I am anchored no more than 50 yards away so those who crowd the railing can see everything clearly with the naked eye. The longboats pull in at opposite sides of the lagoon entrance, and carefully tie up to the rocks. One of the sailors immediately dives overboard, and swims towards the middle of the entrance where he is able to stand with his chin just above water. The day is cold, but presumably the water there is warm. He swims back to the rocky ledge indicating to us by waving his arms and ducking his head that some lobsters are apparently suspended just below the surface, others hiding in crevices above the water line.

Most of the sailors remove their caps and take off their jackets, so they must not be uncomfortable. More slip overboard, while others climb the rocks. The water at the rim is much shallower than expected. Whenever a crewman catches a lobster he holds it aloft and we can make it out in his hand. The claws protrude at one end of his fist, the

267

tail at the other, each section extending three or more inches out from the fingers curled around the animal's body.

Timothy Blaine is definitely an adventurous chap, for he dives in and brings a lobster to the surface that he finds several feet underwater. He hands it to Coubro. Dear old Finsbury stays in his longboat the whole time, placing the lobsters in pails of water as they are handed to him. The pickings are easy, although the south side seems to yield the creatures more readily than the north.

In an hour's time, the 10 men gather 35 of the critters and decide that is enough. They 've had fun chasing them across the rocks and picking them up with their bare hands. On the inside of the southern breakwater, near the open end, the men find one of the proverbial hot springs mentioned by Mr. Nagle. They report later that they could see other streams of bubbles rising to the surface in spots that were too deep to stand. The water is warm around the vent holes, and quite hot right at the sand level, but not hot enough to cook anything. With grins on their faces, and pails full of splashing lobsters, the men row back and happily show their prizes to everyone on deck.

Dinner that night is a treat for the passengers and officers.

* * *

A week later, smiles on the faces of officers and crew are gone, replaced by creases in their cheeks and furrows in their brows. After we left St. Paul, the westerly wind picked up much more strongly than before with serious gusts driving us. Two days out it turned from westerly to north-westerly. As hard as we tried to maintain an easterly bearing we were driven more to the south than east, contrary to our wishes.

The next landmark on our journey was to have been Cape Leeuwin, Australia. Perhaps 'landmark' isn't the right term, because our planned course would have taken us some 400 miles south of the most southwesterly point on the Australian continent. And in actuality we're far south of that planned mark.

The barometer has been falling for over a week as we now enter the Southern Ocean. Yesterday I felt the stinging needles of an ice-cloud pound the starboard hull and assault the sails. Thank heavens none of them ripped. These new lightweight sails the Admiral gave us back in Portsmouth have made my life easier. Very strong, as required, but since they weigh less, the winds blow us faster across the ocean, which is why in recent days we made over 200 miles. I've never traveled that distance in 24 hours before.

It's much, much colder 1500 miles southeast of St. Paul Island. Many of the crew wear scarves wrapped around their faces, tucked into their caps or jackets. A few sport tattered gloves but most have raw hands which stay in pants or jacket pockets until needed. The lookouts change every two hours to avoid freezing in spot. Pipe smoke is welcomed in the crew quarters as it helps add a little heat.

The prisoners complain heavily about the cold. There are no fireplaces to provide warmth below deck. Indeed, it's dangerous to have a fire anywhere on board. I've seen wrecks that show gaping holes in scorched, blackened hulls. Fire leaves its mark readily. The cooking fires in the galley are risky enough but the men who work there are trained to manage them tightly. The heat that rises to the ceiling is piped off to the passenger and officer cabins.

The extra blankets that were distributed to prisoners are held around shoulders even in the middle of the day. Men and women huddle together for extra warmth. Coughs are prevalent. A few blankets have been stolen, but are flushed out quickly and the thieves admonished, receiving fewer rations than normal for several days afterwards. Hot food is very popular.

Despite the fact that the passengers are well supplied with heat in their cabins, they still complain, as the lounge and dining room aren't heated to the same degree. Everyone wears woolen clothes to dinner, often several layers. Sara Goldsmith seems affected more strongly than others. Ten days after leaving St. Paul Island she voices her views yet one more time to the Captain.

"sir, is there no way to make the heat more even? I'd be very happy to have a lower temperature in my cabin and a higher temperature here. Couldn't the engineer partially block the heat transfer pipes to our rooms, so more heat is sent to the lounges?"

Knowing the Captain as I do, he must be grimacing internally. Keeping a straight face he responds. "I've had Mr. Plunkett check exactly that possibility Mrs. Goldsmith. It's an excellent suggestion. Unfortunately, because of the pipe design it wouldn't really help. I'm afraid you will all have to wear sweaters or light jackets to dinner while we make sure the servings are as hot as possible. What did you think of the hot tomato soup with spices this evening?"

"Wonderful, very tasty, and..."

The outer door bursts open and the messenger of the watch rushes in, cutting off Sara's response. He's red in the face from the cold and breathlessly stumbles over his words. "I do apologize Captain and everyone else, but we've just observed an iceberg a couple of miles away off the starboard bow, and thought you all might like to see it."

Lady Hudson-Smythe turns to Matilda. "Get my full-length fur coat and meet me at the door to the deck."

'Good idea', 'We should do the same', and similar comments are heard around the table as everyone stands. Formality is thrown to the wind as officers join the passengers in their excitement to see the monster from Antarctica.

The wind out of the north has driven us farther south towards Antarctic waters than anticipated. The last place I want to be is among icebergs, waiting for them to rip my hull apart. The currents run northward, though their strength is far less than that of the winds. My bow dips and heaves, throwing spray half my length. I hate these kind of seas, and I hate icebergs, even though I've not been among them before. I've heard too many stories of their size and might, the terror they conjure at a distance, and the fatal damage up close.

Paying passengers are on deck, while the prisoners below on the starboard side rush to the portholes to get a glimpse of the towering berg two miles distant. They 'ooh' and 'aah' when they view something they'd only ever heard about in stories. If only they could see what I can see; the frightening, dangerous, and massive size of the underwater portion of the icy behemoth. I want to stay far away from the deadly monster and any of its cousins.

Coubro calls an emergency meeting of his officers in the messroom.

"Men, for those of you with no knowledge of icebergs, let me assure you that the only good iceberg is one you can just see 10 miles away. They present an imposing sight but they are incredibly dangerous to navigation. Hidden beneath the waves is nine times what you see above the waves. Much greater in width and length, colder, stronger, deadly. I want you to double our lookouts, particularly at night. Ships have died here. I do not wish to join them."

Conway, the Boatswain, is one of many who have not seen the icy monsters previously. He speaks up. "'Cor, that's mammoth. Seems a long way away, Cap'n. Won't the winds blow it away from us?"

"Possibly, but where there's one there's usually more. We take no chances. Trust me."

Our Pilot, Nagle, nods his head in agreement. "We are already sailing very close to the wind, but I'll instruct the helmsmen to pinch as high as we can without luffing."

"Do it!"

"What else?" Plunkett, the quartermaster, asks.

"Rotate the lookouts every hour so no one falls asleep."

"Doubt that will happen, Cap'n. It's freezing out there. Ice is forming on the lines and rails."

"No matter. Extra coats for everyone on watch. It'll be a long night. Don't fail me. I'll be with Pilot on the Quarterdeck tonight. Dismissed."

I feel better listening to the discussion. Nagle and Coubro have boosted my confidence. The terrible tales by those who survived disasters due to icebergs are enough to make my timbers feel weak.

More icebergs are sighted the next morning in the distance, and a fine mist settles over us, limiting visibility to about half a mile. A couple of old-timers amongst the crew wager that the mist will become more like a heavy fog, a possible prelude to ice showers. They are right. Conditions worsen dramatically by late afternoon. The fog surrounds us, ominous in its cloak of limited vision, and tiny pellets of ice rip at the sails, beat on the hull, and sting any bare skin in their path. Ice builds on deck planks and sailors move extra carefully across the slippery surfaces. I overhear multiple conversations concerned at the lack of visibility and the deteriorating conditions. The rigging is thickening and becoming more dangerous to climb. Coubro takes in sails to avoid them freezing, and to slow our pace so we can better avoid a surprise iceberg. New crew members heed advice dispensed by wizened old hands.

Twilight descends early. We struggle on blindly, like a ghost-ship, moving from one dark space to another, casting no shadow, leaving only a small wake behind. Nagle and the helmsmen have been successful in re-setting our course as the winds fall away. Everyone breathes a little easier, although I think it's too early to relax. As the dark of night dominates, the lanterns along the deck produce small circles of light that illuminate the ice pellets that fly almost horizontally before the wind. We grope forward slowly, anxious to get past the trailing edge of the storm.

Nagle tests Coubro's resolve.

"Should we heave-to, sir, and wait?"

"No, all our observations earlier in the day show us well clear of any obstacles ahead. We should be fine. Keep on."

Men on watch in the chains and at the bowsprit are nervous. They stamp their feet, call out "all clear", and sing shanties to stay alert and awake. Coubro spends time with them, encouraging them with his presence.

We proceed this way throughout the evening hours. Just before midnight, the wind increases slightly and the ice rain and fog disappear. For a few minutes the world is clear, stars appear, and the moon reflects off the small wave-tops. But just as the mugs of welcome hot coffee are passed around, the wind drops and the fog descends once again, far thicker and more oppressive than before. It lies in sheets along the deck, so encompassing that one cannot see from bow to stern or from deck to crows' nest.

Stunned by the rapid change in conditions, Nagle asks again about heaving-to. Coubro orders more sails furled to cut speed, determined to maintain steerage way. Shanties and forced camaraderie disappear. All those on duty peer into the eerie grey, concentrating on detecting anything unusual or any foreign movement. The men are edgy and scared, so conversations are cut short or disparaged quickly. Two hours past midnight, Coubro orders a change of watch, and replaces coffee for those standing down with cups of steaming hot rum. Fresh and warm sailors are ordered to the bowsprit.

The hours wear on without change. This fog is cold, wet, choking, and blinding. Men on watch curse, rub their eyes repeatedly, stamp up and down, swing their arms around their chests, grab the rail then back off. Small movements are designed to keep the blood circulating and to avoid falling asleep, or freezing in place. The only sound beyond their grunts is the gentle swish of waves along my hull.

Suddenly, a watcher at the bowsprit yells "Iceberg! Two points on starboard bow. Hard to port."

A voice from the starboard bow adds, "90 yards, passing towards starboard quarter." A giant white set of icy cliffs looms out of the darkness, the top unseen, shrouded in fog. Below the water line I see its lethal teeth not 60 feet from my hull. I hold my breath.

Men spring into action. Coubro directs the helmsmen to turn five degrees to port. The sails shudder as we pinch our wind.

On deck the northern edges of the floating precipices fill our view. I watch below the surface as my keel passes within 40 feet of the monster's underwater base. I know we're safe, but on deck every man listens in absolute quiet, holding his breath, hoping not to hear any crunching sounds emanating from below.

We survive, barely. There's no celebrating however, just a few whispers of relief. The crew knows there's no rest ahead. No one knows if this is a rogue berg, or one of many in a flotilla barring our way forward.

I'm annoyed and concerned, as somehow I missed that the berg we just eluded was so close. No leviathans of the deep warned me it was coming and I guess its silent approach was something totally undetectable. No wonder icebergs have such ugly reputations.

Everyone is apprehensive, scared by the near collision and anxious about proceeding. Only when the sky begins to lighten and the fog thins do the tensions start to ease.

We sail on, slowly, carefully.

* * *

During the night conditions worsen again. For many long, dangerous hours, a dark cloak enfolds us. But shortly after seven bells the morning lookout yells down that he sees a patch of blue sky through the mist. His words spread and provide hope that our miserable iceberg ordeal will soon end. Indeed, forty minutes later, the sky opens, and suddenly we are bathed in bright light. This transformation is incredible. The crew can see miles ahead. No shiny Antarctic ice mountains in sight. Cheers run the length of my frame. It's as if God has plucked us out of this maelstrom on the high seas and placed us in a quiet backwater filled with brilliant sunshine. Coubro makes personal visits to the crows' nest men and those who manned the starboard railing and the bowsprit during the night to praise and thank them.

Sailors have a hard life. It's amazing how a kind word from someone high in authority can sustain a man's commitment and morale. Coubro is good at providing it. And it helps his relationship with the officers who disliked the fact that he had Mr. Matheson arrested, making them wonder where they all stood with their Captain. Watch by watch their respect is returning to its prior status.

For the next six days we bask in pleasant conditions. The breeze is strong and consistent, the skies blue, and there are no significant waves to speak of. It is still cold, but noticeably warmer than during our time in the ice field. Sunshine, even when penetrating cold air, is far more comforting than overcast skies. The deck planks absorb the warmth and slowly transfer it deeper into the hull. Everyone's mood is enhanced. The icebergs are miles behind to the southwest, although sometimes they yield a glint off pyramidal peaks.

I've adopted a nice rhythm with the sea, enjoying long, smooth stretches between rise and fall of swells no more than a foot and a half in height. It allows everyone on board to settle into a relaxed, humdrum, easy-going day-to-day repeatable pattern of existence.

We are nearly a hundred miles south of the concave coastline of southern Australia, slowly forging an east-nor-east route moving us closer to land every day. The Southern Ocean here abounds with new varieties of fish. Dinners of snapper and whiting have been a treat for officers, passengers, and convicts alike.

Late one afternoon the lookout sights two large whales off the port side. Word circulates through the ship with amazing speed. It doesn't take long for all the passengers and off-duty crew to line the portside rails. Prisoners crowd the portholes. I take on a slight port list.

The Watch Officer has already ordered some of the top sails furled in order to match the whales' speed as they forge eastward. The lookout up in the crow's nest calls out that there are more whales a half-mile to the south. The whales near the ship are huge, although one is much longer than the other. The onlookers chatter among themselves and presume these two are a mother and calf.

Mr. Nagle takes charge from the Watch Officer and directs the helmsman to within 40 yards of the pair. He returns control to the Watch Officer and heads forward to the passenger group. It turns out he's seen whales on previous trips and has read extensively about them. He's an avid enthusiast and shares his knowledge.

"Those are blue whales," he tells the crowd. He pulls a cap tighter over his hair and continues. "Their shape is much thinner and sleeker than other whales. I think they must be feeding because they can go much faster than our ship if they want to, but they slow down to swallow tons of small krill. They take in a huge mouthful of water then push it out through their baleen, which trap the krill inside. It's strange that these huge creatures dine on such tiny crustaceans."

Mr. Pennington turns and asks, "Just how big do these creatures get? Presumably that's a mother and child. The parent is huge."

"Well, let's see, our ship is 150 feet, bow to stern. The larger one is almost directly alongside now and it looks to me like she stretches well back past our main mast, so she must be close to 100 feet long. That's essentially full size, and at that length she probably weighs over 90 tons. Although I must admit, I've always been amused wondering how scientists ever measured such a colossal weight. Are there cranes that can lift that much? Maybe in railway engineering shops. Did they take a locomotive crane down to some beach and weigh a dead whale?"

Just as Jacob finishes his little spiel, the larger whale sends two giant spouts 30 feet into the air. A few watchers applaud. It's clear that many realize this sighting is a rare treat.

Clarinda Finsbury addresses Jacob. "Aren't there supposed to be Sperm whales in this semi-Antarctic region as well? I thought I read they were pretty big too."

"As I understand it, Madam, while the Sperm whale is the largest of the toothed whale species it's only about half the length of the blue whale. There is another big whale called the Fin whale which can grow to 90 feet, and both Fins and Sperms are indeed found in these southern waters. But this Blue we are watching right now is the Daddy, probably Mommy, of them all for size."

It's Timothy Blaine's turn. "You know a lot about sailing in this part of the world, sir. From Cape Town to St. Paul and Amsterdam islands to the whales and the weather. Plus you have spent time in the new colony. You also have a penchant for passing on information in an easy to understand form. Have you considered writing a book of your experiences?"

"Well, thank you for those kind comments, Mr. Blaine. I like learning about new things and am happy to share what I learn with others, if they are interested. But writing a book? Not for me. It would be a major effort of time, and my penmanship is very poor. I'm a sailor, not an author."

"But you have so much to share and such a pleasant way with descriptions. You have a talent you haven't recognized, sir. Think of the hundreds, maybe thousands, of people who could learn from your stories."

"Thank you again, Mr. Blaine. You make me hesitate. I admit it would be fun to write what I know in a book, for my own memory as much as for others to read. In any event, I have no paper on which to record any writing. If I had the right material this would be a great time to start, as there are many miles to go before we reach Bass Strait."

"I have a huge empty ledger I'd be happy to give you Mr. Nagle. It has a set of columns on each page but you could easily ignore those. And I have a fine pen and some ink as well. And if it would help, perhaps on occasion I could do some of the actual writing for you while you dictate what you want to say."

"I can hardly say 'no' to your persistence, Mr. Blaine. That's a generous offer."

"Well then. That's done." Timothy drops his voice. "And I have no doubt you will be a much finer writer than her Ladyship. Oh dear, she does so struggle."

"Thank you. I will do my best. I heard you were becalmed north of the equator. If you will describe the conditions of that period and the effect on everyone, I will also add that to the book.

"You see, I am a student of ships like this. Some survive storms and weird conditions, some don't. It's a combination of the ship's sea-worthiness and build, plus the captain's skill, versus the ferocity of the wind, temperature and waves. I know the tale of one ship wrecked by storm on the southeastern Australian coast. There were a few survivors and their story was published, but many ships perish without knowledge gained of the reasons for their demise."

"I'd be delighted to tell you of any of the events along our way, sir. I'm sure many parallel those you've experienced, though I can only recount things from a passenger's perspective. I suggest the prisoners may have slightly different versions of tales to tell."

"I understand. I'm sure I can find a source for below-deck happenings, and I may include some of those as well. My recent sailings were all on cargomen. I'm intrigued with how convicts, male and female, survive the arrangements made for them. This particular group seems more adaptable and well-behaved than other convict groups I've heard about."

"The convicts have provoked little discussion in our lounge and dining room circles this whole journey, so I cannot add much. Some do seem less inhibited than others, as I have seen a few dancing naked in the rain and offering boisterous support in the swimming races the sailors put on near the equator."

"You mean, the Captain has let them on deck at the same time as you passengers are present? He must have unusual skills and feelings. I must admit I like what I've learned so far. You and I will spend quite a bit of time together, my friend. I hope I may call you that?"

"By all means. And please make it Timothy. I'm not good at standing on ceremony."

"Fine, I'm Jacob. Now let's get inside and find that blank ledger you mention."

A few hardy souls remain pinned to the railing to watch the whales, but the majority head back to their cabins.

At dinner the whales dominate the discussion. Matilda is like a small child. "I've never seen anything so huge. Must be bigger than the dinosaurs we hear about. To think that that small whale was a baby. It was huge too. 'Alf the length of the mother. I can't imagine being a sailor in a small rowboat going near those things and using a harpoon on them. I'd be scared out of me clothes, that's for sure."

"Matilda!" her Ladyship cries with an admonishing tone. "Decorum, please. Your clothes should never leave your body on any occasion in public. That will be all."

Matilda giggles, waits in expectation for further rebuke, and Timothy Blaine coughs into his hands.

Several of the other women furrow their brows, and the group disperses as if her Ladyship's command applies to them all.

Her Ladyship lingers so that she's the last to leave. As she passes the Captain she puts a hand on his shoulder and asks, "May I come to your cabin in a while to discuss how you manage command of all the seamen aboard? For my book?"

* * *

The knock on Coubro's cabin door is faint, but he calls "Enter," and is not surprised when Lady Hudson-Smythe appears, no doubt somewhat later in the evening than he had expected. She stumbles as she steps over the threshold, but catches herself before falling. Coubro steps forward to help but draws up short, taken aback as he realizes her hair is teased up, and she's wearing a flannel nightdress and fur-lined slippers, with a pretty woolen robe tied loosely about her frame. The ensemble seems unbefitting for the interview he anticipated, and his furrowed brows indicate he is suspicious of something amiss.

The lady's eyes light up at the bottle of port and glasses on the Captain's desk, and she makes a beeline for them, picking up the bottle and slurring, "May I share thith with you, Captain?"

By the look on his face, revelation arrives instantly for Coubro as he frowns. Her Ladyship is totally besotted! Based on her speech, instability, and dress, she has been drinking in her own cabin before arriving.

Did she suddenly remember her request to meet, or is her expectation of receiving encouraging input from Coubro so low that she has to fortify herself in order to interview him? Given her state, he is probably wondering how productive the interview will be.

Coubro smiles, somewhat amused, and says nothing as the woman pours a healthy dose of heavy port for herself, wanders across the cabin, and sits on the edge of his built-in bed. She nearly slides off, but one hand catches the wooden side framework as she takes a large gulp from the glass in her other hand.

Coubro asks, "Did you bring materials to take notes, Madam?"

"Ah, I didn't. I thought if we had a nishe little chat I'd be able to write down the important thinggs I learned in the mornink."

"Well, I can certainly provide you with paper and pencil. I'm sure your recall tomorrow will be much sharper with a few notes." Coubro retrieves writing materials from his desk and lays them on his small table. "Here you go."

Her Ladyship's focus seems elsewhere. "You knoww, Captain, it's much hotter in here than in my cabin. Would you mind if I loosen my robe? It's one of my prettiest. Do you like it?"

Captains are often targets for female companionship and intimacy at sea. The authority, the uniform, the leadership qualities, and the grooming, can be appealing to certain feminine whims. I've witnessed engagements many times over the years.

Here we go again, I tell myself.

I suspect Coubro has been the recipient of both subtle and blatant approaches by ladies many times. Surely he confirms pre-formed suspicions that right now he can forget about any interview. Obviously, a completely different need is coming his way, in a surprisingly less refined manner than he would have anticipated. I perceive as he backs away from her Ladyship that he's not ready to engage intimately with her.

"Your gown is very nice, m'dear, but there's no need to undo anything. I will simply close the heating vent beneath the bed and it should cool down immediately."

He reaches down and shuts the damper. "Now you should be more comfortable. Would you like to sit at the table?"

Lady Hudson-Smythe hasn't moved except to reach up and start twisting several loose ends of her hair. Perhaps it's a sign of frustration at Coubro's responses or a nervousness that is contrary to her behavior at the dining table. Makes me wonder if the displays in the dining room are false bravado and airs. She sips more port.

"No, please sit beside me, Captain. You will be able to appreciate the fine embroidery on both my robe and nightdress better. And you'll notice how my tailor has fitted me perfectly."

Ignoring Coubro's earlier suggestion, she starts removing her robe. Coubro doesn't move to help but in an obvious attempt not to be rude, he confides "Your nightgown certainly shows your charming figure well, Madam."

"Ooh, thachts so nice off you to say. Other men haf found me attractive."

"Well, you definitely have wonderful offerings in front of you. I can see easily."

"Oh, you are such a smooj talker Captain. I musht admit you look verrry handsome in your uniform. But aren't you hot too? I like looking at it, but you'd be cooler and more relaxed if you took it orff. I'm sure it covers a fine physique. Can I see?"

"I'm used to wearing my uniform night and day. It only comes off when I sleep."

With surprising agility Lady Hudson-Smythe slips off the bed, takes two steps towards Coubro, puts her glass on the table, and starts unbuttoning his jacket. "I still feel hot, Captain, and I'm sure you must also."

Instead of retreating or pushing her hands away, Coubro stands mute. His lack of decisive action surprises and upsets me. Has he succumbed to her Ladyship's wiles? Is he thinking "may as well take what is offered?"

As articles of his uniform are removed, he smiles into her face and says, "Since we are being so friendly, may I address you by your first name, your Ladyship? From the passenger manifest I know it to be Mary. Such a lovely Christian name. And you may call me Daniel in here if you want."

I watch, amused, yet at the same time apprehensive. He now seems to be encouraging her, playing into her game. Could he be biding his time, looking for a gentlemanly way out of the emerging situation? I'm far from certain. My apprehension turns into anxiety.

"That would be so nice, Daniel. Sometimes I get zo lonely practicing proper relationships of the upper class. My, you haf a very athletic figure, sir. And I see very interesting mounds in places."

It's at this stage that my conscience (well, as close to that human aspect as I can come,) kicks in.

There's no question where things are headed, and I feel a strong loyalty to my Captain, who has a fine reputation to preserve. I don't want it sullied. I have no doubt he is unaware of the full story behind Mary's presence on board, but if he did, I don't think he'd be entertaining her in this way. Any revelation of scandalous behavior between the two would undoubtedly be another affront to the family were they to hear about it, and very disturbing to the other passengers. Who knows if the Earl has contacts in the Admiralty? Plus, I can see her Ladyship clinging to the Captain for the rest of the trip, in a very possessive way, most likely embarrassing him mightily. Coubro must be aware of this possibility as well.

Despite the many challenges along our voyage, Coubro has maintained excellent self-control as Captain. He can't fail at the hands of the misguided, egoistical Lady Hudson-Smythe, who is struggling to pull her nightdress up over her head. No doubt Matilda usually helps with this task each morning, but the maid has been left well behind tonight.

Earlier, when I noticed Lady Hudson-Smythe stall after dinner and touch the Captain as she left the room, I had a strong premonition about what was on her mind. Some of her intentions had been mentioned by Matilda to Timothy earlier along the voyage.

So, three hours ago, I had a little chat with mother blue whale as she swam beside us. I learned that her calf is a daughter, nearly a year old. The baby was being taught how to catch krill because soon mother's enriched milk would dry up. The pair planned to rejoin the rest of the pod to the south in the morning where there were more mothers with calves.

Having forewarned mother whale, I call to her now, and ask for her help. She has fallen 100 yards behind the ship, but at my bidding she generously stops feeding, increases speed, and rapidly approaches the stern. It's a delicate matter of timing, as Coubro now sits beside Mary on the bed, watching closely as her nightdress is dropped to the floor.

He does not move, and in fact, as I watch, a strange grimace tugs at his features, and his head jolts backward. It's as if an unseen spirit accosts him with a pointed finger, which he is trying to avoid. He squirms. Perhaps his conscience regales him and he's struggling with its message.

He stands and moves to the chair, on the back of which hang his pants and jacket. He slumps into the seat, and his head bangs on the hard wooden table surface, knocking the writing materials aside.

Finally, he lifts his face, strength and pride flooding his demeanor. He states firmly, "I cannot, Mary. As Captain, I cannot. My duty to the ship and passengers prevents me"

Mary, admiring her nakedness, neither sees nor hears Coubro. She rubs a hand across her vulva, fingering her slit, warming to her needs, humming expectantly.

I know I am potentially interfering with natural human behaviors, but just as Mary reaches for Coubro's shoulders, there is a massive impact on my starboard side.

I reel and list 10 degrees to port.

Mary tumbles across the floor and hits her head and left shoulder hard on a solid table leg. A dark red bruise immediately develops on her flesh, but, more worrisome, a trickle of blood runs down from her hairline across her cheek and under her nose. Coubro falls to the floor as well, but avoids hitting anything, and is back on his feet in an instant. He grabs a fresh towel, wets a corner and gently pushes back Mary's hair looking for the cut. Mary moans softly, holding her head in her hands, blood now dripping between her fingers onto her pendulous breasts. She mutters between moans, "Was that a whale or an iceberg that hit us, Daniel?"

Coubro retorts quickly. "A whale I think. The lookout would have seen an iceberg drifting our way, but a whale swimming deep could stay unseen until the contact. Here, keep this pressed on your wound. I'm sorry Mary, but I must inspect my ship for damage. You can stay in my cabin until I return although Matilda may be worried about you."

"My head hurts, Daniel, What a fine mesh thish iss. Just as we were about to get better acquainted. Maybe when you leave you could ask Matilda to come in and help me. She's helped me before. How bad is the cut?"

"There's a gash about half an inch long, now on a good-sized lump. The flow of blood is stopping. I'm sure Dr. Crisp will be able to put a patch on to help it heal. I'm really sorry to leave you, but I must check with the crew. Will you be alright?"

Her Ladyship has the wherewithal to realize the irony of her situation, and laughs. "What rotten timing, Captain, I was so looking forward to knowing you better. Another time perhaps. At leashed you've seen the best of me."

Coubro dresses hurriedly and leaves quickly. He heads to the Quarterdeck, where he's immediately informed "It was that whale, sir. Must not have liked us coming so close today. So far no damage reported, sir. A few of the crew have cuts and bruises but they're all Okay. Dr. Crisp is checking the prisoners as we speak. Guess we found out just how incredibly big those whales really are. We saw her turn and go back behind us, sir, probably back to her baby."

No one is unaffected by the whale mother's giant bulk slamming into my hull. In fact, I wonder if she might have overdone it, but a quick perusal of my starboard hull timbers shows no damage.

I pass on heartfelt thanks to my new friend and wish her luck raising her baby. She slaps her flukes in acknowledgment, but I doubt anyone onboard hears the thunderous clap on the surface nearby.

Below deck there are shouts and cries by people evicted from bunks, upended in the heads, and elsewhere deposited on the floor or slammed into stout timber beams. Cuts and bruises quickly appear in tender skin. The surgeon seeks out those more seriously injured.

The whale and her massive wallop are the talk of the ship for days afterwards. Whale expert Jacob has no suggestions as to why she came back and violently slammed us.

Mary Hudson-Smythe develops strange ideas that the whale somehow didn't appreciate her interest in attempting to seduce the Captain and deliberately intervened. As much as she knows the idea is ludicrous, she can't rid herself of it. She shares her thoughts in sketchy detail with Matilda, who is appropriately shocked, but swears on penalty of death that her lips are sealed with respect to her mistresses' theory.

Inwardly tantalized however, Matilda waits anxiously to find time alone with Timothy again, so she can tell him what happened.

20. *Expectations*

Stories and theories abound about the whale which slammed my hull. Among the prisoners who all felt the massive thump, the consensus is that the mother whale was getting even because we came too close to her baby.

The women especially enjoy discussions about the presence of the baby. For some, the talks bring back memories of their own families, and for others, it makes them ponder whether there'll be a chance for babies in the new land. One day as Jacob Nagle accompanies the Surgeon on his rounds, a number of the women corner him and ask about conditions for female prisoners in Botany Bay.

Before they left England, the women prisoners had heard stories about the penal colony, none of which were comforting. Talking amongst themselves during the trip has not been very satisfactory, as the tales varied enormously. They want to hear from a learned authority about the reality of what they face.

Jacob's message is not encouraging. He reveals that most females on arrival are sent to the women's 'Factory' in Parramatta. He describes a place where inmates make clothing for the convict men in the work gangs.

Women with skills such as baking, teaching, or nursing, might find jobs with free settlers who have approached the government for those skills. There are a limited number of such requests at any point in time.

Generally, a married convict woman is allowed to stay with her man on arrival in Sydney, as couples are considered potentially more stable citizens because of their maturity and family responsibilities. Jacob tells the prisoners a story he heard about a convict ship which carried only women. There, several prisoners established liaisons with guards and crew members, and had the ship's Captain marry them before arrival.

While marriage didn't solve all their problems once on land, those women didn't get sent to the Factory, and usually were much better off than those who were.

His tales scare many of the women, who now worry about the future and wonder exactly what will become of them as prisoners in Botany Bay.

The three women who are pregnant will not deliver until after we reach Sydney, and they are very apprehensive. How they will be treated and how will they provide for their children there? Jacob tells the mothers-to-be that there is a special section in the Female Factory where women live with their children. When asked how women ever get to move on from the Factory he tells them he knows of only two ways. One is to marry, the other to behave well and eventually be declared fit to help free citizens who request their help as maids or governesses.

There are many more male convicts than female convicts in the penal colony and a number of the skilled men come to the Factory to seek a wife. It's not the most romantic arrangement, but sometimes works well for both parties. Yes, Jacob admits, some indeed turn out to be mismatches. In such instances, the woman is usually returned to the Factory. There are no guarantees in the new colony.

Jacob refrains from telling the story of a mass debauchery that occurred when one of the earliest convict ships to the colony full of female convicts arrived. The male convicts raced out of their tents enmasse and overran the outnumbered guards, taking advantage of the unsuspecting women and girls who had just arrived. The government was embarrassed, and executed some of the more brutal offenders. Worse, not all guards were impervious to the opportunity. Several were hanged. No apologies were offered the women. It was a disgrace that officials tried to cover up. The prisoners on board *Lady Corinth* are not aware of the event, but will undoubtedly hear of it at some point after their arrival.

Among the paying passengers, Sara Goldsmith is getting anxious to reunite with her husband. Captain Coubro, with Jacob's help, estimates there are a little over three weeks left on their voyage. In fact, in about five or six days' time they should encounter the islands in Bass Strait, the stretch of water that separates the main land mass of eastern Australia from the large island to the south known as Van Diemen's Land with its distinct, much harsher penal colony. Sara starts to organize her belongings, placing near the top of her suitcase a new pipe and specially selected tobacco for her husband. She works hard at her grooming, avoids the sun, and eats only tiny portions at table. She hand-washes her chemises and dainties and irons her dresses. She wants to make sure she creates the best impression for her man when he first sees her. She longs to be in his arms again, and wonders what the new beard and moustache that he promised to grow will look and feel like.

Lady Hudson-Smythe has taken to sulking after her unhappy encounter in the Captain's cabin. She refrains from most conversations at dinner time and isolates herself in her room, her book about sailors cast aside. Clarinda Finsbury, who helped her with the initial book writing, seems to be no longer sought out as a friend.

The young boys are growing more restless daily. Three months at sea is trying for everyone, but youngsters with boundless energy and enthusiasm grow weary of the lack of new playtime diversions. Their parents have no good ideas on how to stop the boys from either moping or pursuing dangerous adventures in the rigging.

Below deck, Janet Whittington rubs her mounded belly. She's happy with the Surgeon's assessment of the baby's health, and how robust she feels. It's more uncomfortable to walk around in the daytime and to sleep at night, but she realizes that's normal and it's not for too much longer. As a friend of Susannah Moore, who lost her baby daughter earlier in the voyage, Janet is thankful her child won't arrive before they reach land. She anticipates that milk and other suitable baby foods will be more readily available in Sydney than onboard.

She mutters in her sleep sometimes, revealing these and other thoughts. In particular, she's concerned about how her positive feelings for Jacob Nagle dominate her musings. From the moment he first appeared below deck she was impressed. His willingness to visit with prisoners, his lack of condescension when talking to them, his openness in sharing stories and other information with them, these traits all told her he was a man of compassion with high self-esteem and self-confidence.

Whenever he spoke, there was an unusual accent to his speech. She deduced it was part of a newly emerging Australian brogue, a lazy, broad, almost-Cockney accent. Definitely not refined or high-class, but friendly and engaging, especially when combined with local idioms, which he has had to explain repeatedly to his listeners.

Janet and Jacob sit together in the ante room outside the Surgeon's office at the conclusion of her latest checkup. Some time back, Jacob had volunteered to fetch and return Janet whenever a checkup was required. It pleased Arthur to allow them time together, as he found them more mature than many of their peers. Jacob revealed that he had always wanted to have a family, and seemed to hold no adverse feelings about Janet's pending child. It would be a new world where they were headed, and the couple found they had similar ideas about forging a future there, as independently as possible from existing patterns of community and government oversight.

In discussions about their own upbringing and family background, the pair learned they originally came from neighboring towns on the northwest coast of Cornwall. As an adult, Jacob secured a job with the Navy in Portsmouth. After her fisherman father died at sea, Janet and her mother moved to Bournemouth, 50 miles west of Portsmouth. To augment the pennies her mother earned as a washerwoman, Janet worked as a maid in a local pub. Caught with her hand in the till one evening, she was thrown in gaol with little ceremony. She was only 16 and remained incarcerated for a full year before being assigned to the *Lady Corinth*.

Jacob shares his business interests with Janet and finds her a good listener and avid enthusiast. He references the promise of help from the banker, Timothy Blaine, who has provided the blank ledger in which Jacob has begun to record stories. Janet readily recites the experience of the death and sea burial of baby Alison Moore. Jacob pens the episode.

Both Timothy and Janet prove to be wonderful raconteurs, describing with wit and humor many events of the long trip from Portsmouth so far. Jacob finds himself listening carefully and doing a lot of writing.

* * *

As the weather warms and the countdown of days to the entrance of Bass Strait moves from six to five and then four, Timothy Blaine's enthusiasm for life in the new world becomes infectious. He looks forward to his challenge as trusted banker in the new land, and at dinner he talks incessantly about his investment plans to help grow the local economy. The male passengers are impressed with his maturity and openness and ask him to examine their letters of credit the moment they become established in Sydney.

Timothy has another reason for self-satisfaction that I know about, for he and Matilda, Lady Hudson-Smythe's maid, have lain together twice, and both seem titillated with their unions of the flesh.

"*Land Ho!*"

The call comes from the crow's nest and resonates throughout my framework.

"*Land Ho.*"

293

"Land ho."

"Land Ho."

Sailors grin. I hear them talk about how they will be in sight of land for the rest of the journey. Passengers smile. Many exclaim openly about how glad they are that the end of their long voyage is close. Even select prisoners smile. They mumble that they are tired of their confined state, and welcome the thought of fresh air on land, albeit in an environment about which they have some trepidation.

* * *

Coubro's and Jacob's reckoning has been dead on, as the southwest corner of King Island comes into view. We veer eastward to stay well clear of the treacherous rocks and reefs that have claimed unwary ships in prior years.

Bass Strait is reputed to be twice as wide and twice as rough as the English Channel and now lives up to that reputation. I'm experiencing an extremely rocky ride, one that could destabilize many stomachs. This stretch of water is some 300 miles long, so we have at least two days ahead to traverse it completely. Over 50 small islands occupy the Strait, most towards the eastern end. Coubro's intent is to pass north of the Furneaux group, although the winds are not helping and I'm being driven directly towards the islands' rocky shores. We've already passed one distant shipwreck decorating a low-lying reef in front of jutting sea-cliffs. Heaven forbid that I end up there also.

Coubro calls a council of his officers. I'm glad, because 20 miles out I sense trouble ahead if we don't make a drastic change. The winds are increasing dramatically and the rudder movements are becoming less effective. The waves are also building, although it is the wind which I worry about most. It's not only increasing, but gusting as well, much worse than what we experienced at the Cape. It's the gusts' unpredictability that is dangerous. One minute the wind is tolerable, the next it swirls with incredible force from a slightly different direction. It loosens crates and tools, forces hatches open, and throws seaweed into the rigging. When crossing the open deck, the crew has to be doubly cautious. I've already seen a couple of men fall and slide to the railing.

Coubro gives his commands.

"Plunkett, I want to deploy double fore anchors and make an aft anchor ready for quick launch. We're only in 30 fathoms over a sand bottom, so they should have no trouble holding. On my command, when we are firmly anchored you will furl all sails. And I mean all. These winds are inching up to gale force. I don't want to give them an inch of canvas to blow at. We'll hold here until the wind changes, I don't care how many days we need. We will not join those other wrecks on the rocks."

I agree. The bosun's pipe sounds and the crew spring to action. Coubro has won them back. They've never moved so fast. They work harder and smarter than ever and we are soon double anchored, and holding fast. Wind howls through the rigging. Masts creak ominously against lashed booms. I rock violently side to side. Sailors patrol the deck and pick up debris flown in from the waters ahead. A seagull slams into the foc's'le, never to rise on the winds again. A sailor's beret crosses the deck at record speed, headed for one of the islands miles away. The men know that no measure of innate caution can control boisterous, wind driven seas.

Once we are safely anchored Coubro calls the passengers together in the lounge.

"We've entered a part of Bass Strait known to be extremely treacherous, as much of it is still uncharted. There's a group of islands not far off our intended course where too many ships have run aground in the past. Calm your fears and be patient. We will stay anchored here 20 miles or eight leagues away until we are assured of calm weather."

"How long do you think that will be Captain?" Mrs. Finsbury asks.

"Very hard to predict Madam. Storms in this region are legendary. I would expect at least 24 hours before the winds die down. It may take two or more days. As I said, we will remain here until it is safe to move."

Timothy Blaine speaks words that all of the passengers are probably thinking. "After all we've come through it seems ignominious for nature to fight us so close to our destination."

"I agree, sir. But nature is not fair, particularly in Bass Strait. Hopefully this will be our last encounter with her nasty whims, and she'll provide smooth sailing the rest of the way."

Frustration and concern show in every passenger's face, but the talk turns to showing faith in their Captain who has managed well through previous storms.

Below deck the prisoners are fully aware that forward motion has stopped, but have no idea why. They can hear the wind moaning through the rigging and feel swinging jolts as the anchor chains restrict my movement. They see clumps of seaweed fly by their portholes, and as bits of wood hit the hull, the pings add to their concern and curiosity about why we are not moving forward.

Finally, a cook's assistant brings fresh bread rolls and information on why we are anchored. Worries ease a little. Many had guessed we must be facing extremely serious problems, such as a tremendous storm heading our way again. They appreciate the Captain's caution so close to their destination, and do not mind taking extra time to get to the penal colony.

A day and a half later the gusty winds morph into more regular breezes and Coubro gives the order to move on. The rattle of the anchor chains being hauled up is a welcome sound to all. Even the sea shanties sung by the sailors working the capstans seem to be belted out with extra gusto among frequent grunts.

As we turn northeast at the eastern end of Bass Strait, I sense ship-wide recognition that we are entering the final leg of our journey to the new land.

By various means, three couples independently request to be married by the Captain. Two have learned well from Jacob's tales and are heeding his advice. The third couple is Jacob and Janet.

In early days out of Portsmouth, one of the original militia guards and one of the female prisoners found they had common religious interests. Whenever circumstances allowed, they sat together by one of the masts and shared family tales and prayed. The strength of their relationship, sustained platonically over the months, has convinced them that their common interests and mutual affection are sufficient to justify marriage and face the future together. While most guardsmen will return to England with me or on another ship, this is one who will stay in Australia with his prisoner wife.

At the other end of the passion scale, the skinniest, and highly athletic convict, Peter Cooksey, who climbed walls to be with his lover, Betty Willows, has proposed to her, and she has happily accepted. They make an incongruous pair since Betty is large by any measure.

Plus, I suspect her considerable girth may expand further in the months ahead, for she's had trouble keeping her breakfast down on occasion the last month or so.

We sail close to the coastline, less than 10 miles off. Some of the sandy beaches stretch for miles, one in particular taking all day for us to pass. One afternoon we see fires on the beach – presumably natives cooking their fish. Through the binoculars, the crew can see black-skinned figures around the fires but cannot make out details.

Coubro chooses this calm sailing weather to orchestrate the requested marriages. The cook prepares a small celebration with special sandwiches and tarts for the couples and their invited friends.

Jacob and Janet are the first to stand before him. Coubro reads from a modified script taken from the Church of England's *Book of Common Prayer.* He addresses the knot of officers and prisoners who stand in support.

"Dearly beloved, we are gathered here in the sight of God, to join together this Man and this Woman in Holy Matrimony.

"Jacob, wilt thou have this Woman to thy wedded Wife, wilt thou love her, comfort her, honour, and keep her in sickness and in health; and, forsaking all other, keep thee only unto her, so long as ye both shall live?"

Jacob responds quickly. "I will."

Coubro turns to Janet. "Janet, wilt thou have this Man to thy wedded Husband, wilt thou obey him, and serve him, love, honour, and keep him in sickness and in health; and, forsaking all other, keep thee only unto him, so long as ye both shall live?"

Janet smiles at Jacob and answers strongly, "I will."

Coubro tells Jacob to repeat his words: "I, Jacob Nagle, take thee, Janet Whittington, to my wedded Wife, to have and to hold from this day forward, for better for worse, for richer, for poorer, in sickness and in health, to love and to cherish, till death us do part, according to God's Holy ordinance; and thereto I plight thee my troth."

Jacob does a good job, as Coubro separates the phrases to make each easy to remember. Similarly, he tells Janet to repeat her set of words. "I, Janet Whittington, take thee, Jacob Nagle, to my wedded Husband, to have and to hold from this day forward, for better for worse, for richer, for poorer, in sickness and in health, to love, cherish, and to

298

obey, till death us do part, according to God's Holy ordinance; and thereto I give thee my troth."

I wonder how many attendees noticed the difference in the verbal commitments, especially where the wife agrees to 'serve and obey'. Meaningless to us ships, but apparently important for human marriages.

Coubro motions the pair to hold hands and speaks directly to their supporters. "Those whom God hath joined together let no man put asunder. Forasmuch as Jacob and Janet have consented together in Holy Wedlock, and have witnessed the same before God and this company, and have given and pledged their troth either to the other; I pronounce that they be Man and Wife together, in the Name of the Father, and of the Son, and of the Holy Ghost. *Amen.*"

The friends echo *"Amen"*, smile and clap. Janet's friends hug her, while Jacob's supporters pat him on the back, or shake hands with him.

Coubro holds his arm aloft and as the group falls silent, bows his head for the benediction. "God the Father, God the Son, God the Holy Ghost, bless, preserve, and keep you; the Lord mercifully with his favour look upon you; and so fill you with all spiritual blessing and grace, that ye may so live together in this life, that in the world to come ye may have life everlasting. *Amen."*

Laughing with happiness, the men and women move off to the main dining room. Coubro signals to the Surgeon to bring the next couple forward.

The Captain goes through the same process with Peter and Betty, and following them, Colin Stanwood, the militia guard, and his betrothed, Ann Singleton. Each group is shepherded to the dining room, overlapping in part with the previous group. Since the weather is mild, most of the participants head outdoors to eat their treats and toast the brides and grooms.

Since the ceremonies combine convicts intermingling with free citizens, Coubro has employed the militia to keep an eye on the proceedings from a distance. The whole occasion is of course joyous and Coubro has made it clear to the Captain of the guard that he doesn't expect any feelings of ill-will to be passed between participants, so those on watch should be relaxed, but remain alert.

Everyone is well behaved. It's incongruous at the end of festivities however that the couples must separate and return to their respective onboard quarters. No togetherness at this point.

Although they don't have too long to wait.

21. *Arrival*

Two days after the wedding ceremonies a rumor spreads like wildfire throughout my length and breadth.

Sydney tomorrow!

It's on everyone's lips. The end of the journey. They've made it, but what lies ahead? Some fear what they may learn.

Crew members pull their belongings together and pack their sea bags in anticipation of well-earned shore leave. The men have worked hard, especially in the storms. Over the years I've experienced much lazier crews, some of which included individuals who were whipped for insubordination. Yes, there have been a few here who've not pulled their weight to the same extent as others. A good verbal berating by the bosun and some peer pressure usually changed attitudes. That and the threat of time alone without food and water in the onboard gaol.

First-class passengers have their luggage brought up from storage. They rearrange the contents with fresh clothes on top, last-minute soiled attire hidden at the base. The boys reluctantly pack their game boards and movable pieces, trying to attain a smidgeon of tidiness, all incredibly excited to be reaching their destination where they will leave sea-living behind.

Lady Hudson-Smythe gives instructions to her maid. "Matilda, I will want to look my very best when we disembark. Check that my black dress is spotless and freshly ironed. It shows off my figure to advantage."

"Yes, ma'am. Which necklace and earrings do you plan to wear?"

"The same as I wore when we first boarded, the pearls my dear mother gave me. And do make yourself presentable. The blue and white tunic I think will help make you look demure and in your rightful place beside me. And I don't want to see a straggly hair anywhere. We have standards to declare and portray. The officials we meet need to be reminded of where we all come from and the practices and societal mores we hold dear."

"Yes, ma'am. I washed all your undergarments in my basin and they are now dry, and all your shoes are scrubbed clean and wiped shiny where required. You will look regal, I am sure. No doubt gentlemen's heads will turn in admiration."

"I certainly hope so. Where are the letters of introduction to the Governor and Lieutenant Governor? I shall want those close by."

"They're safely tucked away in the large handbag I will carry for you, my Lady. You should only need your dainty purse with the silver clasp and chain. I love that purse. It is so delicate and elegant."

"I may well leave it to you, my dear, since you like it so much."

"Oh thank you my Lady. And may I ask, should I carry your notebook with the start of your Sailor's Life story, in your handbag, in case you want to show it to someone? It shows a side of you others won't know about."

"That's an excellent idea, Matilda. Here, let me get it out of the drawer for you. Anything else you can think of?"

"Not for me to say your Ladyship, but it may stand you in good stead to personally say goodbye to Mr. Blaine, the banker, in case you need his services at some point and also to Mr. Winthrop, the publisher. He seemed quite intrigued with your reading that evening."

"Bless you child. That's very thoughtful. Of course I must also repair my relationship with the good Captain. That will require more forethought."

302

"If I may be so bold your Ladyship. If you visit him in your going-away dress he will be very impressed and delighted to visit with you. Just be careful if he proposes a goodbye kiss. Don't let his hands stray. You are very attractive to men, as has been well proven."

"Thank you, my dear, and as much as I am usually hesitant to confide in you, I would take straying hands as a definite compliment. We'll see." A slight blush forms on her Ladyship's cheeks and there's a twinkle in her eye.

While the paying passengers trade contact addresses, there is little for the convicts to do except settle bets, promise to remember each other, and wish friends good luck in the new land. The three pregnant mothers get extra wishes for safe delivery of their unborn. Nerves get the better of some women and tears flow freely as they worry about what awaits them. Men prone to quarrelling are silent, moody, and anxious. A few shake hands, but often without fervor. I suspect most anticipate hard times ahead.

Young Diana is confused. "D..dear Lord, p..please make Mummy laugh again now we have arrived. No more crying."

On a sun-drenched morning, with the four young lads cavorting at the bowsprit, Coubro turns us towards the west to enter Sydney Harbor. As we come abreast of the north and south heads, the crew gives a grand cheer. "Hip hip, hooray. Hip hip, hooray. Hip hip, hooray!"

The noise is heard below where prisoners crowd the portholes to get a glimpse of the harbor-defining twin buttresses. I admit they create an impressive entrance. I feel majestic sailing between them. In times to come, as civilization expands, I imagine there will be groups of people on the cliffs waving at ships like me as they welcome us to the new land. It's wonderful to finally be here after traveling so long on the open seas.

On deck, passengers gaze gratefully at the calm waters, framed by alternate rocky shores, sandy beaches, and trees that crowd to the water's edge. They clap and shout as a forward anchor descends noisily to the sandy bottom. There is little wind, and as the rattle of the chain ceases, a soft silence falls upon us.

We have arrived!

It's a moment to savour. More than four months battling the elements as we passed through King Neptune's realm are now behind us. We are safe. We've made it. Everyone pauses, momentarily reflecting on a journey few want to repeat. This harbor is our refuge from the wilderness and terror of two giant oceans.

We are at peace. Unbelievable peace. For how long we know not. But for the moment, it surrounds and enfolds us. No matter what lies ahead, we have made it safely. Something to be well thankful for.

The silence and peacefulness is broken abruptly as the militia fire two signal cannons. It's the Captain's announcement to authorities further west that he needs a Pilot ship to guide us the rest of the way in to Sydney Cove.

While all aboard wait impatiently, I've already made contact with two ships at the cargo wharf in Long Cove, a little beyond our ultimate anchor point. The ships tell me there is no other ship in Sydney Cove at the moment, which is the stretch of water directly in front of the Governor's mansion and the commercial center of town. They promise to let me know when the Pilot ship is launched.

I don't have to wait long. My new acquaintances tell me that any new arrival such as ours generates enormous excitement in the town. Officials are always anxious to quickly determine whether they will be welcoming convicts, free settlers, or assorted cargo, or some combination of same. Inspecting the cargo is their preferred task, as goods from home generate commerce and taxes. Officials who deal with people experience bureaucratic drudgery in answering the multitude of questions the newcomers raise and painstakingly preparing required government records and forms.

On the other hand, local residents wonder if they might know some of the passengers, or even some of the convicts, and are always anxious to hear news from 'home'. By the time we sail a couple more miles into Sydney Cove proper there'll probably be a hundred people gathered at the quayside waiting for us.

I'm told the small Pilot's boat is on its way.

Two hours later, following the Pilot's guidance, we anchor directly in line with the single jetty serving Sydney town. Beyond the wharf a small stream empties into the harbor. To one side are multiple large tents with groups of uniformed soldiers who stand outside under trees which provide heavy shade. Beyond the tents are a limited number of wooden huts. From a distance they look rough and primitive. On the other side of the creek and just beyond the circular shoreline there are more buildings which comprise what looks like a shanty town of sorts. Muddy trails meander between trees, buildings, and rocky outcrops. Residents in dirty clothes line the tracks along the shore, and shield their eyes against the sun. Some wave enthusiastically, and a number are clearly shouting, although their voices have trouble carrying distinctly against the breeze, creating a cacophony of undecipherable greetings. Smoke rises from two chimneys and blows away. And as if to provide a message of what lies ahead, a gang of shackled men in striped convict garb is marched through the throng of onlookers led by several guards with muskets and machetes clearly visible.

There are no fine buildings visible as there were along the banks of the Thames. Nor is there any hint of commerce other than carts on the jetty and a few horses ready to transport newcomers' goods to unseen destinations. Tents and more tents dominate the view of those onboard, although beyond the blazing white canvas shelters, out of view from the water, a small township of multiple buildings exists, and it's here that the passengers will find hotel accommodation, stores, and official government entities.

Three tenders are tied up against my port hull. Numerous Immigration and other administrative officials have climbed on board. Four confer with the Captain, the Surgeon, and the Militia Commander about the prisoners. Two officials are talking with lesser members of the militia, while another is asking the Boatswain and a couple of seamen for details about the cargo and the passengers' belongings. Two more administrative clerks roam amongst the passengers lining the port railing, checking their names against a ledger from Coubro's office.

I strain to listen to multiple simultaneous conversations with officials, while also minding questions the prisoners are raising among themselves about what they see onshore.

The chief Immigration officer welcomes Captain Coubro, Surgeon Crisp and the Militia Commander Tomkins, to Sydney and Australia, and listens patiently to a summary of the trials and tribulations of the voyage we've just completed. With pleasantries behind them, and congratulatory glasses of rum downed, the ranking official asks to see the four ledgers for crew, militia, passengers and prisoners.

Coubro summarizes the information they hold. "Prisoner count, sir. In Portsmouth, based on the Surgeon's examination of convicts delivered to the ship, eight women, one with child, were denied passage. Seven men were too ill or weak to be transported. Names were recorded. We left England with 62 women, 93 men and three children for a total of 158 prisoners. Four women were known to be pregnant."

"Births, deaths, along the way, Captain?"

"A baby girl was born, sir, but perished within days. The other three women are still pregnant. One of them married my Pilot enroute."

"We'll go through the ledger in detail later Captain. What about paying passengers?"

"We have four married couples, sir, with four boys aged around 11 or so, one lone married woman coming here to be with her husband, a single man who is a banker, and a single woman travelling with her maid. Twenty in total, a reasonable group, even the boys who had each other to keep themselves occupied."

"Anything else we need to know about? Anyone important, friends or relatives of government officials or politicians back home?"

"The woman with a maid is Lady Hudson-Smythe, daughter of a Count from Wallingford in Berkshire. Pompous and self-important. She probably expects special treatment. As will Mrs. Goldsmith whose husband works in the Governor's office."

The Immigration officer turns to one of his subordinates. "Lieutenant, let's get them ashore this afternoon. I see they've already been marked present. Take the ledger and sign them off individually. Since there are so few, you should be able to prepare their landing papers while they wait at the office onshore."

The lieutenant's timing may be propitious as Sara Goldsmith is having a mini tantrum. She's indignant that her husband didn't arrive on one of the tenders. She stamps her feet and rudely assails one of the clerks assigned to the passengers. "My husband is the military liaison officer in the Governor's mansion. Why wasn't he brought here on one of your little boats? He outranks all of you officials. This is preposterous."

The official being addressed smirks and can't hold back. "Well, high and mighty lady, perhaps he doesn't know you are on this ship. Did you consider that? How long ago did you write to him? It's been five weeks since the last passenger ship arrived here. I suggest you hold your tongue or you'll be the last one landed this afternoon. Now step back."

307

Lady Hudson-Smythe is livid. She flounces forward. "That's no way to talk to this lady, young man. We're not riff-raff prisoners, but free citizens anxious to do good here. Treat us with respect or we'll see to your dismissal. Where is your senior officer?"

"Good luck in finding him, missus. Take your uppity airs to him and see what he says. His job is to manage the ugly criminals on this ship. You people can fend for yourselves once you are on shore."

Her Ladyship starts to retort. "You wretched..."

She's cut off as James Winthrop takes her arm and pulls her aside. "Ignore him. He's not worth your ire. We'll work with someone higher up and more respectful shortly."

A smart suggestion on Mr. Winthrop's part to withdraw, but from what the other ships tell me, civil servants here relish their trifling elements of authority, and arrogance is found in every level of bureaucracy. The traditions of civil English society do not yet exist in this place.

As if on cue, the lieutenant arrives. "What's going on?" he asks.

James Winthrop responds. "Mrs. Goldsmith had hoped her husband would be on one of the tenders, sir. I see you have the Captain's ledger. We're all anxious to be landed. Do you have the authority to send us ashore?"

"Yes, sir, I do. Please step forward and sign next to your name when I call you and we'll get things under way."

He reads the 20 names, and all sign, including the boys.

"Congratulations all of you. Welcome to Sydney. We'll take four of you at a time with your immediate goods. Any household commodities you have in storage will be unloaded in a day or so. Now who wants to be in the first boat?"

"I do," Sara exclaims. Pointing to the rude clerk, she adds." And don't let that crude fellow touch me or my belongings."

The passenger cabins will be empty in a few hours, and the occupants will miss dinner. It dawns on me that I will miss them. Each of them takes me for granted, as should be the case. But I wonder who will linger in my memory longest. Lady Hudson-Smythe, or Matilda and her beau, Timothy? Silently, I wish them all well. Adieu, fine travellers. Good fortune be with you. Perhaps a couple will whisper thank you's or goodbyes, and stroke my rails or my rigging as they leave.

Back in his cabin, Coubro is working with the Militia Commander to explain to the Australian officials the change of guards in Cape Town. He takes full responsibility for dismissing the original commander Mullens, and the guard, Millstone, who beat a pregnant convict. Two other guards, loyal to Mullens, left voluntarily. The new Commander, who is present in the meeting along with Corporal Tomkins, was hired along with two new guards, making the contingent one man fewer than when it started out in Portsmouth.

The incident with Mullens' insubordination is a blur, as it happened on our first day under sail. Millstone's actions, however, still make me shudder, metaphorically. What a gross individual he was. I am not sorry that he is gone. I'm thankful that Sarah Grainger suffered no long term physical issues from his attack. In fact, I admire her tangible leadership of the women prisoners. May she receive special attention at the Female Factory and in life beyond. She should deliver in just a few days, I have heard.

Coubro provides information on his crew, making special note of the seaman who died as a result of a fall from the rigging and the two washed overboard by a freak rogue wave. He also describes the incident where another able-bodied seaman had part of his left arm amputated below the elbow after his hand and wrist were severely crushed. The Immigration official takes hold of the crew ledger and indicates that over the next three days each man will need to stop by the office to sign papers.

The Immigration officer stands back from Coubro's desk and asks, "Can we move to your dining room, Captain, where we can sit and examine the prisoner ledger together? From what you stated earlier, we have 158 names to check and copy to our official books. That will take several hours. Perhaps your cook might provide some biscuits and some more rum?"

"I'll see to it, sir. I'm sure the prisoners are wondering when they will be sent ashore. Any estimate I may share with them?"

"Based on past experience, Captain, we will be able to call a muster on deck mid-afternoon tomorrow. At that time, we should be able to start unloading the female prisoners. I'd suggest mothers and children first. And – oh yes, we need to place the three women with new husbands in the passenger cabins temporarily. Our local doctor will board tomorrow and talk to those women and the pregnant ones in the main group. He has the final say with respect to prisoner health for bounty accounting purposes. Understood?"

"Certainly, sir. Let me give Pilot this information. He can then visit the prisoners with one of your men and inform them of the disembarkation procedure and timing. Pilot seems to have a special rapport with many of the prisoners, I might add."

While examination of the prisoner records gets underway in the dining room, I listen to Mr. Nagle and the Immigration clerk talking to the convicts below deck. The official answers a few questions about the process to be followed on land. He indicates that the men will be marched up the main street the morning after next to a set of barracks, where they will await the Governor's visit the following morning, at which time they will be informed of their dispositions. Those with skills needed by free settlers will be immediately released to their assignments, the remainder will be taken to different working groups in the afternoon.

Women prisoners will be accommodated in large tents overnight with minimal sentry postings. The guard callously notes that he's sure the male convicts tented nearby will welcome the women's arrival. It's the first hint for the women that the limited respect they experienced on their long journey will soon be history, obliterated by the needs and wants of mean and desperate men. The women share their feelings with one another, most revealing severe trepidation at what lies ahead.

Nothing I can do for them of course, but I've come to know many over our four months' association and I regret their situation. Society was definitely unkind to most of them back in England. It sounds as though that will still be the case here.

Dinner, surprisingly, is a somber affair. I had expected the crew's officers to be relieved at the absence of passengers, so they could be themselves and feel more relaxed. From the conversations that ensue, however, it seems as though most of the men are anxious for shore leave, just as they were in Cape Town. They have arrived at the end-of-the-world, and are curious to learn what this place, Sydney, is all about.

While some want to satisfy sexual needs, others will head directly for the waterside pubs, to seek rum or beer and local food. All will rejoice in some way at their safe arrival. Mr. Nagle provides advice on where to find the best grog and vittles. He apologizes for not joining them, indicating he will stay on board with his new wife.

The men implore him to come along, and after much banter back and forth, he good-naturedly agrees to do so, but indicates his need to return onboard earlier than the others.

And so the day winds down. Immigration officials return to their post, prisoners bunch together in small groups quietly repeating their goodbyes, the last of the passengers are taken ashore, and remaining crew members sit on deck where they enjoy the evening air and the gentle swaying around my anchor chain. Night falls slowly.

* * *

I pause in my assessment of what is happening onboard and reflect on what I've accomplished. It's been nearly four months since I sailed out of Portsmouth Harbor destined for Australia some 14,000 miles away. I remember passing the sad prison hulks, regretful insults to both the inmates on board them and all vessels which love the high seas.

On the world's waters, I held the responsibility for safe passage for a new crew, 20 high-class citizens, and one hundred and fifty or so scared convicts. We headed for new paths, new experiences, and new unknowns with a handful of charts, two recently calibrated chronometers and two good sextants, one with the captain, another with the pilot.

The ships in Long Cove ask me for details about the voyage. I respond with pride. We survived scorching heat for days near the equator, massive storms in the Atlantic and Bass Strait, a flood in the hold, rats and cockroaches, mean and violent soldiers, a collision with an over-friendly giant whale, the presence of icebergs and ice storms, and a rough transition around the Cape of Good Hope. Through it all we only lost three young crewmen, and a convict baby, although another sailor was seriously injured.

My listeners love the story of my becoming, temporarily, a floating courthouse in Table Bay, Cape Town, and the prisoner Robertson's revelations, although they regret learning of Pilot's deceit. A pilot and his ship are like a team working cooperatively with each other to choose the best route forward. The pair get to know each other more intimately than most can imagine. The pilot's directions to the helmsmen, his decisiveness, awareness of wind strength and needs for sail deployment govern the ship's responses to his commands. No ship wants to fight the pilot's direction, although that does happen at times. I worked with two different pilots on our voyage, a somewhat unusual happening. I get credit for doing so from my listeners.

I wonder what's in store for me. Once all persons who are going ashore are gone I will head to Long Cove for maintenance and repairs. I imagine after that it will be back to England with a load of wheat, maybe a few bales of wool, probably some soldiers and bureaucrats, as well as a few pardoned convicts or regular citizens heading homeward. I look forward to whatever Captain Coubro can arrange.

Speaking of whom, he's on his usual evening walk around my circumference. He chats briefly with the able-bodied seamen who are about, attentively checks the rigging, watches wavelets gently sliding beneath my frame, examines the dark shoreline to the north, and counts the candle lights in the small buildings on the south shore. Several fires from aboriginal camps can be seen along the shoreline back towards the heads.

Tomorrow I feel certain that Coubro will venture ashore and see some of the natives up close for the first time. I've been told that some of them are learning broken English and help the administration track down escaped prisoners. Apparently, the aborigines are an unusual people with no written language and a nomadic existence. They also wear no clothes which many whites find embarrassing.

The Surgeon wanders out on deck and joins the Captain. They've become firm friends and walk together for a while before retiring to Coubro's cabin. Coubro's steward retrieves his finest port wine and pours two glasses.

"You've done an excellent job, Arthur, not only bringing all the prisoners through in good health, but managing injuries to crew and passengers alike. I thank you for your dedication and concern. I'd be happy to have you with me on any ship I command.

"Do you have any interest in staying here, or, like me, look forward to returning to England?"

"Well, sir, I'm interested to learn about Sydney and the attendant economy here, but *a priori* I am not thinking of staying. Mr. Nagle paints it as a fascinating place with much opportunity, and I imagine a doctor could readily find a good clientele as the place grows. But I like England. My interests are satisfied by my surroundings there, a civilized environment in which our heritage is always present and history just a touch away. I don't need to create a new future."

"I have similar sentiments good doctor. Perhaps a function of age. I've seen a lot of the world but am always happy to return home.

"In any event my friend, let's pay thanks to God for our safe passage, and to Sydney for the promise of a new future for those we will leave behind."

Coubro hands one of the glasses to the doctor and they raise them towards the ceiling. I'm sure Coubro's toast reflects his thoughts.

"To us, and this town. We have a month to explore it before heading homeward. Let's see if it holds promise to be the starting point of a better Britain."

22. *New home*

It's now three and a half years since I first anchored in Sydney Cove and much has happened since then. Captain Coubro, Dr. Crisp, and 95 percent of the original crew sailed back to England with me on the return trip, although Mr. Nagle stayed behind, which required Coubro to recruit a new Pilot. The 30 days in Sydney between arrival and departure were some of the busiest I have ever experienced. Maintenance, cargo loading, and training new crew members kept us all busy. Several military personnel and a few private citizens also sailed back home with us.

Beyond preparations for the return journey to England, there were dramatic business negotiations.

You may remember some of Mr. Nagle's business plans, which included becoming a freight forwarding broker and the possible purchase of a ship. In cooperation with Mr. Blaine, the new banker, the pair pulled together a small group of entrepreneurs willing to invest in the purchase of a convertible passenger/cargo ship, and to finance the construction of new waterfront warehouses for commodity storage and brokerage management.

When I learned that Mr. Nagle wanted to purchase me as his ship of choice, I was really pleased. And when I heard how many thousand pounds I was worth, I was flabbergasted. Of course, since I belonged to a firm back in England, I carried the purchase proposal back to London with Mr. Blaine's parent bank as the agency of record. The bank's solicitors negotiated an agreement with the merchant owners, and on return to Australia nine months after my first trip, ownership was formally transferred to Mr. Nagle's consortium.

On the return trip back from England, Captain Coubro was my master again and a second ship traveled with us. Nearly four hundred convicts were delivered to the authorities. I could tell that Mr. Coubro had mixed feelings when he shook hands with Mr. Nagle at the handover ceremony. My old Captain made a special tour around my deck, patting my railing and entwining his fingers in the rigging in many places. I still treasure the words he offered to Jacob as he climbed back down to the dock.

"Look after her well, my friend. She's one of the finest ladies I've ever sailed. I'll be back to check on her as often as I can."

So now I am owned in Sydney, and I must say I'm pretty happy.

For me, it was sad to part company with Captain Coubro and most of his crew, but the Captain has returned to Sydney three times in the years since, and each time he has made a point to come and visit with Mr. Nagle. He makes sure to greet me directly. He stands at the helm, turns the wheel slowly, and declares, "Good to see you, old girl. You look and feel wonderful." One of the world's finest gentlemen for sure.

He's actually here at the docks right this moment while his new ship, 'Admiralty Crown,' is undergoing maintenance and minor repairs in preparation for the trip back to London. I've listened to his conversation with Mr. Nagle. Jacob's wife, the former convict Janet Whittington, has just left Jacob's maritime office with their three year old boy Arthur, named after the Surgeon Dr. Crisp. Such a curious young soul with a happy gurgle for a laugh and enormous blue eyes.

I think Janet's presence caused Coubro to ask about other passengers and selected convicts on the original trip of the *Lady Corinth*. Jacob fills him in.

"Do you remember the other two couples you married as we sailed along the south coast? The religious couple opened a small boarding house and the other pair with their incongruous size differences opened a pub. The boarding house has had some interesting residents according to stories on the street. A couple of homosexual men were thrown out by the owners, and two women used it as a brothel for two nights, only to be discovered by the owners when their beds were creaking far too much. The stories actually helped the place's popularity. On the other hand, the folks who opened a pub aren't doing so well. The best pubs are in The Rocks area. Theirs is a half-mile distant.

"On a more successful note, Mr. Winthrop, the publisher, is editor of one of the newspapers. And he's about to send my story of the voyage to his old company in England for publication. I'm excited about that. Lady Hudson-Smythe never finished her book about sailors, of course. Probably just as well methinks."

Jacob pauses and strokes his chin. "Let me see. Who else do I know about? Oh, yes. Remember the convict woman, Susannah Moore, who lost her baby early on? At some point before I joined you in Cape Town. She was chosen by a farmer gentleman who came to the Parramatta Female Factory. I heard she recently brought a fine daughter into the world. I forget her name.

"And, speaking of babies, Sarah Grainger, who was beaten by that guard, had her baby at the Factory soon after we arrived. Moreover, 12 months later, her boyfriend Rodney from back home, was finally transported here. They married immediately and he now works as a butcher on an estate west of Sydney. I tend to remember the good things that happened to people. Conversely, I'm sure many of the male convicts we carried are having a horrible time on the chain-gangs.

317

"It's sad in a way Daniel, because from what I know, the majority of those men were convicted of petty crimes. To me, their punishment is out of proportion. Yet, I feel a little guilty in being thankful that they help build strong wharves for our ships. Let's stretch our legs and wander along the dock for a bit where you'll see a group at work."

Coubro watches as a massive piling is hauled into place and connected with chains to the piling beside it. Another two feet of dock space secured! The heavy thump it renders on the deck beneath his feet brings back a memory. "Jacob, you mentioned Lady Hudson-Smythe. Whatever happened to her?"

"Well, she continued her snobbish ways on land. With all her guile and uppity social bearing, it didn't take her long to wheedle her way into the Governor's mansion as a full-time guest. I hear she has a suitor and is a socialite who spearheads a couple of charitable causes."

A big smile brightens Coubro's face. "Let me share a little secret with you, Jacob. Her dear Ladyship tried to seduce me one night. She was very drunk and the effort was clumsy. Thank heavens I was rescued from an awkward situation. Do you remember the whale that crunched the hull one evening? She stopped an event in progress so to speak. I'll ever be grateful."

Jacob's eyes light up. "She did have some attractions, sir, but glad you didn't succumb. I'll treasure that little piece of information. Not that I'll probably ever see her again. Although, I will undoubtedly see her maid, Matilda.

"Matilda was cast aside at Government House because her Ladyship came to favor an existing maid-in-waiting in the mansion. However, I'm happy to report that Matilda and Mr. Blaine, the banker, married soon afterwards and a year later produced a baby boy."

318

Coubro interrupts. "Yes, they named him Daniel, after me apparently. I felt honored when I received their letter in London. Very nice. I will try to visit them. Given how industrious young Timothy was, I'm sure I will be able to find him at his bank. And, just so you know, Matilda certainly was aware of her Ladyship's and my escapade. She had to help afterwards as Lady Hudson-Smythe suffered some cuts and bruises from the whale's strike against the hull."

Jacob grins. "Your secret is safe with me, Daniel."

Coubro pauses and the pair turn and head back to Jacob's office. Coubro grimaces as he tries to recall other travellers on the first trip to Sydney. He struggles, as he has made three round trips since. His brows furrow and he shakes his head. Suddenly he mutters, "...Robinson. Whatever became of him?"

"Robinson? Don't remember that name..."

A pause, then Jacob asks "Do you mean Robertson, the prisoner who was exonerated in the shipboard court case at Cape Town?"

"Yes, that's the chap. I remember my exchange with the police and the magistrates here, and handing him back the belt. Most unusual fellow. He was clearly wronged. I hope he made good."

"Last I heard he works for a lawyer writing up prisoners' requests for expedited pardons, and free settlers' justifications for land grants. With some success, I might add."

"Good for him. He was the most articulate prisoner I ever met."

Another name registers. "How is my old quartermaster, Padraig Plunket, doing? He was the only other crewman who left me and joined up with you. Is he around to say hello to?"

"He's a great trader. You and he did very well with the extra supplies the two of you bought in Cape Town on that first trip, I know. He continues to have a canny sense of potential demand for various items. As manager of my warehouse, I couldn't do without him. And of course, he manages the crew whenever we leave port. Sorry I stole him away from you. You'll find him at the back of the warehouse checking a load of corn that's just arrived."

"I gather you are prospering, Jacob. I see from the loading dock that you are shipping elephant-seal oil and seal skins back to London. I'm sure the trade has been financially rewarding."

"Yes, it has, although the hunters say the seal population has almost disappeared in Bass Strait. Which is why some of the cargo now originates from the islands at the southern tip of New Zealand.

"But there's another prospective cargo I'm intrigued with. And that's wool. Several bales of wool produced on the other side of the Blue Mountains sold in London last year at an excellent price. Its fineness more than matched that of wool sourced in Europe. There are huge farms being established on fertile pastures near Camden that run a new breed of sheep called Merino. Many knowledgeable agricultural experts say conditions for growing ultrafine wool here are excellent. They predict bigger things to come. This country has so much to offer the world, Daniel. I'm pleased to participate in its growth."

Jacob's fervor is catching. I've watched him closely over the intervening years. He's not only a skilled ship pilot and captain, but an astute businessman as well. He is at ease when he negotiates with merchants and government officials, always thoughtful about the direction he wants to take his commercial interests. While the number of business offices in the center of the city is increasing, it is out here in Cockle Bay, previously known as Long Cove, where Sydney's international efforts and future trading wealth are centered.

* * *

When I first arrived in Sydney, Major-General Lachlan Macquarie was Governor of the colony. He still is. The previous four governors were all navy men who staggered through short terms of leadership. Macquarie has already been here nearly seven years and is playing a major role in transforming New South Wales from a penal colony into a civilized settlement. He's helping create a vibrant new society in this land. It's wonderful to witness the results of his efforts. I hear merchants and ship owners uniformly praising him in their dockside conversations over beer and sandwiches.

A panorama of major change is taking place. Back in 1788, 11 ships of the First Fleet from Portsmouth arrived in Botany Bay, then moved north a few miles to Sydney Cove, carrying 754 convicts, 306 crew members, 245 marines, 54 marines' wives and children, and 14 officials and passengers. In total, close to 1,400 individuals were assigned to the development of an end-of-the-world penal colony for the worst types of criminals found in British society. Captain Arthur Phillip was the appointed Governor of this new civilization.

Just over thirty years later, 17,000 people now live in the State of New South Wales, and 3,000 live in Tasmania, previously known as Van Diemen's Land. Some 7,300 are convicts and their children. The remainder are soldiers and free citizens. Convict ships arrive regularly. New towns such as Parramatta, Windsor, Liverpool, Newcastle, Penrith, Bathurst and Hobart have been settled, major rivers have been charted, hard surface roads between towns are being built, agricultural products flourish, the route over the Blue Mountains to Bathurst has been improved, a banking system is in place, and foreign trade is an everyday aspect of business activity.

Certainly, life in Australia is not perfect, and I understand it is a long way from offering the gentler social aspects of British living. But widespread opportunity, a fast-growing population, clear, sparkling blue skies, minimal aboriginal skirmishes, and abundant water and space, contribute to an enthusiastic outlook for most of the non-convict settlers. I'm in awe at how innovative, resilient, and progressive these people have been in forging a rewarding future. I'm happy to have a role in transporting new materials, machines, and goods that aid the exciting growth progress all around.

On the other hand, life for many convicts is far from pleasant. Groups form and rebel, and are severely punished. The work gangs which create roads, buildings, and sea-walls work at hard labour. Many men are ill-treated and die from beatings or poor nourishment.

Public floggings have been eliminated. All the local whippings now take place inside the grounds of the soldiers' barracks. But I hear all the horror stories because I've now made several trips between Sydney and Tasmania carrying those prisoners who've committed a second crime in Sydney, which causes new penalties to be added to whatever burden they were already facing.

I don't like these journeys, as the prisoners are surly, mean, and desperate. Their carvings cause damage to my timber supports in the hold and they fight among themselves continually. Many are flogged by the soldiers guarding them. I'm always glad when the convicts are finally put ashore in Hobart.

It's the voyages back and forth to London that I enjoy most. Every trip allows us to bring new information to Britons about the fledgling society we are creating 'down under'. A new world with amazing potential is emerging here. I wish more of my sailing ship acquaintances had the opportunity to visit this place. We deliver new products from a new country that helps add value to an ancient one. Seal fur is in demand for felt that goes into men's hats and boots, while seal oil is used for lighting, and lubrication in manufacturing.

The outward bound trips from Sydney to London are my preference as there are no convicts on board. Sometimes we have a few fare-paying passengers on their way 'home', and they are usually excited to be heading back to family or friends. In nearly all cases we'll have a contingent of soldiers who have completed their tour of duty, sometimes bureaucrats and associated officials are onboard. They are relaxed, and the crew operates smoothly with no obligations to serve prisoners located below deck.

Many of the crew are also homeward bound, which usually means we have to pick up new sailors for the return trip to Sydney. Outbound from here, the crew members work easily as a team because most of them have come to know each other and me.

Inbound, however, we end up with a wide range of experience among the able-bodied seamen. Some sailors are making their fourth or fifth trip to the Antipodes. At the other end of the spectrum are the new chums. Wannabes who think a sailor's life is glamorous, being paid to see the world, no flat or house to look after, all meals provided, amenable girls in foreign ports, and plenty of mates with whom to drink beer or rum when sailing for weeks or months between ports.

Two or three days of lurching through rough seas that produce roiling stomachs and stained clothes from vomit, grease, and bloody cuts quickly transform new chums' dreams into harsh reality. Sleeping in cramped quarters, working through rain, fog, and cold, and standing for hours on night watch drive some young men to despair, while others respond positively to the challenges, and show traits of leadership and maturity much earlier than others.

I always carry a large load of cargo on the journeys back to Sydney. Agricultural equipment heads the bill, then building materials, marine tools and parts, small industrial machinery, miscellaneous domestic items such as paper, clothing, jewelry, cutlery, dishes, other kitchen and household implements and non-perishable food items. The contents in my hold seem to get a little more sophisticated each trip we make.

It's always the prisoners that create the extra work on the southbound journeys. And no two groups are alike. I believe that as the messages about how prisoners are treated on arrival in Sydney become more uniform and realistic in the English and Irish press, convicts have greater trepidation about what lies ahead. Compared to my first trip to Sydney with Captain Coubro, they complain more often, and exaggerate their concerns.

Contrarily, paying passengers are more informed and more excited to travel with us. They look forward to establishing a new life in a climate of opportunity.

Captain Nagle gives the Militia Commander a lot of discretion in managing the prisoners. Far more than did Captain Coubro. One big change from early days is that all the wooden partitions in the prisoner deck have been removed, which means that the prisoners now exist in one big room. Fights for the best locations are frequent. The only exception is when we have both male and female prisoners. Then a dividing wall is added to separate the sexes.

By removing all the partitions that created smaller individual areas, Captain Nagle has made it easier to store cargo on the trips that leave Sydney. Wool bales are large, approximately 30 inches by 30 inches and 50 inches tall, and weigh anywhere from 250 pounds to 450 pounds depending on the density of the wool. They take up a lot of room. Each bale holds about 60 skirted fleeces, and the finer the wool, the more valuable the fleece. Wool is Captain Nagle's preferred cargo item, followed closely by barrels of seal oil. Traders pay well for timely, efficient transport of both commodities.

Speed is important in both directions of course, but it always depends on the winds. While the winds are unpredictable, we save a few days' time southbound by no longer stopping in Cape Town. The port there was relatively unprotected and disliked by many captains because of the ferocious winds that could test the anchorage at times. It means we carry extra quantities of food and water when we leave London, but so far we've had no problems managing supplies for the complete journey. Sydney and Cockle Bay is my home now, and I'm always happy to return after a visit to other ports.

* * *

In November of 1821 Mr. Blaine and two of the bank's top investors meet with Jacob in his shipboard office. Timothy states the reason for their visit. "Jacob, the board of the bank is impressed with how you've grown your commercial interests over the last four years. Combining convict transport with cargo delivery using *Lady Corinth*, increasing your warehouse space for the wool trade, and placing buying agents in the field have been highly intelligent business actions."

A faint blush flitters across Jacob's countenance, and he dips his head in acquiescence to the compliment.

Timothy continues. "You've benefited from your decisions and strategies. So much so, the bank would like to offer you the chance to double your loan to help you further expand your business."

Jacob smiles warmly. "Gentlemen, that's very encouraging. I am anxious to hear what extra information you have that will help me understand your reasoning."

"Very astute, sir. Confidentially, we are aware of some potential commercial endeavours that may be of interest to you. As you know, in the last two years Governor Macquarie has been seen publicly to concentrate on civic progress. Among other activities, he's had barracks built in Hyde Park and Parramatta, approved the construction of Presbyterian and Anglican churches, found financial support for the renovation of the main medical facility, the Rum Hospital, and approved the development of a town at Port Macquarie.

"Behind the scenes, and far less public however, the region around that particular town has shown the potential for sugar cane. In fact, a very large crop will be available for harvest later this year. As well, next year we shall see the first Australian wine from the Hunter Valley exported back to the mother country. We all think that produce off the land will become more and more important for international trade, and that will result in major rewards."

"I'm intrigued, gentlemen. Tell me more."

The bankers shuffle their feet, look at one another, heads nod, and an older, balding gentleman responds.

"Another upcoming commercial venture is that a regular stage coach service will be established shortly between Parramatta and Sydney.

While it plans to provide passenger service at first, there's little doubt that it will pave the way for regular, reliable freight transport as farms near and beyond the Blue Mountains grow in number. Penrith, at the base of the mountains, will beget an approved church and thereby become an official town where staging will occur."

"Gents, I already receive wool from several farms west of the Mountains. It's a long tough haul for the bullock teams. I hope the Governor is planning to further improve the road soon because we have had to repack a number of bales after they fell off the wagons. There are still stumps of trees which catch the wagon wheels, despite the extra width of the track."

"Actually, Mr. Nagle, there's a rumor of a second route across the Mountains opening up. Not officially confirmed yet, but perhaps that will help. In any event, there is fervent belief that our country has much to offer the world with its fertile agricultural resources. Indeed, a number of smart agriculturalists and government advisors are forming a new Agricultural Society. The society will have a charter to create an English company that will invest substantial money to promote various forms of agricultural development and other land management opportunities in our colony. Indeed, a load of honey-producing bees is on its way to Sydney as we speak."

The older gentleman who has been speaking passes several printed papers across the table, which presumably provide detail on the projects he's been talking about. The titles of companies and names of individuals involved have been redacted to preserve a form of confidentiality. Jacob scans them quickly then places the heavy sextant from his desk on top of them.

I can tell from years of watching Jacob's body language that he is actively engaged, and that his mind is racing ahead. I'm not surprised

327

when he stands to speak. With a twinkle in his eye, he turns to the gentlemen seated around the table and whimsically says, "Perhaps another transport ship would be appropriate, sirs. Along with more warehouses and storage sheds."

The three wise bankers nod their heads appreciatively. "We have plans we'd like to share with you, Mr. Nagle. If you are interested."

"Let me get some glasses, gentlemen and a jug of beer."

* * *

In the months that follow, Jacob gives up providing passenger and convict transport between Sydney and London and also between Sydney and Hobart, leaving the latter local trade to various 'packet boats' that are now being built in Hobart and Newcastle. His primary focus is to provide international freight haulage.

He spends money to convert me into a pure cargo ship, able to handle a variety of agricultural products and miscellaneous freight. My holds can now be configured in various ways, depending on what we are to carry. All passenger and prisoner accommodations have been removed, and crew quarters minimized. Even on deck I can now carry cargo due to the placement of embedded iron hooks and use of strong canvas straps that can secure heavy crates in a variety of arrangements.

I like my new 'character'. It took three months for a team of carpenters to alter the holds below deck, and then a few minor adjustments after our first trip back and forth to the UK carrying freight only.

No more prisoners or passengers onboard is fine by me. No more special foods, no more cleaning up after their journey, no more worrying about their sensitive stomachs when we hit troubled waters, no more noise or persistent demands made of crew members, the Surgeon or Captain. Freight sits there quietly behaving itself for as long as we sail.

Don't get me wrong. I really like most people but convicts in general are sad beings. Many had their families broken up, many regretted their crimes, many were mad they'd been caught. And I have always felt that most of the prisoners we transported received sentences much too harsh relative to the seriousness of their crimes. The majority were starving wretches who stole goods in order to pawn them and buy food for their families. I felt sorry for the ones in that category. Even some of the women convicted of prostitution were mothers trying to earn money to buy food for their children.

Yes, we certainly carried serious criminals as well. There were rapists, arsonists, murderers, torturers, and child abusers. There were fraudsters, hucksters, impostors and con men who took advantage of decent folk. I had little time for prisoners in these categories. Always, shipments of prisoners were unpleasant. They were despondent, complaining individuals, terrified of what the future in a strange land may hold, managed in many instances by illiterate, punishment-prone guards, often chosen for their cruel streaks. And while I felt deeply for many of the convicts we ferried across the oceans, voyages without prisoners were far more enjoyable.

My first trip to these Antipodes with Captain Coubro was atypical, for he and his officers were men of unusual compassion. On trips where the militia were left to manage the convicts, they perpetuated the prisoners' woeful land-side gaol terms and experiences.

I don't miss most paying passengers either. Most of those passengers considered themselves at the opposite end of the economic spectrum and social strata that applied to those traveling enmasse in the hold. Many paying passengers thought the ship was primarily for their benefit. A number were snobs, rich philanderers. Some had committed high-level white collar crimes - embezzlement, illicit liaisons, family incest. Others had exploited the common people with misleading investment, or other get-rich schemes.

On the other hand, there were educators, religious leaders, and successful businessmen, plus some elegant rich folks interested in exploring a new land. All of them, however, thought they were important and wanted to be heard, admired, respected, even loved. The crew who served them laughed behind their backs at their pomposity, arrogance, and sometimes narcissism. So, while these passengers respected each other, their common nemesis was the crew. Demanding favors, repairing items, changing arrangements were the norm in their behavior.

There was always less tension when there were no passengers. Crewmen could concentrate on their jobs. Frankly, when we are under sail, life is still busy. Men are constantly watching for debris and whales and checking the wind and waves.

It's nice not to have unwanted distractions.

* * *

Time speeds by. Three years ago, in December 1822, the authorities back in England appointed Governor Brisbane as the new ruler of the colony, replacing Governor Macquarie.

It is clear that the original intentions associated with the Botany Bay penal colony have changed markedly in the 30 plus years since the First Fleet arrived.

Britain is extending its colonial empire to include and enfold Australia.

To that end, the new government has introduced several positive changes. In particular, the new Governor has had a marked impact in creating a legal infrastructure, based on that in Britain, to look after citizens' rights.

After three years of his tenure, the colony in 1825 now has an Attorney General, a Legislative Council, a Supreme Court, and Trial by Jury. These are excellent tenets of a progressive society and are welcomed by nearly all free settlers.

On the other hand, somewhat counter-balancing, Governor Brisbane is a strong believer in law and order. He has little empathy for convicts. He likes the examples set by the treatment of inmates in the Macquarie Harbor penal colony on the West Coast of Tasmania. Convicts sent to that settlement had usually re-offended during their sentence, and were treated very harshly, labouring in cold and wet weather, and subject to severe Corporal punishment for minor infractions. Their prime function was to harvest valuable Huon Pine timber for furniture making and shipbuilding. But the prison had the added advantage of being almost impossible to escape from, most attempts ending with the convicts either drowning, or dying of starvation in the bush.

As the number of second offenders in the State of New South Wales continues to grow, Governor Brisbane is establishing separate penal institutions for them. The newest one is to be found on Maria island in Bass Strait. In the quest to create harsher punishment facilities for second offenders, six months ago the Governor sent the brig 'Brutus' with its two masted square-rigged sail arrangement to Norfolk Island, 1000 miles northeast of Sydney. The ship carried 34 troops, six soldiers' wives and six children, along with 57 convicts. These people, under

Commandant Turton's charter, were to be the vanguard of a revamped second penal colony there, the first having lasted from 1790 until 1814, before being abandoned.

Maria Island and Norfolk Island colonies are designed to hold "the worst description of convicts". It is still the case that back in Britain the system of justice has hardly progressed in 40 years. More Irish convicts are sent here now, and as a group, they seem to have committed more serious crimes than English convicts. Newspapers back home in Britain still publish stories of how depraved the convicts are that are sent here and how their punishment is just.

As I hear Jacob converse with his friends about the two new harsh colonies, I have some sympathy for their creation. Mainly because a new type of criminal has emerged in our fledgling society. A few 'second crime' convicts who have escaped from prison have become what are now called 'bushrangers'. These are desperate men who've 'gone bush.' They set up camps in the forests from which they raid farms for sheep and supplies, sometimes raping the women and killing the farmers. The worst of these outlaws use stolen guns. Many rural residents are terrified and fear for their lives. The government has started using aboriginal trackers to help hunt these despots down, but it appears that their numbers are increasing. Those caught are publicly hanged. It's hoped that deporting the worst criminals to the toughest penal establishments will limit the number of new bushrangers. I've wondered if any of the bushrangers were men I carried on my various trips from London. But I simply don't remember all the transported convicts, so I've given up listening for recognizable names.

In general, I've felt some limited pity for British convicts, most of whom I believe were 'over-sentenced'. But I have no time for these hardened local criminals. Just as Britain sent its criminals far away, Australia is now doing the same with its heavy criminal class. I am pleased that I'm not involved in transporting them.

The business of business runs the daily lives of Jacob's team of workers and crewmen. A shared interlude occurs as the year comes to a close, for we have two new 'births' to celebrate. A month ago Jacob's wife, Janet, brought her baby, Elizabeth, only four weeks old, down to the docks to show her off to the friendly workers here. Elizabeth brings the Nagle children to three, trailing behind Arthur, nine years old, and Timothy, four. I can tell that Janet is delighted to have a daughter.

The second celebration relates to a new ship in the harbor. Six months ago, Jacob's syndicate bought a sister barque, 'Lady Warwick'. She's a couple of years older than me but we've already established a good friendship. She tells me that Jacob has also retained the current Captain named Robert Lewis, and many members of his crew. I hear that my new sister will also eventually be converted to carry freight only. At the moment, she's fitted to carry cargo, passengers, and convicts, just like I was originally. I wonder just how big Jacob's fleet might become over time.

A government official is in Jacob's office and I listen closely. "Mr. Nagle, His Excellency the Governor would like to lease your two ships to transport freight and convicts to the Kingston settlement on Norfolk Island."

"May I ask when this is to happen, sir? Are there no government ships available for the purpose?"

"The Governor is anticipating a departure around the first of March, Mr. Nagle. At least 120 convicts of the worst type are to be moved there. As well, we need transport for at least 50 soldiers and their families, plus approximately 20 government officials and families. I believe your recently acquired ship, *Lady Warwick*, can handle that number of passengers, yes?"

"Yes and no, sir. We would have to build extra accommodation for that many soldiers and bureaucrats on the assumption they would not care to be housed together, and even more so since each group is larger than our current cabin setup.

"We could do this, but I am most reluctant since my intentions with *Lady Warwick* are to convert her to freight only, as I have done with *Lady Corinth*. Why should I invest in more cabin arrangements when I really want to tear down what already is in place?"

The official effects a sympathetic mien. "We understand Mr. Nagle, but our need is urgent and there is no other appropriate ship available. I have authority to offer you full payment for adding new cabins, and also for removing them on your return. Would that change your position?"

"That would be essential in order to meet your needs. But I'd need more. Cash up front to pay the extra carpenters, and purchase the wood. And I would own the wood when the cabins are destroyed. Also, I would need more than two months to get ready. The Governor must be prepared to accept a departure date at least a fortnight later than March 1."

"I'm authorized to approve up to a two-week extension, Mr. Nagle. So be it. Now, may we get into details on our freight needs, and discuss operational terms?"

I'm stunned. The government hasn't used our services for years, and now they want to deploy both ships at the same time? I feel proud that Jacob's business is so respected, and happy that it would be *Lady*

Warwick, not me, ferrying the prisoners to their new location. But I wonder. *Lady Warwick* will become a freighter, too, and so won't be available for repeat convict transportation in the future.

Requiring me as well as my sister ship for the voyage suggests that I will be stocked full of building supplies, heavy industrial and agricultural equipment, plenty of food and drink, probably animals as well. I suspect the authorities are planning to make the penal colony on Norfolk Island huge, incarcerating the worst criminals we have in our midst here as far away as possible there. If true, the citizens of Sydney and the surrounding countryside will be very happy to hear such news. Little is known about the island but it does not sound appealing. Mountainous, with rocky cliffs down to the sea in all but a couple of spots. No major water sources. Thick forests and undergrowth. Limited land for agriculture, the only semi-positive aspect being that the climate is subtropical and mild. But not a place from which one escapes.

Captain Nagle talks to many officials and other sailors in an attempt to learn more about our destination. His findings reveal that treatment of convicts there is very harsh. British law on the management and treatment of prisoners is interpreted in contrasting ways to what applies in Sydney. I've overheard Jacob on more than one occasion tell Captain Lewis on *Lady Warwick* that at times he wishes he'd never agreed to the journey.

But it's too late to change. Time passes quickly and preparations progress well. It's now the week before we plan to depart. In the middle of the day my attention is drawn to the sound of unexpected footfalls on the boarding planks. They are not the usual reverberations of heavy workmen's boots, but involve some hesitancy and a meter of insecurity to them. A lady's head appears at the rail, alongside that of

Captain Coubro. Such a delightful and unexpected surprise! I'm tickled pink and I'm sure Jacob will be as well.

But who is the lady travelling with my old, wonderful master? Is this a Mrs. Coubro, or simply a friend? My curiosity runs at peak levels. Jacob is quickly summoned from the warehouse. I must hear him greet his old friend and learn about the primly dressed lady he's brought along.

Typically unassuming, the Captain has dropped by with no other intention than simply to say hello. We haven't seen him in a year, but he looks the same as then. When Jacob finally appears, the thrill of meeting is doubled, as Daniel announces that the lady by his side is Mrs. Chantal Coubro. They've been married for eight months and both seem to be extremely happy. Chantal smiles demurely, extending her right hand in welcome to Jacob. He kisses the back of her fingers in a charming gesture of respect and admiration.

I'm sure my old Captain has shown his lovely wife many other ships, but he's very gallant as he offers to show her some of my special features. He gently turns to face her and humbles me with some loving words.

"My dear Lady of the Land, I'd like you to meet an esteemed old friend, my Lady of the Sea." He places Chantal's hands on my starboard railing just as he's done with his hands on so many visits in the past. I feel the warmth of their gentle grasps and am overwhelmed with affection and pride. What wonderful memories I hold of serving the man who brought me to this fine land. I'm sure he'll come by again on his next trip to the Antipodes.

Jacob leads the couple to his cabin, and, basking in the glow of Daniel's remarks, I decide to only pay half attention to their conversation.

Beside which, there is an altercation spilling on to the wharf from the warehouse that has men gathering.

Tom, one of the three aboriginal shed workers has declared he won't come to work tomorrow as he will be 'going walkabout'. This happens not infrequently with the natives, whose natural environment and life is one of nomadic wanderings. The call of nature is in their blood and when it surfaces there is no way to offset it. It's something I've heard white men supervisors complain about often. Reliability of aboriginal workers is not guaranteed. They are not used to working for a wage, and they miss the freedom their bush homes allow.

In this case, Tom's timing to go 'walkabout' is very poor since we are filling up with the supplies for Norfolk Island. Everyone is working hard, two shifts a day. But I know Padraig will work something out.

He does, and four days later on the fourteenth of March we sail from Cockle Bay. I am looking forward to visiting a place I haven't been before, even if it is destined to hold a tough penal colony.

On the way out, we pass Sydney Cove and my mood darkens. For there off to starboard is the wreck of the *Phoenix* which last year was converted to a prison hulk after she ran aground on the Sow and Pigs reef. Memories of the line of hulks in Portsmouth Harbor crowd freshly into my mind. Those sad remnants of once-fine ships dismasted, with their sails, rigging, rudders, and cannon removed, and extra anchors added. Formless, characterless shadows of former glory, now despised and neglected, relegated to serve as overcrowded prisons for ill-treated wretched convicts. I rekindle my long-held hope that I will escape that ignominious fate, for it hurts to think about ending my days in such an inglorious state.

There's no wind in the cove but I heel over a little causing the Officer of the Deck to tell the helmsman to mind his helm, who answers that he made no rudder changes. I do it again, causing consternation around the wheel. My way of trying to tell Jacob how I hate that hulk.

To take my thoughts away, I scan the shorelines and notice that a number of small villages are emerging. Years ago when I first arrived here, there was nothing but pristine forest running down to the beaches or cliffs at the water's edge. The aborigines owned the harbor shores then, not white man.

Lady Warwick leads the way through the Heads. I concentrate on following her 400 yards astern and slightly off-line from her port hull. We turn to the northeast, and set full sail on a direct course to Norfolk Island. It's almost exactly 1000 miles away from Sydney, a mere speck on any map of the huge Pacific Ocean. As such, its remoteness is incomprehensible to English citizens. I sense the stories of its primitive lawlessness make Jacob wonder what he'll find there. He doesn't seem anxious to rush and find out.

Out in the open sea a light breeze whispers. The waves are slight, there are no clouds, and the sun is warm, not yet hot.

It's a perfect day for sailing.

Exactly to what is unknown.

23. *I do but serve*

Nine uneventful days later we anchor in well-protected Spin Bay on the east side of volcanic Philip Island, four miles south of Norfolk Island. Apparently, there is little good anchorage available at Norfolk.

In the morning, the sailors are enthused to see many giant green turtles as we pass by Nepean Island, less than a thousand yards south of our destination, Slaughter Bay. Captain Nagle tells a small group of men around him that the name of the bay is not as ominous as it sounds because the word "slaughter" comes from an Old English word that means "slow-moving water.*" While that may indeed be the case, I don't like the word. It connotes savagery and carnage.

Slaughter Bay is wide open to the south, with an extensive reef less than one hundred yards offshore, to the right of a channel. Inside the reef, the water is indeed slow-moving. Outside the reef, the limited charts the captain has collected portray strong currents which run east for three hours, then reverse themselves to the west for nearly double that amount of time. Such a marked change is surprising within a cove.

Both *Lady Warwick* and I heave-to several hundred yards off the reef, although our anchors have little impact beyond their heavy weight due to the rock-like bottom. They do not dig in to soft sand as we prefer. Not an ideal situation.

I feel ill at ease. This is not a friendly cove in which to dally. Its ominous reef, the vacillating currents, and sharp, hard coral provide a challenging setting for our rendezvous.

We carry no cannon to announce our arrival and it is two hours before our presence is finally recognized onshore. Two scraggly residents there help guide the first of *Lady Warwick*'s longboats, which holds guards and convicts, on to the beaches. There are numerous huts at the tree line, but many seem in disrepair, and first reports back to *Lady Warwick* by the rowers indicate large rats running free through the undergrowth.

Captain Nagle goes ashore to meet with government officials, who finally arrive at the beach from the local barracks. It's not like Slaughter Bay is a regular port of call for sailing ships. Most of the officials are unkempt in appearance and look surprised by our presence. I'm sure Captain Nagle is passing on details of the cargo we're carrying. On return from the beach, he indicates he wants to start unloading immediately. To quartermaster Plunkett he says, "All yours, Padraig. Not the most welcoming of men. Don't expect much help from them. What do you want to unload first?"

"All the foodstuffs and cooking utensils, sir. Plus some of the household niceties. That way the soldiers and officials being taken off *Lady Warwick* will have the tools, and plenty of time to prepare an evening meal for themselves as well as the convicts. Maybe a few of those buildings can be cleaned up a bit. No one will need their baggage until tomorrow, so that can wait."

"Good man, Padraig."

"Let's hope they send those huge tents ashore that *Lady Warwick* is carrying, Cap'n. They will help keep the convict group organized and disciplined."

"Right you are. I'll go hail Captain Lewis right now and remind him. Carry on!"

Between the two ships we've brought along hundreds of different necessities. They range from tools and building supplies to eating utensils and food to help establish quarters and meals for the convicts we're about to deliver to this remote place.

Unloading the household provisions takes only eight hours, thanks to Padraig pushing his men. Sailors of the current crew are all relatively new and he's been enjoying breaking them in. He hasn't had to do that since our last trip back to London eight months ago. As my cargo is transferred to shore I sit higher and lighter in the water. There's a narrow stretch of water between the end of the reef and the western shoreline of the cove. The longboats are maneuvered with extra care through the gap.

Finally finished, the men stretch and relax, downing their rum rations in quick time. They watch waves break ever more violently over the reef even as the tide recedes to its low point. Spumes of froth ratchet upwards as the waves pound the coral. To me, the spirals of foam provide warning signals. At high tide the reef is invisible beneath the waves. But at low tide its menacing presence is all too obvious. I'm wary.

All the prisoners that were on *Lady Warwick* are now ashore, so as the light begins to fade Captain Lewis leads us back to Spin Bay where we intend to anchor and spend the night at anchor again.

The crew of both ships, including many sailors with blistered hands from rowing heavy loads repeatedly through the currents to shore, are in a surprisingly jubilant mood. The main reason? Our load of prisoners with their constant complaints and despair is gone. Peace reigns. And unloading the freight that remains tomorrow should not be that hard.

We anchor back in Spin Bay, and as soon as we are sure we are holding, sailors not on watch relax. They swim back and forth between Jacob's two ships across the cool water of the bay, sharing tales of the animals, vegetation, and other things they saw on Norfolk. At the end of their exertions they swill plenty of rum, a just reward after a hard day's work.

Morning sun reveals a few clouds. Starting early, the day is to be spent unloading all the agricultural and building supplies from both ships. Once the small volume of goods is emptied from *Lady Warwick's* hold, many of her crew will be assigned to help my crew. That's because I am laden with implements ranging from huge two-man saws used to fell timber, to fertilizer and fence posts, giant coils of wire and rope, metal gates and grids, hand-held shears and digging tools, to bags and crowbars, lead shot and powder, along with a multitude of other items for farmers and builders alike.

As well, I have 40 head of stock that need to be transferred to land. Ten horses, ten cows, a bull, 10 sheep, and 9 goats. The crew use well-adapted slings to hoist the animals overboard into water that is approximately 12 fathoms deep. Sailors beat and cajole the larger beasts to swim to shore, guided by men in a boat alongside, along with a specially trained Border-Collie who rounds up stragglers. Smaller critters, the sheep and goats, fit comfortably into long boats without a problem. The men seem to enjoy swimming alongside the cattle and riding on the backs of a few of the calmer horses.

I like animals. Far better behaved than humans on board, unless, of course we are in rough seas, in which case they become as scared and uneasy as any non-sailor. The only thing I don't like is the mess they leave behind. Captain Nagle insists that my decks be thoroughly cleaned once all the animals are off.

Finally, the furniture and baggage of guards and free-settlers is removed from my hold and I ride even higher in the water. My waterline is a good twelve inches above the surface. It's as if I've been put on an overnight diet. I feel good, ready to dance with the waves, rather than plow through them.

We finish all the unloading ahead of schedule so the captains decide to do some adventuring and sightseeing by circumnavigating the island clockwise. It's a straightforward, hassle-free trip. We make a brief stop outside the Cascade settlement on the north coast, before continuing back to Spin Bay as night falls. The trip makes me understand better why we unloaded in Slaughter Bay. Elsewhere, this island's shores are rocky bases of near vertical cliffs. There is no other place to unload as much material as we've carried. It helps me feel more accepting and relaxed over heaving-to in the windy open southern cove.

Next morning dawns fair and pleasant, and we stand-off in Slaughter Bay. We are waiting for the emancipists, convicts who've completed their sentences and are destined to return to Sydney, along with four regular passengers, and some sample produce to be loaded on *Lady Warwick*. Two of her longboats are already onshore. I am hove-to with my main aback and foresails drawing, my bow facing shoreward in 13 fathoms of beautifully transparent water, while *Lady Warwick* is somewhat behind me resting in 20 fathoms. The offshore wind offsets a tiny swell from the south, keeping us in place without need for an anchor. About fifteen sailors in my crew, temporarily relieved of work, are standing at the rails fishing for groupers. They are having much success at the current depth, and constantly challenge each other to see who can land the first, the largest, the longest, and the last.

Well out in the ocean I observe a small rising swell rolling in our direction. The peaks and troughs seem a mile away, providing a gently undulating landscape that's soothing to the senses. I know too well however that the sea can conceal its effects in its great depths, and particularly how the immense power of a long swell from a distant storm can react with an irregular sea-bed to deliver surprising effects on shores.

Suddenly there is a strange surge on my stern. It's unusual enough to catch my attention. It must have risen unheralded from the depths, for it is surprisingly strong and not obvious near the surface. I'm alarmed, for it has arrived without notice! Not even the officer on watch detects its presence.

The surge nudges me towards the reef as this unheralded, forceful swell overrides the offshore wind. I sense imminent danger. My bow rides up and down in an unfamiliar movement as small but confused waves lap at my stern.

I know what must be done, but need the crew to act. Captain Nagle needs to know this immediately. The Officer of the Deck should have noticed the change but has been distracted by the fishing fun. Real danger threatens us. It's high tide, so there are no breaking waves and blowing spray from the nearby reef to signal its presence to the relaxed fishermen.

Oh God, no! The reef! It's between me and the beach...

Our situation needs urgent attention.

The relaxed, off-watch men who are fishing are totally unaware, and the captain and on-duty section have been distracted by difficulties getting the ship to lie still hove-to. Fluke circumstances.

I flex the rudder in an attempt to shift broadside, hoping the pronounced swinging motion I create will register the danger with someone. But it's no use. My actions alone are not enough. I need men at the helm. Now! Or we will be in serious trouble.

"*Lady Corinth*! Ahoy! Ahoy! Look smart!"

"Ahoy there!"

"You're drifting toward the reef!"

"Look out!"

344

I welcome these strident shouts. Men are hailing us from the *Lady Warwick.* Crew there have sensed my movement and are trying to warn us. Thank God they've noticed our plight. They see the danger but are helpless to aid us.

"You are too close in!"

"Trim your sails and move away!"

"Turnabout!"

"Hurry!"

Their cries are short and direct, urging fast and furious action.

Our crew drop their fishing lines as one. The Bo'sun sends them racing to the sheets to trim sail and gather headway. He calls 'All Hands' from their quarters. They smoothly trim sheets with all the skill and finesse developed over our long cruise to this point. Soon men aloft have stretched extra canvas on the yardarms to catch more wind so we can sail smoothly away from the reef. We need to turn 180 degrees and face south into the waves currently riding up against my stern. One chap climbs furiously to the crows-nest atop the main mast. His report is not encouraging.

"The swells are gaining in size out in the Pacific."

Not only that, I also feel a swift change of current. The active watch has failed their assignment. Captain Nagle steps calmly onto the quarter deck as others attentively ease the wheel to come onto the wind. I start to swing about to port. Encouraged, Nagle orders the bow anchor dropped. He hopes to hold the bow steady and swing my stern, but the coral cuts the rope lead. The swell is now much stronger than the wind. I'm shoved shoreward half broadside, caught in the heavy west-flowing current. It helps me turn however and I am halfway around.

The crew struggle to send off two longboats. They row awkwardly away towards *Lady Warwick,* joining up with the long boats she has launched. They pull on lines attached to my hull to further help reverse my direction. There aren't enough men. The swell is too strong. Waves pound my frame. The rowers can only watch open-mouthed as I flounder in the heaving surf.

Their efforts are to no avail.

I'm helpless.

My stern rams with wrenching, grating screams hard into the reef. I feel and hear a sickening, tearing sound. A major coral head claws a gaping hole between my after timbers. Rocklike coral rips into my keel despite its copper sheathing. I am stuck fast. The eerie noise and unusual pain is excruciating. I hurt horribly as I twist in the angry water and grind against the needle-like outcrop.

I slew around further and my after starboard quarter is torn to pieces. Bits of wood rise up from the depths and float away. I am in terrible agony. I shriek inwardly. A jarring sensation runs along my frame from stern to bow. Deck planks rise and fall, in small, then larger sections. It's as if some unseen giant is mauling me with his powerful hand, and slowly crushing sections of me at will. I'm scared. This ugly, vicious reef taunts me with its immovable presence. Angry waves plough into me forcing me farther into the reef's clutch.

There is no escape. Cold, clear salt water combers into my lower hold. So much water below deck quickly overwhelms our single pump, and cannot be pumped away. We have failed, as I am now locked against the coral in an inescapable embrace. I feel desperate, powerless to help myself. I am doomed.

Nagle heads to the stern. Shakes his head. Realizes that I am wedged firmly and that each large incoming swell pins me even harder against the reef. He sees the massive spikes of coral that impale me.

There is no hope of setting me free.

I hear his terrifying order. "Drop the masts. Cut the starboard shrouds between the deadeyes*. Don't get hurt. Watch out for falling rigging."

I understand this action of his is designed to keep my wreckage stable on the reef. He wants to salvage whatever he can from me. But it means I am to be abandoned. In an isolated and unfriendly bay that rarely sees visitors. I fear I will be very much alone. Abandoned at the end of an honorable career. Nothing but a statistic for Lloyds....

The nimble crew quickly drops all sails, cuts away the rigging, and eventually drops the masts. Dodging between reef and hull, longboats capture each of the three masts and tow them towards the beach, against the tide, away from my starboard side. They are anchored far from the ship, to avoid further bashing the hull, while retaining hope of later retrieval.

I loathe the consequent disfigurement. My heart breaks.

My pride is crushed, like my hull.

* * *

An hour after impact the tide starts to recede. Soon, two feet of the top of the reef will be visible, and waves will break even more heavily over it. It's time to try and get men and supplies to shore.

I hear women wailing on the beach. I wonder for a moment if they wail for me. They cannot tell that all the men are safe. I'm thankful no-one has been hurt or lost overboard. Many of the crew gathered their belongings from the hold, bundled them, and threw them overboard, hoping the current would take them to shore. Alas, it sent them seaward and only a few bundles were saved by *Lady Warwick's* sailors in the longboats.

Captain Nagle stands with his crew. "Get me the longest, lightest rope you can find and tie it to a fair-led hawser. A small empty barrel as well. And I need a volunteer to accompany me in a swim to shore."

He peels off his shirt and boots, the muscles in his arms and chest rippling with strength. A wiry older sailor steps forward. It's Roger, the chap who won the long-distance swim race in the becalmed waters just north of the equator. "I'll go with ye Captain."

The pair dive overboard near the bow, as far away from the reef as possible. The barrel floats with the rope attached, and they strike out for the shore. The current tries to push them well away. Their struggle is evident and the crew shouts encouragement. Stroke by stroke, they inch forward as their strength prevails. At last they reach a longboat, which ferries them past the end of the reef to the shore. I'm glad they get there safely, but I worry. Will Nagle come back, or is that his last exit from my deck?

Soldiers on the beach race to help. The light rope is pulled to land and when the next heavier line to tow the hawser follows, it is made tight around the trunk of a sturdy pine tree. Now the revitalized crew begins to tow a strong hawser between ship and shore which can be used as the support line of a system to move men and salvageable cargo.

Our strongest crew in a longboat carries Nagle back along the line to take charge again. I'm relieved. His example is not lost on the crew. They have already been at work creating a second line to pull men and supplies back and forth between beach and ship. They have removed a large grating from the hold, big enough for four men to sit upon. It serves as a platform on which they stack barrels of rum. All four men swiftly secure the barrels, then feed out slack line as the crew ashore pulls precious cargo from ship to beach.

Surf pounds against the reef, sending spray high in the air. And as much as I think I am stuck irrevocably fast, I am slowly slewed around by powerful underwater surges and the now east-flowing current so that my bow faces almost eastward. Part of my port hull is rent away. I watch as longboats chase down chests, drums and barrels, boxes and pieces of wood with hardware still attached floating by, salvaging everything possible from my wreckage.

I vacillate between conflicting emotions. I hurt, and feel ashamed at my demise. My days will end here. Ignominiously grounded upon a foul reef. On the other hand, the crew is not abandoning me. They salvage whatever they can. Parts of me will live on. That gives me hope and some comfort. My three masts are towed to the beach and dragged up high on the sand. I hope the wood in them and the attached stays will be put to good use.

My new position hard against the reef has created more problems, for now the hawser runs directly across the reef. The connection at my end is moved from bow to stern, and the crew carefully erects a large wooden triangle on the reef to keep the hawser high. Even so, slashing waves make it almost impossible to keep loads of goods upright and stable.

The wood, iron, and copper alloy bolts that constitute my main deck were the finest available when I was built. They now remain in good stead for the men who still remain onboard, for while waves wash over the main deck during the night, the men stay dry in the foc'sle and will move useful items to the beach during low tides.

* * *

349

It has been four days. The remaining supplies are all ashore. Boxes on my top deck are empty, as sails, tools, spare parts, and rigging lines have all been removed. Two anchors remain, but with masts and rigging all akimbo, there is little left of my original splendor.

Captain Nagle visits me often. We have both suffered a major loss. There are days when his shoulders slump as he walks around the deck where planks are still firm and stable. Once I was his primary freight carrier. Now, I must quickly be replaced.

He mutters to himself as he strolls the deck, his upper torso bare, all of him wet from the swim. "I will sorely miss you, my fine friend. Ten years, we've been to so many different places, carried so many people and cargoes, survived so many challenges."

His hand, calloused but gentle, rubs along what little is left of my railing. "At least parts of you will be ever present here for the folks of this island. And faithfully remembered by all those who have sailed with you in the past."

I think of Coubro.

"All those from the past." I pause and ponder. I imagine many convicts will not have happy memories of me, but even they have helped me learn about men's ways, their fears, compassion and anger, their venality and love, their pride, diligence, and commitment.

We ships have souls. I reflect on all my journeys and feel proud. I've sailed across vast oceans where the only guidance is the wind, the current, and one's faith in a captain with his compass and sextant. I have proved myself worthy of the trust the Admiralty, captains and passengers placed in me.

But now I must make peace with the reef that destroyed me. The pride in my soul is strong, for I have served my masters well. Here, for years to come, I can still serve man and his needs. I will be able to provide wood, iron nails, chains, and rope lines to islanders seeking shelter and industry.

As the days pass, I come to accept my fate. At first, I struggled to free myself. Now, I realize I am irrevocably bound to my final resting place. At least I'm not an unseen wreck in deep waters in the middle of the ocean, but a visible form, blessed by sunshine, clear water, and curious little fishes, swaying with the tides, reliving my memories of a term well served.

I watch Jacob talk to his crew at the edge of the beach. There, the sand is soft, the water warm, the air aromatic with the pungent scent of pine trees and the heady fragrance of passionfruit vines.

Finally, my Captain can tarry no longer as he must return to Sydney. He swims out and climbs aboard. "I've come to say goodbye, my Lady. You have been a wonderful, faithful companion in our adventures, carrying me thousands of miles across the major oceans of the world. You are the finest Lady of the Sea I know. You have served me well."

He pauses, then offers another thought.

"You and I have come through so much. The terrifying storms, the cauldrons of clashing currents, the dangerous iceberg fields – not one of them bettered us. We beat the best and worst that nature threw at us. "Yet, despite all that, we are given no victory honors. The sea never forgives. She is always waiting to take her due."

His voice falters a little as he looks heavenward.

"Be at peace with her, my friend."

He reaches down and opens a wooden box he has brought with him. "I've brought you a goodbye gift. It's your bell. The crew took it ashore, but it belongs with you. It has your name, *Lady Corinth*, engraved around its lip." He hangs it in its old spot and the sunshine sparkles on the polished brass.

I'm overwhelmed with his thoughtfulness. I will treasure the bell as a constant reminder of the man and his goodness.

He walks to the bow and prepares to dive in and swim away for the last time. He turns, faces backward, and cries into the wind, "Adieu, my Lady, and God Bless."

I watch as my Captain swims away from me through the sea, and climbs aboard the *Lady Warwick*. As she sets sail and I say goodbye to her, he waves to me from her stern.

Summoning up every last ounce of energy I can muster, I ring that bell over and over again – my final farewell - over and over and over and over, until my Captain is completely out of sight.

Ding Ding,

    Ding Ding,

        Ding Ding,

            Ding Ding...

24. *Limited glossary*

Bells that keep time: The use of the bells to mark the time on a ship stems from the period when seamen could not afford a timepiece. The bells mark the hours of the watch in half-hour increments through 6 phases, each four hours long. The seamen would know if it were morning, noon, or night. Each watch* is four hours long and the bells are struck as follows:

Notes: ** - The period from 1600 to 2000 is split into two dog watches. These watches run from 1600 to 1800 and from 1800 to 2000. This

Mid	Morning	Forenoon	Afternoon	Dogs**	First
0030 - 1 bell	0430 - 1 bell	0830 - 1 bell	1230 - 1 bell	1630 - 1 bell	2030 - 1 bell
0100 - 2 bells	0500 - 2 bells	0900 - 2 bells	1300 - 2 bells	1700 - 2 bells	2100 - 2 bells
0130 - 3 bells	0530 - 3 bells	0930 - 3 bells	1330 - 3 bells	1730 - 3 bells	2130 - 3 bells
0200 - 4 bells	0600 - 4 bells	1000 - 4 bells	1400 - 4 bells	1800 - 4 bells	2200 - 4 bells
0230 - 5 bells	0630 - 5 bells	1030 - 5 bells	1430 - 5 bells	1830 - 5 bells	2230 - 5 bells
0300 - 6 bells	0700 - 6 bells	1100 - 6 bells	1500 - 6 bells	1900 - 6 bells	2300 - 6 bells
0330 - 7 bells	0730 - 7 bells	1130 - 7 bells	1530 - 7 bells	1930 - 7 bells	2330 - 7 bells
0400 - 8 bells*	0800 - 8 bells	1200 - 8 bells	1600 - 8 bells	2000 - 8 bells	2400 - 8 bells

alternates the daily watch routine so sailors on the mid-watch would not have it the second night, and, the split also gives each watch-stander the opportunity to eat the evening meal.

* - The end of the watch is at 8 bells, hence the saying "Eight Bells and All Is Well."

http://www.navy.mil/navydata/nav_legacy.asp?id=212

Chiak: To taunt or tease in jest.

Deadeye: A circular wooden block with a groove around the circumference to take a lanyard, used singly or in pairs to tighten a shroud.

Emancipist: A transported convict who had been given a conditional or absolute pardon after serving his time in Australia.

Gybe: To change course by swinging the sails across a following wind.

Halyard: A rope used on sailing ships to raise and lower a sail, spar, flag, or yard.

"Haul Away Joe" lyrics:

When I was a little boy and so me mother told me,
Way haul away, we'll haul away Joe.
That if I did not kiss the girls me lips would grow all moldy.
Way haul away, we'll haul away Joe.

    Way haul away, we're bound for better weather.
    Away haul away, we'll haul away Joe.
    Way haul away, we'll haul away together.
    Away haul away, we'll haul away Joe.

King Louis was the king of France before the revolution.
And then he got his head chopped off. It spoiled his constitution.

Saint Patrick was a gentleman. He came from decent people.
He built a church in Dublin town and on it put a steeple.

Once I had a German girl, but she was fat and lazy.
Then I had an Irish girl. She damn near drove me crazy.

I courted next a Spanish gal, she took things free and 'aisy,
But now I've got an English gal an' sure she is a daisy.

Way haul away, rock and roll me over.
Way haul away, well roll me in the clover.

Khoikhoi: The hunter-gatherers, also called 'bushmen', were the earliest inhabitants of Africa. There were probably about 120,000 living in South Africa around 1500.

Knots: A knot is a measurement of speed defined as one nautical mile per hour. It is approximately 15% faster than one land mile per hour.

Laudanum: An opium based pain killer used to treat various ailments in Victorian times.

Macpherson's Lament: This rare old rant is said to have been written by the notorious freebooter, Jamie Macpherson, while he lay under sentence of death in the fall of the year 1700. After holding the counties of Aberdeen, Banff, and Moray in fear for a number of years, MacPherson was seized, tried, and convicted of being "repute a Gypsie and vagabond, and oppressor of His Majesty's free lieges, in bangstre manner." When brought to the place of execution, on the Gallows Hill of Banff, on November 16, he played on his violin the stirring tune he had composed in the condemned cell, and then asked if any friend was present who would accept the instrument as a gift at his hands. No one coming forward, he indignantly broke the violin on his knee and threw away the fragments, after which he submitted to his fate. [Various Internet sites].

Nautical miles: A nautical mile is defined as one minute of arc of the equatorial circumference of the Earth. In the third century BC, a Greek scholar named Eratosthenes, who was a scientist, mathematician, and philosopher, worked out the distance around the globe at the equator by taking measurements of the angle of the sun's shadows at different equatorial cities at the same point in time. He came up with a measurement of 250,000 'stadia'. Stadia was the length of a Greek stadium back then. At some point, centuries later, it was determined that a stadia was almost identical with a tenth of a mile, and that the equator was therefore close to 24,900 miles long. To calculate the length of an arc at the equator, consider the circumference as a big circle. Divide the 360 degrees of the circle into equal sized one degree segments radiating from the center – like the pieces of a pie. Now decompose each of the degrees, or pie pieces, into 60 minutes. That yields 21,600 equal sized tiny slices, each one defined by a small piece of arc of the circumference, or a 'nautical mile'. Dividing the 24,900 miles of circumference by 21,600 bits reveals that each arc is 1.15 miles long.

Pollywog: A sailor who has not yet crossed the equator.

Shellback: A seaman who has crossed the equator and been initiated into the realm of King Neptune.

Slaughter Bay: Most likely named after the villages Upper and Lower Slaughter in the Cotswolds, and an old English word for wet land, slough, slothre, or muddy water. The two small villages lie near a little stream.

St. Paul Island:

Tack: To change course by swinging the sails across a head wind.

Tenements: The word usually refers to sub-standard flats/apartments in poorer districts. In Scotland, the word doesn't have the less salubrious connotation, essentially when applied to multi-family buildings with several floors of flats. Most indeed were in poorer neighborhoods, but many were rented by physicians and citizens of superior socio-economic backgrounds and standing.

Teredo (Navalis) shipworms: Saltwater bivalve molluscs that eat wood, sometimes called 'termites of the sea."

www.ingramcontent.com/pod-product-compliance
Lightning Source LLC
Chambersburg PA
CBHW061313170626
46817CB00001B/166